ACROSS THE VEIL

ACROSS THE VEIL

Leann M. Rettell

Copyright Notice

Across the Veil Copyright © 2017 Leann M. Rettell

All rights reserved. No part of this book may be reproduced in any form by any electronic or mechanical means including photocopying, recording, or information storage and retrieval without permission in writing from the author.

This is a work of fiction. All the characters and events portrayed in this book are either products of the authors' imagination or are used fictitiously.

Melissa Gilbert, editor
Susan H. Roddey, interior design
James Christopher Hill, cover art

ISBN-13: 978-1545284650
ISBN-10: 1545284652

*In Memory of my grandma,
Ora S. Pilkington,
who has always been my light.*

*In Memory of my mother,
Mary Arlena Haydon,
who has always been my rock.*

Acknowledgements

Many thanks to Melissa Gilbert at Clicking Keys for being with Ora through all of her growth and making her better at each step.

James Christopher Hill, an amazing artist, who gave Ora a face.

Dallas Hughes for all your support.

Cheri Prince for always encouraging me to never give up.

Faith Hunter, mentor and friend.

And to those who read this. Thank you.

Chapter One

"Thank God. A seat," I muttered to myself.

"Thank God. A Starbucks." Charlene "Charlie" McCurry, my best friend, replied and vanished to the right, disappearing behind the glass door of Starbucks, the smell of roasted coffee grounds wafting out behind her.

My salvation was a fancy wooden bench with wrought-iron legs and ornate caved letters of DU in the center. DU for Dalley University. The prestige of the bench was diminished by the full trash can to one side. Not that it mattered. It was a seat and the opportunity I needed to figure out where I was going next in this jungle of a campus. The first day jitters weren't calming down. I even had this weird tingling sensation as if an electric current ran underneath my skin.

I placed my computer bag on the bench beside me and unzipped the side pocket. I rooted around and pulled out the folded map of the campus and a copy of my schedule, already thin and well used from the amount I stared at it over the summer. I'd finished Physics 101 and next was Biology 101 at 11:00 a.m. in Douglas Hall with Dr. Joseph Zitalee.

A shadow fell over me, followed by a gasp. Charlie towered over me. Well, as much as she could with her five feet, four inches. She held a Starbucks cup in each hand. Her head jerked side to side, her eyes darting around while moving one cup to pin it between the hook of her arm and body. She snatched the map out of my hand, crumpled it, and tossed it into the nearby trashcan.

"Charlene!" A wave of annoyance passed through me manifesting as a sparkling light coloring the edges of my vision with tinges of pink, purple, and blue. *What the?*

Her mouth fell open. "Excuse you!"

Sweet revenge. She hated her real name and always went by Charlie. She took a seat beside me, still eyeing the courtyard. "You're going to make us look like nerdy freshman!"

Across The Veil

I shrugged and took my drink from her, sipping the iced chai latte. "We *are* nerdy freshman."

She scowled, and I smirked back, deepening her scowl. "How are we supposed to find our way around without a map?" I asked, unfazed by her concern over what people might think of us. The courtyard was full of students of every age and race. They weren't paying us the least bit of attention, but there was no telling Charlie that.

She nodded at my bag, separating us. "The school emailed us a copy of the map at orientation. Check your phone."

Hands back in the bag searching, my aggravation rose again. Charlie had talked me into wearing this ridiculous sunflower sundress with spaghetti straps instead of my usual jeans and t-shirt. If I'd dressed the way I wanted, I would have pockets. My phone and keys wouldn't be buried in this bag.

Charlie was all about changing our high school images of the nerdy, top of the class, loner chicks who never had any dates to…well, I guess popular, fashionable hotties with the boys lined up. I hoped her ploy would work for her, but I couldn't care less. I was who I was and had accepted that a long time ago.

Sure, I had potential to be the things she wanted. I'd always been called pretty and people envied my long, curly red hair, freckles, and flat stomach—which unfortunately matched my chest—but there was something about me that turned people off. I didn't know why, but that was the truth of it. There would be no popularity for me, and as for the guys, there was only one who had ever shown any interest. That relationship hadn't ended well.

I located my phone and slid my finger across the screen. I'd missed a text. *Odd.*

"Hey who texted you? No one ever texts you, except me. Did Grandma Perdita actually figure out how to send texts?" Charlie peered at my phone, and I turned it out of her view.

I punched the notification on the phone. The text was from John. "Hey! Hope your first day rocks. I think we should talk when you come home on Friday."

I hit delete before Charlie could see. The text from John made my heart flutter. *We should talk*, a loaded statement if I ever heard one. Charlie was waiting for me to reply, and I lied. "No, she didn't get a phone. It was from the school. A survey or something about orientation."

She took a sip of her mocha frappe and frowned. "I didn't get one."

As I opened the link for the map, I said, "Think it said randomly selected or something like that."

"Ah." After a long pause, she muttered, "So… I signed us up for a sorority pledge. It's Friday at seven."

I groaned. "Charlie, we talked about this. I don't want to be in a sorority, and we're supposed to go home this weekend. I promised Grandma I'd come home *every weekend*."

"Come on O, we just left home a few days ago. We're only an hour away, so we can go on Saturday morning. This is our college experience. We've got to live a little. Try it. For me?"

I caved at the pout on her lips, even though her green eyes sparkled with mischief. My shoulders slumped in defeat, and her pout transformed into a smile. She did a half clap, adjusting her cup to the side.

I gestured with my chai. "How much do I owe you?"

She shook her head. "Nothing. I used our gift cards from Melissa."

When she saw the confused look on my face, she rolled her eyes. "Our R.A. Honestly, O, you're terrible with names."

R.A., Resident Advisor. Right.

My eyes trailed around the courtyard. Students milled about everywhere. Some carried bookbags; others had laptop bags like mine. It was a warm August day in West Virginia with a soft breeze blowing over my arms. The fragrance of blooming flowers filled the air, mingling with the aroma of fried meat and burnt grease from a nearby student cafe. Checking the map on my cell and the time, I said, "Come on. We better go before we're late."

I stood and lifted my bag to my shoulder. I turned my face to the sun, warming it like a lizard. I hated having to go back inside the frigid buildings.

Charlie called from the sidewalk, "Don't forget your jacket."

It had slipped out of my bag onto the bench. I flung it over the bag and headed for Douglas Hall, holding my phone, map at the ready. While phones were convenient, I preferred paper and real books instead of electronic files, but since my lovely friend threw my map away so we wouldn't look like nerds, my hands were tied. Several other students held maps in their hands, looking around, and part of me wanted to point it out to Charlie, but I held my tongue.

Charlie sucked the last of her frappe dry with a slurp and tossed it into the trashcan. She nodded toward my jacket. "I can't believe it's eighty degrees out and you're carrying a jacket."

"What? It gets cold inside when they have the AC cranked up."

"You and the cold." She shook her head, but held a half smile.

I couldn't help it. I hated being cold, especially in the summer. My favorite place in the world was in the woods, dangling my toes in the rushing water. Even better if there was a warm rock and a soft breeze.

The memory of my last trip to the river turned my thoughts to John's text. Guilt swarmed in my head like stinging bees. I'd kept my relationship with Charlie's brother to myself. My guilt rose because I knew I'd be skipping her Friday night sorority meeting. John wanted to talk. *That* I wouldn't miss.

Chapter Two

DOUGLAS HALL WAS A GRAND FIVE-STORY RED BRICK BUILDING with eight white steps leading to the front entrance and large white pillars holding an overhanging roof. I stepped inside and was surprised the building was missing the familiar smell of crayons, chalk, Elmer's glue, and that odd rubbery gym smell of my high school. Instead, a faint scent of formaldehyde and ether carried on the air-conditioned air. This was the smell of college. Charlie and I made our way to the classroom.

There was a large whiteboard in front with a wooden podium for the professor to stand behind. The rest of the classroom was stadium-style seating with steps on either side. Each row held a large semi-circular desk that extended across the span of the room. Along one side of the stairs, various doorways led out of the classroom. Each student had their own black leather computer chair with arm rests. *Fancy.* We made our way to the third row and took our seats a quarter into the row. I pulled my laptop from the bag, plugged the cord in one of the sockets lining the floor underneath, and pressed the ON button.

The classroom filled with an ever-increasing chorus of chatter. At three minutes to eleven, an older man, who I could only assume was Professor Zitalee, entered the room. He was of medium height and build, had round horn-rimmed glasses and a large mustache. He wore a long white lab coat that billowed behind him as he whisked through the door carrying a stack of papers. At the sight of him, the chatter in the classroom trailed off. At exactly eleven, he spoke. "Good morning. I am Professor Zitalee, but you can call me Professor Z. This is Biology 101. You should have gotten an email with the class syllabus and my contact information, but I have some printed versions here in case I missed anyone."

Professor Z walked around the podium and handed the large stack of papers to one of the students in the front row. As he turned back to the podium, I noticed a round shiny bald spot on the top of his head. Behind the podium once more, he said, "On top of the stack is a seating chart. Please write your name legibly and do not change seats for three weeks as I attempt to learn your names." He pushed his glasses farther up his nose with the back of his hand. "Okay, let us begin. Can anyone tell me what biology is?" he asked, his nasally voice carrying a northern accent I couldn't place.

My hand rose at the same time as Charlie's. The professor pointed to Charlie. "Biology is the study of life," she said.

"Correct. Biology is the study of life and living organisms, including information regarding their structure, function, growth and reproduction. But don't forget, biology is a science, so first we need to talk about science. Can anyone tell me what science is?"

Someone behind me must have raised their hand because Professor Z pointed. I heard a boy's voice, but his reply was lost as the seating chart was passed to me. I wrote in my best handwriting, Ora Stone.

I looked up in time to hear Professor Z say, "Science is derived by a method that all scientists follow to learn about the truth of the nature of the world and our universe."

Leaning forward to take in the lecture, my hand rose absentmindedly to my neck, and my heart dropped.

My necklace was missing! My hand flew to my chest where my family's amulet usually rested, but instead, my fingers found only the thin fabric of my sundress. A chill of dread rushed through my veins, and I pushed myself away from my desk, my eyes turning to the floor, searching between the sneakers and sandals of my classmates for the faintest hint of gold. Nothing. Grandma's voice echoed through my memory. "Ora, you must never take it off. If you do, you will be in grave danger." And now it was gone.

Charlie elbowed me in the side and asked, "What's wrong?"

I righted myself and leaned toward her. "I can't find my necklace." Her eyes widened. She scooted her chair back and searched as well, but it was no use. My necklace was nowhere to be found. My neck felt naked without the necklace's familiar weight. On my eighth birthday, Grandma had given me the amulet, giving me protection, and I had worn it every day since. And now it was gone.

Even though it may only have been a silly superstition, wearing the necklace made me feel safe, and I'd promised Grandma when she gave it to me that I would never remove it. I stood, my eyes searching the area in front of the door to the auditorium, in case the necklace had fallen there when we'd come inside.

Charlie tugged on my dress. My gaze shifted to her, and she jerked her head toward the professor, whose lips were pursed. "Excuse me."

"Yes, sir?" I blurted, my cheeks flushed red.

"Have somewhere better to be, do you?" Professor Z asked.

I shook my head. "No, sir. I'm sorry, sir." Relief washed over me as his eyes left mine and he resumed his lecture.

"The third step is experimentation," Professor Z continued.

I ignored him. I tried to remember when I last saw the necklace. Reacting to the anxious look on my face, Charlie gave me her most encouraging smile. "It's okay. We'll retrace our steps, and if we don't find it, we'll go to lost and found."

I nodded and wiped a tear from my eye. I chanted silently, *It's only a necklace. It's only a necklace…* But my heart pounded in fear, and I felt an overwhelming sense of danger. My own words echoed in my memory. *I promise. I promise I won't ever take it off.*

I remembered that night as if it were yesterday. Images of our backyard in Michigan and the decorated gazebo roaring in flames flitted in my mind's eye. I ran through the fire, escaping through the other side unburnt. Grandma picked me up and ran with me to our car. We drove and drove and finally checked into a hotel. Grandma left me there alone and returned late that night with the necklace.

Now, conflicting emotions raged inside of me. Should I leave the class on my first day of college? Attempting to ignore my rising panic, I tried to pay attention to the lecture, but the flickering lights from earlier returned with my panic. *I must be hyperventilating.*

My thoughts raced as the light continued to rage at the periphery of my vision. Memories from my childhood flashed before my eyes. In waves of image after image, memories returned. A teddy bear shrinking in a store, a wintery meadow melting into spring, flowers blooming in seconds in my hand, and water boiling when I got angry.

Across The Veil

"Are you okay?" Charlie whispered in my ear.

I shook my head, clearing away the images. I then nodded, but it was a lie. Something was very wrong. I didn't know what. I couldn't put my finger on it. My eyes squeezed shut, and I forced myself to take a deep breath. *You're just freaking out. Having a panic attack or something. Get a grip.*

Opening my eyes, I focused on Professor Z. "Now, a law is something which has been proven over and over again. The best example we have is the Law of Gravity. Now, see, if I pick up this pen, and I drop it—"

The pen started to fall. The world stopped with a sound like a large engine revving down. A funnel appeared around the pen. I could see how every molecule of the pen fit together and how it was connected to the world around it. The entire world transformed into an intricate nautilus forming the tunnel. Something inside me reached out, both familiar and foreign. And it grabbed the pen. Its descent to the ground halted.

The inner design of the pen was fascinating. It wasn't static, but ever-moving in a three-dimensional wave. That foreign *thing* inside me moved again. In response, the pen spun in a slow circle but soon increased in speed. A girl behind me screamed, breaking my trance. The world revved back up. I flinched and the pen crashed to the floor.

A few of my classmates stood with their mouths agape, eyes wide. Someone screamed, "What the fu!" Their words were cut short. A faint rippling rainbow vibrated and sizzled in front of the door. No one but me noticed it.

Other students laughed, the sound nervous.

"Great joke, Professor," said a girl in the front row.

The rainbow at the door shimmered, growing in intensity. The hairs on my arms stood on end, and the nervous laughter flitted away.

Charlie grabbed my arm and pointed. Inside the rainbow, four shadows appeared. She whispered, "What is that?"

With a faint pop, the rainbow vanished leaving only the shadows, each growing more solid. The assumption that this was some sort of joke thinned as the shadows sharpened.

The world turned chaotic. Screams filled the room. My classmates scrambled over one another to get to the doors. The professor was nowhere to be found. Laptops crashed to the floor. Charlie pulled on my sleeve. "Come on! We have to get out of here!"

I stood and made it the bottom step before the other students halted, knocking into each other. Four shadows solidified, blocking the exit. Two men and two women stood there, each wearing a different color of skintight leather.

The panic rose, jolting the students back to life. Some sprinted toward the other doors, individuality lost, a stampeding herd. Others stood where they were, eyes wide. A few had their cell phones up, recording.

"Stop!" One of the men held out a hand. An echoing snap sounded, loud despite the screams. The snap of the other doors locking.

Two panicked students tried to push their way past the strangers but were blasted back and slammed against the far wall. The rest of the students froze, knocking into each other, panting.

"Now, sit down!" The other man marched in front of the classroom glaring like a lion at prey. Fear prickled along my skin. Massive muscles bulged underneath the purple leather of his uniform. His red hair waved in an artificial breeze. Charlie and I, along with a few others, shuffled back toward the front-row seats and sat, waiting. The rest stood in place, frozen by shock. It wasn't everyday people materialized out of thin air wearing leather head to toe.

The man in purple glared at those who remained standing and said, "I'm not going to repeat myself."

Moving as if in slow motion, the crowd found seats. The strangers moved too fluidly and stood too still to be human.

The woman closest to the door had long blond hair and had a model's figure. Miss Runway gazed around the room with guarded blue eyes. Her bluish green leather creaked when she shifted her body to better inspect my classmates. She looked at the first man who spoke, a dark-skinned body-builder clad in blood-red leather.

Miss Runway asked him, "Corporal, did you see anyone escape?"

"No one gets by me!" the man in purple snapped.

The blonde rolled her eyes. "Corporal *Allyn*," she paused stressing the man's name, "did you *see* anyone escape?"

Allyn looked at each of us one by one, and when his fierce brown eyes focused on mine, I shivered. His eyes moved on, and I exhaled the air I wasn't aware of holding. Allyn continued to look at each person and finally answered, "No, Lieutenant Sun."

Across The Veil

This had to do with the pen; I knew it. Whatever I had done with the pen had brought these people here, and they meant nothing but trouble. I looked for the nautilus, but it had disappeared.

"Quiet," the other woman said. Even though her voice was hardly more than a whisper, the ragged breathing from a handful of terrified students stopped immediately. The air around her sizzled as she spoke again. "I'm Commander Stewart, a Protector of Sphere." She paused, letting what sounded like a title resonate. Not that I had any clue what it meant. "It has come to our attention that the magic of the House of Sphere was used today in front of humans. The Concealment Code has been breached. I ask you all now: is there someone here from Sphere illegally?"

I braved a look around the room, but no one answered her. *Protector of Sphere? Concealment Code?* I was lost. Commander Stewart, dressed in chocolate-brown leather, crossed her arms over her chest. "If whoever performed the levitation will come forward, it will go much easier on you."

Charlie grabbed my hand. My fear and confusion were mirrored in her eyes. A scrawny boy with brown hair whimpered. "We... we don't know what you... you're talking about."

Lieutenant Sun answered, "Most of you are innocents. I assure you that once the guilty one has been found, the rest of you will be set free and your memories of this entire incident will be erased. There is no need to worry."

She was talking about magic or some sort of alien or secret military tech. Maybe it was a joke, holding a pen with my mind? It's ridiculous. Maybe it was some sort of daydream or hallucination? But no. I knew I'd done it.

Allyn smirked. "Unless you are a Nip."

At the word, the four strangers tensed. At their reaction, my mouth went dry.

Another boy stammered over his words. "Ma'am, what... what is a Nip?"

"A Nip is a human who steals magic, a vile creature that must be destroyed. And that is all you need to know." Allyn paced in front of the main entrance, glaring at my classmates as if daring us to try to escape. I could only assume the other doors were still locked.

The Commander turned to Sun. "You start questioning these witnesses, and I will go and make sure the Imation Team has arrived."

"Yes, Commander. It will be done." Lieutenant Sun bowed. Stewart turned and left without a backward glance through the main entrance.

"Right, let's get started." Sun made her way to front of the classroom clasping her hands behind her back. The Lieutenant's eyes found Charlie. "Can you tell me what happened here today?"

"You mean the pen thing?" Charlie nodded toward the pen lying ever so innocently upon the floor.

"Yes, the pen. What happened?" Sun leaned her body closer encouraging her to continue.

"I'm sorry, I... I don't know." Charlie looked down and shook her head.

"I think you know." The second man pushed the Lieutenant aside and was nose to nose with my friend. "Where is the witch you did this to? Did you think it would be amusing to show off her power this way?"

This second, more aggressive man in lavender, grabbed Charlie by the arm and jerked her out of the chair and over the desk. Our hands were ripped apart. Books and computers crashed to the floor. Several of my classmates screamed.

"Bizard, stop." Sun moved between them. "I am your superior. Step aside."

Bizard shoved the Lieutenant and glared at Charlie with a look of complete loathing. "You knew what would happen. Why did you do it?"

"I didn't." Charlie's voice cracked, and she gripped his arms trying to break free. Tears welling in her eyes. My mouth went dry, and I couldn't speak. Couldn't move.

"Then who did?" Bizard grabbed her by both shoulders, spun her around, and shook her. Her head whipped back and forth with a snap.

Charlie sobbed. "Please, sir. I don't know. Don't hurt me."

"We'll see," he said. He took a slow, deep breath and exhaled a long stream of smoke. Once released from his lungs, the smoke turned in small circles, quickly gathering speed. They turned faster and faster, hanging in the air, separating Charlie and the Corporal. Charlie's back was to me, and I couldn't see her face. With a nod of his head, the breath came to life, shooting directly at Charlie.

The whirlwind landed on top of Charlie's head. Her hair flew around her, attacking her. Blood splattered from Charlie's face spraying the floor. Her screams ripped through me. I sprang over the desk, shouting. "Stop it! Please stop it! I did it! Do you hear me? I did it! Leave her alone!"

The mini-tornado died away and vanished. Charlie fell to the floor, whimpering and shaking. It had all happened so fast. I knelt at my best friend's side, pushing the hair away from her face with shaking fingers. My murmuring words of consolation meant nothing. I couldn't fathom the amount of blood covering her in such a short time. Deep gashes exposed the stark whiteness of bone.

"Damn you, Corporal," Lieutenant Sun cursed him, her fair skin even paler. "You're always so reckless."

"What the hell is going on here?" Commander Stewart returned, throwing the door open with a bang. During Charlie's attack, a few students had moved to the side doors. They halted trying to shove it open when they saw the Commander. Her face filled with rage. She raised her hand, and the chairs levitated, corralling my fellow classmates and prevented them from leaving.

"I'm sorry, Commander, but during the questioning, Bizard here," Sun nodded toward the Corporal, "disobeyed me and used his magic to interrogate a witness."

The Commander raised an eyebrow. "Sometimes force is necessary, Lieutenant. You are too forgiving sometimes."

Lieutenant Sun's lips pursed, and her hands clinched into fists at her sides. "The questioning had hardly begun. The girl had barely even answered. And she didn't know anything. Bizard has put us all at risk. He used magic unnecessarily. If the Human Representative Association hears of this—" She left the unfinished comment hanging in the air between them.

Stewart raised her hand and shook her head, discouraging Sun from continuing. She turned and looked at Bizard. "Is this true?"

Bizard shrugged. "Technically yes, Commander," he said. "But the other girl there, the redhead, admitted to the crime. So even though Lieutenant Sun doesn't agree with my timing or my methods, they are, nevertheless, effective and quick. The Imation Team can now begin the dememorization, and we can get on with our lives." Corporal Bizard finished his speech with a smug smile.

"She admitted it?" Commander Stewart's eyebrows rose.

"Yes, Commander," Corporal Bizard smirked.

"While I commend you on a fast discovery, I do not, however, condone your non-compliance with Lieutenant Sun's orders. This will be investigated. You will take full responsibility for your actions. Understood?"

Corporal Bizard nodded once. The four strangers turned and surrounded me. Corporals Allyn and Bizard grabbed my arms and jerked me away from Charlie. I screamed for them to let me go and realized my hands were sticky with blood. *Her blood.*

"You have to help her!" I jerked my arms back. "Please, help her." Their arms were like steel. My stomach churned at the thick, metallic smell of blood.

"She'll be okay." Lieutenant Sun's hand was gentle on my arm. "Our Imation Team will heal her. But you will come with us."

Allyn squeezed my arm even harder. "You should have thought about her before, you worthless human."

Bizard leaned forward and whispered into my ear. His hot, rank breath smelling of day old onions blew against my cheek, and my stomach rolled with nausea again. "I'm going to tell the Imation Team not to heal your precious friend. You'll live what is left of your pathetic life knowing she will be scarred forever because of you and your treachery." He blew a breath, but this time no tornado appeared. Instead, a mist flowed outward through the door.

His words washed over me as if a bucket of ice water had been poured over my head. Tears sprang to my eyes. Why would they do that to Charlie? She hadn't done anything. It was me, but what was the big deal of keeping a pen suspended in the air a few moments? I hadn't meant to do anything wrong. It was a simple mistake. I didn't even know how I'd done it.

Across The Veil

"It's time to go." Commander Stewart looked at a device on her wrist. "Allyn, will you go and tell the Imation Team that the suspect has been found? They can begin the dememorization." She inclined her head toward the Lieutenant. "Has the official arrest been performed?"

"No, I'll do it." Bizard pulled my arm even closer to him. His fingers bit into my flesh, and I winced.

The vile man in lavender, who I had already begun to hate, blocked Charlie from my sight. I stared at his chest, but he grabbed my chin, squeezed hard, tilted my face up, and forced me to look into his malicious eyes. "By the order of the Counsel and the Magical Detection Agency, I, Corporal Jabez Bizard, a Protector of the House of Tempest, arrest you for violation of the Concealment Code and improper use of Sphere magic. You shall be escorted through the Veil, to Conjuragic, where you will be held at the Nook until your trial begins. And now we travel."

Chapter Three

BIZARD PUT A CLOSED FIST TO HIS LIPS, LET OUT AN EASY BREATH, and opened his palm. A small bluish orb of air hovered above his hand; only the edges were fuzzy. The temperature around him dropped at least ten degrees. He looked at the Commander and nodded his head. She reached into a pocket of the brown leather outfit. When she removed her hand, it was balled into a fist. She placed her hand in front of the stream of air, and as she opened it, a small amount of glittering sand shimmered like diamonds.

The sand blew from her outstretched hand and merged with the blue orb. At first the orb and sand resisted each other, but as if the two material objects came to an agreement, they merged. The ball pulsated with a golden brilliance. Bizard dropped his hand. The ball shot forward a few feet before halting and flattening out as if it hit an invisible wall. The remnants hummed and expanded into a shimmering curtain, stretching from left to right, with no beginning and no end. It appeared to be made of water that had trapped a thousand rainbows in its depths. Its colors were an ever-changing matrix of beauty, a living painting thin as paper dividing the room. It appeared to fall from beyond the ceiling, absorbed by the floor. Bizard and Allyn took a step and pulled me forward into the curtain of rainbows. Before stepping through, I turned my head for one last glimpse of my best friend.

Charlie hadn't moved from the floor, curled in a fetal position, her face an emotionless mask. She appeared locked away within herself, trapped in a nightmare and unable to escape. And it was my fault.

From the moment the strangers appeared in the doorway, I'd been afraid, but nothing could touch the fear now rolling through me. They were taking me away, and I had no doubt I would never return. My best friend, my grandma, and John were lost to me forever.

The curtain fell over me. In a heartbeat, the world dissolved. Simultaneously I was falling and being ripped apart. I was everywhere and nowhere. It was as if every molecule, every cell of my body was separated, and that same foreign limb inside me awoke with fury. It spread outward, coiling around me like a snake, preventing me from becoming lost in a void of nothingness.

In this place, time held no meaning. There was no one and nothing else. The thing inside me reveled in the feeling, wanting, needing. It terrified me. As if sensing my fear, it sighed and things became solid once more. A new, different light stung my eyes. I covered my face in reflex. Every movement took great effort. I stumbled and would have fallen to my knees had the strangers not pulled me upright. After a moment, my eyes adjusted.

The classroom was gone, replaced by tall, sleek white skyscrapers looming over me. The buildings and cobblestone streets were a river of shimmering light that pulsated and flowed from one building to the next, connecting the city together like a living thing. A new man's voice said, "Welcome back to Conjuragic, gate six-seventeen. I trust your journey through the Veil was pleasant. Magical identification, please."

The owner of the voice was a dark-skinned man dressed in red robes with a gold necklace that held a strange, circular, flame-shaped ruby in the center. Allyn had the same kind connected to his belt.

Each of my four captors turned their right hand palm up, and the air above their hands hazed. The haze swirled, coalesced, and dispersed again. The greeter put a thin wooden stick with a crystal tip into the haziness above their palms, one at a time. The crystal beeped, and each time a different smell radiated from it. Allyn's smelled of burnt marshmallows. Bizard's reminded me of the wild, unpredictable smell before a thunderstorm. A salty sea breeze came from Sun, and fresh cut grass from the Commander. The greeter, apparently satisfied, put the stick away. He dipped his head. "Thank you."

Then he turned his dark eyes on me. At first he appeared curious, but his eyes narrowed with suspicion. "Palm up."

"She can't." The Commander spoke for me, moving closer.

The greeter jumped backward, dark face paling. "Is she a Nip?"

"We're not allowed to discuss open cases, Bryalan. You know that." The Commander looked at the band on her wrist again.

"She must be branded. *You* know that." Bryalan smirked at me, a hint of danger in his eyes. "Which color shall be used?"

"Black, of course. Now get on with it," Stewart waved.

The maliciousness in Bryalan's eyes grew as he disappeared into a red booth, returning with a long thin piece of metal with a black jewel on the end. "Hold her arm out and keep her still."

Sun held her hand up in protest. "Wait, you're supposed to numb her first."

"Well, we could," Bryalan said, holding my arm tighter.

"But we won't," Bizard finished for him. The men laughed.

Before I could react, Allyn grabbed my shoulders tighter, and Bizard extended my left arm. As Bryalan was about to stab my arm, Sun gasped.

The Commander took a step toward Bryalan and yelled, "Stop!"

But it was too late. Bryalan thrust the metal deep into my arm. Heat and cold mingled into pain like I had never known. I must have screamed, but there was only pain. The rod hit bone, and he pressed a button. He yanked the metal rod out of my arm, leaving the black crystal in its place. The pain subsided to a dull ache. Sweat prickled on my brow, cooling but doing nothing for the nausea or panting. As soon as the rod ripped backward, vines reached up behind him, grabbed him around his throat, and pinned him to the ground.

Bryalan squirmed in the vines and yelled, "That was a dirty blow, Stewart." Instead of answering, the Commander flicked her wrist, and the vine covered his mouth, muffling the rest of his words.

My attention jerked away from the vines. The evil black jewel wiggled deep in my arm, penetrating and searching, taking up roots in my flesh and bone. It grew and twisted, scorching like lightning through my nerves. First, it spread tentacles down to the palm of my hand. After finding a dead end, it started a new branch traveling up my left arm, crossed my shoulder, and turned inward. Slithering deeper, searching for the life force of my beating heart. My screams tore through my throat, but there was not a noise I could make to adequately release the anguish. After what felt like a millennium of pain, Sun pushed the men aside and forced a cold liquid into my mouth.

"Drink," she commanded.

Across The Veil

I choked and sputtered, but as soon as the liquid touched my lips, the screams vanished. I drank and drank, desperate, as if my life depended on it. The icy fluid entered my stomach. Its arctic fingers spread throughout my body, demolishing the pain, but not the terror. I stared at the wooden floor of the platform as the jewel grew within me. My heart raced like a spooked horse, and no amount of air could soothe my lungs.

"You're animals!" Sun glared at the men.

She sat down beside me and whispered, "You're okay." Although the pain was gone, I couldn't hold back my sobs, and I was blinded by tears.

"I want to go home," I sobbed, covering my face with my hands. "Please, please let me go home. I never hurt anyone. Just let me go home, and I'll never do anything again."

"We're animals," Allyn spat at Sun, "and what about the Sphere this Nip is murdering? Why should you care what happens to her? You are a disgrace, Lieutenant, betraying your own kind for this disgusting thing."

Sun jumped up from the ground pointing a finger in his face. "*I'm* a disgrace? We don't know what happened in that classroom. What if she is innocent? What are you then?" She shot them both dirty looks.

Stewart interjected with the same calm, commanding voice. "Corporals, our mission is to capture the person who has violated the Concealment Code. We have done so. Our only concern at this time is transporting the prisoner to the Nook. She will undergo trial for her crimes. Until that time, she is, as the humans say, 'innocent until proven guilty.' As you well know, it's against departmental policy for unnecessary harm. Bizard, you already have to answer to the department for your actions during the arrest. You don't want to push your luck. And lower your voices; we are drawing a crowd."

Bizard scowled but bowed to her. "Yes, Commander."

"With all due respect, Commander, how can she be innocent?" Allyn asked. "She admitted it."

"Only after Bizard used his magic to hurt her friend. What if she only confessed in order for him to stop? You have never had any self-control." Sun shoved a finger in Bizard's chest. "You're a danger to the Quad, and to our entire race, Corporal. Not only the department, but the Council will hear of your gross misuse of power. You're not worthy of the rank of Protector."

Bizard's eyes narrowed and his nose flared. "Careful, Lieutenant. You know my connections."

The air around the platform surged with static electricity, raising the hair on my arms. The Commander stepped between Sun and Bizard. "Enough." She faced Bryalan, who was still being held in place by the vines; one was covering his mouth, muffing his protests. "And you will have to answer to the department as well. Release." She flicked her wrist, and the vines slithered beneath the platform.

Springing to his feet, Bryalan ran his hands over his body, as if feeling for more vines. The Commander rolled her eyes. "The Imation Team should return shortly. You'll contact me if there are any problems or delays in their return. Understood?"

"Yes, Commander, I'm at your service." Bryalan bowed low.

"Let's go," she said to the rest of her team.

The Corporals dragged me to my feet. My legs wobbled as if I'd run a marathon. Squeezing my eyes together, I wished this was all a dream, but the nightmare was real.

The Commander and Sun strolled ahead down the three steps to the cobblestone street.

"Stewart, wait," Allyn said.

The women whipped around, both glaring with the same expression of indignation. "Commander Stewart," Sun snapped.

"Commander. The prisoner requires a net."

"A net? She can barely stand. You really think she is going to run?"

"Protocol. Isn't that right, Commander?" Bizard challenged.

The Commander nodded, indicating the men should join her. The men pulled me down the stairs, my toes hovering mere centimeters from the ground.

The Commander whispered to where only the five of us could hear. "This is your first and last warning. Any more disobedience or defiance, and connections or not, you will be off my Quad. Understood?"

Bizard's jaw clenched. "Yes, sir."

Commander Stewart stretched out a hand. The men yanked my arms in front of me, placing a hand over each of my wrists. Sun's hand extended as well. The same haziness appeared in their hands. It lasted a second before an invisible rope swirled around my wrists and waist. It moved, rolling and flowing, at times like air and others like water. Warm in places and icy in others.

The Protectors turned as one and pulled me farther into the road. They led me through the city. People lined the streets, coming in and out of various shops. Each wore robes with a talisman necklace very similar to Bryalan's, but like the Protectors, there were four colors: brown, purple, red, and blue. Their talismans differed as well. Those in red had the ruby flame. In brown a green orb; purple, a tornado; and blue, a teardrop.

When we were spotted, the people's eyes went wide, or they pointed, clasping a hand over their mouth. A woman with young children hurried them inside a building.

The roads were narrow. No cars or horses were present. No indication of how people got around. The city streets were clean and flat, and the way the city shimmered made me feel as though I were walking on water. The names of the businesses were strange, and I wondered about these places to take my mind off the lingering pain in my arm.

Along Fay Avenue, the Fairy Unemployment Agency loomed over the other shops. What appeared like little women flew in front of the building, zooming in and out. They were too small and moved too quickly for me to be sure. Fairies. Real fairies.

On the corner of Troll Lane, delicious smells of seared meat and spice drifted out of the open doorway to The Human Eatery. With a name like The Human Eatery, I wasn't sure I wanted to know exactly what meat they were cooking. Another five minutes' walk took us to the edge of the city. The cobblestone stopped, and beyond, a sea of grass separated a vast hill. The change was so abrupt, my senses couldn't take it in. It was almost as if the place was pieced together like some giant jigsaw puzzle. We stopped walking at the last shop, Wonderful Witches' Potions, and stood in front of a large wooden post. It was once a large tree, but it looked out of place in this white city. I think perhaps this was done on purpose, making it easier to see amongst the buildings.

The Commander pulled out a card, placed it into a slot in the middle of the large post, and zipped it in and out like a credit card. The post split along the middle, above and below where the card was inserted, until the split was a foot in length, and then stretched open. A few moments later, a fairy zoomed up from inside the depths of the post into the round hole made by the card. "Good afternoon," the fairy squeaked.

My mouth fell open as I took in his appearance. He was like a miniature caveman with a ragged beard and matted, tangled hair. He wore black pants that were little more than rags and a loose red shirt that was covered in tree sap. His wings were like a moth's, dull and boring. "You can't possibly be real?" The words were out of my mouth before I realized it.

The fairy's face contorted, and he zoomed out of the post, stopping in front of my nose. "Of course I'm real. And, yes, there are male fairies, too. Bet you thought we're created every time a baby laughs for the first time! Ha! No, we use—" He moved to the waist of his pants.

"That will be enough of that." Sun swatted at him.

"Trying to hit me, are you? I have half a mind not to even call the Transport and make you walk. Yes, that's what I'll do. Disrespectful witches…" He zipped back into the post, disappearing into the darkness below.

The opening started to close, and the Commander stuck her hand in preventing it from sealing. "Excuse me." When there was no response, she said again, "Excuse me!" and knocked on the post.

"If you lost us our ride, you'll be sorry," Bizard whispered into my ear so no one else could hear him. "This will not be a pleasant walk for you." I doubted anything here would be pleasant for me, but I didn't say so.

After a few minutes, the little fairy reemerged from the post. "Oh, it's you again. I'll not help you. Do you hear?" He pointed his small little index finger at me.

"I'm Commander Stewart, leader of this Quad." She nodded her head toward me. "We are escorting a prisoner to the Nook. We will get a Transport, or you will be joining her there."

His mouth opened in surprise. "Yes, ma'am. I'm sorry, ma'am. Right away then, ma'am," he stammered as he zoomed away, weaving between the buildings and out of sight.

Allyn shook his head and sighed. "Stupid fairies. How dumb can you get? He didn't even notice that she's being held by a hook! They think we owe them something because they warned us a hundred years ago about the centaurs." The other three nodded in agreement.

In the distance, a repeating deep sound reverberated along the buildings. A *womb, womb, womb* noise like something between a large machine and beating wings. The sound grew louder with each passing breath, accompanied by a rush of wind sending the settled dirt in the grass flying. The Protectors were unconcerned, looking more bored than anything.

Leaning forward, I looked toward the sound. A huge machine, larger than a train, sparkling in the sunlight, zoomed toward us. "Finally," Bizard said.

The Transport slowed, turning the womb sound into a slow hiss. The stark white cars seemed endless, flowing with that same energy as the city that I couldn't explain. The Transport's sleek frame swam through the air, running not on tracks but skimming the surface.

The Transport halted at the post, and the little fairy returned seconds later, panting. "Sorry for the wait, Commander." He saluted her before returning to the darkness of the post, and the hole closed behind him.

No doors could be seen, but after a faint pop part of the side of the Transport vanished, revealing a dark opening. Two little black platforms floated outward and ended in a cascade. The Commander ascended the steps first. She spoke quietly to the conductor before waving the rest of us to board. The steps weren't wide enough for Bizard, Allyn, and myself, but as soon as my foot touched the step it extended outward, accommodating us with no problems.

The conductor fidgeted with her red hair, trapped in a bun at the top of her head, trying her best to avoid looking in my direction. She cleared her throat and turned her soft green eyes upon Allyn and gestured behind her. "Security car is in number fifty-four. Step on the wheel and you should be there momentarily."

Bizard jerked my arm and stepped on the black pathway running down the middle of the extremely long train. One heartbeat, the floor was stationary; the next, we were speeding down the corridors in a blur. I swayed as the cars passed, and Sun put her hand on my shoulder to keep me from crashing to the moving floor. Just as fast as the floor moved, it stopped, and I sped forward, crashing into the Commander's back. Allyn yanked me backward.

"Sorry." I couldn't meet her glare.

The disembodied voice of the conductor said, "Car fifty-four, Security."

Another pop and an opening appeared to my right. Without being told, I followed the Commander inside. A straight-backed, sterling silver seat sat in the middle, facing a magnificent window, and two plush cream couches sat on either side. They pushed me to the central seat, hard and impersonal, before taking their own seats on the comfortable-looking couches. No matter how much I stretched, twisted, or repositioned myself, the silver chair wouldn't give an ounce of comfort.

The Commander passed her arm over a panel beside the door, and with another pop, the opening disappeared, leaving us sealed inside as it hissed closed. The Transport rolled forward, but if not for the window, I would never have known. No movement could be detected, and even the *womb, womb* I'd heard earlier was absent.

My thoughts turned to Charlie. She'd been hurt badly. Would they have healed her or left her like Bizard had said? And what about my grandma? How would she ever find out where I'd gone? I'd seen enough to know I wasn't on Earth anymore, at least not the Earth I knew. Any hope of rescue was hopeless.

The Transport picked up speed. The grasslands where we'd boarded ended in the same odd way as the city. We moved into the edge of a massive forest that bulged with strange and welcoming trees beckoning me to come and live amongst their branches. They invited me to share their view from the top of the world and sleep in their loving limbs. As the forest started to dwindle away, a sign read, "You are now leaving The Willow. Come Back Soon."

The trees thinned and merged onto soft feathery-white sand. In moments, a sea opened before me. The water as clear as crystal, cleaner than any I'd ever seen. The waves caressed the shore with a gentleness the human world's oceans could never hope to achieve. Birds far more colorful and larger than sea gulls swooped toward the ocean, and dolphins jumped upward, meeting as if playing a game. Wanting a closer look, I leaned forward, but before I could stand, Allyn shoved me backward.

"It's beautiful, isn't it?" Sun smiled, gesturing to the water. "It's called the Severn Sea, and it's my home. The Haven is beyond those rocks there." She pointed at what she called rocks. They were nothing like the hard, dirty stones I'd seen my entire life. These "rocks" looked like huge pearls, smooth and perfectly round with small flat areas where you could sit. The water didn't stick to their slippery surface.

Without warning, the Transport did a one-eighty, heading out into the Severn Sea. I screamed as the great metallic beast flipped vertically and dove into the blue water. We remained in our previous positions, not flying out of our seats as I expected. The Protectors remained aloof, as if nothing was out of the ordinary, except for Bizard, who smirked as I panted. The room swam around me as I tried to take it in. Outside the window, water slipped by. My eyes darted around as I waited for our car to fill with water. None came.

The voice of the conductor chimed overhead. "Next stop, Syreni Antro."

The Transport righted itself, and my head spun again. At the conductor's announcement, Sun gave a small humph of surprise. "The mermaids are leaving the sea? Something big must be up."

"Today is the Creatura Tribus. Everyone who's anyone is going to be there." Allyn mumbled the last.

Recognition flashed in the Commander's eyes. "That's right. You two were supposed to get off early today."

Bizard glared at me, as if it was my fault he had to work late. I averted my eyes and instead peered out the window, trying to catch a glimpse of these mermaids. I wondered how they would be traveling. Was there a cart somewhere filled with water or something else even more miraculous?

"Who's your money on?" Allyn asked Bizard.

Bizard straightened. "Socin, all the way."

Allyn laughed and covered his mouth with his fist. "What? Socin?" He leaned back shaking his head. "Nedra. Now there is someone to be reckoned with." He shook a finger toward Bizard.

Bizard scoffed. "A centaur over an elfish prince? You've lost your mind."

Sun interjected with a smile. "I heard Elvis is playing tonight."

"Isn't Elvis dead?" I blurted out without thinking.

Bizard rolled his eyes. "Stupid human."

Out of the corner of my eye, I caught movement. A mermaid swam before our window. She had a pale greenish face and a long thin body that tapered into a shiny tail, covered in various green, blue, and purple scales. Her hair was a forest green and floated around her head like a mass of seaweed. She paused for a moment to stare back at me, before smiling and waving with her long, slender, webbed fingers.

Much too soon, we left the Severn Sea and entered another forest, this one dark and foreboding. Its trees were twisted and broken, and instead of calling to the world for companionship like those in The Willow, these warned only of death and pain. Fog filled the forest giving it a haunted look. The Transport slowed to a halt, and the conductor announced, "Stop number nine eighty-three. The Shadow Forest." The four Protectors stood.

Of course, this was our stop. This time, I steadied myself and didn't fall as the corridor moved or stopped. Before we exited the Transport, the four Protectors grabbed gas masks from a hidden bin and put them on. There wasn't one for me.

Bizard and Allyn shoved me out of the cart, and I landed hard on my knees.

"Bizard," the Commander yelled.

"What? She tripped."

Breathing in the foggy air, I watched as the trees blurred. Pain sprang up around my head, squeezing, pulling nausea from deep in my belly. My heart picked up speed, beating faster and faster. From beyond the tree line, yellowed eyes with vertical pupils stared out at me. From all around came growling and snarling. Cries of pain rippled through the air. Visions of women and children ripped apart by beasts filled my mind's eye. For the first time since my capture, I ran, desperate for escape.

The rope constricted around my wrist, yanking me around, and I lost my balance. I slammed into the ground with a thud and gasped as the air escaped my lungs. The pain medicine Sun had given me at the gate was wearing off. My arm throbbed along in time with my heartbeat. Looking at it for the first time, I screamed and clawed at my skin, unable to do much with my wrists bound. The black stone had imbedded itself in me, marking my skin like a black tattoo of evil vines.

Hands yanked me to my feet, forcing me forward. Unable to focus, they dragged me along an uneven path overgrown with weeds and strewn with pebbles. Unseen things slithered and screamed in the forest. I couldn't break free.

"You better watch out, Nip," Bizard shouted at me through his gas mask and laughed. "There're werewolves and goblins in this forest, and they love the taste of human flesh."

"Are you sure you want to run away from us and go in there?" Allyn's face appeared in front of my eyes.

The fear settled in my abdomen, and vomit spewed from my mouth. Allyn jumped out of the way at the last second, but some of the acidic bile hit his shoes. He cursed.

With every breath of the mist, the panic grew. They dragged me farther into the forest. Time meant nothing. It could have been minutes or days. We stopped without warning. Allyn held his arms out wide. "We're here, Nip. Behold, the Nook."

My head raised, and the blackness took me.

Chapter Four

Perdita Stone rocked in an ancient chair on her front porch. The rhythmic thumps it made upon the wood chased away the shortness of breath she'd been battling ever since Ora had moved into her dorm. Her silver hair was still streaked with the blond of her youth, but her once-flawless pale skin was now touched by time. Worry shadowed her green eyes as she attempted to lose herself in the sunlit afternoon, a light breeze rustling the tree leaves.

Her granddaughter had finally left home, away from her protection. Perdita played through her mind for the hundredth time the arguments leading up to her reluctant permission for Ora to go away to school. Perdita understood Ora's arguments. Ora would be with Charlie, so she wouldn't be alone. And she did need to get away, to start fresh where everyone didn't think of her as a "freak," as Ora put it. Perdita knew she should be encouraging Ora to move on to the next phase of her life. This was the norm in the human world. But Ora had no idea the danger she could be in, and no one was to blame except Perdita. She should've told Ora the truth, but she'd been a coward, like always.

Perdita's blood ran cold, interrupting her thoughts. Something was wrong. She cursed herself. From behind her eyes, she saw a flash of Ora's eyes wide open in terror, then Charlie's, covered in blood. A blood-curdling scream rang in Perdita's ears. Inhaling, she smelled the distinct scent of fresh rain, mud, and the pungent chlorine smell of ozone—the Veil.

Perdita's jumped from the chair and ran through the screen door into the house. Evelyn McCurry's face wavered behind Perdita's eyes as if through water. Perdita's hand was on the phone receiver seconds before it rang. "Evelyn, what's wrong?"

Evelyn's voice on the other end was shaky. "It's Charlie. She's been attacked. We're on our way to Dalley Hospital. We're sending John over to get you." There was a pause on the other end of the line and then, "Perdita, no one knows where Ora is."

Perdita swayed, balance gone as if the floor had dropped out from under her. She knew this day would come; she had hoped against it, ran from it Ora's whole life, and despite all her efforts to keep her safe, here it was. If only Ora had listened, if only she had stayed. If only she had warned her. But there wasn't time for regrets. Perdita took a deep breath, forcing herself to be calm. "Okay, Evelyn, I'll be waiting."

Thirty minutes later, John, Charlie's brother, sped up the driveway in his beat-up old pick-up. Perdita grabbed her purse and suitcase and climbed in the truck. "Let's go." John pulled the truck out of the driveway without a word and headed for the interstate.

"Tell me what you know." Perdita looked at his young face, and it was hard for her to believe this handsome young man, now twenty-two, was a boy only a few short years ago.

He was tall with skin turned golden-brown by the sun and toned muscles from working at his grandfather's dairy farm. His brown hair was cut short, and his eyes were like warm chocolate, normally kind and smiling, now filled with worry.

"Not much," he said. "I was working this morning when I got the call from Granddad. He told me the school called around one o'clock because they found Charlie." His voice broke, and he fell silent. He drummed on the steering wheel. "They said she must have been attacked, and her face is—" He couldn't continue and shook his head before saying, "They were taking her to the hospital by ambulance. That's all we know."

Perdita's heart ached for him. "I'm so sorry. Was there any more news about Ora?"

"Grandma asked about her, but they said Charlie was the only one found. And Grandma insisted they check on Ora, too."

"Well, they wouldn't be allowed to tell Evelyn anything anyway. She isn't related to Ora." Perdita wrung her hands.

"But they're roommates."

"John, they're in Dalley. No one knows them there."

"How can no one know where Ora is? Granddad figures something must have happened to her, too."

"After I hung up with your grandmother, I called the school and asked them to check on Ora, to send someone over to their dorm room. I was told hundreds of parents have already called requesting information on their children, and they don't have the resources to check on every single student at the school."

"What? Not every student was best friends or roommates with the girl who was attacked."

"I know, but what can I do from Raleigh? I'll have to go myself once we get to Dalley."

"I'll go with you."

Perdita shook her head. "No, let's go to the hospital first. You need to be with your family."

"Ora's my family, too."

She shot him a questioning look. He squirmed in his seat. "We, she and I... We, sort of, well, we used to..."

Perdita let out a small gasp. "John, when did that happen?" Ora and John, a couple?

"At the beginning of summer." He shrugged as his cheeks flushed red. "But it doesn't matter right now. I have to find her."

"I know." Memories of the Veil's scent returned. Perdita's eyes burned as she prayed she was wrong.

"No, Grandma Perdita. You don't understand. I, we, had this fight and kind of broke up before she left. I didn't want her to leave me. I told her I wouldn't wait for her." He trembled, looking too old for his young age. "She walked off without saying anything to me. I'm such an idiot. I, of all people, should understand everything she has been through. Always teased by these ignorant redneck hicks."

Perdita said nothing as John spoke. Under any other circumstances, he would never divulge this information, especially not to Ora's grandmother, but his worry had relaxed his tongue.

He scowled. "She wouldn't even look at me when they moved in." Perdita recalled the icy silence as he carried in box after box, but she'd been too distracted to pay much attention.

"I was going to apologize this weekend. But now she's missing." His voice trailed off. After a few moments, he murmured more to himself than to Perdita, "She's got to be okay."

Across The Veil

Perdita didn't know what to say, so she kept silent for the rest of the trip. She couldn't fathom how she missed Ora's summer romance. Perhaps she'd been too worried about their separation. And she had good reason to be worried. She prayed silently to the gods, repeating the words she'd heard her own mother speak, and ended the prayer with her own plea. *Please don't let Ora be in Conjuragic.*

In less than an hour, they arrived at the hospital. Evelyn and Jacob McCurry sat in the waiting room on the third floor, skin pale and ashen. Evelyn rocked back and forth in an unconscious attempt to comfort herself. In a corner chair, Jacob watched the news on TV. His gray hair stood up on one side where he'd grabbed it in agitation. He turned his green eyes to Perdita and touched his wife. "Evelyn." He nodded toward Perdita and John. He and Evelyn stood and hugged Perdita and John.

"What's happened?" Perdita asked.

"We still don't know exactly." Jacob looked as lost as Perdita felt. "We got a call from the school saying Charlie was hurt. These imbeciles don't have any idea what happened. They said when the students arrived for the one o'clock class, they found her." Jacob's voice cracked, and Evelyn let out a sob. Perdita pulled Evelyn to her shoulder.

"She was alone, hurt, and they rushed her to the hospital. No one saw or heard anything." Jacob wiped away the dampness on his lashes.

Evelyn trembled. "The doctors came and spoke with us. They told us that Charlie is in shock. Her face has," she brought her hands up in fake quotation marks, "numerous lacerations."

Jacob finished, "She's getting stitched up now."

"Any word about Ora?" John asked as he crossed his arms over his broad chest.

Evelyn went to John, and he wrapped her in his arms. Jacob pulled on his hair again, making it stand up further. "No. Not a word. The school wouldn't tell us anything. She's still not answering her phone?"

The slight nod threatened Perdita's feeble grip on her emotions. "I've spoken with the school already, but they're refusing to send anyone to check on Ora. I need to head over there."

"Why wouldn't they check on her? She's Charlie's best friend and roommate!" Evelyn's face contorted. Her normal steadfast manner wavered in the roller coaster of emotions.

"I know. Don't put any more on your plate. I'm headed over to the school. If Ora's there, I'll let you know." Perdita checked the clock on the wall, after three o'clock already. She'd have to hurry before the school's administration offices closed.

"Thank you, Perdita." Evelyn brushed the tears from her cheeks with the back of her hand as Jacob kissed his wife's forehead.

Perdita smiled, feeling the slightest tinge of jealousy at their affections. "If you'll both excuse me, I need to call a cab."

"Nonsense. John, take Perdita to the school." Jacob turned to his grandson, who had slumped into a chair as if in a daze. "Call Grandmom's number if you find out anything, and we'll call you if she turns up here." John stood and joined the small group, and Jacob hugged him in a tight embrace.

"Will do," John said, his voice muffled by Jacob's shoulder.

Perdita walked up the concrete steps of the girls' dormitory, passing the dim gray and depressing walls. The air inside the building was stale, as if no one ever bothered to dust or open a window. Perdita couldn't believe it had only been a few short days since she helped Charlie and Ora move in.

The girls' room was on the fifth floor, half way down, number 515. Most of the girls were in their rooms, every door open except for one, and they sat together whispering about an attack. A young girl of medium height and build, about twenty years old, met them in the hallway. Perdita recognized Melissa, the R.A. "Can I help you?" Melissa asked.

"Yes. We've met before. My name is Perdita Stone. I'm Ora's grandmother. And this is John McCurry, Charlie's brother. We're looking for Ora. She's gone missing. We were hoping to check their room."

The whispering from the girls grew louder at this. Melissa visibly paled. "Yes. I remember you now. I'll get my master key." Melissa disappeared into a room at the beginning of the hallway.

Across The Veil

Perdita leaned against the wall opposite Ora's room, hoping she would find her inside, but she knew the room would be empty. Melissa returned with the key and knocked briefly before placing the key in the lock and swinging open the door. *Empty.* Melissa excused herself and retreated.

The room hadn't changed much since move-in day although they had put their things away. Two twin-sized beds were on opposite sides of the room, and the small desks at each end were covered in new books. Their spines were intact since they hadn't been opened yet. Perdita wondered if they ever would be. The room boasted a large armoire that held the girl's clothes, and above it they had plugged up a TV. The room smelled of Ora's perfume, and Perdita felt tears well in her eyes.

At the foot of the bed, covered with Ora's blue and gray comforter, Perdita spotted light glinting off Ora's necklace. She bent and retrieved it while John's back was turned. The chain had snapped, the magical binding released. Ora's magic had returned. Perdita slipped the necklace into her pocket with a sickening finality. Pain squeezed at her heart, and she felt as if there wasn't enough air in the room. Any remaining hope that Ora was safe evaporated in an instant.

Perdita's cell phone rang in her purse, making her jump. She answered on the second ring. A man's voice was on the other line. "Hello. I'm trying to reach Perdita Stone."

"This is her."

John shot her a questioning look, and she shrugged her shoulders.

"Yes, this is Gordon Miller, the president of Dalley University."

"Have you found Ora?" Perdita blurted, and John stepped closer, trying to listen in.

"Um, no ma'am. We have not. I was calling to set up a meeting. Ora's roommate—"

Perdita interrupted him. "I already know about Charlie. I'm on school grounds now. Where do you want to meet?"

"Oh, um... I'm at Douglas Hall, in the biology auditorium."

"I'm on the way." Perdita hit the end button, looked to John and said, "We're meeting with the president of the school."

Perdita and John left the dormitory and found Douglas Hall. Police tape blocked the entrance to what had to be the biology classroom. The door opened, and two men stepped out. The lecture hall flashed as men in police uniforms snapped pictures. A pool of blood was visible for an instant before the doors shut.

The two men introduced themselves as Professor Zitalee and Mr. Miller. Both men's faces were constricted under stress. A deputy joined them from a spot across the hall that had been made a temporary break room. The smell of old coffee and stale cigarettes followed the deputy.

"Good afternoon, ma'am. I'm Deputy McGraw. I presume you are Ms. Stone?" His blue police uniform was crisp, and he removed the hat, placing it under one arm, revealing a balding head.

"Yes."

"You're aware of the circumstances that went on here today?"

"By 'circumstances' you mean how my sister was attacked?" John glared at the man, his voice coming out like a growl.

"Ora Stone is friends with the victim, and they're roommates?" Deputy McGraw said, ignoring John.

"That's correct. No one has been able to get in touch with Ora."

Professor Zitalee, a middle-aged man in a bad suit, spoke. "Someone wrote her name in the seating chart this morning."

"So, she was in your class today? With Charlie?"

Zitalee squirmed, looking as if he'd wished he hadn't spoken. "I can only say her name was written down. I don't remember."

"She's got long red hair. She does tend to stand out!" Perdita held out Ora's high school picture for the men to study. The man didn't even bother to look.

"I'm sorry, Ms. Stone, but I don't remember her," Zitalee said, shaking his head. His hair stood on end, and his skin paled. In other circumstances, she might have felt sorry for him.

"How do you know you can't remember her?" John grabbed Ora's picture and shoved it in the professor's face. "You're not even looking."

"John, calm down." Perdita pulled him away from the professor. "You're not helping."

Across The Veil

"Ms. Stone, I'm sure she is fine." Mr. Miller's condescending tone enraged her. A portly man with greasy, thinning hair combed over to one side to try to cover his bald head, the deputy opened his mouth to speak, looking doubtful.

Perdita jabbed Ora's picture at him like an accusing finger. "Fine? She's fine? Are you out of your mind? Charlene McCurry, Ora's best friend, was attacked *at your school,* and no one knows what happened to her. And now my granddaughter, another student in the same class *at your school*, is missing, and you say everything is *fine*?"

"Uh, well, I..." The man's gaze fell to the floor, and he shuffled back and forth. His eyes darted side to side as if deciding if he needed a lawyer.

"I don't remember the class at all. Nothing," Zitalee said, more to himself.

The dread that had been building all day spiked. Everything pointed to the truth, but she didn't want to believe it. Why else would he remember nothing if he hadn't been dememorized? "Get out of my way," Perdita said as she pivoted, and asked John, "Can you take me to the police station so I can report my granddaughter missing? Officially." She glared at the deputy.

"Do you really think that's necessary?" the president interrupted, reaching for her elbow to stop her from leaving. "There really isn't any evidence, and the attack already has the students afraid."

"Yes, it's necessary!" John said as he yanked Perdita away from Mr. Miller's grasp.

"Honestly, you don't care about Charlie or Ora; you only care about your school's image and the money you will lose because of Charlie's attack!" John shouted as Perdita stormed out of the building. John followed close behind her, calling out obscenities.

They left the school, got into the truck, and headed toward the police station. As they drove along a winding road, Perdita stared out of the window into the trees beyond, caught up in her own thoughts.

John abruptly laughed. He glanced her way. John's grin faded into sadness. "I remember the day Ora came home with Charlie. I remember I told Grandmom I had inherited another sister. I complained one was bad enough."

Perdita smiled. She, too, remembered how quickly the girls became close. "But now, I would give anything to—" He couldn't finish.

Perdita understood. Ora and Charlie had grown up together. For a long time, Ora had been like another sister to John, and then this past summer, she had blossomed and become something much more. And instead of staying at home, Ora left. She lost her amulet, and her powers had returned. Now Perdita had to find a way to get across the Veil to find her. She recalled something that might work, if only she could remember that woman's number.

Chapter Five

After a very disappointing half hour, Perdita and John left the police station. The police had offered them little help, but at least she was able to fill out a missing person's report.

"I can't believe they're going to sit on their asses and do nothing!" John said for the tenth time. Perdita nodded. A plan had been forming in her head, but it was dangerous. Too many things could go wrong, and she might put Charlie and her family in further danger.

Perdita needed help if she was going to get across the Veil to rescue Ora. She would have to explain some things to John, but she didn't know how much of the truth he could handle. His reaction was vital. If she had any chance to save Ora, she would need his help. She knew he would be willing, if he believed her, but humans were so reluctant to see the truth.

"John, pull over at the rest stop coming up."

John shrugged, pulled into the right lane, and then turned into a deserted rest stop. Perdita surveyed the area. A forest situated behind the weigh station would be perfect. It was isolated and close to the road. It would probably only show up as a minor blip on the Magical Detection Agency's radar. Perdita turned back to John. "Kill the engine. We need to talk."

He looked worried but did as she asked. The vibrations of the truck's engine faded. Perdita clasped her hands in her lap, looked down, and sighed before speaking. "There are things you don't know about Ora and me. Things even Ora doesn't know. I have never told anyone what I'm about to tell you now. When you hear the truth, be patient, and the answers will come. If you have more questions when I'm finished, then I will answer them, but we have to act quickly."

John regarded her, his brown eyes full of questions. "Okaaaay."

"Ora and I are witches," Perdita said.

Whatever he was expecting, it clearly wasn't this. He shook his head and laughed. Before he could speak, Perdita held up her hand to silence him.

"I know what you're thinking. I'm a crazy old woman, off her rocker. But as I said, let me finish before you make your decision. I assure you, Ora and I *are* witches, but she doesn't know it. I've never told her. I was waiting until she was ready, but I've lost my chance now. It's my fault she's in danger," Perdita admitted aloud for the first time. She lowered her head in shame and felt the full weight of her guilt on her shoulders.

"You know where she is?" John asked. His amusement died.

"Yes, I do. At least I think I do. I'm going to try and save her, but I will need your help. And you need to understand the danger she's in, and the danger we'll be putting your family in if you decide to help me save Ora. But please, let me explain. Okay?"

John said nothing.

"Okay, where to begin? I'm from a different world. I guess you could describe it as a different dimension or realm." She paused for a moment, gathering her thoughts. "I was born there and was a slave my whole life."

"Wha—?"

She waved her hand as if swatting a fly. "When I found out I was pregnant, I knew I had to protect my unborn child. Ora." She looked at him, waiting for the realization to hit him.

"Wait! What? Your unborn child was Ora?" He reeled back in shock.

"Yes."

"So that means you're her…"

"Her mother."

"Holy shit!" John gawked at her with utter disbelief. "But you're so old."

She smirked. "Thanks."

His cheeks flushed red. "Oh. Um. Sorry. No offense or anything."

Perdita cleared her throat. "Yes. Well, I escaped into the human realm before she was born. She, of course, was a witch as well, but since she was only a baby, she couldn't control it. Every time her magic would slip, we would have to run to avoid the Quads."

"Quads?"

"A Quad is a group of four witches or wizards called Protectors. There's one person from each of the magical Houses, and they come here to investigate unauthorized or improper use of magic. Anyway, where was I? Oh, yes. When she would slip, we would have to run to avoid being captured by a Quad. That was why we moved so often when she was younger."

"But what changed?"

"I found an ancient form of magic that protected us: our lockets. She wasn't wearing it today. The chain broke." She reached into her pocket and pulled out Ora's necklace, the one she had worn every single day since he met her, and understanding dawned in his eyes.

He opened his mouth as he finally understood what had happened to Ora and Charlie. "She used magic."

"I believe so, yes."

"And she has been taken by a Quad."

"Yes," she said.

"And taken to your world," he finished. The words hung between them for a few moments. John eyed Perdita's own necklace. "And this prevents you from using your magic?"

She nodded.

"How does it work?"

She avoided his eyes, turning to peer out the window of his truck, looking not at the scene around her, but into the past. "The last time she lost control of her powers was at her eighth birthday party. She caused the yard to catch on fire, and she did it in front of about a dozen people. I knew the Quad was only a few seconds behind us, so we left everything we owned behind."

"Wait, wait? She caught the yard on fire?"

She turned back to him and rolled her eyes. "Witches, remember?"

"I know but fire... really?" His grin was lopsided and still unsure, as if he wasn't quite sure if he believed her.

She huffed. "Do you want to hear this or not?"

"Yeah. Sorry."

Perdita turned back to the window. "After our escape, I realized she was becoming more powerful. So, I left her in a hotel room, went to an isolated area, and performed..." She tried to pick her next words carefully. "Three spells. First, I put a blocking spell in her locket. It prevents her from using magic as long as she keeps it on. I also placed a siphoning spell on my own amulet. I can't use my powers, even if I take it off or lose it."

"Why didn't you do a siphoning spell for Ora, too? Then it wouldn't matter if she wore the necklace or not."

"A good thought, but the siphoning spell can only be performed on yourself. If you do it on someone else, they will die."

"Why?"

"A witch cannot live without her magic. It is tied to her life force, but if you willingly put it elsewhere, you can survive… with consequences."

"What consequences?"

"My youth. But you're right. I knew trusting Ora to keep her amulet on would be nearly impossible. So, I added another spell to my locket, a guarding spell. It prevents any magic from being performed within a thirty-mile radius."

She ran her thumb along the silver amulet, tracing the swirls that connected into a strange and twisting path that led to the crystal in the center. Heat seeped from the crystal pulsating in time with the pearly white smoke that filled it.

John leaned in closer and for the first time saw the smoke. He gasped. "Is that your magic?"

"Yes." She clutched at the crystal, blocking it from his view. A fourth spell had been added to each of their lockets, a sort of disillusionment charm. Humans wouldn't see anything more than a necklace, unless it was brought to their attention.

"It's amazing. I've never noticed the smoke before. Was Ora's smoky?"

"Humans ignore magic. It's in their nature. But to answer your question, yes, Ora's looked like mine." She pulled Ora's amulet from her pocket and held onto the only thing she had left. Ora's was silver and gold with a similar pattern.

John studied Ora's amulet, his eyes narrowed. "Why isn't it smoky now?"

"Because she isn't wearing it."

He looked up, staring out of the truck, his forehead constricted in concentration. "That's why you didn't want her to go away to school. Because only your amulet has the guard spell."

She nodded only once.

"Then why didn't you add a guard to hers?" he asked, his voice rising.

Perdita's shoulder slumped, making the old leather of the truck's seat squeak. "I didn't think about it at the time, and since my magic is locked away, I couldn't add one before she left. Plus, I haven't actually been trained to use my magic. Remember, I grew up as a slave. I was only allowed to use my magic for one purpose. And I have been afraid to use it in this world. It was by chance I actually created these lockets correctly." There was no way to explain the complexities of the spells she had done. The ancient books she had been given when she arrived in the human realm helped. But she had been warned magic without training or the tech used to focus the energies was dangerous. Not only so she wouldn't get caught, but to anyone around as well.

"Right. Sorry." The statement was empty, not because John was cruel but because he couldn't fathom what her life had been.

"What purpose did you use your magic for?"

His question dredged up the past with force. In an instant, she was back inside the rocky walls of the volcano. Sweat running down her back while the guards watched, whips ready. "We were forced to attempt to make an enchanted stone to fulfill a prophecy."

"Prophecy?" He smiled like a school boy listening to a fairy tale.

She shrugged. "I don't know. I never heard it." The pain of the whips every time she and her partners failed the master slashed across her back again. She shuddered.

John's eyes lowered to Perdita's necklace and glazed over. The insane hunger to possess it had begun already. *Fast. Too Fast.* She had to move now.

Perdita recalled the extreme danger of the amulets from the spellbook. How many humans had stolen amulets over the years, killing the owners, only to die because they did nothing but stare transfixed at the magic within? They forgot to eat, sleep, and even move. And they would become violent if anyone tried to take the amulet away from them.

"So what happens now?" John asked, eyes clearing. *He's fighting it.*

She rolled the window down, and the sweet smell of grass greeted her. The crickets were already singing their steady cadence of chirping. "We'll have to go to Conjuragic, the magical city."

"Then let's go." He placed his hands on the key ready to restart the truck.

"Hold your horses. You can't drive to Conjuragic. And I can't go back and say, 'Hey! You've made a mistake, please give me back my daughter.' For one thing, I would either be hunted by my former master, or Ora and I would be killed because of what we are."

"What do you mean what you are? I thought you were witches. Isn't it a city full of witches?"

"We *are*, but we're different from the others. Our kind is forbidden."

"What! Why?" he asked. The poor boy had thought this would be easy.

"You don't need to understand it all now. I need you to understand it will be dangerous for me to go get her. Yes, that's what I am planning on doing." She answered his questioning look. "But it'll take planning and help. It'll be dangerous, and if we're caught, we'll die. And I have no idea what they would do to you."

"So what're we going to do?" he asked, shoulders slumping. His eyes flickered to her necklace and away in rapid succession.

"First, I need to get my magic back." Her fingertips grazed the amulet.

"You can do that?"

Question of the day. "I hope so. I need to break the crystal." *And it's going to hurt like a mother.* Ora's words almost made her smile. *Almost.*

"But won't the... What did you call them? The Magical Detection Agency notice?"

"Probably. That's where you come in. You see, they can't detect magic itself, but they somehow measure the reactions humans have to it. The more people and reaction, the greater the detection. Understand?"

"Kind of." He scratched his head.

"Ora and I were lucky at her birthday party because we managed to sneak out. We barely made it away. But if I'm correct, she did magic today in the middle of class. There were over a hundred people in her class, which means a major detection. The Quad must have shown up in a matter of seconds." Her hands fidgeted in her lap. She was eager to get started, and John's questions were wasting precious time.

"But if she did it in class, then why didn't anyone remember it?"

"Because the Quad probably erased their memories."

"Oh, right. Of course, erase their memories. Why didn't I think of that?" He threw his hands up and rolled his eyes. "Fine, what'd you need me to do?"

"When I break the crystal, it might be noticed. And they may decide to send another Quad because of what happened today with Ora. I need you to wait in the truck while I go over there," she pointed into in the forest, "and release my magic. I need you to be my getaway driver."

He looked at her as if she had gone crazy. "That's your plan?" She gave him a sheepish smile, and he could only shake his head in exasperation. "Fine. Whatever." He leaned over and opened her door. John's eyes wandered to her amulet. Her heart skipped a beat because of his closeness. Until she could release her magic, he was a threat. But once the amulet had been destroyed, his desire to possess it would dissolve, or so she hoped.

She pushed him back to his side of the truck. "Before you decide to help, I need to tell you one more thing. When I'm done, we're going to drive back to the hospital. Hopefully, by then, we'll be able to get in and see Charlie. I need to talk to her."

"But you heard my grandparents. Charlie's in shock. She can't talk with you."

"Witch, remember? I may not be trained, but I know ways of reaching her. We have to make absolutely certain Ora did magic and was captured by a Quad. No need to put anyone in danger if I'm wrong." Her eyes never left his face; she had to make sure he understood every word.

"Okay. Do what you have to so we can go," he snapped, agitation growing with each passing minute. The obsession had to be near the tipping point. He kept glancing at it, hungrily licking his lips.

"John," Perdita whispered. "Charlie was probably attacked by the Quad. She may've been trying to protect Ora. If the Quad comes back, Charlie might get hurt again. And they might also hurt your grandparents, or you. I'm asking you to help me, but these are the full consequences that you or your family may have to pay. I want you to be fully aware of what might happen before you make your decision."

For a few long minutes, he stared only at the amulet, and then with a jerk of his head as if the movement took great effort, his eyes found hers. "How sure are you Ora was captured by the Quad?"

"Very."

He gazed up at the twilight sky, quiet in his own thoughts. The crickets sang their song as the owls hooted in the distance, rising from their daytime slumber. A lifetime seemed to pass in the truck before John sealed his fate. "I'll help. Whatever happens, happens. Go on. I'll be waiting."

Perdita patted his arm. "Thank you. Now let's hope this works." She slid out of the truck and walked with quick steps into the forest beyond, her journey just beginning.

Chapter Six

SABRINA SUN WAITED FOR THE OTHERS TO EMERGE FROM THE Shadow Forest. They'd dropped off their prisoner in the holding cell and filled out the necessary paperwork. She adjusted her mask to keep from breathing the fog, distraught with today's events. Despite wearing the mask, which prevented the misty air from reaching her lungs and causing hallucinations, Sabrina felt a chill race up her spine. She was on constant guard, looking for things slithering in the shadows.

Leigh Stewart strolled out of the woods, looking beautiful despite her gas mask, and stood beside Sabrina. After a few more moments, the men appeared as well. Sabrina doubted she could continue working with Bizard. Perhaps the Council would reassign him, if not dismiss him all together, despite his connections.

Bizard and Allyn laughed, exchanging playful banter and discussing the Creatura Tribus through muffled voices due to their masks.

Their discussion trailed off when they saw their Commander waiting for them. "That has got to be the fastest Nip arrest in history," Allyn said to Bizard, punching him in the back.

"All thanks to me." Bizard stuck out his chest with an air of superiority. Sabrina had the overwhelming urge to blast him with a wave. Her skin buzzed, her power rising to the surface. A definite sign she'd reached her limit with him. Her magic hadn't risen without her call since she'd been a girl.

"Right," Allyn's smile faded, replaced by a scowl.

Bizard didn't seem to notice. Sabrina turned her back to them, rolling her eyes and calling him the worst of curses in her head.

Leigh spoke in her Commander's voice and said, "If you're done boasting, we need to move. Paperwork isn't going to fill itself out."

"Yes, Commander." Allyn bowed. "Are we taking the Transport again or shall we materialize?"

"Materialize. You two go on ahead." Leigh gestured to the men to leave. "Lieutenant Sun and I will meet you there in a few moments."

"Yes, Commander," the Corporals said in unison. Allyn bowed again, but Bizard merely inclined his head. Leigh scowled at his obvious insubordination. The men straightened and vanished. A high-pitched whistle and a slight gust of air followed them.

After the two men disappeared, Leigh motioned for Sabrina to follow her. "Let's materialize closer to the city, and then we can talk for a bit without these masks. I hate sounding like Darth Vader."

"Yes, Commander." Sabrina bowed before closing her eyes and vanishing. She reappeared seconds later at the edge of The Shadow Forest and removed her mask. She pressed the button hidden on the side of a Transport post revealing an opening. She dropped the mask inside, and it disappeared, returning to the Transport storage. Her Commander appeared, and she bowed again.

"At ease," Leigh said.

"Thank you." Sabrina's shoulders relaxed. They strolled along the outskirts of The Shadow Forest. The streets of Conjuragic were surprisingly empty for this time of day. Probably because of the tournament.

Sabrina thought she knew what Leigh wanted to talk about but waited until Leigh was ready. It had been a hard transition for her to start calling Leigh Commander. They'd been friends since forever.

Leigh was a natural leader and had sped through the ranks. She'd always had the ability to silence any room when she spoke. She didn't need to yell or repeat herself. Her tactical skills were in the top of the class, and not even the most hostile situations could break her calm demeanor. People respected her, and it didn't hurt that most of the time, people agreed with her.

Sabrina, on the other hand, found that people didn't like what she had to say. This didn't go over well with her commanding officers, and she suspected it was her friendship with Leigh that had kept her in the military. Sabrina questioned her superiors and disagreed with their methods. She had skirted outright insubordination but had come close to dishonorable conduct once. Not that she would do anything different. There were some lines she couldn't cross. *Again*. How she had made Lieutenant was a miracle. The MDA didn't have a habit of putting friends on the same Quad, but it had been assumed she would obey a friend more than a stranger. So far, they'd been right.

Leigh said, "As you have probably guessed, I don't like discord in my Quad. Between you and me, Corporal Bizard is an ass, but he's, nevertheless, popular with the Council and their advisers, even those of your own House."

"Councilors Talon and Cilla Souse don't approve of Bizard," Sabrina disagreed, immediately regretting her insolent tone.

"The Councilors of Naiad may not approve of him, but Mathesar Enoch does, and he's their most trusted adviser. In fact, Mathesar is drawing more support by the day. It is rumored he will be the chosen as the next Councilor of Naiad House, so you should do well not to step on his toes," Leigh advised.

"Yes, Commander, I know I should. But, I don't trust Bizard. He completely lacks concern for other people. He shoved me aside today, and I'm his superior. I don't mean to overstep my bounds, but as your friend, I have to tell you that he isn't following your orders. He could not only endanger our Quad, but our entire world."

"Lieutenant Sun, I'm aware of what goes on under my command. Trust that his actions today will be addressed. I don't need your assistance in that matter," Leigh snapped. Sabrina had crossed the line.

"Yes, Commander. I apologize and put my trust in your leadership." Sabrina halted, bowed, and fell back in line behind the Commander. Leigh raised her hand and waved her back to her side for a second time.

As they walked along the streets, they heard shouting at the corner of Magic Boulevard and Roman Street. The Protectors hurried toward the sound of voices. Two young boys, both Tempests, shouted at each other. Magic gathered in a sweeping cloud around them. School should be over this time of day, and there was no reason they should be on this side of the city.

"Come on! Magnus said they'd be bringing the Nip this way. Don't you want to see one?" One of the boys, taller with a face covered in freckles, yanked on the other's arm, pulling him closer to the road.

"I'm telling you he lied to us." The second boy had eyes so green they shone like emeralds. He hadn't mastered control of his gifts yet.

"I'm going to check it out. If they have a Nip, then I have to see..." The boys froze when Leigh cleared her throat. White faced, they bowed to the Protectors and said in unison, "Honor to our great city's Protectors. May we always trust in your leadership and the wisdom of the High Council." Their words were stuttered, pulling on memory of the proper greeting.

Leigh waited for a moment, receiving their pledge, and then responded, "Thank you, dear citizens, for your trust and the honor of protecting our fair city. You may rise."

The two boys straightened and didn't meet the Protectors' eyes. Leigh watched them for a moment and then tilted her head to one side. "What, may I ask, brings you two pupils so close to The Shadow Forest and so far away from your western home in The Meadow?"

The two boys both shuffled their feet and mumbled something unintelligible. Leigh crossed her arms and said, "Surely you are learning to speak better than that at the Conjuragic Academy."

The tall one met her eyes, his face flushed with embarrassment, and answered in a strong voice. "We heard a Quad has arrested a Nip today, and we—" The shining-eyed one elbowed him in the side. "Ouch! Oh, all right! *I* wanted to see one."

"And I was trying to stop him."

"I see." Leigh shook her head, putting a hand to her chin. "What are your names?"

"I am Carlin Rafala. House of Tempest, first born of Bruce and Violet Rafala," the tall one said.

Emerald eyes muttered, "I'm Tom Rafala. House of Tempest, second born of Bruce and Violet Rafala."

"Would your parents be pleased to know you were not on your way home to The Meadow?"

"No ma'am," they murmured together.

"Your concern shouldn't be for a Nip or any other arrest. You should be focused on your schooling and how to bring honor to your House. Is that understood?"

"Yes, Protector," they said in the unmistakable monotone of children being reprimanded.

Carlin blurted, "But I want to be a Protector when I grow up."

"Good. We can always use brave Tempests, but you must also follow rules. Now, I think it best you get back to The Meadow. Do you need us to call the Transport for you?" Leigh asked.

"No, Protector. We can walk back to the school and take the Recreator," Carlin answered, shuffling on his feet, clearly anxious to get away.

"Very well then. Go on," Leigh told them. The boys turned and ran away almost before the words were out of her mouth. Before they turned a corner, Sabrina heard Carlin say to Tom, "See, I told you Magnus wasn't lying. That was two members of a Quad. I bet we just missed the Nip." Then the boys rounded the corner, and Sabrina could hear them no more.

"How do rumors spread so fast?" Sabrina wondered aloud.

"It may not be a rumor."

"You really think that girl is a Nip?" Sabrina couldn't believe her ears.

Leigh shrugged, resuming her steps. "What happened today was mysterious and dangerous. We haven't seen a Nip in almost ten years, yet the fear is as powerful as it always was."

"I think we should have made peace with them." Sabrina crossed her arms over herself, thinking hard.

Leigh chortled. "This old argument. You and your bleeding heart."

"Is it so wrong to want peace?"

Leigh halted and turned to fully face her lifelong friend. "You've seen the reports, the old footage. You know what Nips can do to us."

"Just because they can doesn't mean they would."

"Just stop. It's not up to you and me anyway. Our job is to capture criminals and punish them. If you want change, you should've taken the track to be an Advisor."

Sabrina didn't bother arguing. Even if she had gone in politics like her great grandparents, no one listened to her. Her opinions on humanity, Nips, and even the Forbiddens fell on deaf ears. Her thoughts turned to the girl. Was she really a Nip? There was something off about her, but Sabrina couldn't put her finger on it. The girl sent so many conflicting images. Her surprise in the magic she saw today was clearly the reaction of a human, but she resembled a member of Tempest House. But the magic done at the school was Sphere magic. Sabrina didn't know what to think. Curious, she said to Leigh, "I guess we're lucky to have made such a quick arrest today." Sabrina hoped she sounded casual.

"Yes," Leigh murmured. "We were lucky." Uncertainty flashed in Leigh's eyes for only a moment, and then it was gone in an instant, replaced by her usual self-assured expression. If Sabrina hadn't been looking for such a reaction, she would have missed it.

"We should get back." Leigh turned on her heel. "See you there." With that, she vanished in a gust of wind. Sabrina was left standing alone on the corner. She looked back in the direction of the Nook and prayed they had not made a terrible mistake. Then she, too, vanished.

Chapter Seven

A SECOND LATER, THE GUIDANCE HALL LOOMED OVER SABRINA. The Unity Statue was poised at the top of the building. The ivory statue was of the four great mothers who stood in a loose circle, their hands joined with heads tilted back, eyes closed. Above them hovered a crystal sphere filled with a bright light that connected to the Hall by an ivory column of power. The light moved from the center of the crystal, down the column, and into the Guidance Hall, spreading throughout Conjuragic before returning to this very spot. The four cores of magic coursed through the city giving it the shimmering light.

Sabrina adored the Unity Statue and the love and sacrifice it represented. She knew the words on its plaque by heart, drilled into her at Conjuragic Academy.

> The four great mothers, one from each House, brought peace to the land by forming the Guidance Hall. Of all the powerful wizards who fought in the House Wars, none could bring peace and end the suffering. But these witches knew, the only way for the magical world to continue was for the Houses to work together in harmony. They met in secret and planned the city of Conjuragic. They intended the center and heart of it to be the Guidance Hall. They designed the High Council, which would be formed by two representatives from each of the four Houses. These noble witches envisioned the Guidance Hall to be a place where the High Council would reside and work together in harmony to ensure the safety and unity of all of the cores. They wrote the peace treaty and formed the Unity Bond.

The treaty, displayed in the lobby of the Guidance Hall, outlines all their wishes for their Houses. They made history by building the Guidance Hall together because it was the first time all four Houses had ever worked in harmony. At the completion of the Hall, the four great mothers made the final and most magnificent addition to the future site of Conjuragic. They climbed to the top of the Guidance Hall, formed a circle, and placed all their magic, and with it their lives, into the Unity Statue. They sacrificed themselves to protect the city and ensure the alliance of the four Houses.

Sabrina smiled to herself, kissed her hand, raising it to the statue, and bowed her head, offering her respect to the statue. She turned away and walked into the main lobby of the Guidance Hall.

Upon entering the building, she hurried after Leigh, who had turned down a corridor up ahead. The afternoon bells were ringing in the distance as she passed the Magical Creature Liaison office, and she turned a second corner by the Magical Detection Agency headquarters, catching up with Leigh at the top of the stairs of the east wing.

After passing through the Dangerous Magical Weapon Concealment scanner, or DMWC, they made the final left turn and entered the Conjuragic Protector department.

Simeon, one of the department's overworked clerks, sat at the front desk. He had worked for the department for twenty-five years, and he knew his stuff. Sabrina doubted if anyone else could handle the amount of work that came through this office from their Quad alone. Luckily for them, however, Simeon was only fifty years old. Unless he decided to get a new career, he would be there for a long time.

As if to prove his usefulness, Simeon chatted on the communicator dealing with a dispute in The Sierra, the Ember homeland, sorting the mail with his left hand, and filling out the paperwork for an upcoming raid in The Meadow with his right. Even doing all that, he still managed to look up and wink at Sabrina.

Sabrina and Leigh strolled past his desk overflowing with paperwork and continued down the hallway past other Quad offices. Deluge, a Naiad and member of Quad Thirty-Two, stuck his head out of his office and shouted as they walked past, "Congrats on the arrest! That isn't going to look too bad on the record, is it?" His laugh was more of a hiccup.

Leigh murmured her appreciation but continued down the hall to the last office, marked as Quad Room 1. Just inside the office, they found Bizard and Allyn playing their ongoing game of crystal warfare. The two men glanced up as Leigh and Sabrina entered the office. Allyn stood. "Commander, the Council has requested our presence for a full debriefing as soon as you return."

Leigh paused for the briefest second. Sabrina sensed her annoyance that they had been notified instead of her directly, and instead of working, they were playing games.

"Fine. Are we ready?" Leigh asked. When they all nodded their agreement, she left without another word. She really was mad.

Sabrina followed Leigh with Allyn close behind, and Bizard fell into his usual place in line. When they reached the entrance of the MDA headquarters, Simeon nodded his head as they approached, giving Sabrina his usual wink. Leigh surprised them all by stopping at his desk. "Messages for my Quad are to come to me. Understood?"

The reprimand, especially a public one, shocked everyone. Simeon nodded once, unable to answer while on the communicator arranging for another Quad to be sent to The Willow; apparently, someone had stolen some Journey Dust.

After passing through all the additional security measures, they stood in the foyer of the Councilor's Chamber. The foyer was an elegant circular room, the marble walls covered with the portraits of past Councilors. Glass cases along the periphery of the room displayed the various laws that the Council had created and signed over Conjuragic's three-hundred-year history. The dome-shaped crystal ceiling filtered in sunlight and warmed the room.

Two grand ivory doors led into the Councilors' Chambers. The door on the left had a carving of a Sphere tree with leaves blowing by the Tempest wind. The right-hand door pictured a Naiad lake with a small sailboat with a lantern on a hook lit by Ember.

The most interesting part of the room was the huge aquarium floor covered with glass. The fish swam beneath Sabrina's feet within the coral reef below. It reminded her of home.

The Quad crossed the aquarium floor and stood before a large oak desk located off to the right of the doors. Leigh took one step closer and waited a few seconds for Phoebe, the Councilor's secretary, to acknowledge their presence. Phoebe was a mousy little witch who kept herself busy by shuffling papers on her desk. When Phoebe failed to acknowledge Leigh, the Commander cleared her throat. "Quad One, reporting as requested."

The little witch jumped and looked up with nervous eyes. "Yes, Commander," Phoebe squeaked, knocking over her drink. Sabrina sent a gust of power into the liquid so it rose from the table and placed it back in the secretary's cup.

Phoebe sighed appreciatively. "Thanks." She picked up a communicator and spoke into it, "Pardon me, High Council. Quad One is here." She listened a minute before setting the shell-shaped communicator down. "Just a few minutes."

Sabrina stole a glance at the hourglass; it was almost four o'clock, and the staff would soon be leaving for the day. She smirked to herself, figuring Phoebe was only pretending to be busy until quitting time.

Leigh stepped back, taking her place in line, and Quad One stood at attention, awaiting their audience with the Council. Sabrina resisted the urge to look around the foyer at the portraits of the past Council members. She longed to look for her ancestors, Sam and Catrina Sun, the first members of the Council from Naiad House, and more recently, her great grandparents, Claire and Tobias Sun. Sabrina had often wondered if they would be proud of her. She was a member of the first Quad, after all.

The two great doors leading into the Council's Chambers opened. The sweet smell of roses, magnolias, and jasmine wafted through the air. Commander Stewart waited until the doors were fully opened before entering the Chamber.

Sabrina crossed the threshold, and she stood within the circular room of the Council's stronghold. The dome ceiling was directly underneath the Unity Statue's crystal ball. The light and magic from the crystal flowed into the Chamber; the separate cores unwound in this room to display the magic of the various Houses, and then at the marble floor, they rejoined and went on to flow throughout the city.

Naiad's magic took shape as a waterfall on either side of the entrance doors. The water flowed from the dome down to the floor and then moved in two directions; first underground to the aquarium underneath the foyer, then around the circular room to the garden.

Across The Veil

Across from the lanterns, the Council awaited them at their massive half-moon table. Their golden headpieces came to a point on the middle of their foreheads, symbolizing their position. Their delicate silk robes were golden, and instead of the usual House jewel, a golden ankh hung from their neck. Their departures from the usual attire of their Houses separated them from the rest of the citizens and represented the unity of the Council.

Sabrina marched in line to the front of the Council's table, facing the garden. Leigh ordered an about-face. As one, they twisted and faced the Councilors from their own Houses.

Once in place, Leigh called out. "Quad One, Pledge on my count... one, two, three." Sabrina and the rest of the Quad dropped to their knees, bowing until their foreheads touched the floor. They chanted in unison, "Honor to the High Council. May we always trust in your leadership and wisdom. Guide us, lead us, and protect us."

Sabrina, as was customary, remained bowed until the Council said together in a bored tone, "Thank you, Protectors, for your trust and for the honor of leading our fair city. You may rise."

Sabrina stood, musing at how stupid these formalities were, and stared straight ahead, focusing on no one.

Dharr Drecoll, Sphere Councilman, raised his hand and said, "Silence." The muttering in the room from a few of the advisors faded, and all eyes turned to him. Sabrina watched as he straightened his robes and then addressed Leigh. "Commander, we received word this morning there was an unauthorized use of Sphere magic at approximately 11:22 a.m." He spoke slowly, his tone never more than barely above a whisper. "In addition, the MDA informed us the Concealment Code was breached today, in front of," he paused to pick up a piece of paper from his desk with a shaking hand and squinting to read the writing, "exactly one hundred and fourteen humans. We, the High Council, authorized your mission to the human plane to investigate."

He coughed into his hand and took several long minutes to regain his breath. He bent down and dipped a small ladle into the stream. He returned to his sitting position and sipped from the ladle. "Where was I? Oh, yes. We authorized your mission to the human plane to investigate at 11:24 a.m. We were informed by gate," he squinted at the paper again, "six-hundred seventeen, that Quad One had returned at 11:37 a.m. and brought a prisoner back with them." He looked over the top of the paper at them. "Quad One left gate six-hundred seventeen at 11:58 a.m. Paul Mariposa, the Nook Warden, sent word a female prisoner arrived at 1:12 p.m., and you departed at 3:43 p.m., after filling out the commitment papers. He also informed us, according to your statement, this girl," he checked the document again, "Ora Stone, confessed. Now," he rolled up the document and pointed it at Leigh, "I want to hear about your mission directly from you. Leave nothing out."

Sabrina felt her muscles stiffen, but Leigh retold the tale of the arrest including Bizard's use of force and his insubordination. Leigh even told them about Bizard, Allyn, and Bryalan marking the girl without the use of the anesthesia potion. Leigh left nothing out, except their private conversation. When she finished, the Councilors turned to each other and whispered amongst themselves.

After a few minutes, Dharr Drecoll's wife, Mira, spoke. "I think I can speak for all of us when I say the girl's confession is a bit questionable considering the interrogation methods. Corporal Bizard's use of force was inappropriate. I think we'll leave it up to Tempest House for the reprimands with input from the CPD and his commanding officer."

The Tempest Councilors and their advisers formed a small huddle, whispering together before turning back toward the Quad. Nissa Kefira said, "We've decided to discuss this within the Tempest House separately. Jabez Bizard, you will report to our office when you are summoned."

"And if a mistake was made," Mathesar Enoch held up his hand, "then your Quad will be held accountable." *Isn't that interesting. Political favoritism at its finest.* Wonder how much gold his father shoved in pockets. Anger flashed in Bizard's eyes, "Yes, Councilor."

Mira Drecoll continued. "As for the arrest. At this time, Ora Stone has no known magical ability. If it was her, then it is likely she is a Nip. Due to the inappropriate action of Quad One, her confession is invalid. A trial will now have to be held. A public Defender will need to be assigned and the district Accuser will need all information."

The words stung, growing worse with every word. The fast arrest would now be their biggest blunder, a blight on Quad One's record. An investigation now would be near impossible.

Dharr Drecoll finished for his wife. "The investigation will begin tomorrow. At first light, we'll assign a Quad to the investigation. The trial will begin in three days. Quad One dismissed."

The Quad bowed, and Leigh called out orders to about-face and march. Cilla Souse, Naiad Councilwoman gave Sabrina a small gesture of farewell. Sabrina smiled before continuing out of the Chamber and into the foyer beyond.

Leigh led them out of the entrance hall before halting the Quad. "At ease." No longer bound by formalities, they made their way back to headquarters. Simeon handed Leigh a message when they entered without a word. He didn't even give Sabrina her special wink. She wished she had an excuse to talk to him, but those thoughts would get her nowhere.

Leigh opened the message while they worked their way back to the office. Inside, she turned to Bizard. "Corporal Bizard, you have been summoned to Tempest Councilor's office for a disciplinary hearing."

Wow, that was fast. Sabrina admired how Leigh could refer to this hearing in the same tone of voice she would use if he were going to have a lunch with good friends. Sabrina stifled a laugh, hoping he was getting suspended or, better yet, discharged.

Bizard, however, had neither expression nor emotion in his voice. "Yes, Commander." Without a word, he left.

Leigh watched him walk away, and like Bizard, her face displayed nothing of her thoughts.

Leigh closed the door behind them, going to her desk. Sabrina and Allyn went to their desks. Leigh, instead of sitting, paced in front of the large window overlooking the city. When Leigh faced them again, her face was devoid of emotion.

"Corporal Bizard may or may not return to us. It doesn't look as if we will find out until tomorrow. However, I want us all to be prepared for a replacement until he returns."

"Do you think he will be back?" Allyn asked frowning with worry. The two men were friends, even associating outside of work. Allyn was a good guy and Protector. Bizard was a bad influence, and Sabrina couldn't understand how he could stomach him.

"I don't know," Leigh said with a shrug. "We'll have to wait and see. But we have other matters to consider, namely Ora Stone. We'll receive word tomorrow whether we are the primary investigators of her case, or if, because of the nature of her arrest, it will be given to Quad Two."

Allyn gasped, even though Sabrina had already gathered that possibility during the meeting with the High Council.

Leigh nodded. "It would be a great dishonor if that happens. But, if we are put in charge, she'll need to be questioned again, and if it comes down to that, Lieutenant Sun and I will go alone."

"Permission to speak freely?" Allyn asked, gripping the armrests of the chair. Leigh nodded for him to speak. "If I may ask, why only the two of you, Commander?"

"If we're questioned further regarding her arrest, you will be implicated in her abuse at the gate. I don't want the defense to have anything else to use against us. We're already on a thin line with the Council, and I don't want any further doubts about us. And frankly, Corporal, after the way Corporal Bizard and you treated her today, she might be more likely to speak with us if you weren't there."

At this, Allyn flushed and looked away, his questions silenced.

Leigh's voice softened. "We're a unit, Corporal. You're an outstanding Protector, but since Bizard has joined us, you've changed. And not for the better. If and when Bizard returns, you do well not to follow his lead. And if anything like today happens again, I'll be recommending to Ember's Councilors that you be reprimanded as well. Understood?"

"Yes, Commander." He sounded like boy being scolded by his mother.

Leigh patted him on the shoulder. He nodded but didn't meet her eyes. Leigh glanced at the clock. "I think that is all for today. As soon as all the paperwork from today is turned in, Quad One is dismissed."

Allyn left the room and disappeared down the hall, not speaking to anyone. Sabrina guessed he'd gone to the community office to fill out his paperwork or he'd done it already.

Today had been a hard day for them all, but she could only hope he would take Leigh's advice.

Across The Veil

Leigh turned to the window again. Sabrina pulled the dozens of forms from her desk. The ticking of the clock was the only sound in the room as Sabrina filled out form after form. When she finished, Leigh still hadn't moved, even as she bid her friend goodbye. She turned in the forms before leaving the office. Simeon was updating Rific, the evening clerk, about the day's events. When he saw Sabrina coming out, he thrust the handful of papers at Rific and walked out right behind her.

Simeon always made a point to try and walk with her whenever he could. A few times, he had even waited for her before work so he could walk in with her as well. Sabrina enjoyed this more than she should. With a day like today, she had to remind herself not to let her feelings get the better of her. They could never be anything more than friends. The Houses had to remain pure. A Naiad could never be with a Tempest.

They exchanged small talk on the way out of the Guidance Hall. After this horrible long day, his smile and private wink always made her day. Before they parted, she wished him a good evening.

"Thanks, same to you, Lieutenant." She might've been mistaken, but thought his voice held a tone of longing. Those walks were always too short. She was so stupid. He turned to the right and she to the left, and they went on their separate ways. At the corner, she stopped and stole a glance back at him. He watched her from the corner. A blush rose to her cheeks. With one last wave, she rounded the corner and vanished, arriving at the edge of the Severn Sea. She took careful steps atop the water until the lights of city underneath shown bright. Letting her magic move from under her feet to surround her like a bubble, she sank, falling deep into the sea, untouched by the water, to The Haven, her underwater home.

Chapter Eight

Deep in the forest, branches crunched beneath Perdita's feet. She viewed each rustling of nearby leaves as an unknown attacker. Unsure what she was waiting for, she halted, removing the long golden chain from around her neck. Gripping her necklace, the familiar weight pressing into her palm, a strange sadness filled her. This had been her protection for ten years. The first she'd ever had in her life.

Perdita risked everything to get out of Conjuragic, to keep Ora away from slavery or worse. She'd do it all again. Without another thought, she grasped the chain, and with a great swing, smashed the amulet against the nearest tree. She squeezed her eyes shut, and her body tensed against the expected flash of pain. But nothing happened.

She opened her eyes one at a time. The amulet, still intact, mocked her. She threw her head back and roared with laughter. She hadn't really expected that to work. And cursed herself for bad planning. Why hadn't she thought to go home and consult the ancient books? She tried again and then a third time. It still didn't work. The amulet dangled on the end of the chain, unscathed and swinging from her grasp. She swore out loud.

She laid the amulet down on a nearby tree stump and searched the ground for a large rock. She found one covered in thick moss. It was twice the size of a brick and even heavier. It took all her strength to drag it along the muddy ground until she reached the base of the tree stump, feeling all the fabricated eighty years the spell had given her. She sank to her knees, using every muscle to lift the monstrosity with her frail arms. High above her head, her arms trembled, the sagging skin jiggling as if in a dance. She murmured her mother's prayer, and then she dropped the rock.

It fell slowly, almost in slow motion, to land upon the necklace with a loud *thunk*. Perdita released a breath she had been unaware of holding and pushed the rock to the ground. There upon the stump, the necklace didn't even have a scratch on it.

She swore again, louder this time, grabbed the necklace, and staggered to her feet before vaulting it into the trees. She slumped back to the ground, cradling her head in her hands. She had no idea what she would do now. She couldn't risk being near John to drive back home. She couldn't talk to Charlie or free Ora without her magic. All the days of her life she'd cursed her magic, wishing to be nothing more than human, and now when she needed it most, karma decided to pay her a visit.

"Grandma Perdita?" John spoke in the darkness.

She jumped and turned toward him. She'd been so absorbed she hadn't heard him approaching. *Had the hunger taken him already?* He hadn't taken his eyes off her and didn't seem to be searching for the source of her power.

"You were taking a long time, so I thought I'd come and check on you."

Her heart raced, drowning out the chirping crickets. She must not let him find the amulet. She glanced sidelong at the trees, searching in the general direction she flung her amulet, and for an escape route, just in case. She'd been so stupid to throw it. The large branch she'd used to try and break the amulet lay a few feet away. If she could reach it, perhaps she might be able to hit him to stop him. If it came to that, she'd steal his truck and head back home to her books. After the amulet released her power, she could find him again.

She leaned toward the branch, but John didn't seem to notice. He'd spotted the amulet laying a few feet away in the woods. As Perdita scooted farther, she realized John was taking no notice of her at all. When she grabbed the branch, he still didn't even glance her way.

She snuck around him, holding the branch in her hands like a baseball bat, adrenaline aiding her weak arms, and swung. As the branch neared his head, John bent, her swing missing by a few inches. He picked up a cantaloupe-sized rock and strolled away. Perdita swayed, almost falling over from the momentum of her swing.

John scooped the amulet into his hand and laid it upon the root of a wide oak. Perdita considered grabbing the necklace and making a run for it. But John grunted, and as his arm rounded in a great arc, the rock he held flew downward. It connected with the crystal in the center of the necklace. Perdita felt more than saw it crack with a flash of light, followed by a thunderous boom. For one heartbeat, nothing happened. Then with a roar, the magic ripped from the crystal. It flew toward her, knocking her backward. It pinned her to the ground. Her body swelled and morphed as power invaded every cell. Agony like she'd never known took her. The magic screamed as it entered her, or was that her own screams? The pain escaladed as the world blacked out.

Chapter Nine

Perdita's eyes fluttered open. Her lids felt heavy, as if weighed down by lead, taking great effort to open. The forest was gone. Instead, she stared at the dashboard of John's truck. She'd no recollection of how she had gotten there. The faintest snores attracted her attention. John dozed beside her, a small dribble of drool on his chin and a tiny cut beyond his hairline.

She tried to sit up but moaned instead as her head swam. John jumped and stared at her wide-eyed and confused. He stared at her face, and it took a few moments for recognition to set in as he awoke. His shoulders fell in relief, and he gave her a bright smile.

"Are you okay?" His concern both surprised and delighted her.

"Oh, I've felt better," her voice croaked as if she'd gargled ground glass. She tried again to move, but she ached all over, and no strength was left in her muscles. She'd felt better when she'd had the flu. John wrapped an arm underneath her waist and held her arm as he eased her into a sitting position. She held her breath to avoid her own protests. She kept her eyes closed and breathed in and out until her head cleared. A bottle of water touched her lips, and she drank. When one bottle was gone, she had the strength to take the other John offered her. As she drank, she didn't think anything had ever tasted so sweet on her lips as the cool water washing out her mouth. "What happened?" Already her voice had improved, and the water replenished her. Her stomach growled. She was famished.

An ambulance siren reached her ears. Through the windshield was a wide brick building. The back side of Dalley Hospital. The morning sun was touching the top of the building, outlining it in gold and pink. *Oh gods.* It was morning. They'd lost hours while she'd recuperated. Her memories of the ancient spell were hazy as she'd only skimmed it ten years ago, as she'd never planned to undo the spell, but she'd never expected what had happened to her.

Her head cleared further after the second bottle, and she opened the third. With one hand, she held the bottle; the other rubbed her sore muscles of her neck. She yawned and her stomach growled again. She couldn't remember the last time she had eaten.

"What happened? Man, I was hoping you could tell me," John said. "When that thing broke, it was like a bomb going off. A big old flash of light and a bang that shook the ground. The tree branches exploded. Something slammed into me. And I remember flying backward. I guess I hit my head on something 'cause I woke up with this," he gestured to the cut on his forehead, "and one helluva headache. Took me forever to find you again. When I got back, the crystal was smoking. I mean like a volcano erupting. It was crazy." He stared at the steering wheel, shaking his head as he spoke. "The smoke was going into your mouth, your eyes, your ears, even through your skin. It was kinda gross." His eyes flashed toward her and back to the steering wheel. "You were screaming and clawing at your eyes. I tried to touch you, but, um, your skin burned me." He raised his hand and held it up. She could see the blisters on the first three fingers of his right hand. "I thought you were dying," he said, voice bleak. "When all the smoke was gone and you stopped screaming, you passed out. I could touch you after that." He glanced her way again, almost as if trying to assure himself she was still alive. "All I could think to do was to pick you up, run back to the truck, and drive us here. I'd have taken you inside, but I didn't know what to say to the doctors."

"You did wonderfully. Thank you. I think you saved my life."

He shrugged as his cheeks flushed. "Hey, um. I'm going to run in and get something to eat. Any requests?" he asked.

"Anything will be fine. Thank you." But at the mention of food, her mouth watered and stomach cramped.

He slid out of the truck and shut the door with a creak before jogging into the main entrance of the hospital. Perdita got out of the truck herself and walked around it, testing her muscles. They ached, and she moved at a snail's pace. Three bottles of water in and she still felt like a dried up old prune. She found a cooler in the bed of the truck and grabbed a fourth bottle of water. Returning to the cab of the truck, she rummaged through the glove compartment and found a bottle of pain reliever. She shook three into her palm, threw them in her mouth, and washed them down with some of the water. Her thoughts wondered. *How had John broken the amulet?*

A disembodied woman's voice whispered in her mind, *"Remember."* With that word, the pages of the book appeared in her mind's eye. A small paragraph about humans.

> Only those humans, pure of heart, can resist the hunger of possession. In an extraordinary show of character, they can even destroy the amulet with mundane means.

John walked out of the hospital, carrying two white Styrofoam containers. Perdita said out loud to no one, "Pure of heart. How about that."

He climbed into the truck and handed her one of the containers. "Thank you," she said, staring at him.

He opened his own container, stopping as he noted her staring. "What?"

"Nothing," she said with a smile and ripped open the plastic to her disposable utensils, popped open her container, and dug in to hospital eggs, bacon, and buttered toast. It was one of the best meals she'd ever eaten.

After a few bites, she asked, "How long have we been here?"

"About seven hours. I called Grandma and Granddad last night and told them we were checking into a hotel so they wouldn't be worried."

"Good thinking. How's Charlie?"

"The same. They stitched up her face, but she's still in shock." He scraped the bottom of his container with his toast, eying her in between bites and opening his mouth as if he were going to ask something.

Ignoring him, Perdita ate every bite and still wanted more. She needed the calories. "What is it?" she asked, finally growing tired of his game.

"Perdita," he said, which she found odd. In all the time she had known him, he had always called her Grandma Perdita. "Um, why do you look…really young?"

She stared at him for a moment, not understanding his question, then pulled down the visor and looked at her reflection. The wrinkles that usually lined her eyes had lessened, and her silver hair had returned to its former blond. She touched her face with unbelieving fingers and found her skin tighter and smoother. She smiled in spite of herself. She hadn't looked this young since Ora was eight years old. Then she frowned; the book had said no one was supposed to remember what she looked like before. She tried to act casually, closing the visor and folding her hands in her lap. "I don't know what you mean."

His eyebrows rose. "Give me a break. Yesterday you were an old woman. Now you're... like forty-ish."

She cursed under her breath. "Fine. You aren't going crazy."

"Yeah. Figured as much. So why are you younger?"

"Because I *am* forty. Well, forty-four to be exact."

"If you're only forty-four, why did you look so much older?"

"I told you the siphoning spell had consequences. In this case, my youth. Now that it is broken, so are the consequences. But you weren't supposed to remember I looked different."

She glanced at her watch. They had lost so many precious hours when she could have been getting in touch with… She paused. The voice. "Remember," it had said. She'd heard it so often over the years, growing accustomed to it with its small nudges, she'd assumed it was her own inner voice. But with her magic again flowing inside, she recognized the subtle difference. Aryiana had always been there. Always watching. "I'll be damned," Perdita muttered.

"What?" John asked, looking around for the source of her words.

Aryiana, the seer, nodded mentally, over the distance. She thought back at her, *"You've been waiting."*

"There is a way," Aryiana thought, sending images of a phone number.

Perdita snatched a pen from her purse and wrote the number on the Styrofoam container.

"Hello? Earth to Perdita." John waved a hand in front of her face. He must've been talking to her.

"I'm here."

"This is too weird. So what'd we do now?"

She stared off into the distance as an ambulance pulled out of the ER.

"The plan?" he asked again.

Streaks of pink stretched across the morning sky, a beautiful morning. She hoped it was an indication of how things would go. "First, I need to talk with Charlie and hope no one notices the change in my appearance."

"Then what?"

"After Charlie confirms what happened to Ora, I have to make some phone calls. I know someone who can help us get across the Veil."

"The what?"

"The Veil. It's what separates the human and magical worlds."

Without another word, she finished another bottle of water, gathered their trash, leaving the container with the seer's phone number, and slid out of the truck. John followed. Birds chirped in the distance. The day was already warm with the promise of high humidity and Perdita's blouse stuck to her. At some point, she'd need a shower and a change of clothes. Her grandma getup wasn't going to cut it anymore. The strong diesel smell of the ambulances going and coming lingered in the air.

"So where do you think she is being kept?" he asked. At first, she thought he meant Charlie, but then realized he was asking about Ora.

Perdita exhaled with relief as the hospital's powerful air conditioning sent a cool breeze over her face. The sticky sweat on her brow evaporated. She held up a finger as they waited for the elevator to arrive. Once the doors slid open, she and John got on, along with two nurses. Perdita kept quiet in the elevator until the two nurses exited on the second floor. "She'll be in the Nook," she finally answered once they were alone.

"The Nook. What's that like?"

She couldn't bring herself to face him. "The scariest place imaginable."

She heard him gulp, and out of the corner of her eye, he ran his fingers through his hair like his granddad. "You can always back out," she offered. "I'd understand."

"No. No, I'm not going anywhere."

"And if something happens to you?"

"It won't be your fault. It's my decision to go. I'm a man. Besides if something happens and you all don't come back, I couldn't live never knowing what happened. I have to go."

The elevator doors chimed as they opened. They made their way down the hall to room 308. Perdita, still sore, took the opportunity to stretch before going into Charlie's room. Despite her protesting muscles, her body was forty years younger than it had been yesterday. Physically, she was stronger than before. If she'd stayed in Conjuragic, her body wouldn't have aged half as much. But aging was a price she'd gladly paid to ensure Ora would be free. She'd only had to pay with age; Ora's father had to pay with his life.

Outside the door, Perdita stopped an aid. "Excuse me. Do you know what time the library opens?"

The young man in black scrubs sighed, not bothering to hide his annoyance. "I don't know. I'll have to check."

"Thank you."

"Why do we need to go to the library?" John asked when the aid disappeared into another room.

"I need a public phone."

He shook his head with a smile on his face and pulled his cell phone out of his pocket and waved it at her. "You can use mine."

She felt her cheeks flush red. "Yes. Right. I knew that." He laughed at her.

They faced the closed door. A sign read, "Quiet Please." The hospital floor was anything but quiet. Monitors beeped and the faint muttering of voices wafted down the hallway. Static from a distant TV merged with the non-stop ringing of phones. Loud, obnoxious snores finished the cacophony of noise.

John knocked three times and opened the door.

A thin body lay in the hospital bed, connected to too many wires and an IV. The patient was unrecognizable with heavy bandages covering the face, only the mouth and two blackened eyes left uncovered. Thin, lank, greasy hair had been brushed backward, fanning out over the white pillowcase. Only Jacob and Evelyn McCurry's presence let them know they were in the right room. Images of a blur around Charlie and the echoes of her screams flashed through Perdita's mind. Charlie's hands also were wrapped in thick gauze. Charlie had tried to protect herself during the attack.

Jacob and Evelyn McCurry dozed on the pull-out sofa bed next to Charlie. Jacob's arm was around his wife, and she was snuggled up close, her head on his shoulder. They looked like they had aged the forty years that Perdita had lost overnight. John moved over to them and touched his granddad's shoulder with a soft hand. "Grandma, Granddad."

They stirred awake with a start. With sleep-filled eyes, they stood and embraced John like they hadn't seen him in a year.

"What happened to your head?" Evelyn asked once she pulled away, her hand reaching up to feel it. He winced as her fingers grazed the cut.

"It's nothing. I hit my head on Charlie's bed. We were searching their room, and I looked under the bed." He lied easily, and his gaze fell upon Charlie. "How's she?"

"Not good. She sleeps a lot, but the few times she's woken up, she just stares off into space. They doctors are keeping her sedated for now." Jacob's words were hollow. He was in his own kind of shock. Evelyn wasn't holding up as well. At his words, she stared at Charlie, a balled-up fist to her lips, grief etched in the lines around her eyes.

"We've tried talking to her, but she doesn't respond," Evelyn explained.

"Can I try talk to her?" Perdita asked.

"Of course," Evelyn said, getting to her feet. She moved to Perdita's side and embraced her. "Still nothing on Ora?"

"No. I've filed a missing person's report. I'll need to check the voicemail as soon as I get to a phone."

"You can use mine," John said. "And after this, you're going to have to get a cell phone."

Evelyn smirked. "Definitely. If use old people can figure it out, then a young woman like yourself shouldn't have any problems."

Perdita caught John's knowing look. They hadn't noticed the change in her age. Perdita moved to the edge of the hospital bed. "Charlie," she whispered, "it's me." She didn't know how to finish. "It's me. Perdita. Charlie, can you open your eyes?" Charlie didn't respond, but her heart monitor sped up. Perdita placed one of Charlie's hands in hers as if she were a doll and kissed it.

Evelyn busied herself folding their blankets while Jacob turned the fold-out bed back into a sofa. John excused himself to go to the restroom.

Evelyn's eyes were haunted. She muttered to herself. "How could this have happened? My Charlie hurt, Ora missing. It isn't fair."

Perdita finally gave in to the sorrow she had been holding at bay since she first got the call. Evelyn sat beside her, wrapping her arms around Perdita as they sobbed together. Jacob stood to the side, uncomfortable; two women being emotional pushed him past his limits, his own grief muted. When their sobs subsided, Perdita's eyes were swollen and red.

Perdita asked Jacob and Evelyn, "Why don't you two go on to the cafeteria and get some breakfast or some fresh air? John and I will stay with her." They agreed, after some convincing, and left hand in hand.

John returned from the bathroom. "Now what?"

Perdita leaned over Charlie, placed her left hand over Charlie's brow, and released a small of amount of magic, pushing it gently into her mind. "Oh child, what you have been through... I'm sorry, but I need you to go through a little bit more." Memories of her past returned. The slaves had learned this little bit of magic. The guards were always watching, listening. By touch, they could sink into each other's thoughts. Their only means of freedom.

Perdita closed her eyes and looked into Charlie's memories, like watching a movie in reverse. Perdita felt her heart clench. Charlie hadn't been able to respond but had been aware of everything around her.

The first images were dark, filled with sounds and smells. Subtle footsteps moving close by, a phone ringing in the distance, and various voices speaking over the hospital's paging system. The pungent stench of ammonia from old urine and the thick commercial scent of disinfectants mingled with the sickeningly sweet aroma of syrup. Charlie's voice, only a whisper, repeated over and over, *Am I dead? Am I dead? Hello? Is anyone there?* Fear and panic laced her thoughts.

Perdita pushed deeper. A woman with kind eyes and a long white coat stood over of Charlie. The doctor whispered to Charlie, "You're going to be okay. Just hang in there." Charlie's voice erupted inside Perdita's mind as if she were shouting into a megaphone. *"Help me! I can't move! I'm here! Please don't shut me in the dark! Ora! You have to help Ora! They've taken her! Please help me!"*

Perdita swayed with the terror that filled the voice. "What is it?" John asked, but his voice was a thousand miles away. Perdita ignored him.

Across The Veil

Perdita went even further into Charlie's day. Pain laced her hands and face. The doctors hadn't given Charlie enough anesthesia when they sutured her lacerations. Charlie had been unable to cry. Charlie's voice was so loud and filled with such pain that in Perdita's mind, it felt as if her ears drums would burst. Perdita traveled further back in time. Charlie lay on the floor in the biology classroom. Charlie heard Ora screaming, but her words were lost.

Perdita rewound the scene a few minutes further. This time, her vision was blurred by something. It took Perdita a few seconds, but then she realized the blur was Charlie's hair and blood, swept around her by a strange wind. Perdita choked back a sob.

"What's going on?" John demanded.

Perdita could only watch helplessly as the tornado flew across Charlie's face, and she fought with an unseen foe. Each time Charlie's hair flipped across her face, ripping into her flesh, Perdita could feel her pain. Worst of all were the screams.

Perdita still didn't have the proof she needed and skipped back in time once more. And there it was. A pen, floating in the air held by nothing and spinning. *This is it,* Perdita thought as she watched the scene unfold. Soon Perdita's fears were confirmed—there, standing before Charlie and Ora, were four Protectors.

Perdita had no doubts now what had happened to Ora. She was across the Veil, no doubt in the Nook by now. They'd have to travel to Conjuragic.

Perdita guided Charlie back to the present, and instead of going into her memories, she changed direction in her brain and searched. Perdita emptied her mind of everything except for happiness, peace, and serenity. When she reached the correct depth of Charlie's unconsciousness, she started to siphon off her loving thoughts into Charlie's mind. Charlie's terror and mistrust lurked just out of reach. If Perdita wasn't careful, she could get locked in Charlie's nightmare.

Perdita had to fill Charlie with love to drive off the negativity that was holding Charlie captive within herself. Little by little, Charlie gave in and accepted Perdita's offering. Charlie succumbed and lapped it up greedily. When Charlie could take no more, Perdita receded from the girl's mind. Perdita opened her eyes. An unnatural light extended from Perdita's body into Charlie. Perdita withdrew her power, and she and Charlie were once more two separate minds. The light had never happened before, but she also had never done that with a human.

John stared at her with his mouth agape. A brief knock at the door brought them back to reality. Jacob and Evelyn had returned. "Was there a light in here?" they asked. But Perdita never had to think of an excuse because at that moment, Charlie opened her eyes and said, "Grandma, Granddad?"

Evelyn and Jacob stared at their granddaughter as if they might faint. They rushed over to Charlie's side, Perdita moving out of the way, and threw themselves around her small body. "Oh, my baby," Evelyn sobbed. "My sweet baby. You're okay." Jacob was beyond words, but tears of relief spilled down his cheeks.

The young pretty doctor who Perdita saw in Charlie's mind entered the room with a knock. She was tall with long brown hair and a white coat hanging to her knees. Her face broke into a wide smile. "You're awake."

"Just now," Evelyn said, wiping her tears with the back of her hand.

"Excellent. Hi, Charlene. I'm Dr. Hamilton. Would it be okay if I examine you?"

Charlie nodded, and the McCurrys stepped aside to give her room. Dr. Hamilton withdrew her stethoscope from around her neck and placed it over Charlie's chest and back. Once she was done, she said, "You sound great. All your labs are normal. Your vital signs are stable. But now that you're awake, I will have to notify the police. They want to ask you some questions. Okay?"

Jacob said, "That will be fine."

"I'm also going to have a psychiatrist speak with her this afternoon."

The McCurrys agreed and thanked the doctor before she left. Evelyn turned to Perdita. "I don't know what you did, but thank you. Thank you so much." She hugged Perdita and wouldn't let go.

John hugged Charlie and said, "You gave us quite a scare." Charlie grinned underneath the bandages, although it didn't reach her eyes. He let go of Charlie and eased Perdita out of Evelyn's grasp. "We'll give you all some time alone."

Across The Veil

John and Perdita left the room. The hallway, for once, was empty. John leaned toward her and whispered, "What the hell happened in there?"

"It's as we thought," she said, her eyes grim.

His eyes closed. "So how do we get there?"

"I still have to talk to Charlie. She needs to understand what happened to her today. I have calmed her, but she will be lost again if she doesn't get an explanation soon. And after that, I can start making calls."

"Okay," he agreed, lifting his chest as if steeling himself for the task at hand. A look of worry flashed in his eyes. "What're we going to do if we can't get there?"

"We'll cross that bridge when we come to it."

John leaned against the wall holding himself up with one foot. Glancing around, checking to see if they were still alone, he whispered. "So, I guess Grandma and Granddad didn't notice your..." his gaze ran over her body, "change... Wonder why I'm the only one who remembers?"

Perdita had wondered the same thing. "I think it's because you're the one who broke it. That's the only thing I can come up with."

They stopped talking as a couple of nurses walked past. When they disappeared into the elevator, John whispered, "What was that light?"

"I don't know. Let's find a place to sit." The water and food had helped, but Perdita was still weak, and it had taken more out of her than she realized helping Charlie.

Back in the family waiting room where Jacob and Evelyn were yesterday, Perdita grabbed a soda, bag of chips, and a large sweet bun. It wasn't her typical diet, but she needed the calories. Various people came and went from the waiting area, so they didn't get much chance to talk. She ate all the food and downed the drink. John stared at the TV not likely watching the game show.

John got up to get himself a drink out of a vending machine and her a second. While he was pressing the machine's buttons, his grandparents walked in the door.

"Hey," Jacob said, the lines around his eyes lessened. "Grandma and I are going to the Ronald McDonald House. It's across the street."

"Absolutely. You two get some rest for a little while. We'll be here," Perdita answered, accepting her second soda from John.

"I grabbed you all some stuff before I left," John said, handing his granddad his truck keys. "I'm parked behind back by the ER. I'll walk you out."

His thoughtfulness surprised Perdita. No wonder Ora had fallen for him. Jacob and Evelyn hugged them both again, disappearing down the hallway.

Perdita waited for John to return before going into Charlie's room. Their footsteps echoed along the hallway. Her room had lost some of the grimness of yesterday. The windows were open, letting in a stream of sunlight. The walls were a light mauve, bare of pictures. Instead, there was a large white board with Dr. Hamilton's name, the nurse's name and number, and goal for the day: Get Well.

The head of Charlie's bed had been elevated. The sight of her face covered in bandages enraged Perdita. Charlie didn't speak or even look at them, but she jumped when an aide dropped a tray outside the door. She screamed and took large panting breaths, repeating, "I can't breathe."

"It's okay," John comforted her.

Perdita took her hand, slipping in more calming emotions. Charlie's heart rate settled back to a slower rhythm.

Charlie met Perdita's eyes. "I saw you in the darkness. You did something. You brought me back."

Charlie, usually so alive, so vital, looked so frail as she shivered in her thin hospital gown. But despite her appearance, Perdita knew Charlie would not stand for mediocre answers.

She straightened her blouse and flattened her hair, preparing herself for the long explanation that was to follow. As she retold their story, Charlie's expression changed from confusion to understanding. Seeing magic made it easier to accept.

Charlie never interrupted once, a lesson she could teach her brother, but instead stared as if transfixed and nodded every so often. When Perdita finished her tale, Charlie's eyes were filled with wonder. "Ora's always been magical to me. But I… When are we leaving to save Ora? And how did you bring me back?"

Perdita had been prepared for the first question, and she regretted that she would have to disappoint Charlie on the second one. "To help you, I had to give you happiness. Your own had been locked away, so I gave you mine until yours finally broke free."

Charlie's eyed her bandages on her hands, not really seeing them. "Okay. And my other question? When do we leave?"

"Charlie, I'm sorry, but you can't come with us."

"What? I have to! I can't sit here and do nothing."

"Charlie. Listen to me. You're not well. The trip across the Veil is hard, and if you're not in top form, it's nearly impossible." Perdita tried to reason with her. Charlie opened her mouth to protest again, but Perdita held out her hand. "The Quad might recognize you, and we can't risk that. If we're found, then none of us have a chance, not even Ora. The last thing Ora saw before she was taken was you lying helpless. Ora wouldn't want you to get hurt anymore."

"But please, I have to go," Charlie begged.

John leaned in. "Charlie, I'm going. I'll find her and bring her back. I would do everything that you would. You can understand that, can't you?"

"Why would *you* go?"

"Because I love her."

Charlie's eyes flashed in shock.

John's gaze dropped, embarrassed. "We didn't want to tell you. Anyone. We didn't want anyone to be weirded out. I'm sorry we lied to you."

Charlie could only nod, still processing everything, before facing Perdita, "I want to help. If I hadn't been there, then Ora wouldn't have confessed, and she'd still be here and safe."

"No. She didn't have control of her power. They would've found her. It wouldn't have mattered if you were there or not. Someone would have gotten hurt, and she would've confessed.

"It isn't my fault?" Charlie asked, voice hopeful.

"Absolutely not," Perdita confirmed.

"But why did she do the spell? Why after so long?"

"Her necklace blocked her from using her magic, and she wasn't wearing it," said Perdita.

Charlie threw her hands over her bandaged face. "Just before it all happened. She'd realized it was missing. She was freaking out."

"That'd be why she lost control. Strong emotions always brought it out."

"Why didn't we leave? Maybe we'd have found it. Before. Before." Charlie broke down sobbing.

"Don't beat yourself up. There's nothing you could've done."

John rubbed her shoulder. "It'll be all right. We're going to get her, and she will be so happy you're okay. And she'll understand that you wanted to help, but couldn't."

"That's… not… it." Charlie hiccupped between sobs. "I told her we would find her locket later, after class. I should've told her we would go and find it right away. It's all my fault."

"No, child. The fault is mine. I should've told her who and what she is. I should've taught her how to control her magic. I left her unprotected and without the most valuable weapon…knowledge."

"But how can you find her?" Charlie sniffed.

John held out his phone to Perdita along with a ripped off piece of Styrofoam. "She's going to get us a ride."

She took the phone with a shaky hand and the white foam, her own handwriting scrawled across it. She dialed the number.

The phone rang. On and on it rang while Perdita's heart raced. Perdita mouthed, "It's ringing."

The ethereal voice answered, clear and strong. "Perdita. I've been waiting."

Relief flooded her. The seer was still on her side.

"Aryiana. I need your help."

Chapter Ten

CONSCIOUSNESS RETURNED INCH BY INCH. A HEAVINESS LAY overtop of me. I'd felt something similar once before when I'd had the flu. Every muscle ached with each breath. Any movement took great effort. The next thing to reach my level of understanding was coldness from the chill in the air and the hard, icy floor beneath me. *Where I am I?* The darkness of the room filled every nook and cranny. A sea of swirling dimness and moving shadows greeted me. And there was whispering. I wasn't alone. The words were incomprehensible. Nothing made any sense. Why would I be on a cold floor instead of a bed? Why was I so tired? Was I drugged? Was I sick? And who was with me? Grandma? Charlie?

The tornado on Charlie's face. Her screams. The blood.

My eyes popped open. I bolted into a sitting position. Screams held on my lips. *Please be a nightmare.*

It hadn't been a nightmare. A twinge of light to my right illuminated what I could only call a cavern. I wasn't alone either. A group of about twenty others were in this strange place, too. The walls glistened with grime, and slime-covered wet rocks hung downward from the ceiling and others sprang from the floor. The names for them drifted upward from somewhere in my memory. Stalagmites and stalactites.

Icy wind blew through the cavern. The thin spaghetti dress covered nothing and gave no protection from the wind. My teeth chattered and arms and face trembled. Trying to get warm, I curled my legs from underneath myself and pulled the dress over my knees, tucking inward.

"She's awake!" one of the others yelled. His voice echoed all around the walls and slammed into my ears like a bomb. My hands flew to cover my ears as my heart sped into a gallop at the sudden noise.

"Let us out of here!" another screamed.

"Please, we don't want to be in here with a Nip!" shouted yet a third prisoner.

The rest of the group joined in, and the attack of voices magnified. How could they stand it? It was so loud. On and on their wailing continued until I couldn't take it anymore. I shrieked, "Shut up!"

They stopped shouting as if muted. I opened my eyes one at a time and took my hands away from my ears to make sure I hadn't gone deaf. How had they heard me over the sound of their own screaming? The only sound that remained was a slow, steady *drip, drip, drip*. In the distance, someone wailed as if tortured. The others remained crowded near the gate, silent.

They all wore robes.

"Where are we?" I asked.

At my words, the shouts resumed. *What is their problem?* I'd been kidnapped and taken to their world, yet they were afraid of me.

"Quiet," I said in the tone I'd heard the Commander use. Again, they fell silent. "Where am I?" I asked again.

"You're at the Nook," a large muscular man in red whispered, his voice shaking. This man's massive arms could snap me like a twig, yet he quivered and wouldn't meet my eyes.

"Please don't hurt us," a woman in brown pleaded, voice cracking if she were going to cry. *Could they be messing with me?*

"I won't hurt you," I said. This was true. I couldn't even if I wanted to, but they didn't seem to know that. "What's the Nook?" I asked to no one in particular.

"Surely you remember when you were brought in?" an elderly man in blue asked. "The Protectors like for you to get a taste of the mist."

I couldn't be in *there*.

The castle the Protectors had brought me to was at least a half a mile wide and more than twenty stories high. Stone statues of men and women in robes, chained and writhing in pain, perched on the corners of the castle. There looked to be at least five hundred windows with fire foaming at their edges. The stones themselves shined red like embers from a dying fire. A castle Satan would've been proud of.

I shivered into my pitiful sundress. How long I had been unconscious — hours or days? It seemed like an eternity since I had woken in my new dorm room, its cinderblocks painted pink, and put on this new sundress, picked out special for my first day of college.

Across The Veil

How I had envisioned this day. Never would I have imagined being trapped in this cave somewhere in a magical prison, my new dress covered dirt, blood, and grime. Tears stung at my eyes, but I refused to cry. Not here. Not in this place.

Leaning back against the jagged wall, the irregular bits of rock digging into my shoulder blades, I fought the burning in my eyes. My left arm throbbed in time with the steady cadence of my heart. The evil black jewel pulsating as if were alive—a life-sucking parasite. Would it get infected? I somehow doubted anyone would treat it if it did. I wished I could clean it. I wished for a lot of things.

Not thinking, my gaze drifted to my arm, looking for redness or pus. I gasped. No puncture wound marked my skin. Instead, there was black vine, like a tattoo, flowing along my arm and shoulder. The stone's malicious roots marked me deep, its evidence reflected from below.

I clawed at my arm. "Get it off! Get it off!" No amount of rubbing could make this stain go away. Thick scratches with bits of pooling blood appeared. This vile thing was inside me, and I couldn't get it out. My eyes burned. I couldn't breathe. My outburst instigated yet another round of the other prisoners screaming.

Our screams mingled. The sound of our misery, like a haunted melody, frightening yet profoundly captivating, built off each other, growing louder and more passionate. A crescendo had to be reached.

Through the screams, a different sound filtered through distracting me from the panic. Our screams faded as the steady tapping of footsteps approached the gate. The others scurried away from the gate to the opposite side of the wall, but I remained motionless in the middle, holding my breath and feeling panic simmer below the surface as I froze, watching and waiting. The footsteps drew closer and closer to the gate in a slow steady pace.

From behind the gate, a loud clanging followed by a grinding metallic sound of something very large turning. A key. Something clicked into place. A ray of light stole its way into the cavern from a tiny crack on one side of the gate. The door opened, and the light blinded me. My eyes slammed shut against the unwelcome sting.

More footsteps followed, entering the cavern. I squinted through the openings between my fingers. Two figures, illuminated by a light from beyond, blacked the doorway. Each held a torch further casting them in shadow. One was at least seven feet tall with broad shoulders and bulging muscles. *Part giant?*

The second person was almost as tall, muscular, but with a curvy waist.

The larger of the two growled, "Okay, prisoners. Get up." The voice was deep and guttural.

As the others and I stood, the shuffling of feet and swishing of clothing were the only sounds. The smaller figure moved farther into the room. In a high-pitched voice belonging to a woman, the other said, "Now get in line behind me." Like trained rats, we scurried to form a line. "You have anti-enchantments on you, so don't bother with spells."

The larger of the two stepped into the light. The part giant towered above me with a face more scar than skin as if wild animals had gnawed on him. Only one small area above his left eye was free of scars.

"You'll wait here." He shoved me to the side.

"Oh God! What happened to you?" I whispered. Mingled feelings of fear and sympathy raged inside me.

His eyes flashed brown as the hair on the backs of my arms stood. His lips pressed into a thin line.

My feet inched backward. Some internal alarm rang inside me. Danger. The man lifted his arm across his body.

My voice quivered. "I'm…"

His hand whipped forward. The back of his hand connected with my jaw. Lights flashed as pain roared outward from my cheek accompanied by a thick crack. The room tilted backward, falling fast. Another blow, this time to the back of my head. A ringing bell hummed next to my ear. Above me wet slimy rocks looked down on me. *How odd? Where am I?* A bounding laugh echoed around the room seconds before the metallic door slammed, leaving me waiting in complete blackness.

Chapter Eleven

Two huge knots sprang up. One on the back of my head where I'd hit the floor, the other on the right cheek. The skin was sticky with dried blood along my jaw and bottom lip. The bone crunched with my gentle probing. And the movements were slow and irregular when I tested opening and closing my mouth. Definitely broken. The cavern felt as if it had been moved to the sea. The walls moved in a steady up and down rhythm. Pain lanced through my skull, and nausea tightened around my middle with the tiniest of movements. Probably a concussion, too.

The metallic taste of blood combined with the swamp-like smell of the cave worsened the stomach cramps. My arm, at first at dull throb, now felt like every nerve from my shoulder to my fingertips protested even the wind skimming the surface. The bottom half of my dress had soaked up a large pool of something liquid. Water? Blood? Urine? Like a broken animal, I didn't care. It wasn't like I could do anything about it anyway. Neither could I do anything about the temperature. Each shiver sent shocks of pain through me, breaking me out in a cold sweat, dropping my core temperature even lower. My imagination roamed. A hot bath. Clean clothes. Warm bed. Motrin. After a while, the shivers stopped, and the pain faded. A part of me realized this wasn't good.

Footsteps approached beyond the gate again. Metal clinked, and the gate swung open. My eyes were closed in anticipation. "Get up," the brute who had backhanded me commanded.

An unknown strength filled me. My movements were slow, but I made it.

"Now listen here," the woman jammed a finger in my face, "Nip. If you manage to attack one of us, the other will kill you, and then it won't matter. Do you understand?"

I nodded. I was using all the new strength to keep me standing, and she thought I was going to attack.

"Good," the woman said. She turned into the light. She towered over six-feet tall with thick defined muscles. Despite that, she was quite pretty, a thin nose and full mouth. Like the Commander, she wore brown leather with the round emerald on her belt and a whip at her side. Although hers was older and cracking in places. "I'm Keeper Malandra. I'm a guard at the Nook. Mark and I'll be escorting you to the processing room. I'll warn you again—try anything and it'll be the last thing you ever do." Malandra caressed her whip.

I nodded again. Even that small movement hurt.

"Answer her!" Mark shouted, his voice reverberating off the walls. When I could only answer with silence, he broke into a sprint, racing toward me with a fist raised. Unable to do more than a meager moan, I ducked to the floor, covering my head with my thin arms, the only shield available. My body tensed, anticipating the blows.

"Mark, enough!" Malandra shouted.

Mark halted, sliding the last inch, fist held above me. "Fine!" he growled, breathing heavy and slow. "Answer her."

"Yuhhuss mum." The words emerged a garbled mess. Malandra trotted over, used one hand to push Mark behind her, and squatted beside me. She placed her hand under my chin and raised my face to meet hers. She stared at my cheek in concentration and gave an experimental squeeze. The bone crinkled like bubble wrap, sending another shock wave of pain through my cheek. She scowled then cursed out loud. "You broke her jaw! Idiot!"

She yanked me to my feet. The cavern around me spun with sudden movement. "Now we'll have to take her to the infirmary and explain your idiocrasy. The bosses aren't going to keep letting this slide."

He shrugged, the utter lack of remorse almost comical. If it didn't hurt like hell… "Why don't you fix it? No paperwork. No one the wiser, eh."

She growled in annoyance. "Fine, I'll try, but not because of you. You ain't taking me down with you. This is the last I cover for you."

Try?

Malandra shoved me back to the wall using the rice crispy treat of my face as a handle. Running on reflex, I lashed out, attempting to throw her off me. As if bored, her other hand knocked my hands away. Her fingers gripped tighter as the lightening pain rippled, blurring my vision. Her fingers probed, at first jabbing and squeezing. Her finger tips grew warmer with an undercurrent of electric power. The sensation shocked me into paralysis. A scorching heat surged through my jaw, followed by grinding noise and a crunch. Nausea and blackness threatened me again as sour bile rose into my mouth.

Malandra shot backward, releasing me. "Oh no you don't."

As soon as she let go, the fire in my face receded. My jaw slid up and down smoothly without pain. She'd healed me.

"Speak." She ordered me like a dog.

My brain jumped into overdrive, as if searching the database of correct responses that wouldn't get me punched or kicked. "Yes, ma'am."

Her shoulders relaxed. She spun to Mark, jabbing at finger at him as she spoke. "Keep your hands to yourself. This was the last time. I'll report you myself. You understand."

He said nothing. She raised her hand, sweeping it toward the door. "After you."

Mark scoffed and marched toward the door. The torch light from some sort of pathway from beyond the gate reflected what once might have been light purple leathers. Malandra jerked her head in his direction indicating I should follow him. I hurried out of the gate while Malandra followed behind.

A series of underground passages led from the holding cavern where the others and I had been held. The dim light did nothing to illuminate the numerous jagged rocks. The paths were narrow, and with each misstep, those rocks took their opportunity to take their ounce of flesh. The cool, damp air clung to me, further saturating the sun dress. The stench of rotting, molding food and deep wet earth clung to me like a cloak, soaking into my pores and strands of my hair.

Mark and Malandra knew every nook and cranny because on our long journey neither touched the wall, but tiny pin pricks of pain littered themselves over my bare arms, palms, shoulders, and even one knee. I'd guess if I had a mirror, it would appear I'd taken a jog through a briar patch.

We emerged into a large cavern the size of two football fields filled with an alien bluish light. The light came from a sequence of long skinny vertical tubes stretching from the bottom of the cave to the high ceiling a hundred feet above. A small platform, reachable by five stairs, sat in the center of the cavern. The platform held a single wide podium. An ancient looking man with long gray hair, mingling into his beard wearing fine velvet blue robes sat behind the podium. His hair obscured his face as he bent forward over a book the size of an end table. Using a feathered quill, his hand flew over the page with quick scratching strokes. Malandra nudged me up the steps of the platform where the old man continued to write without looking up. A golden chain hung around his neck with a sapphire at the end. He looked like he'd stepped off a *Lord of the Rings* movie set. Gandalf peeked his light blue eyes over the rim of his glasses, which had slid down to the tip of his nose. "Another prisoner to be processed? My, it's a busy day." His voice had the rasp of old age.

"Ahh, but this one is special. This one's a Nip," Mark said.

"Allegedly." Malandra sighed, rolling her eyes.

The old man's gazed fixed on me, evaluating me from bottom to top, before turning his attention back to the book, turning the massive page to a blank one. "I see. Very well." Gandalf tilted his head and nodded to someone or something I couldn't see. To the left of the old man, an obese small child waddled to one of the vertical tubes of light and stepped straight through the thin film of what I thought was glass. The child-like thing looked upward and shot up the tube, disappearing into a mist at the top of the ceiling.

Gandalf asked, "Name?"

Malandra bumped her elbow into my ribs. "Ora," I answered.

"Full name?" Gandalf asked.

"Ora Arlena Stone"

"Land of origin?" Gandalf wrote into the large ledger on the podium.

"Uhh…what?"

"Where're you from?" Gandalf waved a feather quill in my direction.

"Oh, um, Raleigh, West Virginia," I answered. I wasn't really sure how to answer. I didn't know where I was born, but Raleigh had been my home since I was eight.

"Spell it."

I did.

"Date of creation?" Gandalf scratched his nose, leaving ink on the side.

"You mean my birthday?" I asked. Mark squeezed my left arm, and I let out a small yelp of pain.

"Yes," Gandalf said. His tone bordered on annoyance. It wasn't as if I was trying to be difficult on purpose.

"June 27."

He sighed. "You wouldn't happen to know the conversion, would you?"

I had no idea what he was talking about. "Um no, sorry."

"No matter. No matter." He waved in dismissal. "I'll look it up later."

"My social security number is 28…"

"Your what, girl?" he muttered at me.

"My social security number. It's for identification, right?" I asked.

"We don't use that here," he grumbled.

"I was only trying to help."

"Don't," he added. He rummaged through some papers, muttering to himself about humans and their idiot notions. "Where's the questionnaire, ah yes, here it is. Okay, nature of crimes. Violation of the Concealment Code, Grand Theft Larceny of Magic by means of a Nip, and Attempted Murder in the First Degree with possible First Degree Murder. How do you plead?"

Shocked reverberated through my body. Murder? No one said anything about murder. And Grand Theft Larceny?

"Not guilty," I said. Mark and Malandra yelled together, "What?"

"But you admitted it," Mark growled. "The Quad told us so."

"I didn't kill anyone, and I didn't steal anything." My temper rose, and the same tingling sensation zipping over my skin from this morning returned. The anger rising inside me died replaced by curiosity. That feeling had begun this morning. I'd thought it was first day nerves, but what if…?

Mark raised a closed fist jolting me back to the here and now.

Gandalf lifted the quill again, waving Mark off. "We have to follow procedure. You aren't in charge of her questioning."

"But, Haskell, how can she admit it and now try to deny it? She's trying to cause us more trouble." Mark grabbed my arm even tighter.

"I've already received word the Council couldn't accept her original confession. I have to follow procedure, and if she states she is not guilty, I must put it on the form." Haskell dipped the quill in a small bottle of ink and scratched my answer.

The child-like person from earlier reemerged. He wasn't a dwarf as I first believed, but an elf. He had pointy ears, a child-like face, but a bulky body on short stubby legs. He stepped onto the platform and held out black robes and a few other things I couldn't make out. "Here you go, boss." The elf's voice rang like angelic bells.

"Thank you, Tyke. Now if you would please go and ready the showers?" Haskell asked him.

"Yes, sir," came Tyke's musical reply. He waddled off in yet another hologram of light.

Shower? How I hoped it was for me.

"Now back to business." Haskell scratched his nose with his quill. "State your defense."

"Wait, don't I need a lawyer or something?" I didn't want to say anything wrong now. I needed to talk to someone who knew the right words, the right procedures, and the laws.

"You have to give me a statement so you can be processed and in order for the tribunal to decide if your excuse is worthy of a trial." Haskell waved the quill in annoyance.

"You mean my fate on whether or not I spent my life in jail is based on what I say right now?" I asked incredulously.

"Afraid so," Haskell replied with his raspy voice.

"It's not that," Mark mocked me, "it's whether or not you get sentenced to The Kassen or get a life sentence in here with me."

"The Kassen?" I asked before I could stop myself.

"The Kassen is a death sentence." The shock rolled down me as if someone had dumped a bucket of ice water over my head.

"State your defense," Haskell repeated.

"I, um…" My mouth went bone dry. My eyes stung and throat grew tight. I wouldn't cry. *Please let me get this right.*

"Okay. I... I've never stolen anyone's magic." Images of the pen spinning returned, and the strange power in me uncoiled and rolled, rising to the surface, curious. "My friend, Charlie. She was hurt..." At the memory of her face, that same power shrank back down to its hiding place. "By one of the Protectors, and she didn't do anything! So I told them I did it so they would stop. I didn't take magic from anyone." The new thing chuckled. Ignoring it, I went on, "I want to go home." My life was in their hands, and my gaze fell to the ground as I waited to hear my fate.

"Is that all?" Haskell asked, and if I wasn't mistaken, his voice was kind.

I thought of everyone I might never see again. Grandma. I didn't even tell her I loved her before I'd left for school. Charlie. I would never find out if she was okay. And John, my sweet John. All the stupid fighting I'd done with him and Grandma. I wished I'd never gone to school. "I guess that's it," I finished with a sad finality.

Tyke popped up again. "Excuse me. The showers are ready."

I jumped at the sound of his voice. I hadn't notice his return.

Haskell turned to me and said, "Good luck." His kind words surprised me.

"Thank you."

Malandra guided me down the podium through another cave, this one surrounded by a waterfall. She pulled me to the side and said, "Strip."

"What?" I wrapped my arms around my chest as if I were already naked.

"Strip, take off your clothes," Malandra commanded as if I didn't know what she meant.

"Does he have to stay?" I asked, gesturing to Mark.

"Don't worry, Nip, your kind don't do it for me."

"Mark, turn around," Malandra urged him.

"Like she deserves any privacy," he murmured but turned his back to me.

I slipped off my daisy sundress and handed it to Malandra, who threw it on the floor. I took one last look at it. It lay on the floor crumpled, bloody, dirty, and beyond recognition. Like a loss of innocence. How very appropriate.

I added my underwear and bralette on top of my sundress. Malandra waved toward the waterfall. I stuck a toe into the waves, and a sharp inward gasp escaped my lips. The water had to be only a few degrees above freezing. Malandra shoved me in the water, and the icy shock made me scream. She threw me a bar of soap. "Hurry up."

The soap hit the floor. I dipped, grabbing the bar with shaking fingers. The artic temperature seeped into my muscles, making every movement an effort. Thirst gripped me, but I choked on the salty sea water. My teeth chattered in a rhythmic *clackity clack clack* almost as loud as the water crashing around me. My hair clung to the small of my back as my hands flew over my face, arms, and legs. The cold did block any stinging from my multiple injuries. I stepped out, and Malandra tossed me a towel. I dried off, rubbing at the water dripping over my goosebumped flesh. Cursing silently, the foreign place creaked open a bit wider as the thing inside stretched. Like a slow rising volcano, heat rose within me, spreading outward. The coldness disappeared, replaced by a subtle heat coming to the edge of being too hot. The thing inside, tired now, slept. How I felt each of these things I couldn't say, but with each oddity accumulating through this long, long day, my shock lessened.

"Now come here and lean over," Malandra commanded.

With the towel wrapped tight around me, I went to her side and bent over, thankful my behind was facing the waterfall. Malandra pulled my long hair forward, over my head, the tips dangling above the cavern floor. "Hold still. This might tingle a bit."

Before her words even processed, an intense tingling spread across my scalp, the feeling both familiar and alien. The tingling arced in a sharp zap before falling away in an instant.

What the hell?

Malandra stepped back. "Okay. It's time to get dressed so we can get you to your cell."

Straightening, a cool breeze caressed my scalp, and the familiar weight of my hair was gone. My long red hair spread on the floor around my toes like a hairy animal. "My hair!" I screamed.

Panicked fingers grasped at my bald head, heart racing, as I spun hoping to see the familiar span of hair over my shoulder. It was gone.

Across The Veil

Bald. Beyond bald. Not even stubble remained. Anger swelled inside me, and I reached for that place. It didn't answer. Sleeping beyond my reach as if exhausted. I shouted at the Keeper, "Haven't you done enough? Why did you do this to me?"

"In our world, hair is a mark of prestige. You're a prisoner, and you have none. Now shut up. That is the first and last time you raise your voice to me," Malandra growled. She held a hand outward, palm facing Mark, whose eyes bulged. "I'm the only thing between you and Mark. Now put these on."

She thrust thin, black robes into my hands. I stared at them for a minute as if I'd never seen clothes before. Too much. Everything was too much. How much more could I take?

With fumbling fingers, I slid the robes on, pulling them over my body. The robes reached all the way to my toes and were a little too long. The right sleeve flowed past the tips of my fingers. The left side was sleeveless, exposing the tattoo-like vines from the stone. So much of this place was about status and an unspoken uniform. The color of the robes, the strange jewels, hair length. This exposure and color of the robes was another mark of my status.

Malandra stepped behind me, slipping a long silver chain over my head. I studied the charm at the end of the chain. Unlike the stones of the Protectors, this one had an onyx dagger with cold metal and an unnatural blackness.

"The mark of a prisoner. Let's go."

Malandra led me from the cavern with Mark following. The new locket rested on my breast bone, hanging a bit higher than the necklace I'd lost this morning. *My necklace. My promise not to take it off.*

Stumbling, images sprang up from the hidden place, the crack stretching wider. A field of spring flowers blooming surrounded by trees in winter. A hateful old woman, chest full of black tendrils, evaporating. A dog, near death, healing as a child's hand touched his paw. *Me. That was me. That was magic.*

Another image came. Grandma handing me the necklace and asking a question I couldn't quite remember.

My necklace and magic were connected. And Grandma had given it to me. She has to know.

I ran into Malandra. She'd stopped, and I hadn't been paying attention. She swiped something over a panel.

It beeped.

Above the doorway, a sign read: High Security Cells, Level 218

The door swung forward with a metal grinding. Dust flowed outward, and a layer of thick blackened soot lined the floor. As Malandra stepped through, her footsteps left imprints on the ground as if no one had been down this particular part of the Nook in a very long time.

The cave transitioned from rough cave walls to more rectangular hallways, looking more manmade than the inside of a mountain. But like the rest of the prison, only dim light from occasional torches lit the way. Closed doors with numbers beside them marked different cells.

Instead of taking me to the nearest door, we walked through winding hallways, deeper inside. Our footprints were the only ones. I didn't know if that meant the cells were empty or the prisoners were left to die. Malandra halted beside room marked 120607.

A vague outline of a door faced me, but no door knob. Malandra touched a placard, and it beeped like the entrance to the High Security Cells.

The door moved to the side with the grinding of rock against rock, revealing an opening, pitch-black inside. Mark moved closer to illuminate a small area revealing a small pile of what looked like hay.

Mark shoved me inside, laughing. "Well, here it is. Enjoy."

Chapter Twelve

THE DOOR CLOSED ON THE ECHOES OF MARK'S LAUGHTER. Darkness descended as the door slammed home, sealing with a long snake-like hiss. The complete absence of light had to be the most terrifying thing that happened today. Was the cell empty?

My imagination ramped into high gear. Monsters reaching out of the darkness to grab me. Bugs and snakes slithering toward me. I sank to the floor, crawling on hands and knees, feeling my way in the darkness. My fingers crunched on a long, thin strand. Squealing, I jerked my hand back, reeling away. Nothing moved or rushed toward me. Once the racing of my heart settled, I reached again. Mounds of mounds of the crunching sticks were under my nails. Crawling closer, inhaling, the familiar scent of a barn filled my nose. Hay. It was hay.

On hands and knees, I continued exploring. The cell was maybe ten feet by ten feet. Traveling like an infant in the compete darkness made it hard to judge distance and straight lines. Not large. Just about the size of my living room. The cell was also empty of anything other than the hay. No toilet, sink, or any other rooms. No bed. No food or water. Even the worst human criminals received better than this. At least there didn't seem to be any bugs or snakes.

Crawling into the hay pile, I wrapped the thin robes around me as much as I could. The cell's temperature was like the rest of this place: freezing. Whoever said Hell was a raging inferno had lied.

The pain in my left arm had eased off. Or the new sensations of hunger, thirst, and the need to empty my bladder blocked those other aches and pains. Perhaps the tattoo was healing. Despite the shower, I felt greasy, and with all the crawling on the cave floor dirt, there was no way the robes weren't covered in dirt and dust.

A strange metallic clicking rang out in the darkness. Startled out of an uneasy dose, I jumped, trembling, and waited. The clicking continued like a countdown, or a bomb: *tick tick tick.*

A purplish radiance lined the edges of the cell, at first dim but brightening into a blazing luminescence blinding me. The rocks of the cell dissolved into a whirl of air, lightening striking along the walls. The wind swirled around the perimeter of the room sending the hay flying. The roar of the whirlwind drowned my slight scream. My cell was now inside the middle of a tornado. *What next?* Dust, debris, and hay whipped around the room. I clung to my robes, curling into a tight ball. The already frigid temperature plummeted. If this kept up, hypothermia was a real possibility.

The howl of the wind roared in a mixture of whistling and grinding noises. My eyes remained shut tight, but tears leaked from my lids, trying to clear the dust that slammed into them when the wind first began.

The swell of my bladder intensified. I clinched tighter. I had to go.

In desperation, I risked opening my eyes to search for a bathroom now that the occasional flashes of lightning strikes lit up the room. As before, the room was empty of any bathrooms or sinks. Instead, a cat sat on its haunches inside the cell, feet together, sitting too still to be natural. Blinking and wiping away the dust, I checked again, positive I'd imagined the cat.

Another lightning strike. The cat was black with light green eyes and a tale about an inch long. I rolled into a crouched position, almost falling. "Where the hell did you come from?"

At my question, the cat swiveled its head around the room, as if searching for something, but for what, I didn't know. It yawned, unfazed by the tornado, spun in a circle, and lay down. It licked its paws and rubbed them on its face. When it finished its bath, it rested its tiny head on its paws, watching me with long vertical pupils. I hadn't moved, but the dust assaulted my eyes. I narrowed them to slits, sinking to the ground with small deliberate movements. The cat and I regarded one another. The cat's eyes glowed, even when the lightening inside the tornado was absent.

After a long time, I got curious and stood. The cat mimicked me. I took a step left. The cat did the same. I spun in a circle. The cat did as well, giving me a clear view of, um her, bottom. I jumped, and the cat cocked her head to the side then sprung forward. I screamed and backed away.

Across The Veil

The freaky-eyed thing stared at me. She didn't seem to blink as often as normal, and she didn't look away or move her ears listening to quiet sounds as cats are prone to do.

Feeling very stupid, I spoke to the cat. "All right freaky-eyed little black cat. Are you planning to attack me or what?" The cat blinked, trotted over to me, and rubbed herself on my leg. *Guess that's a no.*

It took all my willpower not to kick her. She vibrated in what I guessed was purring. My eyes ached, and no more tears ran as if I'd used up the supply of my tear ducts. If the cat was going to attack me, it wasn't like I could do anything about it. I curled up once more, and she nestled next to my belly. Closing my eyes, I ran a hand down her head to the nub of a tail. The purring vibrations soothed me, and her warm body seeped heat into me. "You didn't happen to bring me any food, did you? Or better yet, a bathroom," I asked as a wet warmth spread outward.

Freaky Eyes jumped to her feet, hissing, and sprinted to the other end of the cell and glared at me.

"Sorry."

She scowled at me, staying at the edge of the cell, fur rippling in the breeze.

"Don't suppose you'd understand I've been holding that all day?"

She looked away.

My eyes closed, resigned to her dismissal. Not that I blamed her. I wouldn't want to be around me either. Peeing on myself was a new low. The wind continued. I vowed to keep my eyes closed no matter what. My eyeballs were so dry they felt like raisins in my skull.

My thoughts turned to John. We'd kept our romance a secret because we didn't know how Charlie would take her brother and best friend dating. We'd been friends since Charlie and I were eight and John twelve, so he had been like my brother, too, but last summer, everything changed.

The night of the yearly carnival began like any other night. The small traveling group came through once a year. It was the one night teenagers in West Virginia could go out somewhere other than the movies, bowling alley, or the river. It made us feel like the big city wasn't far away.

Charlie and I went together, riding rides, and putting off going to the funnel cake booth until it was acceptable. At the house of mirrors, we'd run into John and his date. We went in together and got separated. I found myself alone with three young men in their early twenties. They weren't locals, strangers in our small town. At first I only saw two of them.

"Aren't you a tasty little thing," one of them had said to me.

"Yeah," said a second one who sniffed the air. "Can't wait to get a taste of you."

I backed away, but a third had come up behind me. I stopped, eyes wide, and heart pounding. The situation was so foreign I didn't know if I should run or scream. They moved closer, and I spun, running forward to get past the third man.

"Where are you running off to in such a hurry, darling?" the third one asked, shoving me backward.

The other two had snuck behind me and grabbed my arms. I tried to scream then, but the third man covered my mouth with his dirty hand, reeking of cigarettes. My screams muffled into his hand, and the man holding me squeezed my arms tighter as I tried to jerk away.

"Shhh, shhh," said the third man. He stank of alcohol, cigarettes, and sweat. My stomach clenched. His eyes were glassy as he searched my face, down my chest, below my stomach, and back up again. His face was within inches of mine, and he licked my face. I screamed louder and fought even harder against the restraining hands. The men behind me laughed, the sound cruel.

The drunken man pulled me up against him and ran his fingers over my lips. I shook my head no and kicked outward, but he jumped away.

"Ahh, you are a feisty one," the man holding me whispered in my ear. He held my arms to my sides, useless. The man in front of me smiled, his teeth rotting, and he swaggered closer, rubbing himself. "This is what you want, isn't it?"

Tears rimmed my lids as he unbuttoned my jeans. Kicking again, the two men holding me pinned my legs together.

"Now, now," the ringleader said, "we just want to be friends."

I knew what was coming. My heart galloped in my chest, but there was nothing I could do. I couldn't move, couldn't scream, could only wait, trembling for the inevitable. John appeared behind the third man.

"Hey," he screamed and yanked the man off me. He spun him around and landed several blows to the man's face, each with a sickening thud. The other two released me as they joined the fight. I sank to the floor. The fight was total chaos. Whirls of fists, kicks, and swearing. Two burly men from the carnival ran screaming from behind me.

John straddled one of the men, flinging blow after blow to his face. The other two would-be assailants were sprawled on the floor, moving slow and moaning. The two carnival workers pulled John off the man. John threw his arms up and said, "I'm good."

They let John go and squatted down beside the passed-out men. One got on a walkie-talkie requesting security and police presence. John knelt beside me and offered his hand. His eyes were cold as he glared back at the men. A small trickle of blood ran across his brow; his knuckles were bruised and covered in blood. His bottom lip was cut. His eyes found mine and said, "Let's get out of here."

In a daze, John led me out of the maze. Charlie called me on my cell, laughing and asking where I was. She was still lost within the mirrors.

Before I could answer her, John took the phone out of my hand and said, "Hey, Ora isn't feeling well, and I'm taking her home." A brief pause, "No, I'm not waiting, we're leaving now." I heard Charlie on the other line, screaming at him. He yelled, "I'm not really asking, Charlie!" And he hung up on her.

He took my hand and led me to the parking lot. The car ride home was quiet. I figured we should've stuck around to talk to the cops, but I didn't say anything. It wasn't the first time I was in his blue truck, smelling of mint and old leather, but it was the first time Charlie wasn't with me. Tears rolled down my cheeks. I hated crying, but I couldn't stop. John didn't say a word but drove very fast, his knuckles white upon the steering wheel. He pulled in front of my house, put the truck in park, turned off the engine, and leaned back against the seat. We sat in silence for a few long moments. Finally, I heard him say, "I'm sorry."

I was so taken aback. I stared at him.

"Why are you sorry? You… you saved me," I said, my voice breaking at the end. I composed myself and continued, "You saved me, and I didn't even say thank you." I buried my face in my hands.

He slid over beside me and pulled me into his arms. My head rested in the crook of his neck, and he wrapped his arms around me. He was warm and strong, and he smelled like soap and after-shave. I felt safe. Completely safe being held in his arms. He whispered in my ear, "I'm sorry I didn't get there sooner." His voice was so sad, my heart ached. I wanted to take away his pain, his guilt.

I leaned away from him, and he kept his eyes cast down, refusing to meet my eyes. I placed my hand on his chin and lifted his head so he would look at me. "Don't you ever be sorry. It wasn't your fault, and if you hadn't come..." I couldn't continue, and instead I said, "Thank you."

I took up his hands, holding them, and kissed his knuckles. Each one, and every time I whispered, "Thank you." I looked at his face and kissed the bruise on his cheek, and I leaned my head in, my heart pounding, and placed my lips on his, kissing his bruised mouth. When our lips touched, my body came alive in a way I never imagined. Our kiss deepened, taking us both by surprise. We broke off when the porch light clicked on, and Grandma peeked out of the window.

"I, um... I have to go. Thank you again. And thank you for the ride home," I stammered, too embarrassed to look at him. I opened the door, slid out to the ground, and bounded inside the house.

Something soft touched my arm, and I jumped. My attention returned to the cell. The cat had snuck up beside me and rubbed her head on my arm, nudging me to pet her. I smiled as the cat licked my arm and meowed. Freaky Eyes bent her head allowing me to run my hand over and down her soft warm body to the tip of her tail. She avoided the puddle around me, but she'd come back. When she was done being petted, she curled beside my neck and purred. This small contact with another living creature gave me a tiny bit of hope. I petted her for a long time, eyes closed, enjoying her company.

When the clicking started again, Freaky Eyes stood, rushed to the edge of the wind, and between clicks, ran straight into the tornado disappearing. I gasped. Two more clicks, and the room changed again. The tornado faded, replaced by a torrent of water. I rose and inched close to the edge of the cell, taking my time. I inspected the wall of rain. A mist radiated outward, leaving a fine coating on my face. The water collected on my cracked, dry lips. The burning in my throat rose, the thirst growing at the nearness of the water. I dashed forward, dropped to my knees, and leaned my face into the water. I prepared to take large gulps, but instead, a shock of electric pain hit my face throwing me backward. I landed hard on my back and grunted as the wind ripped from my lungs. A warm gush of blood dripped down my nose and into my mouth, the bitter metallic taste mocking the thirst. I sat up and pinched my nose to squelch the flow of blood.

The water was yet another torment, so close but not allowed. I couldn't bring the cool sweetness to my lips, couldn't ease the thirst and drown the hunger with a full belly of water. I was on my feet and screaming. Not in terror, but in a rage. I jerked the necklace, ripping it off my neck. I hurled it at the waterfall. I threw handfuls of hay into the air. I ripped at my robes. I fell to my knees to claw at the floor. My fingernails cracked and bled. I screamed. I screamed until my voice broke and my throat was raw. I reached for that place inside me, but it too was denied to me. My screams turned to sobs. The tears didn't last long, and something inside me shifted. Not power. Acceptance.

Motionless on the cold, damp floor, staring at nothing, the seconds turned to minutes, the minutes to hours. The rain continued to fall. A few times, the waves rolled into the room, soaking me in icy seawater. I shivered, but still I didn't move. Lost within myself, like Charlie.

The clicking returned, the water receded, and the room burst into flames with rolling lava cascading down the walls. I recoiled from the intense heat, scrambling to the center of the room, the farthest spot from the walls. The heat rose quickly. At first refreshing, seeping into me, easing the numbness, but soon a prickling pain took over as the feeling returned to my fingers and toes. The temperature rose to sweltering, and sweat rolled off my brow, further worsening the dehydration.

My eye lids grew heavy. I yawned and laid on what was left of the pitiful pile of hay. I pretended I was back by the river in Raleigh, sunbathing. My skin tingled with sweat.

Half aware I'd drifted into a dream, I opened my eyes. The sun shined on the flowing river, blinding me. I slipped on the sunglasses to my side. The forest around me glowed with life. Squirrels and birds chirped. A gentle cooling breeze blew through the trees, rustling the leaves. The mixture of river water, mud, and dirt mingled with the coconut scent of tanning oil. All rolled into a canvas of peace and relaxation.

John stood in the river, the water up to his knees. He cast the thin fishing line from his fishing pole. His muscular, bare back rippled with each movement. My gaze followed downward to his hips, the cut-off khakis pants hanging off his waist. The sight caused a stirring in my middle. A new feeling I hadn't quite figured out yet. Smiling, I whistled at him. He glanced over his shoulder at me; his face lit up with a smile. He waved at me then leaned down, sticking his fishing pole between some rocks to hold it in place. He strolled out of the river while I admired the rock-hard abs. He reached me and stopped, blocking my sun.

He extended one hand down, and I took it. He pulled me to my feet. A gentle breeze brought the scent of his sweat and aftershave as he pulled me close. He brought his lips to mine in a quick kiss. "You're so beautiful."

I giggled, and we kissed again. My heart quickened, as it always did whenever he touched me. He smiled at me, a mischievous twinkling in his eyes.

"What?" I asked, smiling, starting to back away, not prepared to run in my bare feet.

"Nothing," he denied, but his smile kept telling me otherwise.

"Oh no you don't." I pulled away and ran. John laughed behind me. He caught me without any effort, picked me up, and threw me over his shoulder. I screamed and laughed. "John! John! No! Put me down!" I smacked at his arms, playful, as he carried me toward the river.

"John! No! No!" I hollered. His shoulders moved with his laughter.

"This isn't funny!" I yelled, but I loved every moment. And he laughed even harder. As he got closer to the large rock overlooking the deepest part of the river, he stopped walking and ran. My body bounced up and down as I wriggled trying to get away. At the top of the rock, he threw me.

I flew through the air before landing in the cold water. I held my breath before going under. As I rose to the surface, John stood on the rock, his whole body laughing at me. I huffed at him, pretending to be angry. In response, he stepped back from the rock, took off running, hurled himself of the rock, and yelled like a little boy, "Cannonball!" He landed next to me, the splash nailing me in the face. His head popped up out of the water, and he splashed me again.

"I'm going to get you!" I yelled, splashing him as fast as I could. But he was faster and pelted me time and time again. If I could've stopped laughing, I might've done better. I gave up trying to win the splash battle and jumped on his head trying to dunk him. His head dipped under my weight, but before he went under, he shoved me backward, then pounced.

Before I went under, I yelled, "Truce! Truce!" And he stopped. He let go of my head, and I swam away, sank into the water, and came back up pushing the hair out of my face. I wiped the water off my face and looked at him, considering splashing him again.

John floated in the water with his arms spread wide, the sun glistening off his hair, looking unbelievably handsome. He righted himself and looked at me, suddenly shy. "I love you," he told me for the first time.

Chapter Thirteen

PERDITA STEPPED OFF THE GREYHOUND BUS AND HITCHED HER bag higher on her shoulder. She squinted at the bright sun and coughed as the diesel smoke wafted around her head. The roar of the bus faded as it rounded the corner.

The bus dropped her in a rundown section of New Ford, Kentucky, a tiny little town about forty miles north of Frankfort. The brick buildings were established over sixty years ago and now wore the dirt and grime that had accumulated over the years. A train whistled in the distance. On the other side of the street, the metal giant roared its way down the tracks and carried big black mounds of coal from one of the nearest mines. Sand from the black coal streamed behind the train and came to rest wherever it saw fit. It dusted the streets and settled upon the dying grass beside the tracks. Perdita brushed off her t-shirt and shorts.

All the rusted cars parked along the side of the street wore a thin layer of coal dust, and Perdita knew most, if not all, of the men in this small town worked in the coal mine. The big coal companies were the only lucrative means of employment here, so most of the residents had no other options. The women had even fewer choices. Unless they moved to one of the bigger cities.

John cleared his throat. Perdita glanced over her shoulder. John's face was hidden behind his blue baseball cap as he checked the directions and then consulted the map on his phone. A strong gust of wind blew, and John cursed as he almost lost his hat. Perdita cried out when her hair whipped around and hit her in the eye. For the first time in many years, she had worn her hair down, but now she was regretting that decision as she dabbed at her watering eye.

"Right, it should be down Main Street, and then we make a right onto Second Street. Are you ready, *Mom*?" John asked.

Across The Veil

"Yes, *Jack*. Let's go." Perdita pulled her hair back into a loose ponytail.

Aryiana suggested it wouldn't be wise to use their real names. Perdita decided to use Evelyn Hamilton as an alias, a name she had come up with at the spur of the moment. She had inadvertently combined Evelyn McCurry, Charlie and John's grandmother, and Dr. Hamilton, Charlie's doctor's surname. But it was just as well. At least she could remember it.

Aryiana referred them to an underground black market of sorts. Their fronts were many, but this particular avenue was a tour service provided for family or very close friends of witches or wizards. It was only allowed for a selected few and only those who had had stringent screening performed by Conjuragic Protectors, but like most things, there were those who could be persuaded to forge documents if the price was right. The touring company only had to add a name.

Their cover story was simple. She and her son, Jack Hamilton, were the descendants of a wizard whose magic had died off after many years of marrying humans. They wanted to see where they'd come from.

Cantius Abishot and Todd Vulpine, the two men who ran Conjuragic Tours, set them up with no questions asked after Aryiana's call, except, of course, when the check was coming. John and Perdita had arranged their departure for later that day and were on their way to the meeting place.

Perdita had no desire to see any place in Conjuragic except the Nook. But, of course, that destination wasn't on the tour. Ora disappeared on Monday morning, but Wednesday was the soonest tour they could arrange. Perdita could only hope they weren't too late.

As they walked down Main Street, Perdita watched the old cars putter by. Even though this town was barely keeping its head above water, there was something about the simple life, where no one rushed to be anywhere, except perhaps church on Sunday morning. It was one of the reasons she had chosen places like this and West Virginia to keep herself and Ora hidden.

As they turned onto Second Street, they found what they were looking for. The Abishot Antique Store, a front for the two wizards living in the human world. The awning was faded blue and filled with cracks and holes. The glass appeared to have never been properly washed. Spider webs hung in the corners, and as Perdita opened the heavy rusty door, an ancient bell chimed overhead announcing their presence.

The smell of dust and mold greeted Perdita, and she sneezed three times. Through watery eyes, Perdita noted the over-priced furniture, doubting most anyone living in this little town could ever afford to purchase anything at this store. This did not happen often, as there weren't many wealthy people in New Ford except, of course, the wives of the businessmen who ran the coal mine.

From the back of the store, Perdita heard someone yell, "Coming!"

John explored the store, looking at various old lamps and lanterns, and kept glancing toward the back of the store.

Perdita pretended to be very interested in tapestries while she waited, her heart pounding. A noise from the back caused Perdita to turn. She spied an old man of medium build and height, with a full head of white hair coming from the backroom and maneuvering around various odds and ends in the store.

"Ahh, here we are. So sorry to keep you waiting. I'm Cantius Abishot. I know, I know, please don't hold it against me," the old man chortled. "Is there anything that you might be interested in today? We received a beautiful eighteenth-century bedroom suit. It's very rare and beautiful."

Perdita couldn't help smiling at Cantius. He certainly was strange, but she immediately liked him. "No, no bedroom suits for us today. My name is Per…achoo!" Perdita faked a sneeze. She hoped Cantius hadn't noticed her floundering on her name. "Excuse me, now where was I?"

"I believe, my dear lady, that you were about to tell me your name," Cantius offered, extending a hand.

"Oh yes, my name is Evelyn Hamilton. My son Jack and I are here looking for a rare African sixteenth-century flower pot."

He gave them both a knowing look. "Very well, then you are in the right place. Please come this way." He motioned for them to follow him. Perdita weaved in and out of the various tables, rows of old coins, past Queen Anne chairs into the back of the store. He led them into a small conference room and told them to have a seat before disappearing through a door leading farther back.

"That was close," John mouthed to Perdita.

Across The Veil

"I know."

Perdita sat in a brown folding chair. The room was well lit with florescent lighting, and opposite the chair was a huge dry-erase board that covered the length of the wall. A statue of a beautiful woman in flowing robes rested in the corner. Her long hair appeared to be caught up in the wind that was intent on going somewhere behind her.

John dropped his suitcase on the floor with a thud and flopped beside Perdita. "What now?" he asked.

Perdita shrugged. "We wait." John gave a sigh of impatience and slouched in his chair.

He grew ever more irritable the longer Ora was gone. Perdita didn't think his task would be as hard as hers. He wouldn't have to pretend to be amazed by all the magic in Conjuragic, but Perdita would.

She'd seen magic before and had no real desire to reenter the world. It was filled with terrible memories. But John, Perdita predicted, would get caught up in all he would see, and if only for a short while, would forget about Ora and escape from the worry. Perdita could not say the same.

After a knock at the door, another man entered the room. The new arrival was younger than Cantius. But, since he was from Conjuragic, how old he looked was a very poor predictor of his actual age. He was short, stocky, and had long brown hair pulled into a loose ponytail. "Hey there, folks, I'm Todd Vulpine." They introduced themselves and shook hands with Todd.

"It's real good to meet you. I feel I must apologize. You see, I will be taking you on the tour, but my partner will be explaining about the rules and such. I would love to do it myself, but unfortunately, I have prior commitments to attend to." Todd leaned in close, whispering, "He knows nothing of our arrangement, if you catch my drift." He straightened, raising his voice. "He has a flare for the dramatic."

"I heard that," Cantius said with a wink, returning to the room, hands full of large white binders.

"Well, all right then. I'll leave you to it, but you all can holler for me anytime if you have any questions. Just in case the old geezer confuses you all too much," Todd said with a wink.

"Who you calling an old geezer?" Cantius countered, trying unsuccessfully to stifle a smile.

Todd laughed and shut the door.

"Rascal." Cantius shook his head, still smiling. "So, are we ready to get started?"

"Yes," Perdita and Jack said together.

"Good. No need look so serious. This is supposed to be fun, remember?"

Perdita and John exchanged a nervous glance, but Cantius regarded their nervousness as humans traveling to a magical world. "Okay, here we go." Cantius clapped his hands and passed out binders with various information about Conjuragic. For the first hour, he explained the rules. His lecture was very strange. At different points, he talked to the statue of the woman behind him, who he referred to as Mina. Mina didn't answer back, of course, but he pretended she did. This made him appear quite crazy, but Perdita thought the whole thing was hilarious. And for some reason she couldn't quite put her finger on, she was glad he wasn't a part of the black market.

At one point, he waved his hand, and Mina's cold colorless frame transformed. Her robes changed into a flaming red. For a few seconds, Mina seemed to be bleeding, but Perdita understood that she was an example of an Ember. Next, a fire ruby amulet shined around Mina's neck. "This," Cantius explained, "is the marking of a witch from Ember."

Cantius pretended Mina interrupted him. "No, Mina, I didn't say all witches wear red. Weren't you listening? You weren't? What do you mean, what are the other colors? I don't know, but I'm going to find out." He pretended to study the binder and raised a finger as if discovering the answer. "Here it is, Mina. Red, as I said, is the symbol for Ember House, and the other three each have their own unique color. *Does everyone always wear their House colors?* Gosh Mina, I don't know, but I think the answer is on page 19 of the handout. Let's find out shall we?"

This continued until they covered all four Houses. "*Are there any other colors or symbols?* Why, yes Mina, the High Council wears golden robes and their symbol is the golden ankh. But don't go worrying these fine folks about them now. The Council almost never enters the public."

"Pop quiz, Jack. Will a witch or wizard always wear their House colors?"

"No," John answered.

"Great!" Cantius threw him a miniature candy bar. "And Evelyn, when are they required to wear their House colors?"

"Within Conjuragic city limits, which means they can wear any color they choose when they are in their home villages."

"That was mostly right. You forgot in addition to Conjuragic, they're also required to wear their House colors when they are in another House's village. And also when a witch or wizard is in his or her home village, they can wear any color they choose, except for another House's colors. That's very important. But since that was such a great try, you'll get some candy, too." He tossed her a piece of candy.

"Jack, which House wears blue?"

"Naiad."

"Fantastic!"

"And Evelyn, what do Sphere and Tempest wear?"

"Green and Purple."

"Someone has been paying attention, Mina." He tossed both of them more candy.

"Cantius, I have a question," John said, his hand raised.

"Shoot. But if I get it right, can I get some candy, too?" Cantius laughed at his own joke, his belly shaking.

"You keep mentioning the House's home village. What does that mean?"

"Great question! Conjuragic is the central city. It's a place of unity where all four Houses trade, shop, work, just like a city here. Their home villages are separate. I might describe it as being a suburb. It's a place where people of the same House live together in their ancient homes." Cantius leaned against the table, his face wistful and sad. Perdita guessed he missed his home. She knew a House's home village was much more than Cantius let on. She heard once it was a place of regeneration and connection with the core of a witch's power. Some people believed the ancient homes were the source of each House's magic and the reason for the long lifespans of witches who lived in Conjuragic.

"So do the ancient homes have a name?" John asked, interrupting Cantius's thoughts.

"I'm glad you asked, my boy." Cantius scratched his ear. "What, Mina, you mean he wants to know what they are? By George, well, I guess we'll tell him. Better yet, let's show him." Cantius snapped his fingers, and the dry erase board became transparent. "Let's see...Sphere's ancient home is The Willow. It is a mystic forest full of tree spirits and fairies. The trees are kind and have an awareness I'm unable to explain." The board filled with pictures of the most beautiful forest Perdita had ever seen. She had always wanted to see The Willow but was never allowed to leave her prison.

"Tempest's home is The Meadow. It's located on rolling hills and planes and is filled with all kinds of exotic birds." The board changed from pictures of a forest into grasslands with long blades of grass with hundreds of birds flying in an intricate dance.

"Naiad's home is The Haven. Now, I have never been there, but it is an underwater city. Sea life surrounds the place, and you can even ask questions about the future or your love life to the ancient giant sea horse, Myrtle." The board changed again, and Perdita felt truly at home. Her heart longed to enter the underwater city and walk along the crystal streets that were filled with light.

"Ember's home is The Sierra. It's an island with the Pyre, a giant and ancient volcano, but it's gentle and commanded by the wizards who live there." The board morphed once more, and a great volcano appeared on the screen.

Perdita shivered and felt blood drain from her face. A flash of heat flushed her skin, and a distant rumbling followed a grinding noise of rock on rock as the mouth of the Pyre ripped open. Hissing steam filled the night air as lava poured out from the top, spilling down the sides.

Run!

Her husband grabbed her hand, and they ran as fast as they could. The screams of the dying gripped her heart every time the lava reached someone she loved, extracting the revenge of the ruler of the mountain.

As they reached the boat, she and Philo climbed in and looked back. They saw silhouettes of four out of the nine who had escaped with them. One by one, they were overcome by the lava. When the last fell, Philo met her eyes in defeat and pushed away from the shore. Only she and her husband had escaped The Sierra. All her friends and fellow slaves perished in the attempt. And little did she know, her husband would die, too, in only a few short hours.

"Mom! Mom, are you okay?" John shook her roughly. Perdita blinked in confusion and glanced around. "Oh, I'm so sorry. I haven't eaten this morning, and I got lightheaded all of a sudden."

"Madam, I'm so sorry I've made you suffer. Please let us take a," he peered at his watch, "thirty-minute break, and you all can run across the street to the Starlight Café and grab a small bite to eat. It's only ten after ten, and we're way ahead of schedule. But make sure to save room for your wonderful lunch at The Human Eatery."

They agreed and soon were sitting down with their breakfast. The café was nearly empty, and the smell of old bacon grease and burnt coffee hung in the air. The place was well worn, and Perdita had the feeling that at peak hours the food would have been good. John wouldn't quit asking if she was okay. "It was nothing. I had a…flashback."

"Well, you do need to eat, and you haven't touched your food."

She could only manage little nibbles. She pushed around her cold, tasteless oatmeal with a spoon and only took small bites of her toast, which wasn't even warm enough to melt the butter. The coffee was too strong for her taste, so she only sipped on some ice water. Even though she hadn't eaten, she had no desire for food. The memories had stormed in, and she had been unprepared. She'd have to be careful, lest the memories come back at inopportune times.

When they returned, Cantius had dark blue robes lying on the tables. "Okay kiddos. Now that we know about the different Houses and colors, we'll move on to something harder. You see, while you all are in Conjuragic, you will be required to wear these robes." He gestured his hands.

"In addition, you will have to be marked. Now here is where some people get nervous, but don't be. When a human enters Conjuragic, they are allowed a certain period of time to be there. When you first get there, they'll numb your arm and place a small blue crystal into your arm. It won't hurt nor do any lasting damage. It's called a pellucid." Cantius motioned to Mina. The statue had on the blue robes with blue markings on her left arm.

John gulped, and Cantius noticed this reaction as if he had been expecting it. "It's all right. I promise you. But this next part is very important. The crystal will have a built-in timer. If you stay longer than you were allowed, the crystal will make you fall into a deep sleep and send a signal to the gatekeepers. A team will be sent to retrieve you, and you will be escorted back to the human world. If done on purpose, you'll never be allowed to return to Conjuragic. Now, do you still want to go? We'll understand if you don't. If you need a minute to decide, I can step out."

Perdita met John's eyes. "We're still going."

Cantius's face broke into a huge smile. "Excellent. Now let me add that in the unlikely event you all would stay past the allotted time, the deep sleep doesn't do any damage either."

Not unless you fall or if you are in the middle of say…a prison break. Then I think there would be some major damage.

Cantius's smile faded, and he became serious. "Now this is important. You're allowed to leave whenever you wish, but you must let Todd know you want to leave. Because if you don't and jump in with another group of people leaving, you will die before you reach the human world."

Perdita was expecting this. "We understand. What next?"

"We need to sign various release forms, and as soon as Todd is done, you are ready to go." Cantius clapped his hands together.

They signed page after page of various paperwork agreeing if that they were injured, Conjuragic Tours was not to blame. Perdita wondered who in the world they would sue. But she didn't really care at this point. All she wanted was to get to Ora and save her. There was so much at stake that dangerous was an understatement.

Perdita and John gathered their bags and changed into their dark blue robes. Perdita tied her hair out of her face, and John put away his baseball cap. Todd returned from a little workshop down the hall. He wore brown robes and the emerald orb.

"So, last quiz, you two. What am I?" Todd asked them.

"Sphere," John answered.

Todd gave them two thumbs up. "You guessed it. Are we ready to travel?"

Across The Veil

John and Perdita nodded.

Todd pulled a small brown canvas bag out of a pocket. He dipped his hand in and pulled out some sand, which they were taught was Journey Dust. Cantius held his hand in front of him, palm facing forward. The air in front of Cantius's palm turned hazy, like a mirage. The murky air floated out, swirling the Journey Dust, and the Veil appeared.

John stood mouth open, and Perdita pretended to do the same. A feeling of dread ran through her, and she had an overwhelming urge to run. But Ora needed her. No matter what, she would give up everything—her life, freedom, and sanity—to save her daughter.

"You have to hold my hands." Todd grasped their hands. Perdita realized her palm was sticky with sweat. "Okay, on the count of three, we'll step through the Veil. One. Two. Three."

Chapter Fourteen

THREE, TWO, ONE...AND THE CELL TRANSFORMED BACK TO THE cave. The cell changed in cycles. I'd given them names: the cave, the tornado, the hurricane, and the inferno. The inferno was my least favorite of all the different forms my prison took. I dreaded the heat more than anything.

Days had passed since being thrown in here. No one had stopped by to give me food or water. No longer did I have the energy to move. The hard floor had become home, and at times, I knew death was close. Reality lingered just beyond my reach.

The only escape had been the cat. At the start of the last hurricane cycle, I had awoken to the sweet rumbling of her purring on my arm. The sound was muffled, but it calmed me regardless.

I didn't feel so alone when Freaky Eyes was with me, and I looked forward to chatting with her. I told her all about being a prisoner and what I could remember about levitating the pen. I shared stories about Charlie and me. But mainly, I talked about John. Freaky Eyes mostly ignored me but allowed me to pet her. Always a few moments before the room changed, the cat dashed out of the cell.

But she kept coming back. I was never sure if she would return, but I was glad every time I saw her. She would only come in between the cell's transformations. She'd been in every cycle, except for the inferno. Not that I blamed her, it was stifling, and I would have gladly skipped that cycle as well. The heat stole what fluid I had remaining, and my dehydration grew worse. My mouth and eyes were dry, no tears would come, and I hadn't felt the need to use the bathroom for a while now. That was definitely not a good sign.

I'd been sleeping more and more, hoping each time I closed my eyes that it wouldn't be the last thing I ever did. Even sleeping offered no escape. Hours were spent in nightmares of being executed or Charlie being tortured by Bizard. I woke screaming during a dream where the three men from the festival beat John to death. But the most disturbing dream I had was being betrayed by someone I'd trusted. I've dreamed that many times. I stood at one of the entrances to the Nook. It felt as if I were escaping, but someone was there, someone I trusted, but they were against me and trying to stop me from leaving. I could never see the person's face.

Each time I woke, I longed for a release, anything to take away my misery, even death. It wouldn't be long now. Ironic really. The wizards had made such a fuss about a trial and execution, and instead, I was going to die of dehydration and starvation. I tried very hard to care, but I rolled over on the sparse hay and tried to fall back to sleep; at least when I slept, I wasn't sick.

Before I could drift off again, the wind died away, minus the usual clicks. I struggled to rise, but fell. My heart tried to beat faster but failed, staying at the same slow rhythm. I held my breath and waited as the hissing of the door being unsealed filled the room. Every muscle constricted, I waited for whatever was coming. Just as suddenly as the wind died away, an opening into my cell appeared.

Light hit my eyes, stinging them, but no tears sprung from the sides. I squeezed them shut, moaning, and covered my face with my hands. A figure stood in the shadows at the door flanked by two others. Malandra and Mark. The newcomer in the doorway stepped into the room; the light showing the hint of purple robes. In this world, I'd come into contact with two men wearing lavender: Bizard and Mark. Anyone in lavender was my enemy. Yet this man appeared kind. *I'm definitely dying, and this man is an angel come to fetch me*, I thought.

Eager for escape, my arms stretched to him, longing to go with him. He towered over me but squatted so his face was next to mine. His lips were moving, but his voice sounded far away. I couldn't comprehend his words. My hand still hung in the air, reaching for him. The man turned and his shoulder shook from... shouting? Why would an angel need to shout? My hand fell beside me as all the strength to lift it vanished. The world tilted, and my muscles screamed in pain. The angel had finally lifted me in his arms. I leaned my head upon his shoulder, and my body rocked with his steps as we left my cell. My eyes drifted shut. It was time. I listened to my heart beating. Slow. Faint. The rise of my chest was shallow and uneven. Dying. This was dying, and I didn't fight it.

I heard John's voice, and something in me stirred. I thought I moaned his name. Bits of color flashed behind my closed eyes. I saw John. Or rather a memory of him, of us.

It was twilight. I'd spent the day reading, sipping lemonade, and laying out by the pool. But it was finally twilight, and John and I were going out. I showered and blow-dried my hair. On my tanned face, I put only a touch of lip gloss and wore a simple peach t-shirt and brown Capri pants. I put on the bracelet he bought for me and a small spray of the floral-scented perfume he liked.

I waited by his truck, watching the fireflies dance over the rolling hills. The crickets chirped the gentle song of nighttime. The sun had just set behind the trees, but the sky still glowed the purplish blue of sunset in the distance. A gentle breeze fluttered my hair, and a twig snapped behind me. John wrapped his arm around my neck, kissed the top of my head, and buried his nose in my hair, inhaling. He released me, and I twirled to face him, stood on tippy-toes, and pulled him down so his lips met mine. He tasted like mint and smelled of his soap, my favorite combination.

"Hey, babe, you ready to go?" he asked.

"I think so."

He opened my door, and I slid inside his truck. He shut it behind me, got into the driver's side, and turned the key, the engine roaring to life. We pulled away, down the dirt road. I bounced on the seat and laughed as he turned the wheel sharply, hitting a bump, causing me to flop closer to him. He laughed while wrapping his arm around me and gave me a quick peck on the cheek.

"Going public?" He smiled his lopsided grin.

"Yup," I answered. We were headed into town. In our small town, it wouldn't be long before our relationship got back to our families. All summer we had been going to the lake, hanging out in groups, kissing in the shadows, or sneaking out after dark to go riding out to Stoney Point. We ventured out once to the drive-in movies. But tonight, we'd turned a corner. We were going out to dinner together and then to a movie. It would be just the two of us.

"We should tell Charlie." I looked out the window, not wanting to meet his eyes. "She'll be crushed if she finds out from someone else. She should hear it from us."

"Babe, tonight is our night. We'll tell her soon. Okay?"

I nodded my head. My guilt had been eating away at me, but he was right. This was our night to go out in public as a real couple on a real date. We could tell her tomorrow.

We arrived at the restaurant and followed the hostess to our seats. I stopped worrying about who might see us and enjoyed myself. We even grew so bold as to hold hands as we left the restaurant. I spent most of the movie curled in John's shoulder. I was so happy. I forgot we're hiding our feelings from Charlie and our grandparents, forgotten I was leaving in a few days.

I saw a flash from the movie screen and turned my head from John's shoulder to watch the movie, only I wasn't at the movies. Confused, I turned my eyes back to John, but he had disappeared. Instead, my head rested on the shoulder of the man in lavender who had come into my cell. The angel. He'd carried me to a stark white room with metal cabinets and a silver exam table. Not exactly how I'd pictured the pearly gates. He sat me upon the exam table, and I anticipated the coldness of the metal, but it was warm.

Disappointment rested upon my chest like a great weight. I wished I could go back to John. *Why won't they let me die in peace?* I clenched my jaw. In a sudden blinding moment of clarity, my mind screamed, *"John! I can't die! And Charlie and Grandma. I have to live. I have to get back home."*

"Help me," I whispered, though no sound left my lips.

A woman appeared, leaning over me. Her blond hair fell over her face covering one blue eye. She tucked the escaped lock behind one ear as her eyes traveled down my body like a mechanic would examine a car. "She's almost gone," she said.

"Can you help her?" a man's voice asked.

"I'll try. It appears to be dehydration and starvation. She's on the brink, but I'll do all I can."

The man muttered something I couldn't understand and left the room. The blonde walked around me, her blue robes brushing across my tattooed arm. The woman called for help. Two more women appeared by my side. The three women undressed me. I was unable to help, and it didn't occur to me to be modest. Something sharp stuck in my arm as a needle was pressed inside my flesh. Dark red blood was pulled into a crystal syringe. The woman in blue held the needle. She met my eyes and said, "I'm Healer Tekden. I'm going to help you."

The Healer took the vial of my blood and left, disappearing through a doorway. Her assistants put strange devices on my arms, legs, and chest, above my heart. One of the women wore brown robes and washed me with warm water, her hands flying with expertise. The warmth felt nice, but my skin cooled quickly in the open air.

Healer Tekden returned and explained to her assistants, "As I suspected, dehydration. First, we have to give her fluids. Sonya, can you add the minerals listed here, in the exact amounts, to the water?"

Sonya, the woman in brown, answered with a bow. She disappeared from my sight. When Sonya was gone, the other assistant, this one in red robes, pulled off the devices and handed them to the Healer, who studied them. They must have meant something to her because called out to Sonya, "Add forty micrograms more of potassium."

Healer Tekden pulled another needle out of her robe and injected my arm with a pink liquid. My entire body went numb. A great weight pressed on top of me, pinning me to the table, preventing any movement, even breathing.

She placed a tube into my mouth and hit a button. My chest rose in fell in time with a humming sound from behind me. As if sensing my panic, she said, "You're okay. It was an anesthetic. I have to do a procedure to help you, and it would hurt without the medicine. Try to relax. You'll be better very soon." The Healer was neither cruel nor kind. I tried to respond, but couldn't. "Close your eyes and rest."

But I didn't. I managed to jerk my head around trying to figure out what was going on. My vision blurred from the medicine as the Healer and her assistants moved around my body. The one in blue lifted her hands and adjusted the tube and straightened my head, my vision clearing.

Across The Veil

Above me floated a body of water. Before I could react, the hovering water descended fast as if released by something unseen. I expected to be soaked when the water hit, but instead it rolled over me, entering my mouth, nose, and eyes in long snake-like strands. The pressure built quick, filling me like a balloon, more and more until it felt as if my bones would crack. As the body of water slipped inside growing smaller and smaller, the pressure eased until it was all gone. The hollow feeling had disappeared with the pressure, and my thoughts were sharper than they had been in days. Only the tiniest nag of a headache lingered behind my eyes, but I suspected if I hadn't been given the numbing medicine, I'd feel a whole lot worse.

Sonya stood beside me waving her hands over my legs. Up and down my legs, abdomen, chest, and arms were deep one-inch cuts I hadn't recalled getting. On a table beside her were scalpels covered in blood as if the Healers had randomly stuck them in me. As Sonya waved her hands, the wounds healed. The skin pulled together, and the lacerations vanished as if they never existed.

In seconds, every cut and scratch was gone, leaving me exactly as I had been before coming to this place, except for the tattoo, black and ugly. My mouth wasn't dry, and my head had stopped pounding. Sonya squirted something into the tube that tasted salty and sweet with a tinge of acid. The numbness vanished, and the weight lifted. She removed the tube from my mouth.

Healer Tekden appeared on the other side. "Better?" she asked.

"Thank you," I croaked, my voice stronger than before. She nodded her head and patted my hand.

"Overall you're healthy. I see an old stretching of your right ACL and an old fractured mandible. When did those happen?" Tekden grabbed a clipboard and a pen, staring at it as if waiting for my answer.

"I, uh, hurt my knee playing soccer a few years ago."

"And the mandible?"

"What is that?"

Tekden huffed a laugh. "Your jaw."

"Oh, um. That happened here." My heart rate sped, and a coolness spread through my body. I wasn't sure if I was supposed to tell the truth.

Tekden's head shot up, her eyes penetrating. "Here?"

I nodded, gaze not leaving the floor. "Yes. The Keepers."

"I see." Tekden's mouth set in a thin line, and she jabbed at the paper with a purple quill.

"Lindsey, you can bring the tray," the Healer said to the assistant in red who vanished through a door in the back of the room. She returned a few moments later carrying a tray. "Here. You need some food."

Lindsey sat the tray down and pulled me into a sitting position on the exam table, slipping a clean white robe over my shoulders. I twisted myself until my legs dangled over the side of the table. Lindsey handed me a bowl of white paste. It had no smell at all. It looked something like Cream of Wheat. I hated Cream of Wheat.

"I know it doesn't look like much, but you haven't eaten in days. You need something bland, and it has protein, carbs, minerals, and fat. And it tastes better than it looks." She handed me a spoon.

I picked up the spoon, dipped it into the white goo, and put it in my mouth. I let the stuff roll around on my tongue and swallowed. Lindsey was right. It didn't taste that bad. I took slow bites pretending it was banana pudding. It did have a buttery sweetness to it. At first I pushed through the nausea, but I couldn't even finish the small serving. But the food and water made me stronger and able to think straight.

When I finished, Lindsey led me to a shower in the back, handing me a bottle of soap before closing the door behind her. The bathroom had an odd familiarity. No pictures were on the wall, but a tiny mirror hung above a sink, the toilet had a lever instead of a handle, and a porcelain tub with a white cotton shower curtain waited in the corner. The whole place was ordinary. Not at all what I would have expected in a land of magic.

I placed a hand under the running water and found it warm, almost hot. I stepped in, anxious to let the water soothe my skin and massage my sore neck. The bottle of soap, which smelled sweet and earthy, like some sort of flower, ran out in a smooth iridescent purple. It wasn't possible to scrub away unwanted thoughts, fears, and anxiety, but I sure tried. The grime ran down the drain in thick rivulets of blackish brown. My once polished and manicured nails were cracked and broken, but at least the dirt and blood were gone from underneath. It felt strange to wash my bald head and not find any stubble, but at least I didn't have to worry about tangles. I considered asking someone, one of the Healers perhaps, about my hair, but I doubted they would answer. Besides if it had been removed by magic, it might never grow back. I shoved those thoughts away from me, hard.

I lingered in the shower as long as I dared. Stepping out, I found a towel and dried off, finding fresh black robes and flimsy undergarments. The dagger necklace that I had ripped off in my cell was fixed and lying on a nearby table for me to put back on. I sighed and placed it around my neck. I left the bathroom, and Keeper Malandra was waiting for me.

I thanked Healer Tekden again, and I followed Malandra back to my cell. The hay was scattered around the room, but my filth was gone. It was almost breathable in there now. Malandra waved a hand, and the hay levitated into the air, formed a pile, and floated back to the ground. She walked to one corner of the room. "If you step here," she indicated a small stone that looked different from the rest, "you can use the bathroom." She stepped on the stone, and the wall folded out to reveal a privy. She stepped on the stone again, and the wall returned to normal. She walked to the other corner and pushed another similar stone. A table with water in a jug, a glass, and a washcloth appeared. "And if you press this one, you get water to drink or wash."

"Was that always there?" I asked, my voice barely containing my rage. Now healed and rested, the snake inside me writhed matching my anger, eager to rise and aid it.

"Yes."

"And it slipped your mind to mention that when I first got here?" The stone sank of its accord. Malandra jumped backward with a startled scream to get out of the way before being crushed. My vision wavered, closing inward again, like in the classroom.

She glared at me, and the room cleared to sharp precision once more. A cough came from the entrance of my cell. The man in lavender who carried me to the infirmary was silhouetted in the doorway. He strolled farther into the room, gazing around, inspecting. A look of disgust replaced the mild curiosity. The man shook his head, puckered his lips, and waved an arm. The air swirled with a fierceness, attacking one of the walls. A deep rumble shook the ground under my feet. Pebbles sprang from the wall, and a huge chunk of rock broke free and rolled to the center of the room. It wobbled and came to a rest. He strolled over to it, reached into his robes, and pulled out a small red cushion. He placed the cushion on top of the rock and sat. I hadn't realized my mouth was gaping open until a bit of drool ran out of my mouth. Wiping my chin, I hoped he hadn't noticed.

"Really?" Malandra jerked a hand toward the wall with a huge chunk now missing. "I could've gotten you a chair. Now I'm going to have to fix that when you leave."

Ignoring Malandra, the man focused his attention on me. "Hello, my name is Arameus Townsend. I'm your Defender," he said.

He looked at me as if expecting something, but I wasn't sure what. He gestured with his hand. "And you are?"

"Oh, I'm Ora. Ora Stone," I mumbled, quite surprised he didn't already know my name.

He inclined his head. "If you are a Nip, then I would advise you not to attack me. For one thing, it would be solid proof you are a Nip, and you'll be convicted without a trial. And the second, I'm the only one on your side."

"Traitor," Malandra whispered, not hiding the contempt from her words.

"That'll be enough, Keeper. And if I were you, I'd watch your step. You and your partner are already on thin ice."

Malandra huffed, strolling from the cell. "I hope she attacks you."

"I won't do anything," I said.

Arameus smiled. The smile reached his eyes, unlike most of the people I'd met here. The door sealed shut again, and the cell descended into darkness. Arameus cursed and from his direction came rustling of his robes. A scratching sound came next, as if from a match, and then the sharp crack of fire. The Defender was illuminated by a bottle filled with a bluish-orange flame. The bottle lit the entire room. He reached into his robes again, this time pulling out a quill and some parchment paper bound in a notebook. *How many pockets did he have?* He placed the notebook in his lap, quill in hand, and asked, "Shall we begin?"

"Okay," I answered.

He gestured, indicating I should sit down. I gathered up my now clean black robes and sat cross legged upon my pile of flattened hay. He stopped me. "Oh no. No. No. That won't do." He waved his arm, and a second rock carved itself out of the wall and moved directly in front of his. A second cushion emerged from his robes, and he placed it upon the new rock. My lips pulled back in a smile, my first in days, at his kindness, also a first in many days. I took my place on the cushion. Every muscle screamed in protest, aching all over, reminding me how many days I'd spent on cold hard rocks. A moan slipped before I could stop myself. The anesthesia had worn off.

A look of concern flashed across Arameus's eyes, and he reached into yet another pocket, retrieving a bottle filled with clear liquid. He extended his hand, offering me the bottle. I took it with an uncertain hand and placed it in my lap.

"Drink," he urged.

My fingers pulled at the top of the bottle, which came out with a small pop. I tilted the rim of the glass against my lips and poured. The familiar feeling of something cold entered my stomach, and within seconds, all my aches and pains subsided. This must be the same stuff Lieutenant Sun gave me when the gatekeeper marked me. I rubbed my left arm without being aware of it.

"Thank you," I said, grateful for his kindness.

He stared at me as if trying to decipher some hidden meaning. I wasn't sure if he heard me, so I said louder than before, "Thank you. For this." I wiggled the now empty bottle. "And thank you for being so nice to me."

His expression changed as if he were deciding to tell me something or not. "I'm sorry what's happened to you." His words sounded genuine. "In Defender school, they talked about the prejudice against Nips. I didn't really believe it. But now… Well, I wish you wouldn't have seen us at our worst."

I wiggled, uncomfortable at his words. I didn't know what to say, so instead I asked, "What do you want to talk to me about?"

My words, it seemed, brought him back to himself. His back straightened, and his face became a mask, his professional face, I guessed.

Clearing his throat, he put quill to parchment. "Like I said before, my name is Arameus Townsend. I'm your Defender. I doubt anyone has informed you, but your preliminarily trial will begin tomorrow. This morning, I'd like to get your statement. If you're going to change your plea to guilty, then that will be all I require. If you're going to keep your initial plea of not guilty, then I will have to gather evidence and prepare our case for tomorrow's hearing. So, the first thing I need to know is, what are you planning on pleading?"

"Not guilty."

My memories were the only things available to me over the last few days, thoughts of the event leading to my arrest and, more importantly, previous history of magic.

He raised one eye brow. "Are you sure?"

"Positive... but can I ask you a few questions?" I remembered every detail, but what I really needed was an expert. An expert in magic.

"You may," he answered raising one eyebrow.

"On the day of my arrest, one of the people that took me away—"

"Protectors," he corrected.

"Okay. One of the Protectors said that a Nip is a human who has stolen magic away from a witch or wizard. Right?"

"Yes."

"Can you tell me how a Nip does that?" I asked, thankful someone was finally answering questions.

He considered this for a moment and replied, "Well, only a Nip can tell you exactly how they do it. But from what we have learned by questioning Nips and doing... tests... is they can sense the magic within the wizard, and are... attracted to it. This much we have confirmed, but after that, the details become murky." He talked with his hands.

"So, could a Nip do it by accident?" I asked.

"From all accounts, they always do it intentionally."

"But is it possible?"

He paused for a moment before answering, head tilted to the side. "There are rumors when they are young, they don't know what they're doing. But the cases I have reviewed indicate as adults, their powers are controllable. But honestly, I don't know. I suppose it's possible."

I sighed in frustration. This wasn't helping. "Okay. Well, how close does a Nip have to be to the wizard?"

"We think Nips capture the magic when a spell is cast at them. Why? Where are these questions going?"

Finally, he had said something I could use. "Answer a few more questions, please. When a Nip steals magic, do they keep it forever?"

"No. The magic slowly starts to leave the Nip and evaporates into nothing if the original owner isn't nearby. Nips can return magic. But, if they do not, the witch or wizard dies."

I thought of one other thing that perhaps may prove my innocence or make me guilty. "So, if the wizard dies, does the Nip keep it then?"

"No."

"How long can they keep it?" I asked.

"Usually only a few weeks to a month. Why?"

His reply to the last was quipped. His patience was running out. "One last question. What happens to a wizard when a Nip steals their magic?" I asked, leaning forward, closing the distance between us.

He glared at me, his eyes full of suspicion.

"Please answer my question, and I will explain everything to you," I pleaded.

He paused as if debating whether or not to answer me. He stood and paced the floor. "When a Nip steals a wizard's magic, they feel excruciating pain, like no other. They scream in agony, and not all of them survive the initial attack. Then they remain unconscious until their magic returns. If they not cared for, they starve to death, but even with care, they can't live without their magic." His voice was hollow.

I couldn't imagine anyone going through that. I finally understood why Nips were hated and feared by so many here. Regardless, there was no excuse for what had been done to Charlie. No excuse for kidnapping me, throwing me in this prison, breaking my jaw, and starving me to the point of death. Nips may be horrible people, but they didn't even bother to prove I was one before punishing me. The power inside me inched upward, seeking revenge.

Arameus's voice broke through my inner rage. "My father was killed by a Nip. He died before we could find him," he said more to himself than to me. He stared at the wall.

"I'm sorry." It was a pitiful reply to something as enormous as losing a parent, but what else could I say?

He was lost in his own memories, so I waited until he was ready to rejoin me. He didn't seem sure why he confessed this to me. He returned to his seat after a time. He ran his fingers through his hair followed by a deep sigh. "Is there anything else you want to know?"

"No, but there is something I need to tell you. I'm definitely sure I'm not a Nip."

He raised one eyebrow in response.

"To confess, I was a little worried that I was and had stolen magic by accident. But if what you say is true, then I know in the last month I haven't touched anyone and had them go crazy or anything. Nothing like what you described happening. So, I'm not a Nip. It's not possible."

His eyes widened in surprise. "Then why did you admit to doing it in the first place?"

"Well, that's the tricky part. I levitated the pen. With magic." The deep pit inside me opened wider, as if acknowledging it made it stronger. "I'm not a Nip. I'm a witch."

Chapter Fifteen

PERDITA, ALONG WITH JOHN, TOOK A BIG DEEP BREATH AND held it. She closed her eyes and stepped forward. The familiar sensation returned as her body and mind stripped into a million pieces, and she fought to keep herself together. Something in the nothingness between the worlds caught her attention, but it was gone before she could figure out what it was. Perdita wondered how many people tried to travel to Conjuragic and never made it, people who didn't have the strength or willpower to hold onto their being. It took great skill, and some people believed you lost a piece of yourself every time you traveled. Perdita wasn't sure if they're wrong.

When anyone crossed the Veil, they left the material plane and entered one of thought. Time did not exist there. For some, traveling felt instantaneous, yet others swore they had lived entire lives in between traveling. But, for Perdita, it was only seconds before she reached Conjuragic—the most dangerous place she had ever known.

"Welcome to Conjuragic, gate one-thirty-three. I trust your journey through the Veil was pleasant. Magical identification, please," a voice said. The owner remained unidentifiable as her bearings returned. She jumped as a loud cry reached her ears.

"Todd! I heard you were making a trip today." A redheaded man and Todd embraced like brothers and pulled back still touching each other's shoulders. "I'm so glad I was working today. How long you in town for, buddy?"

"A five-day tour. Let me introduce you to my customers. This is Evelyn and Jack Hamilton. And this," Todd gestured to the redheaded man, "is my best friend, Ottah Abishot. This is Cantius's youngest son."

"Pleased to make your acquaintance." Perdita shook Ottah's hand.

"Likewise," John said, grasping Ottah's hand with a firm grip.

"Nice to meet you." Ottah released John's hand and turned to Todd. "Hey man, what are you doing for dinner? I thought we could hang out if you're not busy."

"Well, I'm having dinner with my clients at the Feenwell Hotel. If it is okay with them, you could join us," Todd answered, looking questioningly at Perdita.

"The more the merrier," Perdita agreed with a smile, thinking this was a perfect opportunity to get Todd out of the way after dinner.

When her eyes had adjusted to the light, Perdita looked around at the city at its white buildings and pulsating magical energy. She heard John exclaim, "Whoa." She smiled at the astonished look on his face.

"Yup, she's a beauty." Todd put his hands on his hips. "Welcome to Conjuragic, the Wizards' City."

"We'd better get going." Todd bent down to pick up their belongings, and Ottah stopped him. "You don't mean to tell me you're going to carry their stuff around all day, are you?"

"Hey, man, you know how the Feenwell is…check in isn't until five o'clock, so we don't have a choice. I was going to stop by and put it in some storage lockers until time to go to the hotel."

"Nonsense, my girlfriend works there. In fact, her father owns the place," Ottah told him flashing a lopsided grin and sticking out his chest. "Leave their things here, and I will get it there no problem."

"A girlfriend, you old dog!" Todd said as he slugged his friend in the shoulder laughing. "But yeah, that would be great. Thanks."

"Let's get going." Todd stepped down from a platform, motioning for them to follow, but before they could walk off, Ottah yelled, "Just a second. Identification… you know, policy. And I have to mark them first."

"Oh, right." Todd smacked himself in the head and held out his right hand, palm facing forward. The air in front of his palm vibrated as Ottah placed a crystal-tipped wand into the haze. It beeped, and he put it away. Ottah then took another probe and placed a blue crystal into its tip. He reached into his robes and handed Perdita and John vials of clear liquid.

Perdita and John drank the numbing elixir. John flinched when Ottah stabbed his arm but then grinned. "I didn't feel a thing."

Across The Veil

A dark blue crystal, unlike any stone Perdita had ever seen, pierced her arm. It spread the whole length of Perdita's arm, eerie and ominous. But John grinned from ear to ear, turning his arm around at odd angles so he could examine it. "Awesome. I've always wanted a tattoo."

"It'll also offer you protection," Todd said as he waved goodbye to Ottah, and they stepped down from the platform.

"What do you mean by protection?" John asked.

"Well, let's say not everyone here likes humans very much. There's a lot of stereotyping and prejudice. But with the stone, only authorized people can use magic on you. And that will only happen if you do something illegal."

"That would have been nice to know before we left. Does that mean we're in danger?" John eyed his surroundings as if looking for an attacker. Perdita was sure they were thinking the same thing. They had enough to be getting on with without worrying about random wizards attacking them.

"No. No. Of course not. You have to understand, it's like in your world there are stupid people who do mean things. In New York, for instance, how many times have there been reports in the news about a tourist getting mugged? Not to mention all the hate crimes. Same sort of thing here. Rare, but it does occasionally happen. I would say it's human nature, but as we are not human…" Todd finished with a shrug.

"But couldn't we be hurt by something or someone, other than magic?" John couldn't stop looking for trouble.

"Well, yes, that's possible, but the stone offers you some protection. And the likelihood of anything happening is slim. It's an added precaution. If it makes you all feel any better, there hasn't been a human attacked, by magic or otherwise, for more than ten years." Todd ushered them along and tried to change the subject.

The streets were nearly empty along the walk to The Human Eatery. Perdita listened halfheartedly to the conversation between John and Todd. Instead, she chose to drink in the sites of the beautiful city. She had only seen it once, the night she and Philo escaped from within the Pyre. But on that fateful night long ago, they didn't get to stop and admire the city that they'd heard so much about from within their prison. She and

Philo could only run and try desperately to find a gate. A gate to the human world where they could hide their daughter who was growing within her womb.

They rounded the corner of Troll Lane, and there they stood in front of The Human Eatery.

They walked in through a vanishing door, and the place was packed, but Todd told them they had a reservation. They entered, and the conversations dwindled away as everyone turned to stare at the two humans in their midst. Perdita's mouth went dry, but everyone regained their composure and returned to their meals.

Perdita couldn't blame them. The restaurant held a sea of brown, red, purple, and aquatic blue, but only Perdita and John wore navy. It was definitely something one would notice.

There were signs hung on the walls boasting that the restaurant offered the best human food in Conjuragic. John jumped as a large but surprisingly pleasant-looking troll approached them, his footsteps shaking the floorboards. The troll didn't seem to be offended by John's reaction.

When he spoke, his voice boomed, making Perdita want to cover her ears. But despite the troll's volume, his voice was welcoming and even kind. His feet were as large as a baby dolphin and thick as leather and covered in coarse fur. Perdita smiled when she saw he was wearing hair nets on his feet.

The troll showed them to a table in the back where their table was blocked by a half wall. "I thought you all might like to eat without people staring," Todd answered Perdita's questioning look.

Good. The fewer people who see us, the better, she thought.

"So what's good here?" John asked, picking up the menu. "I'm starving."

Perdita felt guilty for even thinking of food, but the sweet smell of cooking onions reached her nose, and her stomach grumbled, betraying her. How could she even think about eating while Ora was...she couldn't bear to think it. But, she would need her energy if she were going to rescue Ora.

"When we travel, it takes a great deal of energy. Usually people lose a few pounds during a trip, and then their metabolism kicks into overdrive. But there is a catch. If you eat a lot before the trip, you'll toss your cookies along the way. Gate attendees hate that. Which, trust me, isn't something you want to see." Todd eyed the menu. Perdita noted his hands were shaking.

"If you wouldn't mind, could I have some of those crackers?" Todd asked, and when John passed them over, he ripped open a package with his teeth and scarfed them.

"Pardon me," Todd said after he downed four packages. "You see, when I travel, I use a significant amount of energy helping my customers cross the Veil. During regular travel, I lose a pound or two, but during tours, I usually lose five pounds or more each time. So I have to eat a lot to regain my energy."

All during this speech, he scarfed another three packages of crackers. And right at the end, their waiter came. Another troll, a female this time. She was tall as well, six feet and muscular. Her voice was sultry and easy to listen to. Her skin held a greenish-gray hue, and her nose was bulbous like a potato. Her bottom teeth rose from her mouth, stuck up like a boar. She had pointed ears with soft hair around the lobes. Long greenish-brown coarse hair curled down her back. She had a round belly with necklaces in different lengths dangling down her chest. Perdita noted her feet were free from hair. Her appearance was overwhelming, but once you got over the initial shock, you could see her subtle beauty.

Once their waitress was out of earshot, Perdita asked in a hushed voice, "So the, um, people who run this place. They're trolls?"

Todd laughed. "Well, we don't call them that. But that's the name they have from human legends. They call themselves Styxes."

"Are they like the trolls from all the stories?" John rested his elbows on the table leaning toward Todd.

"No, in your stories, they are depicted as big, ugly, and stupid. While they are large, you can see they are certainly not stupid or ugly. Sure, in general, they don't like wizards or humans, but they are their own unique species," Todd explained, shoving the last cracker in his mouth.

"So, are there cows in Conjuragic?" John asked Todd. Perdita tilted her head trying to figure out where this random question came from, looked at the menu, and understood.

Todd laughed. "No. But specialty places like this one have it imported. It's a treat for the people of Conjuragic to eat human food. Hamburgers, hotdogs, pizza, stuff like that. It's especially nice for people who studied or lived in the human world for a time. You get to miss it when you're back home and can't have it. There was even a talk of opening a fast food burger place here, but it wasn't approved by the Council." Todd downed his drink, a hot pumpkin tea, in three gulps.

"What sort of things do witches and wizards do when they live in the human world?" Perdita asked. She had always wondered. During her time in the human world, she would occasionally see different people and sense their magic. For obvious reasons, she'd never gotten too close and slipped away if they made a move to talk to her.

"Anything they want. I've a cousin who is a lawyer. Don't judge me. And you know what I do, run an antique shop and do tours. I think there is a witch or wizard in about every human profession. And some people go over there to get further education. You really do have a vast knowledge chemistry and physics. Usually witches and wizards are really advanced in those subjects, mainly because we can apply them to magic, but also because we can see the reactions." Todd craned his head searching for the waitress.

He must have found her because he made a waving motion, and she returned to take their order. Perdita excused herself and went to the restroom. She was relieved because the bathroom looked like a human bathroom. She washed her hands with a color-changing soap that left her hands soft.

She returned to their table in time to hear John ask, "I was wondering how do you all do magic? Do you have spells or is it just thought? Or what?"

Before Todd could answer, their food arrived, and no one talked much while they ate. They were all famished, but no one more so than Todd. During their meal, Todd managed to eat two cheeseburgers, a medium pizza, three hotdogs, nachos, French fries, three hot pumpkin teas, and a salad.

At the end, the fork made slower trips to Todd's mouth and he could talk more. "As I was saying while you were in the restroom, wizards both live and work in the human realm. Between our two species—well, technically five species—we've advanced technology on both sides. And some are used only here because they have obvious magic. Like our medicines."

Todd paid their bill, waving away Perdita's cash. "It's covered in your package. Besides they don't accept human money." Perdita slipped her cash away, not in the least bit sorry with the small fortune she'd forked up to bypass the questions. Watching Todd interact with the Styx, she found it hard to believe he was involved in the black market.

After lunch, they waddled their way to a Transport pole, bellies full. A small lady fairy signaled for the Transport. John's shocked expression never wavering the whole time the fairy was around.

The little blond-haired fairy glared at his back when he whispered, "She looks like Tinkerbell."

Perdita could only give her an apologetic smile and follow him onto the Transport. The moving platform whisked to cart twenty-one. As they got their seats, Todd said, "Oh, you wanted to know how we do magic."

"Oh yeah!" John said.

"Complex magic requires a spell or melding with technology, but small bits of magic only require concentration. Like this—" He stared at a small circle on the floor, and it turned from a marble tile to a slab of wood and back again.

"Cool!" John pumped a fist in the air.

"I have to concentrate to control it. You know, to make sure I don't hurt anyone or anything. But if you're going to do major damage, like an earthquake, then it is just like breathing. You don't even think about it. Actually, the older and more experienced you get, the less you have to concentrate."

"Why would you need to cause an earthquake?" Perdita asked, regretting that she asked it out loud.

"Actually, no one has done that in a very long time. About three hundred years ago, the four Houses were at war. They are called the House Wars now. Spheres would cause earthquakes. Naiads would cause tidal waves. Embers would blow things up, and Tempest let loose tornados."

"What were you fighting about?" John asked leaning forward, his elbows on his knees.

"Who was the better House? The most powerful? Who should rule? More land. You know the usual things wars are about." Todd stood from his seat to gaze out the window.

"So, what ended it? Now you all have the city and work together, right?" John asked, standing to join him.

"Yes, the wars ended, and Conjuragic was created. The great thing about the city is it's protected by all four cores of magic. There's nothing that could make the city fall. No natural disaster or magical attack can ever harm it."

"Ahh, but there are other ways a city can fall that have nothing to do with buildings," Perdita said, thinking of the government falling.

"True. Very true," Todd agreed. "But enough of that. Let's have some fun."

The conversation ended, and Perdita watched the country side roll past. The Transport left the white buildings, glowing with the magic of the four cores, and soon trees appeared, growing denser with each passing second. The trees were high and thick, and Perdita wanted to climb, something she had never wanted to do before.

The Transport slowed as they reached their destination, The Willow. The conductor announced this magically, without the use of a speaker, according to Todd anyway. They stepped off the Transport, and the forest welcomed them with wonderful strange birds flying over their heads singing the most peaceful songs. The birds' voices soothed the nerves with a sweet melody. Perdita caught glimpses of beautiful sparkling sprites scampering along the bark and limbs. John touched her shoulder several times and pointed things out. His enthusiasm amused her. She smiled at him and nodded her head letting him know she saw them too. They reached a large clearing, perhaps a few miles into the forest.

Perdita's eyes lit up as she beheld the homes of the people of Sphere. They made their dwellings in the trunks of the trees, high in the air. They had circular windows with no glass. Perdita's skin tingled with energy emanating from the very ground.

Across The Veil

Perdita returned her gaze from Sphere's tree houses and looked upon a sea of faces. Unlike the city, the people here are dressed in all different colors, mostly dark greens, pumpkin orange, and buttery yellow. It looked like they were having a festival. There were people dancing in a large circle, spinning with their arms spread out. They had small bells attached to their wrists, and when they turned and entered a new position, they would ring together.

While some danced, others played a game that looked something like chess, but Perdita didn't recognize any of the pieces. Children ran around laughing and chasing each other. She heard one of them yell, "I got you!"

Some children made snails hover and spin until an adult came along and scolded them. An old man sat upon a stump with a group of the young and old alike sitting on the ground by his feet. He was telling them a story about a strange beast he battled in what sounded like the Antarctic.

Perdita asked, "Are they having a celebration?

"No. Why?" Todd asked.

"Wait. You're telling me this is a normal day?" John stared, perplexed.

At first no one took much notice of them, but as they traveled deeper into the clearing, more and more people stared, and the sounds of voices hushed. Todd greeted a large round-faced woman. "Hey, Auntie Sarah. These are my new clients, Evelyn and Jack. This is my Aunt Sarah."

"How do you do?" Perdita said in a soft voice and shook hands. The woman didn't meet her eyes and gave a brisk handshake. She wasn't exactly warm, but polite enough.

"Say, have you seen Mom? I have some of the supplies she asked for, and I noticed she wasn't home when I got here." Todd looked up and to the left, apparently to his mother's home.

"She went into town today. She should be back soon. I don't know what's kept her."

"Okay. When you see her, tell her I stopped by, and I'll be back later tonight. We'll be here for about an hour, and then we will need to be moving along." Todd hugged his aunt. Her face wore a scowl that Perdita didn't understand.

"Are you staying here tonight then?" Sarah asked.

"Don't I always?" he grinned, unabashed by her rudeness. He kissed her cheek and bid her farewell.

A few people floated down from the tree homes to the ground below on what looked like a raft, wicker by the looks of it. Perdita, John, and Todd made their way to the bottom of a tree. Todd stepped on one of the rafts and motioned for them to join him. When Perdita hesitated, Todd laughed and took her hand, easing her onto the center.

"I thought you would like to see one of the homes. I'm going to take you to my parents' house. It isn't one of the larger ones, but the theme is basically the same. Besides most people like the ride."

"Is it safe?" Perdita asked.

"Perfectly." Todd smiled reassuring her.

"Come on, Mom, where is your sense of adventure?" John bounced up and down on the raft, testing its sturdiness.

Up they went. She gripped Todd's hand until her knuckles were white. There wasn't anywhere to hold on, and Perdita swayed until Todd steadied her. At first it was very frightening, being lifted without ropes or pulleys to rise a hundred feet into the air in a matter of seconds. It was, by no means, her favorite way to travel, but once she got centered, the view was nothing short of spectacular. The sea of trees stretched out before her, and the tree sprites waved from a neighboring tree, sweet smiles on their tiny faces. Strange winged bugs flew beside them, racing them to the top.

The entrance of Todd's parents' home held a walkway and a rounded door. The tree was oak, and the wooden floors shined like glass. A fresh scent lingered in the air, like sawdust and lemons. The furniture was all large, soft, and comfortable. A painting of a building Perdita didn't recognize hung above a couch dug out from the inside of the tree.

There was a light breeze blowing through the windows making the lace curtains rustle. A peaceful and relaxed feeling stole over Perdita, and she felt at home. The house was full of character with a high ceiling and archways that led from room to room. Perdita could almost forget she was hundreds of feet in the air in a hollowed-out tree of a magical forest. Almost.

Todd gave them the tour, stopping to tell hilarious stories about the family pictures placed throughout his childhood home. "And this was when we went to The Meadow and went sky diving and my dad peed in his robes!"

As they were about to leave, Todd's mother came in, calling her son. When she saw him, she threw her large arms around him, cackling. She was a corpulent woman, full of life and charm. Perdita liked her at once.

"Sarah said you were here, but she thought you might've gone." Todd's mother's voice was jolly as she embraced her son. She pulled away, spied Perdita, and walked over to her, throwing her arms around her and hugging her as if they had been friends forever. "Hello there, darlings! I am Delicia Vulpine, Todd's mother. But everyone calls me Del. I know y'all will have a great time visiting. Y'all have to stay for some afternoon tea and freshly made cinnamon buns. I know how much traveling takes out of my boy." Del reached over and pinched Todd cheek.

"Ma, you know we're on a schedule," Todd said as he rubbed his reddening cheek.

Del faced Perdita and pouted. "Come on, say you will stay."

Perdita smiled. "We'd love to, Mrs. Vulpine."

"No, no, no, my dear, call me Del. I insist." Del put her arm around Perdita's waist and led her to the kitchen. She sat them down for a delightful little snack and an even more enjoyable visit. The cinnamon buns were sweet and hot, leaving Perdita's fingers sticky. She sipped a hot tea, spiced and sweetened with honey.

Del talked the entire time. "And the other day Julie Sutton tripped over her dog and broke her leg." It was hard to follow most of what she said because she talked about people and places as if Perdita was already supposed to know who and what she was talking about. John stared at her in disbelief, and Todd kept telling her with exasperation, "Ma, they have no idea who that is."

"Oh, I know," Del would say and keep going. Todd shook his head and covered his eyes with one hand. Perdita pursed her lips to keep from giggling. Finally, Todd had enough. He stood from the table, sending the chair tipping over in his haste. He righted it and said, "Sorry, Ma. But it's indeed time to go."

"Oh, do you have to? You just got here." Del pouted with frosting-smeared lips.

"I'm afraid so. We still have to visit the Guidance Hall and check in to the hotel. Besides, they didn't pay for a tour to come and visit with my family."

"We don't mind, do we, Mom?" John laughed. He had been doing a fabulous job pretending to be a nothing but a visiting tourist. But Perdita had never been a good actress. Her face always betrayed her every emotion. Ora often joked she could read her like a book. Perdita always replied, "If you're happy, you smile; if you're sad, you frown; if you're angry, you scowl. Simple as that." At the thought of Ora, she knew she had to do better at pretending. This cover was vital to saving Ora. She wouldn't let the sacrifice she, Philo, and her friends made be for nothing. Perdita was only waiting for the coming of darkness, for tonight was the night. She must not fail.

Suddenly, as if from far away, Perdita heard with extra syllables, "Moooom."

"What?" Perdita snapped to attention. Her eyes found John and realized she hadn't been paying attention. "I'm sorry, I must have been daydreaming. That cinnamon bun made me sleepy. What did you do, Del? Bake a sleeping spell right into it?"

That took the attention off her as they enjoyed a laugh at her expense. John glared at her when the Vulpines weren't looking. She shrugged in response. When the laughter died down, John asked, "Well, what do you think?"

"What do I think about what dear?" Perdita asked. And Todd and Del burst out laughing at her again.

"We were just talking, and Todd suggested perhaps we go straight to the hotel. So we can get some rest," John explained.

Todd added, "I really think it would be best. You look absolutely worn out. I thought we could go check into the hotel and relax for a while. We don't have a full day scheduled tomorrow, so we can always see the Guidance Hall then. What do you think?"

"That would be wonderful. I would love to lie down for a spell." Perdita thought this would be a perfect time to plan for tonight. They said their goodbyes to Del and made their way back down the raft to the forest floor below, slower this time. Perdita was glad. She didn't know how she would handle speeding to the ground. They hailed the Transport and boarded another cart.

Their little group was quiet, Todd giving them time to watch out of the window. They soon arrived at the Feenwell Hotel. It wasn't very large, only about twelve stories high, a dwarf building compared to the other buildings in Conjuragic. For what it lacked in size, it made up for in grandeur. Sleek walls with large ornate windows showed on the outside, and the lobby held marble floors speckled with flicks of gold. Large pristine crystal chandeliers hung from the ceiling, lit by thousands of burning candles.

Twenty minutes later, they checked into their hotel, after some discussion. Check in wasn't supposed to be until five o'clock, but after Todd mentioned in passing to Perdita that for future tours he might have to make different arrangements for his clients to stay at the Rama Hotel, the management agreed to let them go to their rooms early.

They planned to meet Todd in the lobby later that evening for supper and said farewell at the door to their room, number 1207. When Perdita first stepped inside, there was a small foyer. Leading off to the left were two large bedrooms with a connecting bathroom.

She left the second bedroom and entered the common room with plush white carpets, beige couches, and cherry end tables. Opposite the couch, a screen took up half the wall. It might have been a TV of some kind, but Perdita didn't see any wires. To the side of the common room was a library filled with books lining the shelves top to bottom. She wished she had the time to explore the titles. In the very back of the hotel room was a small kitchen with appliances like she had never seen.

Perdita walked back through the room and found John in the bedroom nearest the door. "I feel horrible because we are definitely going to get Todd and Cantius into trouble. They may even shut down their company."

John's shoulders slumped. "I know. I was thinking the same thing." He opened his suitcase.

"But I'm hoping we can get Ora back without them finding out who helped her. It would be much easier than having to fight our way out of here." Perdita sat on the side of his bed.

"I hope so. I really like those guys. I don't want them to get into trouble because of us."

"Me either."

"Do you think we can do it? Do you think we can save her?" John flung himself on the bed, staring at the ceiling.

"I don't know, but we have to try."

"I hope nothing happens to my grandparents or Charlie if they find us."

"I'm going to do everything in my power to get us all home. I promise you that."

"Thanks," he murmured, but he sounded numb.

"We need to discuss the plan."

Since getting to the hotel, John wore a grim face, and his frown only deepened at those words. "Right, what's the plan?"

Perdita stood, walked to a window, and looked in the direction of the Nook.

"Break her out of prison."

Chapter Sixteen

Shock flashed across Arameus's face. He closed his mouth, furrowing his brow. After considering my words, he stammered, "Well, there are legends of human-born witches, but they're really rare. Even more rare than Nips."

This news sank my hopes. Of course, a human born witch would be rare. It was my only answer. My head sunk in defeat. "I'm frightened no one will believe me because it'll be easier to call me a Nip."

"It's definitely a fear that is well warranted. Killing you would be the easiest thing for people. It'll take some time to prove you are a human-born witch, and we'll have to convince the tribunal tomorrow to let us investigate further."

The quill flew across his parchment paper with a frantic scratching as he spoke. "Luckily for us, the Council has thrown out your initial confession due to the circumstances of your arrest. Had they not done so, well, I wouldn't be sitting here. Tell me, do you have any other incidences of you performing magic before two days ago?"

Half a dozen little things flashed before my eyes, all predating my move to Raleigh. The first thing I thought of was my eighth birthday party. In our backyard filled with an enormous garden, underneath the gazebo, opening presents. The last gift was filled with holes. The box trembled as I opened it, and a kitten paced inside. I screamed, unable to contain my excitement. But right after, the gazebo and all my other presents caught fire. The image of stepping through the flames, unburnt, flashed clear and bright, stronger than mere memory. The newest part of me, the source of my magic, shivered with pleasure at being remembered. Grandma and I got in our car, amidst the screaming of the other children and parents, and fled. We never went back to the house. That was the night she gave me the amulet and made me promise I would never take it off.

The necklace must have blocked my power and somehow the memories from before. There were only now returning, little by little. My eyes met Arameus's, and I considered telling him of the fire. A true story of my power. But the magic inside me struck like an asp. For some reason, it warned me against telling Arameus this particular memory.

Instead, I searched for more memories. "Well, I remember when I was three, I was at a store with my grandma, and I saw this humungous teddy bear. And I wanted her to buy it, but she said no. She said it was almost Christmas and maybe Santa would bring it to me." I smiled, embarrassed at the silly story. "I threw a hissy fit so she'd buy it for me. When that I didn't work, I looked at the bear. It vibrated, and then shrank. It went from this big," I held my hand out about three feet above the floor, "to small enough to hold it in my hand. So I, uh, shoved it in my pocket."

"Excellent, excellent. And at age three...impressive," he said, as he wrote down the details.

Feeling more confident, my voice grew calmer. "Most were small things. I could make flowers grow from seeds. I made a tree bend over to help me over a fence. And I could make the best sandcastles when we went to the beach."

The next several hours passed as I retold details of small events that happened in my childhood, and a more in-depth look into my life and family. At the end of the interview, his parchment was full, and his kind green eyes were alit with purpose. Before he left, he asked me if I had any questions. I had only one. "Arameus, is a Defender like a lawyer?"

He laughed. "Yes, a Defender is like a lawyer. I'll defend you, protect you in any way that I can." He gave me a small nod of his head, and with that, he turned and raised a hand. The door vanished, and he faced me once more before leaving, giving me a gentle smile, and said, "Until tomorrow."

"Until tomorrow," I said before the door closed and the waterfall appeared. This time it was a gentle stream instead of the hurricane. I looked around my cell and felt hopeful for the first time. Arameus left me the two cushions and the light in the jar. I was no longer in the dark. No longer alone.

Across The Veil

A few hours later, at the start of the inferno, the lava vanished, and the entrance hissed and opened for the third time. I hoped it was Arameus, but I was disappointed. Instead, the two women Protectors who arrested me entered the cell. They wore the same leather uniforms as before, and neither looked happy. Commander Stewart fanned herself with her hands. The heat from the inferno hadn't dissipated yet, and it was still hot. But I found the room much cooler, especially with the door being open, releasing some of the heat. The intensity of all the room's phases had decreased since meeting my Defender.

I did my best not to fidget. I didn't know what these women wanted nor was I sure I wanted to find out. The two Protectors sat on the cushioned rocks, and the Commander waved her hand for the door to close again. I stood in the middle of the room, my hands clasped in front of me waiting for directions, not wanting to do anything wrong that would give them cause to hurt me.

Commander Stewart motioned for me to sit, and I took my old place upon the bent, sweet-smelling hay. "I trust you remember us?" Commander Stewart asked me.

"Yes," I said.

"I don't believe we were introduced properly before. I'm Commander Leigh Stewart, and this is Lieutenant Sabrina Sun."

I nodded, not answering. *If you would've taken the time find out more information before bringing me here, you wouldn't have to introduce yourself,* I thought.

"You must wonder why we are here. We're Protectors, but more specifically we're members of the Magical Concealment Division. Since you have withdrawn your confession, we're now investigating further, and we want to ask you some questions," Stewart said.

I could only stare at Stewart. I really didn't care what division they were from or what they had to ask me.

Mistaking my expression of disinterest as confusion, Lieutenant Sun explained, "Excuse me, Lei…Commander, but I think she needs more background information. This is all completely new to her."

A look of irritation passed across the Commander's face. "I agree it will be much easier if she understands more. But only what she needs to know. You may proceed."

I watched the two women and wondered what their deal was. I had the impression the women were friends but were supposed to act differently at work. And Lieutenant Sun sometimes forgot.

Sun smiled at me. "Like Commander Stewart said, we're Protectors. This is more of a general title. We work for the Protector's Department, which is like the military, I believe."

I had guessed as much but didn't say anything.

"The Protector's Department has many divisions. We work for the Magical Concealment Division, which as the name implies, enforces the concealment of our world from yours."

Again, I had already worked this much out on my own, but at least my suspicions were confirmed.

Sun continued. "When the Concealment Code has been breached, we cross the Veil into your plane and investigate. We also send a team to erase memories and remove all evidence. We do this so that humans won't find out about us."

Despite my mistrust, this conversation was piquing my interest. Today, it seemed, was a day for some answers. "Sometimes the Concealment Code is broken by a Nip. In case you have forgotten, a Nip is a human who has stolen a witch's magic."

"No, I haven't forgotten," I said. My tone came out as sarcastic as I dared.

Commander Stewart in one fluid movement stood, hands bald into fists. She loomed over me. "Don't you dare be so flippant to a Protector." The move was calm and calculated without a hint of over emotion.

"Understood," I said, tone even.

Lieutenant Sun peeked at the Commander, and the two women reached an unspoken understanding. Commander Stewart returned to her seat and warned me, "You should be wary, child. You're locked within a high-security cell, defenseless and alone. You don't have many supporters, and no one would care if you had an accident. Others who come may not be as forgiving."

Across The Veil

An unwelcomed chill of fear swept over me, and I broke out in a cold sweat. For a few hours, I'd escaped my fear, and now with a few words, I was reminded of my reality. I really hoped after Arameus left, everything might be okay. I didn't realize how difficult it would be to convince people of my innocence.

Nips were feared here, the kind of senseless fear that drove honest and upstanding people to do horrible things. I didn't quite realize until that very moment what grave danger I was really in. I was so lost in my own thoughts that when Lieutenant Sun cleared her throat, I jumped. "Shall I continue then?" she asked.

I cleared my throat. "Yes. Please."

"As I was saying, sometimes a Nip breeches the Concealment Code. This is a very serious crime, one punishable by death. Not only for breaking the code, but to steal magic is an unforgiveable crime."

Lieutenant Sun leaned forward, placing her elbows on her knees. "In this circumstance, we cross the Veil and investigate. Usually, this takes a great deal of time, so we isolate everyone involved until we find the guilty party. This is why your arrest today was such a surprise. It happened too quickly. Nips usually run."

"Lieutenant," Commander Stewart warned.

Lieutenant Sun nodded. "Your original confession has been deemed inadmissible. The statement you gave at processing is what is on file. We're here to ask you some questions about what happened on the morning of your arrest, in order for us to start a new investigation."

"I'd like to ask you one question first," I asked, surprised by my boldness.

"Careful." Commander Stewart straightened her back.

"Excuse me, Protector, but the Council is throwing out my original confession because of *unusual circumstances*. I think that is a really funny way to describe torturing my best friend. I think you all owe me at least one question. Don't you?" My power drifted closer, sliding through every muscle, steeling me for a fight.

Lieutenant Sun and Commander Stewart exchanged a look. Stewart waved an arm in my direction. "Fine. What's your question?"

"What is the purpose of your investigation?"

Shocked is not an adequate word to describe the look on Commander Stewart's face. When neither Protector responded, I continued. "Because it seems to me that if your team effed up during my arrest, then you would be in trouble, yes? And in the pursuit of self-preservation, y'all would do anything to prove I'm guilty. So why should I tell you anything?"

Stewart spoke for them. "Our investigation is to discover the truth. It's true we would be punished if we made a mistake. But I intend to find out the truth, no matter what. If you're innocent as you say, then my entire Quad will apologize, and we'll take the punishment that is coming to us. If, however, you are guilty…" She left the rest unsaid, but the threat was undeniable.

It was my turn to falter under Commander Stewart's gaze. Power radiated out of her. The force of it hit my skin, and goosebumps spread over my arms and legs. The magic inside me spat, reminding me of one house cat hissing at another. As quickly as it came, it vanished. I wasn't sure if there was any change, or if it was my imagination. "I would rather talk to you with my lawyer present."

Lieutenant Sun's brow clinched in confusion. "Lawyer?"

"Oh, erm, I mean my Defender."

"Our rules are different than yours. We may be asking you to speak with us, but it isn't really a request. Protectors are allowed access to any information while investigating," Commander Stewart informed me.

Nothing in this magical world was fair. "Fine, what do you want to know?"

"Tell us what happened on the morning of your arrest," Lieutenant Sun said.

I retold them the story of that fateful morning. And when Commander Stewart looked convinced of my guilt, I told them about the things that happened when I was a child. "You see, I had to find out more information. I knew that I'd done magic in the past. But when Ara…my Defender told me what happens to a witch when a Nip uses their power, I knew I couldn't be a Nip. The only explanation we could come up with is that I'm a witch myself."

"That's preposterous!" Commander Stewart scoffed.

Sun touched her chin. "Not necessarily. I remember reading something years ago about an anomaly that sometimes happens with humans. It's very rare, but sometimes a witch or wizard can be born from human parents. The children themselves are usually found in childhood though."

"Only in legends and children's stories," Stewart argued.

"Perhaps her ability was dormant and only emerged recently?"

"You honestly think that is possible?" Stewart crossed her arms over her chest.

I watched the two women discussing me as if I wasn't even there. But I thought if I could convince Stewart, then maybe I could win over the jury, or whoever was to decide my fate.

Stewart waved her hand, stopping their conversation. "Regardless of our opinions, we have to investigate her story. Ora, you must give us as much detail as possible. If this true, then the MDA might have a record of it. Although I'm not sure how long the MDA keeps records. That has got to be what, at least fourteen to fifteen years ago?"

"Yes," I said.

"Sun, get a quill. It seems we are going to be here a while."

Sabrina and Leigh sat in a regular car on the Transport watching the passing of the grasslands of The Meadow. They'd taken the Transport instead of materializing to give themselves longer to talk. Sabrina asked, "What do you think about her? Think she's a Nip?"

Leigh was quiet, considering her thoughts, and then said, "I hope for our sakes she is because I'd hate to be wrong. The Council would be very angry with us. But whether she is a Nip or not doesn't really concern me, only if we made a mistake. I worry because the arrest was so quick. But no matter what, we'll get the bottom of this."

"Leigh, forgive me, but I say this as your friend. Never once in all the time we have been Protectors have you ever second guessed or worried about an arrest." Leigh's eyes flashed with anger, but before she could say anything, Sabrina added, "This is between us. I'm sorry you think that I was out of line, but there is something different about this girl. She doesn't feel like a Nip to me, and I know you don't think she is one either. But she not human either. Tell me you felt that in there?"

"I say this to you as your friend and your Commander, you're never to repeat what we say here in confidence."

"Of course."

"You're right. This girl feels different, but I can't put my finger on it. I have no idea what that was, but I've never been scared of a prisoner before."

"Me either."

"The stone blocks all magic. There was power in there, and the stone didn't shut it down."

Sabrina nodded, relieved she wasn't alone. "That's exactly what I thought, but there's something else. She's kind. I don't think she'd willingly hurt anyone."

"Yes, but despite our feelings, we have to conduct this investigation in an objective way. We can't allow ourselves to be tainted, so stop thinking of how you feel about the matter and worry about what information we can find. Besides, we're far too late for the Council already. For now, let us drop this and speak of it to no one. Agreed?"

Sabrina nodded, and her head swam with this strange a new mystery.

Later that evening, I paced in the cell, the bottle of light still shining bright. The light never diminished, but it did nothing for the growing anxiety. I had a preliminary trial tomorrow. I couldn't sit still. I wrung my hands, scratched at my itchy, bald head. I wiped my sweaty palms on the black robes. Many hours ago, I'd chewed off my fingernails. Fantasies about the events of tomorrow plagued me. Perhaps they would proclaim a mistake was made and send me home, but I knew this would never happen. But the worst thought that kept coming back was that they would find me guilty and that would be that. Then I'd be executed. I shivered despite the heat of the inferno, which had been blazing for the last few hours.

The hissing sound of my door being unsealed interrupted my pacing. The door vanished for the fourth time today. Another elf, much like Tyke, entered my room carrying a small tray. The tiny elf looked no more than a boy. His skin was flawless like that of a baby cherub. Blond curly locks brushed along his forehead like a gentle kiss. His small cherry lips curled into a small smile, and his eyes twinkled with happiness. *He definitely works in the wrong place*, I thought.

The elf handed me the only thing upon the tray, a small bowl filled with a similar mush as before. My hand shook as I grabbed the bowl and thanked him. No spoon, I noted. The mush was somewhat better than the first time, but still nothing I would've picked for myself. I thanked him again. He smiled back, not speaking. One thing I liked about all the visitors, besides not being alone anymore, was they interrupted the cycles of the cell, so I hadn't had to be in the inferno a full cycle since early this morning.

When I finished my small but pitiful meal, I placed the bowl back onto the tray. The small elf turned to leave, but Malandra and Mark blocked the doorway. *Don't they ever go home?* I wondered.

"Come." Mark motioned for me to join him. I obeyed and faced the brute. "Trosh, she needs shoes," Mark said without looking at the elf.

The elf bowed and left with my tray, the bowl clattering as he hurried away. "Ready for another walk?" Mark asked with a sarcastic grin on his face.

I followed Mark into the passageway. Trosh stood nearby, tray gone, with a pair of black sandals dangling in his tiny hands. I took them from him and slipped them onto my feet. Unlike the first pair, these fit perfectly. The musky smell of dampness hung in the air, and a delicate mist swirled beneath my feet. Mark, Malandra, and I turned in one direction, and Trosh went another.

I followed the Keepers through endless passageways, curving into left and right until I was utterly lost. Other prisoners screamed down long, dark, lonely corridors that appeared to lead nowhere. After several minutes of walking, we came upon the sounds of clinking pots and pans, quiet talking with intermittent laughter, and the tantalizing scent of cooking meat, making my mouth water. Guess not every prisoner got nasty Cream of Wheat to eat. Even though I had been given food—if you could call it that—my stomach growled loudly, demanding to be relieved of its emptiness. Mark laughed when he heard my stomach, and I glared at his back hating him. My magic surged forward with a vengeance, yanking itself out of me.

Mark yelled, tripping forward and landing on his face with a loud sickening crack and then a horrible growl. Malandra, who had been quiet so far on the journey, slammed me up against the wall, pinning me there, gripping my throat. "Mark, what happened? Did she do this?" Her grip tightened, and I could barely breathe. The shock of what I'd done sent the power diving back down.

Mark swore as he got to his feet. Malandra squeezed even harder. I grabbed at Malandra's hands, choking and fighting to get loose from under her iron grip. For this, she slammed my head against the jagged rocks. My vision darkened, and a warm trickle of blood ran down the back of my neck.

As my body relaxed from almost being knocked out, Malandra finally loosened her grip. My head rolled to the side and my ears rang. When my eyes found Mark, his nose was crooked with blood trickling into his mouth. The one scar-free spot above his right eye was torn, blood glistening in the light.

"Well?" Malandra gawked at Mark.

"Well, what?"

She looked at him with a mixture of surprise and annoyance. "What happened?"

"I tripped and fell, that's what."

"Oh. But how?"

"Tripping over my own ruddy feet, that's how. Do you have any more stupid questions, or can we be on our way?"

Malandra laughed, followed by several colorful names while Mark wiped the blood off his face indifferent to her insults. When she'd ragged him to her satisfaction, she dragged me from my sagging position on the wall to my feet, where I swayed. Malandra righted me and swore when she saw my head.

Mark shrugged and said, "It's not that bad. It'll look better after we wash it off."

"That damn Defender is sticking his nose all over the place. And Miss Uppity Healer," Malandra whispered as if I couldn't hear her. She tapped back pushing me forward, and we were once again walking along the cold, dark, slime-covered caves that made up the underground premises of the Nook. Mark led me to the shower room, and Malandra followed close behind. I wondered why I was getting a second shower today, but I knew better than to ask.

Like last time, I was ordered to strip, but this time, I didn't bother to tell Mark to turn around. I didn't care whether he saw me or not, and by the look of his swollen right eye, I'd guess he wouldn't be paying me any attention anyway. Once again, I stepped in the icy waters of the artic waterfall they called a shower. It was as big of a shock stepping into the water this time as last. I reached down feeling for my magic. It reached up to my call, rising outward. The water warmed up under its persuasion, not enough to be enjoyable, but enough that I could tolerate it. The wound on my head felt deep, and I'm sure that it would need stitches, although I doubted if I would be able to get medical attention for a second time in the same day. As if following my thoughts, the power moved there, tingling and pulling. *Healing?*

It retreated, pulling back as my fear of it grew. It didn't want me to be afraid of it. I hurried washing myself again. When I was almost finished, my fingers skimmed the wound on my head. It wasn't healed, but much smaller than it had been. Probably a good thing. A healed wound in this place was a bad idea.

I stepped out of the waterfall, and Malandra asked me, "Stayed in there long enough. What are you, a glutton for punishment?" I shrugged, and Malandra shook her head, handing me clean robes and the sandals.

Our little trio left again, walking backward to my cell. At the kitchens, my stomach was thankfully quiet, and the rest of the walk was unremarkable.

I gasped at the doorway of my cell. I backed out of the room believing I'd made a wrong turn. "What do you think you're doing?" Malandra blocked me.

"But what… is all this?" I asked, bewildered. "Is this really the same cell?"

Malandra rolled her eyes. "Yes, stupid girl, it's the same room. I don't approve, but it was your Defender's orders. Now don't make me tell you again. Get in."

Malandra sealed the door shut behind me. My cell was still small, but other than that, it looked completely different. The pile of hay was gone and replaced with a bed, covered with soft blankets and an assortment of pillows.

There was a small fire burning giving off gentle warmth to the room, both in light and temperature. There was a vase full of daisies. I glided over to what looked like a nightstand, but after a closer look, turned out to be a rock, but one that has been flattened to a smooth surface. Leaning over and inhaling the sweet scent of the flowers, I noticed a vial placed neatly upon the makeshift table with a small note underneath it.

Dear Ora,

This drink will help you relax and ease any lingering pain that you may have. Please trust me when I tell you that it will not harm you. I think we have a strong case for the preliminary tomorrow. I would be completely surprised, and disappointed, if we weren't granted a trial. I have spoken with the warden, and he has agreed to suspend the rotations of your cell for tonight. Afterward, they will be on the lower setting. You'll also have meals three times a day, daily showers, and clean clothes. But for now, sleep upon this token and try for once to have a good night's sleep. I'll see you in the morning.

Best,
Arameus Townsend
Defender, First Class

I picked up the vial and sipped it, not thinking twice about it. It was similar to the drink I received from Lieutenant Sun when I was first brought here and again from Arameus this morning. But this was a little sweeter and less syrupy. All my aches and pains melted away, including my newest wound. I ran my hand over my bald head and to the back where my wound now seemed little more than a scratch. Yawning, I stretched and was ready to sleep. It was unclear if my new relaxation was from the drink or perhaps it was the knowledge I wouldn't have to endure the cycles of the cell tonight. *Oh, face it, Ora. It was the note, or what did he call it? The token.*

Chapter Seventeen

"You have to stay here," Perdita said to John for the hundredth time.

"I want to help. What am I supposed to do while you're gone? And what happens if you get caught? What will happen to Ora then?"

"Be quiet, do you want someone to hear?"

John had the decency to look guilty.

"You can't help me tonight. If I can't rescue her, there is no way you can. I know you want to, but like it or not, you're human. I don't know what I'm facing, what magic I'll have to use, and I can't risk you getting stuck somewhere I can't take you. Besides all that, I don't know what's going to happen. I don't know if I can even break her out."

John threw the glass he was holding, shattering it on the opposite wall. "I can't sit here and do nothing. I have to do something to help her."

"Are you trying to get us caught?" Perdita glared, hurrying to clean up the mess.

John growled, stood from his seated position on the bed, and paced with heavy steps as he'd been doing all afternoon. "I didn't come here to wait in a hotel room while you go out and risk your life."

"You are doing something to help her. You're here, risking your life, to give me an alibi." Perdita attempted to reason with him.

"An alibi?" John said, running his hands through his hair again, looking so much like his grandfather.

"You need to stay here and make sure if someone comes into this room, they think I'm here. That way if we're questioned later, we can have a witness to say we were here all night," Perdita said, getting up and crossing the room to put her hand on his shoulder.

"And how am I going to do that?" John shrugged away from her touch. "I can't make someone think you are here. I'm only human. Remember?" He returned to the bed, sat, and put his head in his hands.

Perdita balled her hands into fists. "I've got it covered. I'm going to record my voice and put it in the bathroom. Later, you can order room service, and while the waiter is here, you can press the button, and they will think I'm in the bathroom."

John gave Perdita a look that clearly said *you've got to be kidding*.

"I know it sounds far-fetched, but at least it will give some doubt if we're questioned." Perdita shrugged.

"We ate a huge dinner with Todd. What am I going to order from room service that won't seem odd?"

"You don't have to order food. Why don't you order a recorded play like Todd suggested?"

"So while you are out being the hero, you want me to stay here and watch a movie?" John asked, hands on his hips.

"This isn't about heroism. It's about Ora."

"What am I supposed to do if you don't come back?"

Perdita could think of only one answer. "Run."

John cursed aloud, pacing again, muttering to himself the entire time. Perdita was done with his behavior. "We've already talked about this. The discussion is over. You will do as I say, as we agreed before we came here."

"Perdita..." John said.

"Enough." Perdita silenced him stomping into bathroom to make the recording. She slammed the door behind her and mumbled to herself, "Kids."

An owl hooted somewhere in the darkness. The waves of the Severn Sea crashed upon on the shore, sending a salty breeze up Perdita's back. She crouched behind some tall brush in the dune surrounding the deserted beach. Perdita flipped the hood of her black cloak over her head and stepped out in the sand, pulling the cloak tight around her, and tiptoed with hurried steps toward the mouth of the hidden cave.

A mile beneath the Nook, Perdita made her way along the dark passageways of the cave with no light to guide her way. Invisible, cold, and scared, she took great efforts to quiet her breathing. She traveled along a rough incline, turning in an ever-increasing circle, climbing higher and higher. Her progress was sluggish as she felt along the wall to know which way to go. Each time a sound reached her ears, Perdita froze like prey spotted by a predator. She didn't dare to start a flame, for either the light or warmth, both of which she craved, lest she be found.

Deep within the cave, Perdita found an opening into the Nook, the same opening that was used to sneak her mother out of the prison many years ago. The escape route had been forgotten many centuries ago and rediscovered by her former master, who used it for his own selfish, evil deeds, fueled by the intense drive of the prophecy.

Perdita's mother's rushed words remained with her, burned into her memory by the fire of trauma. She'd spilt this secret and a handful of others before the guards came, yanking her from their cell, their screams mingled as their hands clung together, fighting to hold onto one another. They hadn't been strong enough. Her mother had been ripped from her. That was the last time she'd ever saw her. Her mother's love and uniqueness vanished in the blink of an eye, forgotten by the world, but Perdita would never forget.

"Who goes there?" a voice whispered. Perdita plummeted back into the present. She gasped and clung to the wall, searching for the owner of the voice. Her heart pounded, and the voice whispered again, "I can see you, but you can't see me. What wicked deeds are you up to?"

The voice had no source; it came from everywhere and nowhere at all. She had no idea how someone could know she was here. She'd been standing quite still for a few minutes at least, and she'd cast the invisibility spell as she walked into the cave.

The voice said, "I see what is there and what is not. Tell me, what are you up to? Something naughty perhaps?" It giggled.

The sound turned Perdita's blood to ice. It reminded her of a child excited by the task of misbehaving, but she was unsure of the voice's intentions. She weighed her options to stay quiet or to speak out. Minutes ticked by, and the voice said with a hint of merriment, "I have all night to wait. I know you are here, and I want to know why."

Perdita could hear a sly smile in the voice, if it even had a mouth. There was nothing left to do but speak. "I'm here. What do you want with me?"

"Depends on why you are here," the voice said thoughtfully.

Perdita challenged the voice. "Why don't you show yourself, coward?"

"I am what you see," it replied.

Perdita searched some more, even more confused than before. "I see nothing."

"Exactly," the voice answered.

"Why are you playing games with me? Who are you? Some escaping prisoner? Or perhaps a ghost who has nothing better to do but confuse the living?" Perdita asked with a hint of condescendence.

"Hmm," it responded, sounding hurt. "What am I would be a better question."

"All right. What are you?"

"I'm an oxyagenian," the voice said, its tone haughty.

"An oxyagenian," Perdita gasped in surprise. "So they do exist. I thought it might only be a story."

"You think you know what I am. Tell me then, what am I?" Its voice grew stronger, and the wind stirred around her legs.

"The story I heard was about a certain number of prisoners from the House of Tempest. The Experimenter," her voice dripped with disgust as she said one of her master's other names, "as he is known to only a few, worked an ancient spell on them. They changed. Becoming something else. A being made up of only air but with a voice and, according to some, a mind of its own."

"But how is it you know such information? You must be one his spies. I will have you destroyed," the oxyagenian said.

The air swirled around her body, and the pressure built all around her, growing tighter by the second. "Wait! I know this because I, too, am one his experiments."

The air settled. "And what kind of experiment are you?"

Perdita steadied herself. "A geminate." The word was told to her first by her mother, then by Aryiana. There was no mention of her in any of the spellbooks.

"Are you really? Most do not survive."

"No, most do not."

"I knew he knew how to keep a secret, but one such as this. How many others?" the oxyagenian asked.

"I don't know. I escaped long ago. There were some who tried to escape with me, but they were all killed. There were more we left behind. So as far as I know, I could be the only one, or one of thousands."

"You escaped him. How wonderful," it whispered, sounding pleased. "Then why are you here? Are you here to search for others? Or do you intend to continue to leave them to their fate?"

The wind rustled again; Perdita could tell it was upset. Perdita had often thought of the others, but it was more important to keep Ora hidden from him.

"Do you remember, air spirit, how much geminates are feared? I would be killed for being alive. I've always wished I could've saved the rest of them, but I had something bigger I needed to protect. That's why I'm here now," Perdita confessed.

"And what could be more important than your own kind?" the oxyagenian asked.

"I'm here to rescue someone who is in this prison. If the Experimenter finds out about her, then all is lost. The world as we know it will end. Please, dear spirit, will you help me?" Perdita pleaded. An oxyagenian as her guide would increase her chances of reaching Ora.

"Who are you trying to rescue?" it asked.

"Can I just say… a girl?" Perdita replied. It laughed.

"Who is this girl? I know she can't be another geminate because you may be the only one. So what could she be that would be so dangerous to him?" It mused aloud. It was hard to talk with an oxyagenian because it was difficult to tell if it was talking to itself or to her.

"I'm sorry, but I can't tell you that," Perdita whispered, "but I can tell you she's special."

"I see. Can she destroy him?"

"I believe so, in time. But she can't if he gets his hands on her first," Perdita lied. She had no intention of letting Ora anywhere near the master. When the oxyagenian remained quiet, she continued. "She has no training in her powers, but after she learns, she may have a chance." Perdita left the idea unspoken for the oxyagenian to make its own assumptions, but she suspected if the oxyagenian thought Ora wasn't going to go after the Experimenter, it would never help her.

As if to prove her right, it said, "I will help you. Now tell me, do you know where she is?"

Perdita's shoulders slumped in defeat. "No. Somewhere on the high security ward would be my best guess."

"So you are planning what, to perhaps ask one of the guards where she is?" the oxyagenian asked, mocking, and laughing at its own humor.

"Well, that was before I had an ally." Perdita smiled knowing oxyagenians loved compliments.

The voice chortled, its laughter filled with mischief. "All right, tell me, my new friend, what does this girl look like?"

Perdita breathed a sigh of relief. "She is a young woman, with long red hair and auburn eyes. She is very beautiful." Perdita's voice caught in her throat.

"Stay hidden. I will try and find her," the oxyagenian said airily, and before it was gone, Perdita gushed, "Thank you. If there is any way I can help you, please know I would."

"I know," it whispered.

"Wait! Before you go, air spirit, tell me, what is your name?"

The air stilled, and the spirit was silent for a moment. The silence stretched on until Perdita wondered if it had gone and hadn't heard her. She jumped when it finally spoke. "I don't know my name. When I became one with the air, who I was before was gone. I could have been male or female, young or old. I know nothing of who I once was."

"I'm so sorry. If I live through this, I will find a way to restore you. I promise."

"Thank you. It has been a very long time since I have spoken to anyone not of the elements. Tell me, what is your name?"

Perdita smiled. "Perdita Stone, and the girl we are trying to find, her name is Ora."

"Her name means light," the oxyagenian said.

"Yes, wise one, it does. What would you like me to call you?"

The air spirit thought for a few moments and whispered, "If you would, call me Lailie. She was the last person to care about me, the last one to try and save me. The Experimenter killed her when he found out. No one remembers her now, but I always will. I wish to honor her by using her name. I wish he will know that name when he is defeated."

"Very well, Lailie."

Perdita waited for a long time. The quiet made her nervous. Even the sounds of the Severn Sea couldn't reach her ears.

Lailie returned, but news wasn't great. "She's far from here, and there are many guards along the way. It will be a very difficult task to get to her."

Perdita's heart sank. "I have to try."

She had known it wouldn't be easy. But getting to Ora without being discovered was going to be near impossible.

"Very well. She is marked, and they have removed her hair," Lailie whispered in the cold darkness.

"Removed her hair?" Perdita asked, shocked. "Has she been convicted then?"

"I don't think so, but those on trial for The Kassen have their hair removed."

Shock waved through Perdita, and dread flooded her heart. She fought the ranging battle of her emotions, trying to calm herself. At least she knew what she was facing. It would be a miracle if they escaped, but they had to try.

"Let's go," Perdita murmured, pulling herself together and heading toward the opening. She slipped out of the hidden passageway and entered the processing caverns. The long vertical tubes hummed with their bluish energy. Empty. Perdita shivered when she realized Ora must have been here only a few short days ago. She sensed Lailie surrounding her with a cool caressing breeze. "I'll be close so I can talk without anyone else hearing."

"Which way?" Perdita whispered.

"Up here and to the right. There you will find a set of stairs, go up three steps, and there will be a crevice on the left. Hide there, and I'll go ahead to keep watch."

Perdita nodded and followed the path leading out of the processing room. There wasn't much light, but her eyes adjusted to the dark quickly enough. As Lailie said, there was a tiny cut into the wall where she could slip in and be out of anyone's way if they came down the stairs. She was still invisible so no one should be able to see her.

Lailie left and returned. "Finish climbing the stairs and cross into the passageway directly across from the stairs. But do so quietly. There is a guard at the edge."

Perdita's heart pounded in her ears. She focused on breathing, slow and steady, with soft steps. She reached the top of the stairs and peeked to her right. A guard sat in a chair, apparently sleeping. Instead of a wizard as she'd been expecting, an oversize Styx leaned backward on a huge chair, head tilted upward, drool rolling down its chin. Perdita tiptoed as quietly as she could in the dark, but halfway to the entrance, her toe bumped a small rock, which rolled and hit the wall with a soft clatter. Her breath caught in her throat.

The Styx stirred, lifted his head, and looked around groggily. He mumbled something that sounded like "stupid rats," but his large tusks of teeth coupled with sleep made him even more difficult to understand. He leaned his head back against the wall and closed his eyes again. After a few minutes, his breathing deepened followed by snoring. Perdita's body came back to life a little at a time. Her heart pounded in her chest, and she wanted to get far away from this guard as soon as possible. Styxes were strong, and their skin deflected minor spells. Her only advantage in a fight with one would be her invisibility and her speed. She hadn't known they were also guards.

Perdita forced herself to move and inched into the passageway. The floor was wet and slippery, covered with a slime that made the bottom of Perdita's shoes sticky.

"This will be tricky. The passageway is narrow, and there are guards who periodically walk through here. We have to hope you are quick and lucky," Lailie breathed into her ear. *Great*, Perdita thought.

Perdita hurried as fast as she could while feeling along the walls in the pitch black. Perdita's heart jumped into her throat as the slow pattering of footsteps echoed down the passageway, heading toward her. She froze, rooted to the floor. A beam of light hit her eyes, and she was blinded as the guard walked into view. This one was a wizard. The guard held a lantern and was almost upon her. She backed away, taking small steps, praying not to bump into anything because she couldn't see a thing. She was concentrating as hard as she could to remain invisible. The guard continued moving forward to the exact spot where Perdita had been standing. He stared straight at her, and she was sure he could see her. Then without warning, he turned and walked away. Thankfully he hadn't been a Styx. If so, he could've smelled her, and there would be no hiding if one walked by. These walls wouldn't be wide enough.

Perdita let out a sigh of relief. "Close, that was," Lailie blew. The imprint of the lantern was left upon Perdita's retina causing a temporary white dot that clouded her vision. She hated how long it took for her eyes to adjust to the dark and only a matter of seconds to be completely blinded again.

"Up ahead a few more feet, there will be an opening with many different stairs. Go up the fourth one from the left," Lailie instructed.

"Any guards?" Perdita whispered.

"None for a little while, but I would still be quiet."

Of course she was going to be quiet. She hadn't planned on singing and tap dancing down the passageway. Tension brought out her snarkiness, as Ora often told her.

Once her vision cleared, her pace sped, but she felt her muscles aching from holding herself so stiffly. Up ahead was the hub of stairwells Lailie mentioned, thirteen of them. Her previous annoyance at Lailie disappeared because if she weren't here, Perdita wouldn't have any idea where to go. As instructed, she took the fourth stairwell from her left and ascended.

Lailie spoke again. "We're close, but here is where it gets complicated. You have about fifty more steps to the top. From there, you will take the first left, then turn at the third right, then the second left, the first right, the fifth right, and finally the first right. Her door is the third on the left."

"Are you serious?" Perdita huffed, winded from her climb.

"Afraid so."

"How many guards?" she asked, but she didn't really want to know the answer.

"Sporadically throughout the entire route."

"Figures. Any Styxes?"

"No."

"I'm supposed to watch out for guards and try to remember all those turns?"

"No, I'll blow around you so you will know when to turn. Like this."

Perdita felt the air caressing her right cheek. "The right."

"Yes, and now…" She did the same to her left.

"Okay, I understand."

Perdita continued her journey up the last of the steps. Huffing once, she reached the top, thinking she'd have to hit the gym if they survived. She made it through the first left, but as she passed the second right, two guards came around the corner.

One had fire in his palm, and his red robes fluttered behind him. Perdita flattened herself to the wall and prayed she was far enough away from them. They walked past her, talking about an upcoming game they hoped they could go see, missed brushing her shoulder by a fraction of an inch. They turned a corner, and Perdita breathed a sigh of relief. "You must be lucky," Lailie whispered.

"Let's hope it lasts," she replied in return. A slow steady drip came from somewhere on her right, and for the first time, she heard the cries of the prisoners. A man's deep voice cried for his mother. Another voice, this time a woman's, was crying out for her baby. Perdita shuttered at that. Others joined in, their voices mingled together in misery. Their sadness mixed with Perdita's fear, and she feared she would never be happy again.

"Don't listen to them. I've been here long enough to know the tricks of the prison. Most of the voices aren't real. It's a trap, meant to lull the other prisoners into misery. We have to go," Lailie urged.

Perdita silently thanked the gods Lailie was with her. She would have been trapped here without her or caught already. This was a debt she could never hope to repay.

Perdita held her head high and continued down the hall. She made a turn at the third right, the second left, and the first right. At the next to last passage, a large Styx came stomping out of one of the rooms on the left.

Across The Veil

Oh crap. The Styx, large and considerably less well-groomed than his counterparts at The Human Eatery, walked toward her carrying an oil lantern. Its stench reached Perdita's nostrils, and she almost gagged. Its huge hairy feet rumbled as it moved, shaking the ground beneath her feet.

Perdita squatted trying to get as far away from the Styx's nose as soon as possible and prayed she was still invisible with her concentration wavering. Her armpits were sticky with nervous sweat, and her brow was damp. Her own body odor would surely give her away. An inch beside Perdita, the Styx stopped and sniffed, long and hard through large hairy nostrils. *I'm done for.*

Just then a gust of cold air swept down the hallway. Perdita took a chance and looked at the Styx's face, scowled in confusion. It grunted, shrugged its shoulders, and walked past her down the hallway.

Once the Styx was out of sight, Perdita stood, legs quivering with the surge of adrenaline, head cloudy as if she might faint. She whispered when she felt the cool breeze around her once more, "Thank you."

"We're almost there. Hurry! Hurry!"

Perdita ran face first into a wall because she couldn't see…again. Rubbing her nose, glad to see she wasn't bleeding, she made the final turn. Standing in front of the third door on the left, she was about to use her magic to open the door when Lailie stopped her. "Perdita, no, you can't. There is a tailless cat in there with her."

"No! It can't be. Not her!" she denied with the shake of the head. Dread filled her. A cat with no tail could mean only one thing.

"I'm sorry, but you can't go in. I can't go any farther either. The cat will sense me. She'll tell him."

Perdita walked backward until her back hit the wall. She slid down, tucking her knees to her chest and resting her head on them. She spoke aloud to herself. "He must be watching her, so that means he knows. He knows what she is." Perdita whimpered as a single tear slid down her face. "I'm too late."

"I don't think so," Lailie said, the tone soft and comforting. "You know he uses Nips. His own personal army. If he suspects her of being a Nip, he'll try and recruit her."

A smidge of hope returned to her. If he didn't know about Ora, she might still have a chance. "What do I do now?" Perdita asked softly, unsure who she was asking. She felt so lost. She didn't know what to do or what to think anymore.

"My friend, it'll be dawn in a little over an hour. You'll be caught for sure if you are still here when the day is light. You'll not be able to escape. You must start back now."

"But she is right there, beyond the door. I'm so close. I can't leave now," she pleaded, staring at the door, willing it to open. Helplessness and desperation flooded her senses.

"If you don't, you won't have a chance to save her. If you're caught, then he'll know for sure. He'll have her, and you'll be dead. You have to leave now."

Perdita knew Lailie was right, but still she couldn't make herself stand up, couldn't make herself leave now that she was this close. She fully appreciated now what John went through earlier this evening. She thought to herself that she must remember to apologize to him when she got back, if she got back.

"Perdita, you're not giving up. You're not abandoning her. You're giving her another chance. Please," Lailie begged. The wind rustled and pushed around Perdita trying to get her to stand.

"All right. All right." Perdita stood with useless tears spilling down her cheeks. Her feet carried her to the front of Ora's door of their own accord. She placed her palm gently on its surface and leaned her head against it. "Soon, I'll be back for you. Soon. Be brave. Be strong. I love you."

Perdita stepped back, took one last look at the door, turned, and left before she had a chance to change her mind.

On the other side of the door, Ora stirred. She rolled on her side and wished her dream was real. Her grandma was there, and she was safe. She fell into a dreamless sleep as the cat laid by her feet, awake and watching.

Chapter Eighteen

Sabrina's head throbbed as she walked into the MDA early in the morning. Even the sight of Simeon couldn't take away her stress, but she smiled at him anyway. Heading back to Quad One's office, she almost ran straight into Bizard. He wore a large scowl, more prominent than his usual one. But this time, instead of smugness, his face revealed anger or perhaps embarrassment. She noted a large box in his arms, full of his personal belongings. Dare she hope he'd been fired?

"Morning," she said, pulling all the politeness she could muster into the greeting.

Instead of answering, he grunted and pushed past her. Perhaps it would turn out to be a good day after all.

She entered the office to find Allyn hunched over his desk, looking as if he had lost a puppy. Leigh shuffled through the morning reports, sipping her usual tea. Her lips were pressed in a thin line, which made whatever hope Sabrina had for a good day vanish along with Allyn's metaphorical puppy. Sabrina made her way to her desk, her blue leather creaking as she walked. As usual, she was greeted by handfuls of forms to sign, messages to answer, and reports to review. She held her tongue and waited to be debriefed. Her eyes were itchy and rimmed in red from spending hours in the vault the previous evening. Sorting through fifteen-year-old reports of minor Concealment Code violations was a tedious task. No one had ever told her about the amount of paperwork and well, mere reading, that went into investigating. She had the analytic mind for it, but she much preferred being out in the field, chasing criminals, and kicking some butt using magic.

The dryness of her eyes brought back visions of the girl. Her accounts were genuine, but save for a few minor things, there was nothing that would have caused detection and, therefore, no records. The girl and her Defender, a relative novice, Arameus Townsend, were playing a very dangerous game. Claiming she was a witch, but not of Conjuragic and born from a human, was a defense that would be almost inconceivable to win. But it wasn't Sabrina's job to come up with a defense, only to get statements from the Defender, the accused, and the Accuser, and then look objectively through the evidence. It wasn't even her job to judge the evidence. That would be left up to the tribunal.

Leigh cleared her throat. Sabrina and Allyn looked up on cue. Once Leigh held their attention, she waved a piece of paper at them and said, "I'm sure you must have guessed, but according to this report, Corporal Bizard has been temporarily suspended from the MDA until further notice. He is under investigation for assault with a deadly weapon and use of excessive force. He is currently being released into his own custody, but he could be facing time in the Nook."

Damn!

Sabrina didn't feel sorry for him. Allyn was quiet, looking at his hands. Sabrina wondered if he was worried he would be under investigation, too. She doubted it. Even though he did go along with Ora's marking at the gate, he wasn't involved with the torture of the human.

Leigh continued. "Corporal Askar will be joining us for the time being."

Sabrina nodded as a reply. Corporal Askar wasn't inexperienced, had a reputation for being clever and level-headed, and had always been polite enough. Better than Bizard, with a chip on his shoulder and hungry for power. Allyn again had nothing to say, but Sabrina understood his reaction.

Leigh put the form down and picked up another, scanned it, and looked at her wrist. "The prelim hearing is in an hour. Lieutenant, tell me what you found in the vault."

Sabrina leaned back in her chair and placed her hands behind her head, fingers intertwined. "The accused gave us report of many incidences of magical capabilities when we visited her cell yesterday. Most it occurred in her private residence with only her grandmother in attendance. But I was able to locate of few things that registered. Approximately fifteen years ago in a super market in Rochester, New York, there was minor blip in the toy section of the store. The date was December 7. The Quad on duty reported residues of magic found near a section of stuffed animals, an abandoned cart full of groceries, and a handful of people with apparent hasty memory enchantments. The Imation Team was able to locate a few memories, which I reviewed. They were extremely fuzzy, and the enchantment poorly done, but I saw one clear evidence of a large stuffed animal, which could be a bear, shrinking in size, then a swirl of something red. It could give reasonable doubt this was in fact the accused as a child using magic to shrink the bear, something she described quite accurately."

"Show me."

Sabrina stood, walked to her bag, gathered the crystal shard that held the memory and placed it in the replayer. The image appeared before the screen, seemingly more blurry than yesterday. The crystal itself should be clear, but this was cloudy.

Leigh shook her head after the images played through. "That will be hard pressed to be accepted into evidence. The images leave a lot to the imagination, and the crystal itself appears tampered with. What else did you come up with?"

"Really only one other thing." Sabrina returned to her seat, grabbing her bag along the way. "The accused reported at her preschool in Newberry, South Carolina, that she touched a plant, making it bloom in front of all the kids in the class."

Leigh interrupted her. "That wouldn't have registered. Kids believe in magic, so there is nothing for the MDA to detect."

Sabrina gave a shrug of her shoulders. "I know, but if that plant not only bloomed, but never fell, eventually the adults in the class took notice."

Sabrina pulled out a beautiful flower from her bag, intact and perfect. "This was recovered after a flicker was noted on the radar over and over again from the same location. Eventually someone got suspicious and sent in someone to investigate. It wasn't a Quad, just a trainee, but she posed as a substitute teacher. Eventually she was told about an orchid at the school that had been there for years, but even though no one ever watered it or changed its pot, it never died. One teacher had even put it in a closet where it would get no sunlight, but it still lived. The investigator did some tests, and it had evidence of Sphere magic. When she inquired about where it had possibly come from, the teachers at the school said it had been there for years. The trainee kept going."

"Over a flower? Why didn't she give up?" Allyn asked.

Sabrina shrugged. "A Quad would have, but she was still in training. Anyway, she followed it back to a teacher, Miss Todd, who admitted to purchasing it, but she had no magic. The trainee searched out every student, and those she could reach all said a former student did it. When she asked the child's name, all they could remember was O."

Sabrina put the orchid back into her bag. "The investigator replaced the plant, which eventually died, but brought the original here. It has been in bloom for the last twelve years."

Leigh considered this before saying, "They might accept it, but it's a bit of a stretch. Was there any evidence of the accused attending this school?"

"Unfortunately, no. The investigation was a minor one, and the trainee wasn't given further clearance to try to locate this O. The end of the report says the magic in question has been removed and no damage had been done. Before coming in this morning, I traveled to where this school was located, and it burned down about four years ago. So there is no way to confirm whether the accused ever attended this particular school or not."

"We'll submit it, but I'm not sure if they will accept it or not. What about you, Allyn?"

Allyn leaned back in his chair, crossed his arms and huffed, "Well, I found something, but I doubt it's even worth mentioning."

"It's not for us to judge. What is it?" Leigh asked, crossing one leg clad in brown leather over her other.

Allyn picked up his quill and parchment. "I went to the vault and searched for any mention of someone named Ora or a redhead. I found only one." He read from his parchment. "Ten years ago, on June 27, there was a major detection that went unresolved."

A major detection that went unresolved? That almost never happens. Sabrina and Leigh shared an uneasy look.

Allyn continued. "At a birthday party for a girl named Laurie, the backyard caught fire. She was about eight or nine, from the reports. Same age as our suspect. The detection occurred because there was nothing that could have ignited the fire. And there was a report from one of the mothers that the child walked through the flames and emerged on the other side untouched."

"What other evidence was found?" Sabrina asked, perplexed.

"None. There was questionable evidence of magic used for the fire, but as you know, Ember magic is difficult that way. All you need is a tiny spark and then the fire takes on a life of its own. It doesn't always leave a large amount of evidence behind. The house burned to the ground. There was nothing left to gather. No pictures. Fingerprints. Nothing. But the real mystery is the girl and her mother who disappeared after the fire."

"What about at the girl's school? If she was eight or nine, then she would've been in school," Leigh asked.

"Apparently, the girl and her mom had only just moved to the area at the end of the previous school year. She was absent on picture days. It seems the girl didn't have many friends, and the kids were afraid of her. The mothers claimed they only went to the birthday party because they felt guilty, but they too felt the girl and her mother were strange. One mother was even quoted to say, 'Good riddance, I say. Our town doesn't need weirdos like those to bring the devil to our children.'"

Sabrina didn't know what to think. It was certainly interesting, and whoever the little girl had been at that birthday party, Sabrina felt sorry for her. She knew not all humans were bad, and there were humans who would accept the magical world if they would come to know about it. But there was still ignorance in the human world. But after finding out Ora almost died because the Keepers didn't tell her she could get water or even feed her for three days, perhaps her world wasn't much better.

Leigh pressed her hands to her eyes then said, "Well, we'll present it, but that is evidence for Ember magic. Her defense is going with Sphere. Only the hair color and age is a coincidence. It's time to go."

Sabrina sat in the courtroom with her Quad. The newbie, Askar, joined them even though he only received the quick version of events. He looked like a usual Tempest with red hair, though his was more of a fine rust. He was attempting a beard, but the hair on his chin was more blond than red. But what little she knew, Sabrina felt he would be a good asset. He was quiet, took things in, and when he did make comments, they were useful. The Defender, Arameus, had pleaded to have his client declared innocent and released immediately. She could tell by the look of the advisors' faces this wasn't going to happen. As was customary, each of the Counselors chose one of their advisors to stand in their place during prelim hearings. From Sphere was Idris, Ember was Vesta, and Sheba from Naiad. She wasn't sure of the Tempest's advisor's name. Despite not being chosen, Mathesar, another Naiad advisor, sat in the back. Mathesar's blond hair was so light it was almost white, and his blue eyes were sharp and hawk-like. His mouth was always set in a grim line, and he had a reputation for ordering swift punishment. He was the favorite to be the next High Councilman of Naiad, but she hoped he didn't win. Although everything he did was for the good of Conjuragic and you could never doubt his loyalty, something about him made her uneasy.

She was dismayed to see who the Accuser was, Starmon Lawrence, which meant the Accusers felt this was an open and shut case. He was atrocious, everyone knew that, so he was only given cases he was sure to win. Sabrina knew she should remain objective, but deep down she didn't think Ora was guilty. At least not of being a Nip. Leigh got up in front of the advisors and presented the evidence they gathered from the previous day. First, she showed the clip of the bear, and Idris scoffed, "That is the worst footage I've ever seen, Commander. If you show that in court, you'll be accused of tampering with evidence. It's inadmissible. Next."

When the orchid was brought in front of the court, Idris had the audacity to laugh. "You're reaching. Please tell me you have something concrete and you're not wasting our time."

When Allyn's evidence was presented, Mathesar's eyes narrowed, and Sabrina could almost see the thoughts churning in his mind like butter. But when it was over, he shook his head, and this time, he was quiet. The Sphere advisor, Idris, spoke. "That was Ember magic, and this is a case of Sphere. Inadmissible. Is that all?"

Leigh bowed. "Yes."

Starmon jumped to his feet before Leigh could retreat to her chair and said, "I move that the accused, Ora Stone's, original confession be reinstated. She is guilty and shall be escorted this very afternoon to The Kassen and condemned to death for her crimes. Let's hope we have time to save the witch who has lost her magic."

Mathesar said, "I agree. All those in favor?"

Idris glared at Mathesar. "You are not on this council. Your vote doesn't count." He lowered his hand, but the Tempest advisor's remained up. Vesta, Sheba, and Idris' hands remained down. Idris nodded. "Her original confession is withdrawn. However, based on the evidence today, her innocence is unclear. Therefore, I must insist we proceed with a full trial. The evidence presented here today is not to be used in the full trial. My Counselors, Dharr and Mira Drecoll, have bid me tell the court the High Council themselves will sit in on the trial. But a tribunal will be chosen. The trial will begin on the morrow, and you each have today to prepare for opening statements and new evidence. You are dismissed." Idris swung a gavel upon the table in front of her.

Sabrina's head was reeling. A full trial with a tribunal in attendance by the High Council? It was unheard of.

The day was hot, and the policeman's outfit was uncomfortable. Sabrina wasn't used to wearing anything except leather. Well, at least not during the day. She wore robes in the evenings, so these clothes felt wrong. It was part of the job as she strolled up the walkway behind Leigh. The house was small, a one story with a small porch and two windows on either side. The detached garage was open, and every nook and cranny was full with various car parts, bits of mismatched furniture, and who knew what else. Leigh rapped on the door, and she heard movement inside, followed by an older woman calling, "Just a second." Her voice was muffled.

The door swung open minutes later. The older woman was still pretty despite her age, but her eyes were sunken as if she had been under a lot of stress recently. Sabrina didn't know what to make of that. "Can I help you?" the woman asked.

"Yes, ma'am. I'm Officer Stewart. My partner and I were hoping we could talk to your granddaughter, Charlene?"

The woman stepped aside, allowing them to come in. "Yes. We got home a little bit ago. I thought Charlie had already finished with you all back in Dalley, but she is in the back. Have you found Ora yet?"

Sabrina almost fell from the shock. What in the world did the woman mean, she had already finished talking to the police? Just got home? Had they found Ora? Something was very off. She felt Leigh's eyes on her as she answered, "No, ma'am, we have not."

"Oh dear," the woman muttered, shaking her head as she led them through the living room. It was clean, the furniture older but still in good condition. The house had the faint lingering smell of menthol and artificial flowers. They rounded a corner to a family room in the back. Who could only be Charlie sat on a couch, leaning back with her eyes closed. Hatred for Bizard welled up inside Sabrina. The girl's face and hands were covered in stitches. Her poor skin was swollen and bruised in various hues of blue and green. Leigh glared at her as if asking why she hadn't been healed. With barely a movement, Sabrina silently told her she didn't know.

When they entered the room, Charlie's eyes opened, and when she saw them, her mouth flew open, and she screamed.

Leigh reacted in seconds. She flung a confusion spell at Charlie's grandmother, and Sabrina raced to Charlie's side. She placed a hand gently over her mouth, silencing her. "Shh. We aren't here to harm you. Be quiet."

A man raced from the back at the commotion. Leigh twisted and sent another confusion spell his way. It hit him between the eyes, and he lost focus. She led the two of them to the living room, and seconds later, Sabrina heard the TV come on. Charlie was silent, save for shuttering, under her hand. Her hands were wet, and she looked down to see Charlie's tears running over her fingers. She let go. "We want to talk to you, okay?"

Charlie blurted, "Where is Ora? What've you done to her?"

Leigh returned, her wrist by her mouth and she was talking into her communicator. "Yes, that's right. Send an Imation Team and a Healer. We're going to need a major undertaking."

Across The Veil

Leigh came in, stood before Charlie, and stuttered, "I... I don't know what to say, child. This was never supposed to happen. I'm sorry." The doorbell rang, and Leigh went to answer it while Sabrina stepped back, trying to reassure the girl with distance. Leigh returned with a two-man Imation Team and a Healer disguised as a mailman. The young man smiled, lifting his hands in front of Charlie's face. Charlie leaned back, frightened, but her face shimmered. The bruises faded. The little black bits of string the humans sewed into her face pushed themselves out, and her skin pulled itself together. Within seconds, her face was as unblemished as before her attack. Charlie sat in shock for a long time. She gathered her courage, and she looked down, seeing her hands restored. Her fingertips flew to her face, feeling every inch. She jumped up and ran to a mirror hanging above a fireplace. A small sob, of what Sabrina could only hope was relief, left her.

Leigh stared at the floor, and Sabrina wondered what other atrocities befell those they questioned. Leigh raised her head and told Charlie, "You may not believe me, but people are going to pay for what they did to you. You were never supposed to be harmed. And Bizard is answering for his crimes. And those who were supposed to make you forget and heal your injuries didn't do their job. Let's say they are going to wish they had by the time I'm through with them."

Charlie whirled around, glaring at the two of them. "And what about Ora? Where is she? Did you bring her home?"

Sabrina spoke for them. "No, Charlie. Ora is in our custody. She is currently safe." She dared not tell her Ora had almost died yesterday. "But she is going to be placed on trial for what happened. We came here to ask you if you knew of Ora performing any magic prior to the day in question."

"Why should I answer anything? And what crime? Holding a pen in the air? What the hell is the crime in that?" Charlie spat, her voice rising with each syllable.

"It's complicated. We're trying to find out the truth."

"No, I never saw Ora do magic. You can't even prove it was her who held that stupid pen anyway."

Even though Leigh was battling her own feelings about what happened to Charlie, Sabrina could see her temperature rising at the attitude of the girl.

Another knock at the door, and one of the Imation Team stood in the doorway of the room, an Ember with white hair and her fair share of wrinkles. Leigh motioned to Charlie. "Just have her remember going to class with Ora, and then afterward, they separated, and she doesn't know where she's gone. And when you're done, someone is going to have to answer to me."

Charlie ran at Leigh. "No! You can't make me forget her!"

Leigh flicked her wrist, and a confusion spell hit Charlie, too. Leigh walked away, and Sabrina followed. The Imation Team had finished Charlie's grandparents.

The grandmother stared blankly at the TV but said to the other Imation member, a middle- aged Naiad, in a monotone voice, "Ora is missing. Her mother went with Charlie's brother, John, to look for her. They've been gone about two days. We haven't heard from them since they left."

Sabrina walked outside of the house, following Leigh, who flicked her wrist and a nearby bush withered and died. It had been a long time since she'd seen Leigh need to blow off that kind of steam.

Something Charlie's grandmother said bugged Sabrina. Why did she say Ora's mother? Wasn't it her grandmother?

Chapter Nineteen

The roar of voices reduced to mumbling as I entered the courtroom. The bodies were packed in tight as sardines. I expected the crowd but wished I'd been wrong. How I wished for fewer eyes filled with hate on me. I glanced over at my Defender and felt a tiny bit better. At least I wasn't alone.

The courtroom decorations were sparse but could've been plucked out of any human courtroom. Except for the sea of strange faces sitting in long rows behind a wooden divider, most of the audience appeared human but wore robes signifying their magical House. But the other faces were far stranger.

Arameus told me there were a few reporters in the audience, but I couldn't tell who they were. He and I were separated from the audience by a wooden swinging door. We sat at one of two desks by the door, and the Accusers sat at the other. They represented the Union of Conjuragic and would be trying to convince the court of my guilt.

My chair faced the front of the courtroom where the High Council would sit. Their chairs were currently vacant. To my left sat the tribunal. They would decide my fate. I avoided looking at them.

"All rise." Arameus's gentle hand eased me to my feet. The announcer continued. "The High Council enters."

Eight people walked into the room, four men and four women. All the men were bald, but the women made up for it as their hair flowed down their backs to just above the floor. Golden crowns rested upon their heads. In the debriefing before the trial, Arameus warned me of this, explaining hair length is a sign of rank in Conjuragic.

The High Council stood in front of their thrones. All together they said, "Be seated."

I bowed my head as Arameus instructed me that morning and sat in what they called a chair. It could easily have been a stool on the ground.

I shouldn't complain. It was better than hay on the ground. And after the dismal prelim, I'm lucky I even was granted a trial. It hadn't been a unanimous decision. I wished Arameus wouldn't have shared that tidbit. Fear laced through me. This was pointless. I was no one, insignificant. Even if I was innocent, these strangers wouldn't care.

I leaned over and whispered this to Arameus. He didn't meet my eyes when he whispered back, "Don't think that way. You're not insignificant. Fight for your life, your freedom. I won't give up. I don't want you to either."

He was right. I had to try, but I couldn't help but wonder how many accused Nips who had gone to trial were set free. Pushing that thought away, I felt down for my newfound power. Its presence both comforts and scares me. It's like looking down into a well with no non-corporeal rock to toss inside to see how deep it goes.

"The accused, please stand," the Tempest court announcer commanded. I rose again to the sound of hisses throughout the room. "Walk to the center of the courtroom and stand there." He pointed to a circle platform in the center of the floor. I glanced at Arameus because I wasn't expecting this, and from the look on his face, neither was he. He nudged me, and I walked to the center and stepped on the raised platform. A gate rose from the around the platform to three feet above my head, snapping into place with a metallic clang. I jumped in surprise, and the courtroom attendants laughed. This was definitely not going well.

The Sphere Councilman spoke with a voice that was more cough than words. "We will now hear the opening statements from the Accuser and the Defender."

According to Arameus, since I had been accused of stealing Sphere magic, the trial would be led by the Councilors from that House: Lord and Lady Dharr and Mira Drecoll. The head Accuser stood. I hadn't really paid him much attention before now. A tall man from the House of Sphere. "Your highness." He bowed toward Councilors from Sphere House then bowed again. "The High Council."

"Ladies and gentlemen of the tribunal, fellow witches and wizards, magical creatures, we are here today to sentence this Nip to The Kassen where she rightfully belongs."

"Objection!" Arameus yelled. "She has not been convicted of any crimes, Starmon. That is what this trial is about."

Lady Drecoll waved her hand to get everyone's attention. "Agreed, please change your words, Starmon."

"My apologies your highness." Starmon bowed again. "We are here today to prove this human," his voice dripped the word with contempt, "has committed the crime of nipping. We will prove this girl is not of the House of Sphere. The records of her birth cannot be proven, neither here nor in the human world." It felt as if everyone in the courtroom held their breath.

"Yes," Starmon uttered with a smile, "she has no record of creation. We will prove she has only one known address, and her whereabouts prior to age eight are unknown. We will show no registered Sphere lives near her. It will also be made known that a Miss Neigh Equinos, a young Sphere who was registered to begin work at Dalley University on the day in question, is missing."

This latest announcement was news to me. Arameus told me because no witch or wizard had been reported missing, I had a better case, but now there was a missing witch. I turned to see what Arameus made of this, but the cage blocked him from my sight. I could see no one except the tribunal and the High Council. My Defender, my one sense of hope, was hidden from me.

"We'll prove the magic she used in front of her fellow humans to mock us was deliberate. We'll prove she has stolen this same magic from Miss Equinos and hope this trial goes swiftly. You, the tribunal, will convict her where she will be sent to The Kassen. The stolen magic will be ripped from her, just as she stole it. Then the rightful magic of Miss Equinos can hopefully reach her in time to prevent her death. Although her time is already running short, a team of Protectors continues to search for her in hopes our Healers can sustain her body until her magic is rightfully returned."

"Objection, this trial is not about a missing person and has no place in these matters," Arameus objected.

"On the contrary, Arameus, Miss Equinos could very well be the source of the accused's magic. Her disappearance is a vital component to this case," Starmon countered with a smug grin and ran his fingers through his greased jet-black hair. I wanted to punch his long, pointed nose. My power peered out from my eyes, teeth barred, growling. My body vibrated. Starmon strolled in front of the tribunal with confidence, completely sure of his words, ignoring me.

"Not when there isn't any evidence to show Miss Equinos and Miss Stone ever had any contact," Arameus argued.

"Well, of course there wouldn't be, if she disposed of the body," Starmon said while raising an eyebrow at the tribunal.

"Objection, hearsay and the Accuser's opinion."

"Enough," Lord Drecoll called out in annoyance. "The disappearance of Miss Equinos should be discussed in the case as probable cause. But you may not make assumptions and place vivid images in the minds of the tribunal. The last lines will be stricken from the records, and the tribunal will be dememorized."

A haze swept over the tribunal. *That's useful.*

Starmon continued. "We have expert witnesses from the Creation Department, the Human-Magic Liaison Office, and a noted geneticist whose research has shown humans cannot develop magic without a link to the magical world, which this girl has none." He paused dramatically. "And furthermore, we'll show the accused shows no remorse or concern for the witch whose magic she stole. And we'll be seeking full justice of capital punishment by means of The Kassen."

In my mind's eye, my face appeared on a milk carton. Would they go back and tell my grandmother I was dead? Fear trickled into every limb with each pounding of my fast heartbeat while I clutched quivering hands to my sides. I'd never given serious thought to death before. Charlie had dragged me along with her to church with her grandparents on more Sundays than I could count. But I wasn't human. Did they let witches go to Heaven? Or would there be nothing? Trapped for eternity in a black nothingness?

The magic turned inward, swiping not at the outside, but at me. Its sting ripped through my mind, tearing away the image of John wrapping his arms around me. Its message was clear. John cannot help me. No matter how much I love him or how happy that time in my life was. He was in my past, in another world, and if I ever wanted to get back, I had to fight. My shaking vanished as renewed confidence replaced.

"No further statements," Starmon finished. He flashed a satisfied smile at me as he passed.

Lady Drecoll nodded toward the Defender. "Defender Arameus, your opening statement will now be heard."

A chair scratched along the floor, and soon Arameus stood before me facing the tribunal. When he spoke, the uneasiness retreated a little further.

"My High Council, lords and ladies of the great magical world, I address you today as a servant. A servant of an innocent girl named Ora Stone. Yes, the accused has a name. Or have we all forgotten that? This world and our people have long since feared even the remotest possibility of a Nip. This has caused hatred and prejudice to humans. I've always been amazed how the human world is afraid of magic, and the magical world is afraid of humanity."

Sounds of disapproval from the audience interrupted him.

"Yes," he continued, pointing a finger in the air, "many are unwilling to admit it, but it is true. We all know our history. We lived together in one world, until we didn't want to hide from humanity and practice our birthright in secret any longer. We created the Veil to separate us and created a new world. Our world, a world where magic was the norm and practiced openly."

"Objection. Please stop this history lesson and professing your love for humanity, Arameus, and get to the point," Starmon shouted with annoyance.

"Agreed," said Lord Drecoll.

"My apologies to the court. I'm only trying to remind everyone our fears far outweigh the reality. If you would allow me to finish?" Arameus pleaded to the High Council, his hands together as if going to pray.

"Very well, but be quick about it," Lady Drecoll spat back in annoyance.

Arameus paused and shook his head as if he bore a great weight. "Fear of magic led to witch hunts, and while our magic brethren escaped easily, innocent humans did not. And during this reign, witches and wizards used their magic to take whatever they pleased from the humans, dominating them like animals. Nature decided to counterbalance this dominance, and so the first Nip was born," he stated inciting mumbling from the crowd.

"Tituba, the slave, the first known Nip, stole the magic of Betty Parris, in the fair city of Salem. Tituba used against them what they had used against her. But was she really at fault? Others have speculated. She was defending herself. Captured and taken from her family, enslaved and sold. Tortured, raped, and forced to do their bidding."

Hisses and boos erupted from the crowd, hatred crashing upon Arameus like a wave. The heat rose in the room. If the people here are so passionate about a Nip from long ago, how would I ever be set free? *I have to believe Arameus can make them believe it.*

"Ahh, you disagree. But where are the outcries for Tituba? Was it right for her to be removed unjustly from her family? Was it right for her to be sold into slavery? Raped? Beaten? All by wizards, all because they could? All because they had power and she had none?" He marched toward the crowd, his boots clicking on the floor.

"Tituba escaped and other Nips born throughout the land heard of her and traveled to her village. Together, they learned to use their powers and their numbers grew until, instead of defending themselves, they went hunting, but they were quickly overcome by our Protectors. But we became like the humans, hunting down those with power, power that we did not have. Power we were afraid of and instead of learning to tolerate it and live in harmony, we have always sought to dominate the humans and eradicate any hope they have of gaining their own power. We hunted the Nips, the same as the humans hunted witches, only we were far better at it, and a hundred times crueler."

Starmon interrupted. "And we should have done what? Let the Nips kill us?"

Arameus smiled as if this was exactly what he wanted to happen. "You'll never hear me say Tituba's followers were right in hunting witches and for the countless murders at their hands. But since then, there have only been three accounts of Nips acting maliciously toward witches and wizards. The rest do so by accident, not unlike our own children, possessing magic but not the knowledge of how to control it. And we capture them, bring them here, shave their heads, throw them in the deepest pit of the Nook, and put them on trial. Then when we, as a people, find out they are Nips, they're put to death!" Arameus continued shaking with anger.

"They're powerful and dangerous to us, yes. But don't we, as witches and wizards, possess a danger to every human we meet? But we kill every Nip because they are a threat. Not so different as humans would do to us. But does that make it right or does that make us ignorant? Should we look only at the surface and not at what is within?"

Arameus waved his arm in my direction and said, "Like this child before us today. Can you overlook what is on the surface and see within? During this trial, I will show the lords and ladies of the High Council, ladies and gentlemen of the tribunal, that this girl, Ora Stone, is not a Nip. She is a witch," Arameus said.

Gasps of outrage resounded across the courtroom. After all his discussion about Nips, everyone, including myself, thought he was going to say I was a Nip, one of the innocent ones who used her power by accident, but a Nip nonetheless.

"Indeed, she is not a Nip or a human. I'll prove to this court Ora Stone is indeed a witch. A witch possessing what appears to be Sphere magic, and she is the child of a human."

I thought the courtroom was shocked before, but that was nothing to this revelation—an eruption of hisses and boos, paper flung to the floor. I thought the crowd might have accepted me as a nice Nip who should be taught instead of executed as a better defense than being a witch.

"Objection!" shouted Starmon. "That's impossible."

"Overruled." Lord Drecoll tapped a mallet on the desk. "Quiet in the courtroom." The tribunal and crowd quieted.

Arameus folded his arms, facing the crowd. "Just because we haven't had one in a long time doesn't mean it isn't possible. How many human legends are true but hidden here? Unicorns? Dragons? Mermaids? Magic?" He laughed, and snickers rose from the attendants. "I'll show she was born from humans and uniquely possesses Sphere-like magic. I'll prove she has shown magical powers from a very young age because she has possessed those powers her whole life. She did not steal the magic from anyone, but it is uniquely hers. And when she is declared innocent from this trial, she will receive training to control it. She may choose to remain in Conjuragic or return to the human world with knowledge of our laws and proper registration."

Arameus looked to each and every one of the members of the tribunal making sure they understood him. "Defense opening statement is complete."

Arameus spun on his heel and passed to where I could no longer see him. The people of the court were shaken at his claims. I didn't know if his theories were unfounded or once in a lifetime. I knew it was a desperate plea, and one glance at the tribunal told me they felt the same way.

I could tell they thought my Defender was making up ridiculous claims to win. My chances of being acquitted now were minimal at best. But something Arameus said bothered me more than the fear of The Kassen. He said he was going to prove I was a child of a human. That could only mean one thing. They will go after my grandma.

After the morning's opening statements, the rest of the trial flew by without much understanding on my part. Starmon brought in expert witnesses from the Creation Records department stating they were unable to find any record of my birth and others from the Human-Magic Liaison Office who discussed how the alarm went off when the Concealment Code was breached.

It was interesting watching the memories of my fellow classmates. It was on a screen, and a person from the Imation department brought them in crystal bottles filled with white fog. It was fed into a device beside the screen, and time after time, it showed Dr. Zitalee holding the pen, dropping it, and it stopping in midair. It was still for a few seconds and then began to spin, slowly at first and then quicker. A scream and then chaos. I didn't fail to notice the video stopped before the attack on Charlie. But at least they left out my original confession.

The day ended with a noted geneticist. I tried my best to follow him, but I wasn't able to even after taking genetics class in high school.

Across The Veil

Arameus was great, objecting at all the right moments, making excellent points, and requesting several dememorizations of the tribunal.

I had no idea where my case stood after the day. I rested my hopes in the tribunal, and they were very hard to read. It was evident that Starmon was nowhere near as charismatic as Arameus. When my Defender spoke, everyone in the courtroom was drawn to him.

Most of the day, Starmon appeared bored as if the outcome of the trial was so surely going in his favor that he didn't have to do much of anything. I hoped he wasn't right.

As the day ended, the cage retreated into the ground with the same metallic clinking. I'd been excused, and I walked back over to Arameus wanting to throw myself in his arms or fling myself into the chair. My legs and back ached.

"What'd you think?" I asked.

"No way to tell, it's way too early. Try to keep your head up."

"Okay."

"Come, let's get something to eat in my office so we can discuss tomorrow."

Protectors Stewart and Sun appeared at my side. As they were about to ensnare me in the magical net, Arameus stopped them. "She'll be coming to my office to eat and discuss her case."

"She must be escorted back to the Nook. We can't leave her," Commander Stewart replied with a look that dared arguing.

"Then you'll wait," Arameus said, not backing down. He took my arm and led me out of the courtroom. His tone surprised me. It was the first time, besides when objecting Starmon, I had seen him angry. It was subtle, but very much said he was in charge. How had I gotten lucky enough for him to be assigned to my case? My guess was that if it had been anyone else, I would have been doomed from the start.

We walked through the Guidance Hall with their crisp white rooms, like most of the city, with the strange pulsating light sweeping across the walls. There were marble floors leading up to large marble columns holding up the massive building. We walked up three flights of stairs, my thighs burning and doing my best not to pant, and he wasn't even winded. *Geez, haven't they invented elevators?*

Seeming to read my mind, Arameus inclined his head with a boyish smile. "We could have taken the lift, but I like the exercise." I'd have been able to take these stairs two at a time if I hadn't almost died two days ago. Years of soccer kept me lean, but my energy seemed to have been zapped away. Perhaps I should start doing some exercises in the cell. Lord knows there isn't anything else to do. I was surprised to find a smile coming to my lips. He relaxed me, and I wished I could stay near him instead of going back to the Nook.

His office was warm with dark wood walls, a large desk to match, and a red Persian rug. What caught my eye the most was the large red and brown couch covered with soft-looking cushions.

"Sit." He motioned toward the couch.

I sank into the soft cushions and moaned in pleasure as I leaned my head back and closed my eyes. The first comfortable thing I'd sat on in what…five days? *Had it been that long already?*

"Comfortable, isn't it?" Arameus asked with the hint of a laugh in his voice.

"Mmm." I didn't bother opening my eyes even as papers rustled on his desk and I heard him ask, "Chloe, can you order my usual from…"

A gentle hand shook me awake. "Ora, the food is here."

The light outside had grown dim, and the most delicious smells made my mouth water and stomach growl. He'd let me sleep. I could've hugged him, but wasn't sure if that was appropriate. I took great care standing, yawning, and stretching at the same time.

"Sorry," I apologized.

"No need, you looked exhausted. Let's eat."

He set out food on his desk, and I noted I had many plates on my side of the desk. There were baguettes with an assortment of cheeses. Unlike my usual shy self, I took great liberty and grabbed one and took a large bite. I was famished. This was my first real meal since arriving in Conjuragic. I scarfed four bites then slowed down, savoring the warm crunchy bread with the nutty creamy cheese.

Arameus smiled as if pleased and asked, "Would you like some wine?"

"Um…" I swallowed my latest bite of bread and shrugged. "I've never had any."

His mouth dropped open, but he composed himself and pulled out two wine glasses, pouring red liquid into each glass. "It'll complement our food."

I took the glass and risked a sip. It was surprisingly sweet followed by intense bitterness. I hated it and snatched another mouthful of bread and cheese to avoid drinking any more. But as I chewed, the flavors came alive because of the wine.

"It's good," I lied and took another courteous sip wishing for southern sweet tea.

He handed me a bowl of soup and ladled some into his own bowl. I placed a small spoonful inside my mouth trying not to slurp. It tasted like cream and orange with small bites of tender meat. "Mmm," I muttered, loving every bite.

"It's lobster bisque. Try it with a small piece of the Brie and a tomato."

I followed his instructions. The brie gagged me with its sourness, but I smiled and said, "It's divine," mimicking what I thought my grandma would have said. I didn't think I had ever tasted anything so gross. When I had eaten the entire bowl, he handed me another plate of white meat, carrots, and onion in a red sauce. I shoveled an enormous bite in my mouth. It was delicious. I had trouble chewing with the amount of food I had crammed in there. It tasted like chicken, and the carrots were soft and sweet.

"It's coq au vin rouge."

"It's great!" I wiped my mouth with a napkin as the delicious sauce ran down my chin. *I'm being such a pig.* I stopped myself and only ate half of my bowl. It didn't take much to fill up a stomach that had been relatively empty for days.

"Save room for dessert," he told me. Despite my fullness, I got excited and wanted to hug him again. He finished his *coq au vin rouge* and handed me a small bowl of chocolate mousse. It was delicate, sweet, and smooth. I ate every last bite despite the protests from my stomach. My eyes grew heavy. Nothing like a full belly of good food to relax you.

"Thank you," I said, placing my hands in my lap. "Are you ready to talk about the trial?" I asked.

He shook his head with a kind smile and placed his hands together. He had a sneaky look in his eyes. "No, we did enough talking this morning. I wanted to keep you out of the Nook for a while longer and get you a decent meal."

I was shocked to my core. Tears sprang to my eyes, and I almost lost all my composure and rushed around the desk to hug him. But I held it in and had to make a conscious effort to close my mouth. "Will I ever stop thanking you?"

"I hope there won't be any reason to soon."

I looked at the floor. I could no longer meet his eyes lest I break down crying. He sighed, and I risked a glance. He was looking at his watch. "Unfortunately, I cannot buy you any more time."

He stood and walked around his desk. I knew he was right. I stood to meet him and offered him my hand. He paused, looking at it, then gently took my hand, shaking it.

"Thank you, again," I said.

"My pleasure."

We left his office, and my team of Protectors stood from their seated positions, encasing me in their magical net. Arameus threatened, "If she doesn't wear a mask when walking through The Shadow Forest, I'll hear about it." His tone was full of menace.

"Of course," Commander Stewart replied with an icy clip. I put my hand over my mouth to hide my small smile, but the look on Corporal Allyn's face ended that. Arameus bid me farewell, and I curtsied like something I saw in a movie. "Goodnight."

We took the lift down to the ground floor. It reminded me of an elevator but missing the feeling of stopping and starting. We made our way through the Guidance Hall and stepped out onto the steps overlooking the city. The sky had the warm glow of twilight. My stomach was full, and the sky was beautiful. I smiled, deciding to take whatever joy I may find here.

Chapter Twenty

The days of the trial flew by. Person after person testified against me. The worst was the father of Miss Equinos. He described his daughter—young, smart and adventurous—who had left home to take a job in the human world. And, like me, on her first day, vanished. Arameus objected to this testimony. Listening to his story made me angry as well, looking for someone to blame for the loss of his daughter. Unfortunately, that someone would be me.

Most of Starmon's accusations I couldn't follow. The tech and laws were above my head. At long last he made his closing statement, which was so lame and unmemorable I wondered if perhaps the Imation Team erased my memory.

Today was Arameus's turn. Time to fight back. The team of Protectors assigned to me had disguised themselves as policemen and interviewed Charlie's grandparents. I hadn't heard about this beforehand. The power inside seethed with anger seeing these people near Charlie and her family. The screen showed Charlie's grandma, eyes glazed over and speaking in monotone. "Ora is missing. Her mother went with Charlie's brother, John, to look for her. They've been gone about two days. We haven't heard from them since they left."

My ears pricked up. My *mother* and John were missing? Surely they'd messed her up, too. Why else would she say my mother? But what if a portion was true? Maybe she had gone with John to look for me. I made a mental note to ask Arameus about this later.

Hating myself, I had to force thoughts of them deep inside when Arameus insisted I take the stand to share stories of my childhood, the arrest, and demonstrate my abilities. *The last is where our defense will fall through*, I thought. The power inside me seemed to have a bit of stage fright, at times jumping about like an excited puppy, and other times dark and hidden like a sleeping predator with large claws. Then again, I'd only just discovered its presence. And since my days were filled in the courtroom, surrounding by enemies, I didn't think that was the best time to start exploring. By the time I returned to the cell at the Nook, I was exhausted.

I argued that placing me on the stand was a horrible idea. Arameus knows I can't perform magic on command, but Starmon doesn't and will take this opportunity to prove Arameus's defense wrong. If I fail to use my powers, he'll say it's because the magic I stole has already left my body. And if by some miracle I can perform magic, he will attribute it to the power of Miss Equinos.

What I'm supposed to do is to wait until Starmon declares it impossible for me to still have the magic I'd stolen. Then unleash my power in a dazzling display to stun the tribunal and make Starmon look a fool. *Yeah, right.*

Arameus and I have been practicing at breakfast every morning before the trial begins and at dinner afterward, as best as he can manage to coach me as he is Tempest and I have what appears to be Sphere power. He's been coaching me after putting a brief hold on the pellucid stone that prevents me from using magic. I haven't bothered to tell him the stone doesn't always block my power anyway. I doubted he'd tell the Protectors, but I could be wrong.

I've had meager success lifting small objects, but usually whatever I'm trying to levitate stays stone still, mocking me with its utter lack of movement. It seems only during strong and negative emotions does the power affect the outer world. Thinking back to my childhood, it had been the same way even then. Perhaps my power was like the Hulk, only coming out when I was angry. At least I didn't turn green, but a huge, superhuman, strong monster would've been helpful during the arrest.

Arameus explained in most young wizards, powerful emotions trigger their magic. But the children here are put into school to learn how to use their abilities.

I dreamed of seeing the school. According to Arameus, it's located in the center of the city where the children take certain classes together like history, magical law, and basics like reading and writing. They also have separate times in their own Houses being trained to control their magic, use spells, and make potions.

Across The Veil

I had requested a teacher from Sphere to work with me, but the request had been denied. It would've been useful having someone who was used to teaching children to use their magic. But time had run out.

Today is the day, do or die, literally. I couldn't bear to touch more than a few bites of my breakfast, a tasty meat like bacon only made of a boar-like creature with wings, served with hawk eggs and bread still hot from the oven.

The morning of the trial went well. The tribunal was enraptured with my talented Defender. He recalled the Imation Team to show the tribunal the attack on my friend. He asked the tribunal to put themselves in my shoes—a young inexperienced witch unsure of what had happened, much like when their magic first emerged, but imagine they knew nothing of the magical world. And right after this happened, four beings appeared out of nowhere and began torturing their best friend. Wouldn't they have admitted to anything, even if you didn't know what you were being accused of, just to make it stop? Their expressions changed, considering his words.

He next called Commander Stewart to the stand. He questioned the method of interrogation. She'd been forced to admit it was unnecessary and against protocol. Anger and embarrassment marred her pretty face. During our interviews and the trips from the Nook to the Guidance Hall, I'd gotten to know the Quad, as they called themselves. They were good people, and what had happened to Charlie was an isolated event. I hated it had to come to this, but if this meant my life, then so be it.

The tribunal grew angry on Charlie's behalf. Several of them shot glares at Stewart while others muttered under their breath. Arameus asked, "Commander, Quad One is the highest of all the Quads. If a simple Corporal could so easily disobey you, are you sure you should be its leader?"

Stewart's eyes flashed with anger, a dark pooling of brown. From behind me, Starmon shouted, "Objection! The Commander isn't on trial here."

Arameus bowed. "Statement is revoked."

Stewart couldn't let it go. "Corporal Bizard has been removed from the Quad. He is currently under investigation. Immediately after the arrest, I reported him. He was a new member and untested. I did the best under the circumstances, as did my Lieutenant."

"Very well, Commander," Arameus said with a nod of the head. "You may step down." Stewart stepped down from the stand, strolling beyond the cage.

Arameus met my eyes and smiled. "I call Mr. Equinos back to the stand." My mouth dropped open. Why was he calling him back?

Arameus stood facing the man, arms crossed over his chest. "Mr. Equinos, why did your daughter want to go to the human world?"

"She wanted to see how the humans lived before attending university."

"I see. Isn't it true, Mr. Equinos, your daughter, Neigh, had a history of running away?"

"How do you know that?" he said.

"Her friends and teachers have informed me she was very unhappy at home. She felt you and her mother were strict and overbearing, and she wanted to get away."

"How dare you defile my daughter this way? She straightened up over the last year! Don't speak of things you don't know about!"

"Ahh, her record did improve in the last year, but according to her friends, it was so she would be given permission to go to human world and finally get away from you."

"Objection!" Starmon called out. "Hearsay."

"Sustained," the Councilor said.

"No further questions," Arameus said, meeting my eyes before shifting his gaze to the tribunal. Several of the member's eyebrows were raised. His questioning had shed doubt on Neigh Equinos's disappearance. Perhaps she'd ran away and not been attacked…

Next Arameus recalled the renowned geneticist, Professor Bryson, to the stand. "Sir, you stated previously it isn't possible for a human to breed a witch. Is that right?"

"I didn't say impossible. It is, in my professional opinion, highly unlikely."

"But not impossible?"

"No, not impossible."

The tribunal shifted as if uncomfortable with this line of questioning.

"Can you tell me, Professor Bryson, what is your professional opinion regarding the genetic difference between the four Houses and humans?"

"Well, Defender, if you studied more in school, you would've remembered from our research the four Houses and humans had a common ancestor. After the splitting of the continents and exposure to different environmental factors, we evolved in different ways. From the one common species arose five distinct species."

"Five you say, and that would be Sphere, Naiad, Tempest, Ember, and Human."

"Yes, that is correct."

"And what of Nips?"

"They have evolved from humans."

"So it seems reasonable, and even logical, if we all shared a common ancestor and humans have the ability to produce a mutant gene leading to Nips, it's entirely possible for them to produce a witch."

The question hung in the air. "It's possible," Professor Bryson admitted after hesitating. The courtroom fell into silence.

"And excuse me, Professor, but I do remember from school, where I paid excellent attention I might add, the founder of magical genetics, Professor Goldman, and your mentor, theorized our common ancestor was humans and from them arose six species: Sphere, Tempest, Ember, Naiad, Human, and Nip, not five as you have said. Isn't that correct?"

"The common ancestor hasn't been definitively identified."

"But that was Professor Goldman's theory."

"Yes."

"No further questions."

As Professor Bryson left the stand, face a dark shade of red, Arameus made his most shocking announcement. "High Council, I ask for a short break for lunch. After we return, Ora Stone shall take the stand."

Whispers erupted from both the tribunal and the many unseen people behind me. He'd definitely ended the morning on a cliffhanger. I hoped it was worth it.

We left the courtroom. Starmon had his head huddled talking with urgency to his assistants. Instead of heading to Arameus's office, he led me upstairs, and I gave him a questioning look. He said nothing and instead kept leading the way.

We arrived on the roof of the Guidance Hall, a large open area with a tables and chairs set up as if many of the witches and wizards came out here to eat. A wall just over my waist ran along the periphery of the building, which made me feel better. At least I couldn't walk off the edge without meaning to.

"I thought you could use different scenery," he said.

"I'm afraid of heights, actually."

He laughed, taking my elbow and leading me to the edge. "You're afraid of falling. And you're with a Tempest. There is no need to worry."

I gazed out over the expansive city, my breath taken away. The city glowed from the light that ran through it. Small gardens with flowers every color of the rainbow, and even some I had no name for, perched on some roofs, pools on others, and over the horizon, the sun glowed red.

"What's over there?" I pointed.

"That is the northern part of our world. It is where The Sierra is, the ancient home of Ember. It's a volcano." He laughed at the shocked look on my face. "Relax. It's mostly inactive. It doesn't go off unless the Embers want it to. Over here, the west side is my home, The Meadow."

He pointed, but I couldn't see it. I imagined him there as a boy running through the grasslands. During our meals together, we'd talked about his homeland.

"This way is the south. See the tops of those trees beyond? That is The Willow, Sphere home. If we win this trial, you could go live there," he said.

I knew if I were set free, I didn't ever want to see this place again. It had too many bad memories. Arameus leaned his elbows on the edge of the building staring into what I could only imagine was the future.

I knew everyone here wasn't bad. In any other circumstances, I would've wished to be friends with Arameus and Lieutenant Sun. Maybe even Commander Stewart. I wished it were under different circumstances. Sadness gripped my heart. It would have been nice to look out over this beautiful horizon and think about the future, but I had no future. My only life was the here and now.

"I've seen The Willow. Well, I rode past it on the Transport." I tried to bring him back and distract myself from what lay ahead.

He turned to me, flashing a relaxed boyish smile, and I wished again that I could have met him under different circumstances.

"That's right. And you have also seen the Severn Sea, where The Haven is located beneath the waters." Thoughts of my first time on the Transport came back to me. Lieutenant Sun had pointed out her home. *Maybe if I am acquitted then I could see the city.* I shook my head, clearing it of those reckless thoughts. I was getting ahead of myself, better not make any plans.

"Come, let's eat." He took my hand in his and led me to a small round table where two trays covered by metal lids sat waiting. I nibbled at my food, and it would be delicious if I weren't so nervous. I tried to eat as much as possible, but instead, I spent most of the lunch hour gazing over the horizon of the city, listening to the birds sing and the wind blow. The wind had always comforted me, like a soft hand caressing my face. My appetite picked up, and I finished most of my meal, pepperoni pizza and salad with ranch dressing. Of all things. All too soon, there came a knock, followed by Stewart sticking her head through the door. "Excuse me. It's time to go."

We reentered the courtroom, and the crowd had grown like weeds. Arameus's announcement of my testifying must have reached the public and drawn in the crowd. This hadn't escaped the notice of the High Council. The extra audience was asked to leave, and they did so with loud mutterings.

I stepped back into my cage, and it rose around me as always. The sound of my heart pounded in my ears as Arameus said, "The defense calls Ora Stone to the stand."

The clanging of my cage being lowered and the beating of my heart were the only sounds in the courtroom. I didn't know if I would have the strength to walk up to the stand. For the first time, I was thankful for my long robes since they covered my wobbling legs. I took the stand. Hateful, curious eyes all locked on mine, and I looked toward Arameus. He nodded at me with encouragement. The court speaker told me to sit and handed me a shot glass full of a bluish white liquid. *Truth serum.*

My breathing quickened, and I took the glass, thankful that my hand only shook a tiny bit and none spilled. I touched the glass to my lips even though I wanted to give it back and run away to hide like a child being given medicine. I resisted the urge to hold my nose. It was thick, syrupy, and tasted like week-old cabbage. A quote from a movie popped in my head. *You can't handle the truth!*

Hysterical laughter threatened to escape my lips. I reined it in, but barely. The court questioner left after I handed him the glass, and Arameus walked to stand before me. "Ora Stone, please tell us in your own words what happened the morning of your arrest."

My mouth opened, and the words poured out. "It was my first day of college, and I was distracted. I was in my biology class, and my professor was teaching us about the scientific method."

"Scientific method?" Arameus interrupted, his brow constricted in confusion, distorting his natural good looks.

"It's a way humans study how things in nature work, and they use this method as a guideline. Basically, you see something in nature, and you try to explain why it happened. Then you set up an experiment to see if you're correct. If you are, you repeat the experiment over and over. And if it works enough times, it becomes a law." I delivered my lines perfectly. Why he thought I should be giving a basic science lesson was beyond me. Arameus nodded as if this made perfect sense. He brushed an escaped strand of red hair from his short ponytail.

I looked only at Arameus as we had discussed, and he asked, "And how is this relevant to your arrest?"

I shifted in my seat, reaching to twirl my hair, a nervous habit since childhood, but as my fingers grazed my scalp, I remembered I was bald. I continued. "Well, the professor wanted to give an example. He chose the law of gravity. You know, what goes up must come down?"

Arameus said, "Yes, I believe I have heard of it."

He turned, flashing the audience a bright smile, and they laughed. I flushed with embarrassment. Even though I knew this was a ploy to get the audience on our side, I still felt it was directed toward me. I braved another look at the attendants, and none would even look at me. Arameus cleared his throat, and I snapped back to attention.

"Right. So the professor picked up a pen, and I knew he was going to drop it. And I don't know why, but I thought it would be weird if it didn't fall," I said.

I ignored the angry murmurs and tried to find the right words to describe what happened. "Professor Zitalee dropped the pen. And it was like the world stopped. There was a tunnel that appeared, and in the center was the pen. Only different. It was like I could see inside the pen. How every piece was connected and how it related to everything around it. I noticed if I didn't want the pen to fall, then all I had to do was hold a part of it. I held it and… the pen didn't fall."

I was talking with my hands, and once I started, the words wouldn't stop. "I studied the design, and I could see it constantly moving. And then, to my surprise, the pen started to spin round and round. I didn't notice everyone was shocked until a girl behind me screamed, and the pen crashed to the floor."

The courtroom was abuzz with discussions. People leaned in close whispering to each other. I didn't know if I explained it right or not, but I certainly got a reaction. Arameus suppressed a smile.

"Order in the courtroom!" Lord Drecoll banged the gavel. Conversations ground to a halt.

Arameus paced around the room. "Very interesting, Miss Stone. What you are describing is the molecular structure of the pen. There are some of us who see our magic in such a way. Now, before we discuss what happened next, had anything like that ever happened to you before?"

I could feel the intensity in the room rise as everyone stared at me in anticipation.

"Yes."

He stopped pacing. "Really, Miss Stone. And when was this?"

I steadied myself to give the prepared speech Arameus and I practiced. "Many times actually. But it was when I was a child."

"Can you describe them for me?"

"Yes. Which one?"

"Start with the first one you can remember."

Shifting my body so I could face the tribunal, I spoke. "I was out shopping with my grandma, and it was close to Christmas. I saw a huge teddy bear, and I wanted it. I asked her to buy the bear for me, but she told me no. I remember yelling about it, and the bear shrank. It went from being as big me, well, three-year-old me." I shrugged, offering a shy smile, and the tribunal laughed. Not wanting to lose the moment, I continued. "It shrank until it was small enough to put in my pocket. I grabbed it and carried it out with me."

"Objection," yelled Starmon. "What is the basis of this if there's no proof?"

"You mean this?" Arameus reached into his robes and pulled out my small bear, holding it high in the air so the entire courtroom could see it.

"My bear!" I called out in surprise. He must have done this on purpose to get an honest reaction from me.

"You could have gotten it from anywhere," Starmon tried to argue against the sounds of gasps.

"True. True. But the records will show this was removed from Ora Stone's bedroom during the investigation. But if we are still in doubt, if it pleases the court, we could perform the reversal spell and see if this small bear returns to its previous size."

Lord Drecoll waved Arameus over. Drecoll took the bear. "I'll allow it." He sat my bear upon the High Counsel's desk; the bear turned hazy and grew. Within seconds, it was about three feet tall.

"Enter this into evidence as exhibit F," Arameus called in triumph.

"Objection. There is still no proof this bear belongs to the accused." Starmon banged his hand upon his desk.

"My lord, if you please." Arameus reached for the bear. After receiving permission, he picked up my oversized bear, hugging it around his chest, and strolled over to Starmon with the sounds of snickers from the courtroom.

"Starmon, if you would be so kind, can you read for me what is written on the collar?"

I squinted, trying to see the writing.

Starmon's eyes constricted in irritation before admitting, "Ora."

Gasps of astonishment waved through the courtroom. Arameus, without missing a beat, left my bear on Starmon's desk and strolled to his desk. He leaned back crossing his arms and asked me, "And the other times?"

Feeling more confident, my voice steadied. "Most were small things. I could make flowers grow from seeds. I made a tree bend over to help me get a kitten from the top. And I could make the best sandcastles when we went to the beach."

"Objection, Arameus, these are cute stories, but where is the proof?" Starmon called, his brown robes siding up his arm as he raised a hand.

"Agreed. Arameus, this better be going somewhere."

"Yes, Lord Drecoll." Arameus bowed toward the Councilman.

"Any other times, Miss Stone?" Arameus continued.

"Yes. I used to make my dolls dance. And I remember getting cookies to fly out of the cabinet."

"It is interesting you would have these magical abilities for so long if you are a Nip as the accusation claims."

"Objection," Starmon yelled.

"Sustained," Drecoll droned.

"Miss Stone, you said earlier these incidences occurred when you were a child."

"Yes, Defender."

"Tell me, why did it stop?" Arameus asked. Everyone in the courtroom held their breath. This was where our story got tricky. *Here goes nothing.* "I'm not sure, but I think it is when I got my necklace."

"A necklace? Where did you get it?"

"On my eighth birthday, we moved because our house burned down."

"You say you were distracted the morning for your arrest?" Arameus asked as he resumed his pacing.

"Yes, sir, I was."

"What were you distracted about?"

"I was thinking about my…grandma. I broke a promise to her." I paused waiting for looks of shock from anyone. There were none.

"What promise was that?"

"I promised I would never take off my necklace, but I lost it that morning."

"What would it matter if you lost a necklace?"

"My grandma is very superstitious. She has always told me all the women in my family get a necklace when we turn eight. It's to bring us protection."

"Objection, what does this have to do with anything, Arameus?" Starmon yelled to the courtroom.

Lady Drecoll leaned forward. "Arameus, you have been warned. Get to the point."

Arameus nodded. "Where is your necklace now?"

"I don't know."

"See, Your Honor, he didn't even find this necklace!" Starmon called.

"No, we didn't, but we did find a photo in her room. Miss Stone, can you tell me who is in the picture?"

I looked closer. It was the photo of Charlie and me at her last birthday party. "It's me and Charlie."

"And are you wearing the necklace you speak of?"

I nodded.

"Wonderful, now if we could blow this picture up." Arameus handed the picture to Lady Drecoll. My photo grew larger until it looked like a poster. She handed it back to Arameus, and he walked over to the tribunal. He pointed out my necklace, and the tribunal gasped. I had no idea why and resisted the urge to stand up to see the picture better.

"I would like to point out the charm on this necklace is a magic binding enchantment, which looks very familiar." He turned and brought the picture to me. I looked at it closer and realization dawned on me. My eyes found the tattoo on my arm, and Arameus was right. It was in the same pattern. *But if that was true then how did my grandma give it to me?*

"Thank you, Miss Stone. I have no further questions."

Arameus's part was over, but I was left with unanswered questions swirling through my mind. He returned to his seat looking satisfied. Stage one had been complete, and now it was Starmon's turn, and I was seconds away from my big moment. *Can't worry about the necklace right now.*

Starmon rose and brushed a hand down his robes. He took his time, letting the silence build in the courtroom. He strode over to face me. He smiled at me and my blood chilled. "Miss Stone, what an interesting story."

"Thank you."

Giggles from the audience.

"It wasn't a compliment," he said. "And how old were you when you shrunk your poor teddy bear?" he asked with a faked childish voice.

My anger rose to the surface. *Good, I can use that.* "I was three."

"Three. Well, my dear, that is impossible! Magical abilities do not emerge until age five. But we don't know at what age Nip's abilities begin."

"Objection. Accusation is speculating," Arameus shouted, for the first time sounding angry. The hair on my arms stood at attention.

"I'll allow it." Lady Drecoll waved Starmon on.

"Starmon, I don't know anything about Nips, but I'm a witch, and if I was born from a human instead of another witch, you wouldn't know at what age my abilities would begin either," I explained, my voice calm, surprising myself.

Starmon stared at me in disbelief. If looks could kill, I would have been dead where I sat, but I held my own and made eye contact, not daring to look away. My power inside me stretched, rattling deep as if shaking a non-corporeal cage, rising to meet the challenge. He looked away first, and I knew I had won a small victory. He regained his composure in no time and turned to face the tribunal, all smiles and charm with none of the loathing he'd shown me.

"And why, Miss Stone, did you think it would be funny to show magic to humans?"

"I didn't really think anything would happen. But, somehow, I did it. I'd never heard of your world, and to me, magic was only in fairytales. I did break your law but only because of ignorance and accident, not from any ill will." I explained myself to the tribunal, hoping they would believe I was sincere. I risked a glance at Arameus, and he gave me the slightest nod. I was doing well.

"Very well, Miss Stone. It seems the answer is simple. You need to show us you indeed do have magic. Can you show us? If I temporarily remove the guard."

The courtroom grumbled in nervous chatter, and Commander Stewart walked from her seat to stand behind Starmon. She touched my arm, and it stung as part of the jewel changed in a small subtle way. Starmon took a pen from his pocket, raised it high into the air, and let it fall. It hit the ground.

"Miss Stone, you may have misunderstood me. I'm going to drop this pen," he bent over and picked it up, waved the pen in my face with a dramatic flair, and the courtroom snickered, "and you need to hold it up in the air like you did before. Ready? One, two, three."

Again, he dropped the pen, and it hit the floor. The courtroom roared with laughter. My cheeks grew hot as my temper rose. The power inside me shrunk backward, hiding as I wanted to hide from the laughter. I whispered to it inside my own head, "We have to do this."

Starmon shook his head, bent down, and held the pen again in front of me, mocking me. "Oh dear, dear, dear. Let's give her one more try, shall we?" The room laughed at my expense. For the third time, he raised his hand, dropped the pen, and it hit the floor. The laughter had reached epic proportions, with some leaning over clutching their belly, tears in their eyes. *Not yet.*

"You see, my fellow witches and wizards of the tribunal, you and I both know she couldn't possibly have held the pen up. The stolen magic would have left her body by now." The laughter faded in seconds, and the tribunal had made their final judgment of my guilt. My anger flashed with such intensity I was taken by surprise. From deep inside me, the power reached forward with an invisible hand and snatched the pen from the floor, raising it high into the air to float in front of Starmon's face, threatening like a sword. It was hanging in midair under my control. Now that the power had been set free, it reveled, quivering with need. The pen stripped apart, pulling at its molecules like stripping away petals from a flower. The power wanted more. I wanted more. Its focus turned on Starmon.

The power lifted him from the ground, shoving him backward, flipping over his desk. The Commander touched my arm again. As if being pulled back inside like a vacuum, the power whooshed inside, hissing. Starmon's sleek hair now rose in wide handfuls, and he peered at me over his desk. I raised my head proud. My triumphant feeling was mirrored on Arameus's face with a slight trace of, could it be, fear?

"Any further questions Starmon?" Lady Drecoll asked, face paled.

"Uhhh...no. No further questions." Starmon stood and smoothed his robes and his hair before taking his seat.

Lady Drecoll commanded me, "You may step down now." I stood, distraught to find my legs still shaky. I returned to my cage and heard the familiar snap of it closing.

Arameus appeared at my side facing the tribunal. "The defense calls Lieutenant Sabrina Sun to the stand." Lieutenant Sun strolled to the stand, moving like a graceful cat. Her long blond hair was swept back into a delicate braid, her clear blue eyes shining bright.

"Lieutenant, you and I discussed at the pre-trial the incidents that Ora Stone has confirmed today. Can you please tell the tribunal what you found from your investigation?"

"Yes, Defender, I looked into the detailed report given by Ora Stone during her incarceration. She gave us a relative date and location of the grocery store, the stuffed animal incident. The Magical Concealment department did indeed have record of a cold case in which several humans witnessed a toy being shrank. The approximate dates matched the description by the accused, and her age would have been three years old."

"And did you find any other information, Lieutenant?"

"Yes, when we searched the home of Ora Stone, we found the shrunken teddy bear with residue of Sphere magical properties and the photograph," Lieutenant Sun explained. More sounds of shock and disbelief, but Starmon remained quiet, stunned into silence.

Arameus announced with his chest out in a loud voice, "The defense rests."

Chapter Twenty-One

Perdita's feet ached from walking. She dared not complain lest her good fortune end. After breakfast at the hotel, Todd led Perdita and John through the city. Their first stop was a museum filled with large works of art, sculptures, and music. The music played on tiny screens with instruments unlike any she'd ever seen. Some could only be played by giants, or so she thought, but when she said as much to Todd, he laughed and pointed. "That's a Tempest flute. They control the air flowing through the tubes. This one is a harp best played by a Sphere by manipulating the metal within with strings."

The paintings were also bewitched. There was one of an ocean where the waves moved looking more like a movie than a painting. The sculptures were less impressive, what Perdita called interesting instead of beautiful. The museum was fun, but Perdita felt that using your own hands and not magic was much more impressive.

Next they made their way to the Pyre, Ember's homeland. Beads of fear sweat prickled at her brow. Thoughts of her former prison set her stomach churning. Even Todd noted how pale she had grown while walking past the base of the volcanic mountain.

"The main seat of Ember's power is vacant. The Pyre has remained empty for many, many years. Embers have built these series of tunneled homes out of lava." Todd pointed toward the shiny onyx mountain-like structures as they drew nearer to them.

Yeah right. She remembered spying the homes during her escape. But walking inside one wasn't what she expected. Despite the lava flowing along one side of the stone walls, the rooms weren't hot. If anything, the tour home was welcoming. But she knew she was biased. The idea of this being a nice place while the hidden prison was so close just couldn't fit together inside her head. When it was time to leave, Perdita wasted no time making her way to the Transport.

Across The Veil

The Meadow was their destination for lunch. The homes of the Tempests were dug out of the earth, reminding Perdita of Hobbit holes. The smell of dirt was thick in the air, and Perdita imagined it would be hard to keep anything clean in this kind of home. But when the wind blew, it gave her energy. When one strong gust went through her hair like a lover's caress, Perdita's hands grew jittery like when she drank coffee. Her power filled her, reenergizing her like nothing ever had in her life.

They stopped at The Savanna Cafe. It too was dug out of the earth, the tables carved out of the mud. Soft music played in the background, and the place was nearly empty. Todd, as usual, was good natured, but Perdita couldn't help her wandering thoughts. Ora was on trial and everything was not in place.

Lailie was off today snooping at court. If Ora was acquitted, then there would be nothing to do except end their tour and meet her back home. But Perdita couldn't imagine a reality in which anything would be that easy. They had a plan, but she wished she could be confident in it. There were some huge flaws in the plan, and time wasn't on their side.

The Tempest waitress took her order of dandelion salad and a buffalo burger. The little waitress was pretty with her soft auburn hair and green eyes. She reminded Perdita of Ora, and the sadness in her grew. Even John's happy façade faded when the waitress was around.

John distracted Todd from her mental absence. Every so often they'd break out in male laughter. She would plaster a smile on her face to appear as if she were listening. But she wasn't sure she fooled anyone.

The Meadow was a vast grassland. The city with its large white skyscraper glittered in the distance to her right. But far off to the left was a sparse growth of trees that grew thicker the deeper it went. It was hard to tell as the land dipped behind a large hill. She was curious and asked, "Todd, what's over there?"

He broke off mid-laugh, his brown eyes glittering with merriment. "Oh, that's The Swamp."

"The Swamp? Does anyone live there?" she asked, still curious. She hadn't heard anything about a swamp before.

Todd squirmed as if this wasn't a subject he wanted to discuss. "Um, no. It's a place where most avoid. Wild animals and such."

Lailie spoke in her head. "Lies."

She jumped in surprise, and Todd took her reaction as fear. "Don't worry, my lady. See that hill? No one goes any further than hundred yards from there and even then not very often. We won't be going anywhere near there."

"Oh," she said as Lailie spoke in her ear again. "The Swamp is where they perform The Kassen. The shades live there. So do the Om Gandac and the black-eyed ones." Perdita shivered again. This time in real fear.

The food arrived, and while she nibbled on her salad, her thoughts kept wandering to the hill. The plan was growing sharper in her mind.

Once they paid their bill, Todd asked them if they wanted to go to the Guidance Hall or to The Haven first. Perdita jumped at the idea of going to The Haven. She could feel Lailie was near, and she longed to talk with her, but she couldn't. Not with Todd being so close. Perhaps she was only imaging it, but Perdita sensed Lailie wanted to speak with her as well. But once on the Transport, they were able to speak when Todd excused himself to use the bathroom.

"The trial is not going quite as her Defender had planned. He has taken the defense that she is a witch."

"A witch! Why couldn't he try to prove her an innocent human?" Perdita asked, outraged.

"Would you like me to ask him?" Lailie asked, her tone sarcastic.

"Of course not. It's that is the worst possible thing he could have done. What of the tribunal?"

"The tribunal is of mixed thought at the moment. They're not sure what to think of her. And have you any luck with your part?"

Perdita felt guilt creep along her skin like a bug. "No. I'm working on finding disguises. It's hard with Todd always around."

John leaned forward, crossing his hands in front of him. He appeared to be in deep thought, and then he spoke. "What if we ask to do some shopping? On our own?"

"That might work."

"Shh… here he comes," John said as Todd opened the door to their car. They were rounding the Severn Sea.

Across The Veil

Todd smiled. "Oh good. I'm just in time. Now watch out. This might seem a little weird."

Before Perdita could ponder what he meant, the Transport turned in a sharp ninety-degree angle heading out over the waters, and then flipped again, diving into the water. Perdita felt as if her head was spinning. Her eyes told her she'd turned upside down, but her brain said otherwise. The nausea passed as they sank deeper into the sea.

Todd pointed. "There is The Haven. It's set up like a huge nautilus or a snail cut in half. In the very center is the eye, and swirling from it are three outer shells. These passageways are where the Naiads live. Kind of like apartments. Inside the eye is their common area. They have restaurants, shops, and bakeries. I was thinking you all might like to pick up some keepsakes here. They have some of the best in Conjuragic. Momma Del told me I have to take you to The Sea Horse. She swears by their beauty projects."

Looking into the depths below, Perdita felt excited for the first time. The crystal city sparkled like a torch in the darkness. The Haven was a living thing. Her magic bubbled from inside her and spread along her body. Her skin was practically tingling with the energy as if her power was begging to be released to join its brothers. First in The Meadow and now here. Her skin zinged with power. She wouldn't have been surprised if she glowed like The Haven.

The Transport slowed to a halt outside one of the spirals. Perdita didn't know what to expect when the doors opened, but the water didn't rush inside. Not drowning was a good sign. Instead, the water was pushed out in the shape of a tube connecting the Transport to The Haven. Todd touched her back, encouraging her to take the step. When she did, the water felt bouncy, like a trampoline, but held her weight. She was walking on water. It was so ludicrous that it made her giggle. She'd expected to plunge into the water, so she ran to the other side.

Once inside, the tube closed, and the Transport swam back to the surface at an incredible speed. Perdita stood inside, waiting for instructions. Todd was busy with a young Naiad guard showing him badges, and he gave them clearance to enter. As they walked along the pathways, the bluish light twinkled, and Perdita felt like a queen. The halls wound in a large semicircle with doors on each side. Todd pointed them out and said, "They call these hallways siphuncles, and the living quarters are behind each of the doors. They call their little pods camerae. Some are bigger than others, but they are all nice. The outer walls and ceilings are transparent so they can see right out into the ocean."

"Aren't they worried about being seen when they're changing and stuff?" John asked, his voice echoing off the walls.

Todd chuckled. "They can bewitch the walls and turn them opaque."

"Cool!" John lifted his hand in the air, and Todd slapped his hand.

They reached the end of hallway, where an archway led into the center of The Haven. The Eye was alive with activity. Looking more like a massive bubble underwater than a room, it was filled around the perimeter with hundreds of tiny shops. There were three levels, each with a balcony. The bottom floor, which they were on, was filled with tables and chairs, but in the center there were dancers, jugglers, and a massive water fountain, spraying upward. Music played as the sounds of voices carried around the room growing louder and fainter, making it hard to pinpoint where the sound was coming from. Perdita loved it there immediately. She let her eyes lead her feet, and the men followed. Most of the shops didn't have names but were filled with silk and satin robes of every color. Another store held necklaces, rings, and earrings. She walked through this store, staring at the large diamonds shimmering and dreamed of wearing anything so fine. There were no price tags, so she was afraid to ask what it may cost.

When she drifted into another store holding the usual robes of the Houses, she turned to Todd confused. "Why would they sell robes from other Houses in The Haven?"

"In case someone wants to buy a present," he explained, running his hand down the woolen fabric of a brown robe.

"Could we buy some?" Perdita asked, in what she hoped was her best nonchalant way.

"Afraid not. It's against the rules. They don't want any impersonators. You understand."

John took the hint. "Yeah, but it would have been fun to take home, as a souvenir. Perhaps dress up like a Tempest for Halloween." He pulled on a brown robe. It fit him perfectly, and if Perdita didn't know any better, she would have believed him a Sphere with his brown eyes and hair. Even though his skin wasn't olive naturally, with his tan from working on the farm, he would fit in.

"Yes, and I could be a Naiad." She pulled on a blue robe over her darker blue one. She turned toward a mirror and gasped in surprise. She leaned in closer, and even the fine wrinkles around her eyes had faded. It must be the magic here restoring her. This could be a problem.

"You do look Naiad, except for the eyes," Todd remarked as he appeared behind her left shoulder.

She nodded in agreement. "Yes, mine are green." She slipped the aquatic blue robe off but didn't put it back. Instead, she slipped it over her arm and moved over to another Naiad robe. This one was shorter than the other, but just the right length for Ora. She met John's eyes, and he handed her the brown robe. He moved over to Todd, threw an arm around his shoulder, and said, "I think this clothes shopping is boring. Is there anything manly in this place to do?"

"There is an entire store dedicated to fishing and another for sports."

John's eyes lit up. "Will you be okay by yourself, Mom?"

"Oh yeah, you boys go on ahead. I'll be fine."

"Are you sure you'll be okay?" Todd asked, concerned, but she could tell he was anxious to get away.

"Absolutely. I think I'm going to look for that store your mom recommended. And what about the first store I saw, the one with the different kinds of robes? Could I buy some of those?"

"Oh yeah. Those you can buy. Just don't wear them until you get home."

"Okay. Do you want to meet back by the entrance at," Perdita glanced at a large clock in the store, "about three o'clock?"

"That's great. Then we'll head over to the Guidance Hall. And then decide on where we want to eat dinner." Todd looked to Perdita and John for confirmation. Perdita waved them off, and then spied around the shop.

She didn't want to steal the items, but she needed a disguise. What was she to do? And even if she did decide to leave money for them on the counter, where would she put them? She could shove them into her purse, but then what would she do if she needed to get in there? She was sure Todd would notice her purse bulging. It wouldn't do. She would have to find some other way. Perhaps she could sneak into the hotel's laundry room this evening and steal a few from there.

She left the shop and went in search of the store Todd had mentioned. There were too many stores, so she stopped and asked an older Naiad woman for help. The woman, whose name tag identified her as Agatha, was still quite pretty, though her blonde hair had faded to more of a silver color. Agatha pointed her in the right direction, and soon she stood before The Sea Horse. When she walked inside, she was immediately greeted by a middle-aged woman whose face was caked with makeup. Her bright blue eye shadow made her eyes bug like and she was loud, her voice a high-pitched squeal. "Hello there, darling. You must be a human. Am I right?"

Perdita felt exposed but answered, "Um, yes."

"Excellent," the overbearing woman said, her eyes sparkling. "I have a cousin who married a human. A darling girl from Wish-Con-Shin. We love her."

"Wisconsin," Perdita corrected.

"That's what I said. Wish-Con-Shin. Anyway, welcome to The Sea Horse. You're going to love this store. Come let me show you." The woman put an arm around Perdita, who was still standing in the doorway, and led her inside. She immediately pointed out various items. "This is a godsend for us woman as we get older. It's a brush, but you see this button here? Well, when you push it, you see how it changes colors? You push until you find the one you want and then brush." The woman had set it on a jet black color, pulled the brush through her blond hair, and with each stroke, her hair changed to black. "You see, my dear. You never have to go to a salon again. Pick your color, brush your hair, and you're done. The color lasts for about twenty-four hours, so just brush you hair every day and you're set."

That could come in handy, Perdita thought as the woman picked up a large basket and threw the brush inside. "It also has an insta-curl setting, straightener, and even a conditioner for when us girls get bushy hair from the humidity. Which when you live in the ocean, you get plenty, huh?" The woman chortled at her own joke.

"Let's see, what else? Oh yes, this is a must have. You see this iron? Well, not only does it get out the wrinkles on your robes, or clothes when you go back home, it also does something extra. Have a special occasion and you have a dress that fits you perfectly, but it is a little faded or not the color you need? Well, press this button here over the color you want, rub the iron over your clothes, and they are pressed and ready to go in the color you want. And you can even use it while you're wearing your clothes since it doesn't use heat. See?" She touched the iron to her hand and didn't even flinch. She pulled it away and her hand was intact. Then she pressed the button, held it on Perdita's robe until something beeped, and ran the iron over her own robe, transforming the aquatic blue to Perdita's dark. She threw it into the basket as well.

"Now this I love. Love. Love. Love. Love. Love." She made huge movements with her tongue each time she said the word. She was waving a paint brush. Perdita could only wonder. "Now this is fabulous. You see how your face is so barren?"

Perdita supposed her foundation, light blush, and a splash of lip gloss could be seen as barren compared to this woman's paint gallon of makeup, but Perdita still took offense.

"Well, with this, you brush it over your face." The woman brushed Perdita's face with a rough hand starting from her forehead, going side to side until she covered her whole face. Perdita barely managed to close her eyes before the woman rubbed the brush over them. When she opened her eyes, the woman spun her around to look at her face in the mirror. Perdita had gone from minimal light makeup to ready to hit a night club in two seconds. Unlike the shopkeeper, it was more than she usually wore, but not horrible. At least she didn't look like a hooker.

The woman exclaimed, "See there? Now you look adorable. And if you're like me, you'll see one pass isn't enough and you can do a few more to darken it."

The woman made to brush her face again, but Perdita threw up her hands saying, "I think that's enough for now."

The woman shrugged and threw the brush in the basket. She pulled her along, but Perdita stopped her. "What're these?"

"Oh, those. Well as you may have noticed, the people here all look similar. And well it gets boring if everyone has the same hair and eye color. So, like the brush there, these are special drops to change eye color. There is one for each color."

"Oh, how exciting! Can I try the blue one?"

"Absolutely, dear." She grabbed the bottle, and Perdita tilted her head back as the woman put on drop into her left eye. She gazed in the mirror, and she had one blue eye and one green. Perdita placed it in the bag and grabbed a few more of the colors. She felt the need to explain herself, even though the shopkeeper didn't seem to mind. "At home we have contacts that do something similar, but if you don't need glasses, it's harder to get them."

"Oh wonderful. Take as many as you like. Now those will last about four hours, so you'd have to reapply. That's their only drawback."

"Thanks," Perdita said hoping she had enough money to buy all these things. The shopkeeper pulled her around the store, showing her ways to trim and polish her nails, apply colors, and never have to get a pedi again. Another wipe removed the hair from wherever you wanted in one wipe, and it wouldn't grow back for about a month. Despite the woman's overbearing nature, Perdita was excited about the mounting items in her basket. Perdita threw in a tube of lipstick. When Perdita told her she would have to leave to meet her son and tour guide, the woman helped her with Conjuragic money. She still wasn't sure about the different coins and bills, and she hoped the woman wasn't cheating her. It took a lot less than she had imagined it would. It was only two-thirty, so she had time to run to another shop and buy three robes, but since she had the iron, the color and pattern didn't matter. She paid for the robes and still had some money left.

Perdita met John and Todd at the meeting time. Todd eyeballed all her bags. "So I take it you liked The Sea Horse?"

She smiled. "Oh yes. It was just what I needed."

Chapter Twenty-Two

My lips quivered and my legs felt like rubber as my nerves from testifying dissipated. Arameus had gotten his shocked reaction by my specular display of magic, but was it going to work? What would the tribunal think of my display of power? Although I think tossing Starmon like a doll wasn't what he'd had in mind. The magic curled back in and licked itself like a cat. As if proud of itself. Such a strange and powerful creature it was.

The Protectors pulled me through the front doors of the Guidance Hall. They jerked me sideways to avoid a woman in dark blue robes. The robes drew my eyes more than anything. I'd never seen that shade in Conjuragic before. The woman was so familiar to me. I could've sworn I'd met her before. I studied her face, blond hair, and green eyes.

Where have I met this woman before?

The adrenaline surged again. Suddenly, I knew. This woman was my grandma! But she was so young.

I opened my mouth to speak to her. She followed a handsome young Sphere up the stairs into the Guidance Hall. Grandma, with only the smallest movement, shook her head no. And I understood.

Danger loomed around us. One wrong move and I'd condemn us both. I averted my eyes and made my face a mask, revealing nothing. My group moved down the stairs, and I followed them. The Protectors took no note of her, so I knew she wasn't here to confirm my birth. She was here illegally.

That could only mean one thing. She'd come here to rescue me. *How did she know where I was?*

My thoughts raced. Working out the connections. She was here. She was young. A spell?

She was a witch, too!

I almost tripped and fell, but Lieutenant Sun grabbed my arm, steadying me. That had to be it! Charlie's grandma at the trial—she'd said my mother had gone to look for me.

Mother, my mother, not my grandmother. How could it be? Why? Was I going mad? A thousand questions ran through my mind, but I couldn't make sense of anything. My heart pounded. Blood cooled to ice. Legs unable to move.

"What's the matter with you, girl? Forgotten how to walk?" Allyn yanked his side of the net.

Just then I realized I was supposed to be moving, and no matter how much I wanted, no *needed*, to process this, I couldn't. Not here. Not now. Not with the Protectors so close. But if I left now, would I ever see her again?

I had to keep moving. Summoning all the courage I had in me, I walked down the steps.

At the bottom of the steps, I couldn't help but look back. My mother was about to enter the Guidance Hall. She looked back at me, and we locked eyes again. I remembered leaving the house on my eighth birthday party with my young mother and her showing back up in the hotel an old grandma. I remembered. I saw her slight smile much like my own, and she nodded. She knew that I knew the truth. Tears welled in my eyes, and I had to wipe them away. The sight of her brought my hope swimming back to the surface. I would've given anything to run back up the stairs and throw myself in her arms. But I couldn't. I wouldn't put her in danger.

The net pulled at my waist, forcing me away from my mother. Then I heard the most wonderful sound I'd ever heard. "Hey, Mom, wait up!"

From around the corner sprinted John, and he looked up the stairs to the Guidance Hall at my mother. At the bottom of the stairs, he skidded to a stop, his eyes meeting mine. And I saw it. Love and forgiveness shining just beneath the surface. We stared at each other, motionless, not daring to speak a word. The world had stopped. He was here, and he was with my mother. They were both trying to rescue me.

Commander Stewart growled, "Move along, boy," breaking our trance.

He shook his head and ran his fingers through his hair, a sight I had seen him do a thousand times working in the field. He walked past me without meeting my eyes again, up the stairs to my mother, who he'd called Mom. I wouldn't dare to look again. Following the Protectors' lead, I walked away from them with all the courage and bravery I could conjure. If my mother and John had come here to rescue me, risking their lives to save mine, then I wouldn't give up.

Perdita milled around the Guidance Hall, her face a mask plastered with a fake smile. She said "mmm" and "ohh" at what she hoped were the right places. She was so close. Ora had been shocked to see them, and she knew! She was such a brave, smart girl. She'd lost so much weight. And those bastards had shaved her bald. Lailie had told her, but it was quite different seeing it in person. And those black robes, just like those she'd been forced to wear. The sight of them made her want to puke.

Perdita could only watch, paralyzed, when John had come around the corner. Their eyes locked and each took tiny steps closer to each other. Ora's Protectors were in a lenient mood to let him walk so close to their prisoner, but the dark blue human robes gave him some leeway.

Perdita kept playing the scene over and over again trying to decide if she could've done something different. Was there a way she could have rescued her right then and now her chance was lost? No. No matter how many ways she played the scene in her mind, she couldn't think of any way to get Ora away from the Protectors and across the Veil without a fight. There was nothing she could've done in that moment. But still, it had broken her heart. Ora had been so close.

Todd broke her thoughts, asking, "Is that okay?"

She had no idea what he was talking about but answered, "Yes, that's fine."

"Great, I'll be right back." Todd disappeared around a corner.

John glanced around, and it appeared as if they were alone.

"Oh my god, Per... Mom, she was right there," he whispered with his jaw clenched.

"I know."

"I wanted to grab her and run."

"Me too," she said.

John ran his hand through his hair like his grandfather. He looked much older than he was. He had aged in the last few days. Perdita replayed the conversation from last night through her head again.

As soon as she returned to their hotel room from her failed excursion at the Nook, he'd bombarded her with questions.

"Where is she?" he demanded.

"I couldn't get to her."

"Why not?" He stood with his hands on his hips.

"Because she is being held deep inside a magical prison, guarded by Keepers, Styxes, spells, and who knows what else!" she shouted, eyes hazing a deeper shade of green.

He flashed a looked of embarrassment. "Right... sorry." He sighed and sank on the bed. He put his head in his hands and asked, "So what happened?"

She recounted her tale, including Lailie, who at that moment, decided to speak.

John jumped up with his fists drawn. Lailie laughed at him, and Perdita couldn't help but put her hand over her mouth to stifle a smile.

"Relax, John. She's an oxyagenian."

"A what?"

"I am the product of an experiment. I was a person, and now I am this," Lailie breezed.

"Which is?" he asked. Perdita couldn't blame him. Lailie spoke as if things were obvious.

"She is made of air."

"But how?" John asked, spinning looking for someone with no body. It really was quite funny.

"No one knows," Perdita said.

"Is she going to help us?"

"I am," Lailie answered.

"Good," he said.

It was Perdita's turn to pace. She wasn't sure whether she could break Ora out of the Nook. Lailie and she had discussed it on the way.

"I was lucky to get out tonight. I don't think I can risk it again," Perdita explained. She told him of her failed break-out attempt and all her near misses. He let out a low whistle when she finished.

"So now what?" he asked.

"Well, I think the best plan is to ride out the trial. If she's proven innocent, then we can end our tour and go home," Perdita said, smoothing the fabric of her robes thinking of how they'd have to disappear, in case this world ever found out what Ora really was.

"And if she's guilty?" he asked.

Perdita swallowed. "I'm not sure."

"What do you mean you're not sure? What're you playing at?" John yelled, his voice rising.

"If she's guilty," Lailie said, "that's where I come in."

Perdita and John both turned their heads. Lailie had spoken into their heads again. John shook his head and put his finger into his ear scratching it. "Uhhh, that's weird," he said. Lailie laughed, her voice drifting on the wind.

"Okay, I'm listening," John said, his face still screwed up in discomfort. They'd stayed up late into the night discussing the plan. It was risky as hell but possible. And since it was the only one they had, it had to work.

An announcement jerked Perdita to the present. "Attention visitors, the Guidance Hall will be closing to guests in five minutes. Please begin making your way to the exits."

John thought about the previous night as well. "So, if she's guilty, how're we going to get out of here if the Lailie part works?"

Perdita smiled and stood taller. "Now this something I know how to do."

Today was the day. The verdict. The last morning I'd wake up in the cell. By the end of today, I'd either be dead or home. The prejudice against me was strong, but Arameus had been such a skilled Defender that I might have a chance.

Regardless, the verdict was beyond my control, as it had been since the moment my magic escaped and levitated a pen. A pen. Such a stupid reason to die.

Last night, nightmare after nightmare woke me from an uneasy sleep. Images of my mom and John being captured and tortured. They must still here. What were they up to? Surely if they'd been captured, someone would have told me, but then again, maybe not.

Starmon had berated Arameus because my mom couldn't be found. Even though Charlie's parents told the Protectors she and John went to look for me, he still made it look like I had something to hide. And for once, he was right. I could only imagine how that conversation went, the four Protectors standing there in their police officer outfits with poor Evelyn and Jake McCurry. Of course, Arameus assured me they were professional. I tried to picture it, but I couldn't. I thought about Charlie often. I missed her so much and wished I could talk with her about everything that had happened. Arameus did bring me one piece of happy news. Charlie was awake and talking. She'd been healed so the tornado to her face didn't seem to cause any lasting damage, despite what Corporal Bizard told me.

I slid off the bed that had been left in my cell since the first night Arameus had come to see me. He'd even halted the circulations of the room and instead left it on the hurricane setting, but it had been quieted down to a slow, steady drizzle. Instead of menacing, it was soothing like sleeping through a rainstorm.

Freaky Eyes wasn't around last night, and I'd missed her. She wouldn't come this morning, she never had before, and I wanted a chance to tell her goodbye.

My stomach grumbled bringing me back to the present. I wasn't looking forward to the mush, especially after the decadent meal I had with Arameus in his office again after the closing statements yesterday.

I had thought I wouldn't be able to sleep, but I wondered if Arameus slipped something into the coffee we sipped during dessert. I was often self-conscious around people, especially eating, but I found myself pigging out whenever we shared our dinners together. We talked some, but there was a lot of comfortable silence between us. It was very nice to be able to sit with someone, eat, and listen to soft relaxing music without the need to fill it with unnecessary conversation.

Last night, he was different though. He asked me about my life. He knew so much about me already to be able to defend me, but these questions were different. What was it like growing up without magic? I couldn't help but laugh at him. "It was normal. Magic was something in fairytales or in movies, not real."

He asked, "What was it like to ride in a car? And how does a television work?"

Across The Veil

I answered the best I could, but honestly, how can you describe to someone who had never been in a car what it's like? "I guess it's like the Transport, the feeling, but you can feel more movement than on the Transport."

He was fascinated by the idea of central air and heat, but he really got excited when I told him about roller coasters. He'd never even heard about them! "So they take you high in the air then you fall and twist and turn and flip upside down!"

It wasn't a bad way to spend possibly the last evening of your life. I spent most of the time laughing at him. He was very funny, like a little boy. "Yeah, pretty much," I told him covering my smile with the back of my hand. I asked, "Don't you have anything like that here?"

"Each House has their own similar kind of thing. Tempest flying is really fun. It's like your roller coaster, but instead of being harnessed into a track and cart, your body is surrounded by wind and you are pushed around by a Tempest controller."

"What? You're not telling me you are flying around in the air with nothing holding you up."

He laughed, his shoulders shaking with the effort. "Well, you're being held up by magic."

"That sounds terrifying!"

"Oh, come on, Ora, you'll get on a rickety metal monster, flipped around by electricity, and if something goes wrong, you'll go crashing to the ground? Tempests control the air, darling. You aren't going anywhere."

"I guess you have a point."

He smirked at me with eyes full of mischief, lifted one hand, and the air swarmed beneath me and lifted me into the air like a feather. I screamed in surprise.

"Arameus, put me down!"

He laughed and flew me around the room. After the initial shock, I spread my arms wide and enjoyed the ride, feeling like Peter Pan. He dipped me, nose-diving to the ground. I screamed again, and the door burst open. The four Protectors ran into the room, their positions at the ready for trouble. Arameus lost his concentration, and I fell onto the couch and rolled to the floor.

We looked at the Protectors with guilt, and both of us laughed. I fell back to the floor, hugging my stomach in uncontrollable laughter. Commander Stewart put her hands on her hips, turned on her heel, and marched out of the door. "Come." The team turned to followed her, and through my laughter, I spotted the grin on Lieutenant Sun's lips.

I smiled at the memory. I'm pretty sure he'd done that to distract me, to give me one night of fun and peace before today. As always, he'd been kind. He had such a big heart, and I hoped if we lost today he wouldn't take it too hard.

My bladder constricted, sending a sharp pain in my lower belly, forcing me to get out of the comfortable bed and step onto the icy floor. I tiptoed over to the wall, stepped on the switch, and relieved myself in the toilet. My brow furrowed at the memory of my first days here, starving, living in my own filth when this was here only a few feet away and no one told me. There came a hiss at the door, which could only mean one thing: the Keepers. I felt my blood boil as my hatred of them roared beneath my veins. I jumped to my feet, not wanting to be caught with my robes hiked up.

The door vanished, and Mark and Malandra entered, looking smug as ever. At least I wouldn't have to see them ever again. "Come, Nip," Malandra ordered.

"I'm not a Nip!" I yelled, surprising even myself.

"Why you little—" Mark flung his hand, backhanding my face. Pain erupted across my cheek as I fell backwards onto the bed. When I stood, the room swayed. I couldn't quite remember where I was. Mark glared at me. I steadied myself, wiping the blood off my mouth with the back of my hand, and smiled. "Say goodbye to your job." My magic vibrated deep inside, begging to be set free, but I held it in check. This was more justice.

Mark paled. He knew I was right. Arameus threatened their jobs if they abused me again, and he'd handed it to me on a silver platter. His face fell as this realization sank in. He rushed toward me again. Before he could throw another blow, Malandra flicked her whip. The leather snatched Mark's wrist. He slowed, looking at it stupidly. With a yank, Malandra pulled him to the ground.

"Do you want to end up in here instead of working here?" she scolded him as he lay on the floor, his eyes wide.

"But she... I," he stammered.

"Leave it alone, Mark. What's done is done. You'll have to face the consequences, but don't make it worse," Malandra told him as he dislodged her whip from around his wrist. She wrapped it back in a loose circle and tied it to her waist.

He stood to his feet, pointed at me, and uttered, "You're one lucky girl."

I decided I had pushed my luck enough and said nothing. My jaw throbbed, but I didn't give him the satisfaction of rubbing it. My head swam but was clearing. I was grateful for the pain because it meant Arameus could force him out of his job. He had no right to treat prisoners this way, and I hadn't even been convicted. I couldn't imagine the treatment of people who were stuck here for sentencing. At least I had to be presentable for the trial, so I wasn't allowed to have any bruises, must be clean, and kept fed.

"Come on, girl," Malandra ordered me. She ushered Mark out first, and I was made to follow him. I looked back only once at the cell. I remembered the hours of starvation, the torment of the rooms. I shuddered at the memory of the inferno, but the tornado wasn't any better. I looked away and followed Mark along the pitch-black caverns for the last time.

We reentered the processing room, and the old wizard stood in the center of the room at his podium. A different set of Protectors stood before him with a new prisoner, this one bloody, and the Protectors looked a little ruffled themselves. I guessed this one put up a fight.

We strolled past them and stood in front of one of the tubes. They were tall, extending from floor to ceiling. It looked like glass, but Mark walked right through it. He shot up and away like a rocket. The tube hummed, and Malandra pushed me inside. It felt gelatinous and rubbery, but popped out into the center. The air moved around me toward the ceiling. I put my hands down to keep my robes from flying up and showing my underwear. Malandra squeezed in beside me and said to no one, "Keeper Malandra, Infirmary."

It felt as if the air was sucked around me, constricting my body. Out of nowhere, I felt a rumble beneath my feet and a torrent of air blasting me upward. I flew up the tube, Malandra beside me, and screamed. We blasted into the air, rising a hundred feet in a matter of seconds. My stomach felt like it relocated to inside my toes. I couldn't quit screaming. "Quiet, girl," Malandra shouted at me over the howling of the wind. We stuttered to a halt and stood outside a metal door. She shoved me out of the tube through the jelly again. Mark stood beside the door glaring at me.

"That was interesting," I muttered, more to myself.

We walked through the silver door. I was again in the white clean room of the infirmary. Healer Tekden sat at her desk looking through a microscope. She looked up as we entered. "Oh my." She stood and ushered Mark and Malandra outside to wait.

Mark gave her a look of concern. "I will be safe, Keeper. You may go," Healer Tekden told him while shutting the door in his face.

"Remove your robes and underwear and sit." She pointed to the metal exam table. It was clean and shiny, reminding me of the inside of an operating room. Charlie and I had shadowed a surgeon, and her table looked a lot like this. I removed my robes, my cheeks flushing red, slipped down my underwear, and took my seat. I used the dirty robes to cover myself, trying to find some privacy, wishing I could have at least kept on my underwear. The Healer walked over, grabbed my robes, and dropped them on the floor without a second glance. I covered my breasts and looked at the floor. *This is so embarrassing.*

She looked me over with scrutinizing eyes, examining every inch of me. Her face held no expression like she was examining a piece of furniture instead of a human being. I guessed to her that's all I was, a collection of parts. She paid particular attention to my jaw and muttered to herself. "Well, at least you've been eating and drinking. Your daily baths have helped, too. What happened here?" She asked while touching my swollen tender jaw.

"Keeper Mark."

She shook her head. "Of course. Well, should be easy enough to fix, then you can shower. After that, your Defender will be escorting you to the Guidance Hall with the Protectors."

"You'll tell him what happened?" I asked, uncertain. It would be better coming from her.

"Of course," she assured me.

She glided over to a cabinet on the wall, unlocked it with a key, and returned with two vials. One the small bottle of clear liquid I had taken before, the pain medicine, the other was in a brown bottle and looked thick. It reminded me of cough syrup. *I hate cough syrup.* My nose wrinkled in disgust. Healer Tekden saw my expression and smiled. "It's not that bad."

She poured the thick liquid into a cup. It was brown, thick, and smelled disgusting. She handed it to me, and I looked at it and felt like a five year old. Tekden put her hands on her hips, just like my grandma… no, my mom…did while growing up. That did it. I pinched my nose, put the liquid to my mouth, and poured. It oozed into my mouth, and I didn't know what she was talking about. *It isn't that bad, my foot.* I coughed and sputtered as she handed me a drink. I took a large gulp and found it was a juice but nothing like I'd ever tasted. It was wonderful and cleaned my mouth of the taste right away.

She handed me the vial of pain medicine, but I waved the bottle away. "It's okay. Do a lot of people get addicted to that?"

Tekden regarded me with a questioning look before answering. "Yes, we've had similar problems with this, but ours is safer. Fewer dangerous physical side effects, but the mental abuse is comparable."

She studied me, this time looking into my eyes and not surveying my body. I thought I would prefer her looking at my body because she could read me too well. "You're a very interesting young woman."

"Thank you," I said not really sure what she meant.

She guided me to the shower and started it for me. I was grateful for the privacy. I saw my reflection in the mirror, bruised and swollen. The pain in my jaw had faded, but it had begun to tingle. I stood transfixed before the mirror. As the tingling intensified, the swelling reduced, and the bruise faded. I smiled in delight. *Magic is so cool!* Maybe I would learn to use it. Instead of a doctor, I could be a Healer. *All right, Stone, if you live through the day, then you could make plans.*

I stepped into the warm shower, its jets washing away the last of my cell. My muscles relaxed, and I stretched my neck letting the water beat on my shoulders massaging them. I pressed a button, and I was flooded with a foamy soap that smelled of gardenias and jasmine. I rubbed the soap all over my skin and my bald head. I was surprised it hadn't begun to grow back in, but I'd imagine it's because it wasn't meant to. I figured it must be a form of magic, keeping me in my rightful place. I pressed a different button and was rinsed by warm clean water. All too soon, I stepped out, wrapped myself in a large soft towel, and dried off.

I slipped on my customary black robes and looked with disdain at the black tattoo on my arm. *Today is the day,* I thought, so I looked away from my arm and left the bathroom. As I slipped on my sandals, Arameus appeared in the doorway. Healer Tekden strolled over to meet him. He looked angry, and I realized she must have already told him about Mark. When he noticed me, the anger left his face, and he smiled. It didn't reach his eyes, and I knew he was worried about today as well.

"Good morning, Ora. Ready?" he asked me and extended his hand.

"As I'll ever be." I took his hand. His fingers gripped mine, extending a note of calmness. We left the infirmary, and Mark and Malandra were nowhere to be seen. I was glad and hoped to never see either of them again. We met my usual Protectors outside the door where they encased me in the net.

We left the Nook, and as we boarded the Transport, I removed my gas mask and took one look back. It was still as scary, but without the hallucinogenic gas from The Shadow Forest, it wasn't terrifying—a long, tan brick caste with about a hundred windows. My anger flared at the Protectors for not putting a mask on me, but Arameus explained it was customary for the first time. It let prisoners experience what it would be like to try and escape.

We arrived at our destination and were greeted by hundreds of people waiting outside the Guidance Hall. I looked at Arameus, and he squeezed my hand again, offering support, and explained, "Reporters come when the verdict is due."

There were people who came to protest. They had signs waving in the air. I caught sight of one that said *Death to the Nip* and I read no more. I kept my head down, and I walked into the Guidance Hall on unsteady feet, past the shouts and flashes of light from photographers. Instead of the courtroom, I was led to Arameus's office. The Protectors left us as had become our custom.

I looked at Arameus confused as to why we were here. He shrugged. "I thought you'd like some breakfast."

I didn't know if I could eat. The nerves had gotten to me, twisting knots in my stomach. Even my power had sunk into the deepest part of its hidey hole. He led me to my usual spot across from his desk. He pushed my shoulders with a gentle hand, encouraging me to sit as my body had forgotten how to move. He placed a bagel in front of me with sweet cream cheese and berries on the side. I had a large glass of the juice I'd had in the infirmary. I nibbled on the bagel the best I could, and we didn't talk much. All too soon, we heard a knock at the door.

The blood drained from my face, and I looked up at Arameus. I noticed he'd had a light breakfast as well. His face was set, and his mouth in a thin line. He took a deep breath, stood, and walked around the desk to take my hand and lead me to the door.

He opened it, and Commander Stewart said, expressionless, "They are ready." He nodded his head once and squeezed my hand. I stumbled on wobbly legs surrounded by my entourage. I entered the courtroom, bulging with people. We made our way down the middle aisle. I turned to the left, Arameus took his place beside me, and we stood and waited. I glanced at the tribunal and could read nothing from their expressions.

"Please rise for the High Council," the court announcer called, and I heard the scuffling of chairs as the spectators rose.

The High Council entered the courtroom. The tension in this room was thick, and other than an occasional cough and shuffling of feet, the only sound was the Councilors' feet upon the ground. They stood before their seats and said, "Be seated."

The people in the courtroom bowed and sat. I knew my eyes were wide in panic. And as much as I want to be strong, I couldn't suppress the overwhelming panic. Arameus reached over and took my sweaty hand. He was being strong for me, and I had the urge to lay my head on his shoulder like a child.

"Has the tribunal reached a verdict?" Lord Drecoll asked.

A young Naiad man stood, his blond hair brushing across his forehead. "Yes, your highness, we have."

"State your name for the record." Lord Drecoll's tone was drawn out and bored. *Bored*! She spoke as if my life and the outcome of this trial were of no consequence.

"Jim Mosby."

"State your verdict," Lady Drecoll said.

My heart pounded. The room swayed, and my body felt numb as if I'd drank the anesthesia potion. The chair shook beneath me. Thank God they hadn't placed me in the cage. Arameus still clutched my hand, holding my sweaty palm steady. *Please. Oh please.*

"We the tribunal in the case of Conjuragic versus Ora Stone, find the accused…"

I held my breath as he paused. The tension was so thick I felt I could cut it with a knife. I saw a faint flicker of sadness pass across his face. *No. No. No.*

"Guilty of all charges."

Chapter Twenty-Three

GUILTY! I FELL BACK INTO MY SEAT AND CLOSED MY EYES. CHAOS erupted around me, tears poured down my face, and I fought to suppress the sobs that were threatening to overtake any of my remaining dignity. Arameus threw his arms around me and whispered in my ear, "I'm so sorry. I'm so sorry. I failed you."

His anguish was nothing to the torment inside me. His words held no meaning. There was nothing and no one else in the world. I was beyond reaching. My mother's face appeared in my mind's eye. It was too late for me. I pushed down against all emotions. Shoving them deep, packing them into a tiny box. The tears subsided enough to get through the last of this. I opened my eyes and pulled away from Arameus, touched by the tears in his eyes.

"Arameus, listen, I need your help," I whispered into his ear so only he could hear me.

"The verdict is made…there is nothing else I can do." He hung his head in defeat.

I shook my head. "You did your best, but I need something else. I can trust you, right?"

"Absolutely."

"My mother and my… friend, John, they're here. I think they've come to rescue me."

His head jerked away from me, and he looked at me in surprise. He said nothing but nodded his head indicating he understood. He leaned back in so I could continue whispering in his ear.

"They're wearing dark blue robes. Does that mean anything to you?" I felt him nod against my face. "I want you to make sure they get home safe. Okay?"

"Yes," I barely heard him say.

"And my friend, Charlie, the one they hurt the day I was arrested, make sure she is okay. Make sure she is completely healed physically as well as mentally, healthy, happy. You can even wipe their memories of me." Eying the ground, he shook his head yes. "And tell them how much I love them." My voice broke.

"I will. I promise." He raised both of my hands in his and kissed my knuckles.

"Thank you for everything," I whispered as someone grabbed my arm.

I looked up as Corporal Allyn pulled me to my feet. I jerked my head toward Arameus. "Right now?"

They were taking me to be executed right now! He managed only the slightest nod. I would be dead within the hour. My panic returned, and a stab of queasiness swarmed in my stomach as my meager breakfast churned.

"Wait!" Arameus shouted. He threw one arm around me, and the other grasped my hand. "Goodbye, Ora." He stepped away, and I felt a cool piece of glass he'd slipped into my hand during the embrace. I tightened my fist around it. I didn't know what he'd given me, but it was a final act of kindness. A huge burden lifted from my shoulders knowing Mom and John would get home safely and Charlie would be okay. *I love you. Goodbye.* The four Protectors led me out the courtroom. To my surprise, Lieutenant Sun had tears in her eyes, and even Commander Stewart looked forlorn. Corporal Bizard was still absent, and for that, I was thankful. They surrounded me with the magical net for the last time. I followed on shaky legs out of the Guidance Hall.

As we left, we were bombarded by shouts and curses and blinded by flashes of light. Some people in the crowd were taking picture after picture of me, but the rest stared with hate in their eyes. I saw no hint of humanity in them, and I knew it wasn't because they were a magical species. They'd become an angry mob. An overwhelming wave of pity swept over me for these people. I knew my life and my death would not mean anything to them, but still I pitied them.

I held my head held high and continued to the Transport. Relief flooded through me as we left the crowd behind. I didn't even mind the security cart as I took one last ride around the beautiful city. I was quiet, but Lieutenant Sun sniffed and wiped her nose.

Across The Veil

"Quiet, Lieutenant," Commander Stewart ordered, voice hoarse.

I should have been feeling sad or scared, but I was numb. My mind blank, I was doing nothing but enjoying the view. Mere seconds before we reached our destination, the Transport slowed, my panic returning. My fingertips grew numb. Commander Stewart and Lieutenant Sun had to pull me to my feet. I exited the Transport and was again blinded by cameras.

We walked deeper in the woods along a winding path. The crowd of photographers grew thicker with each passing step. They had the decency to keep their mouths closed and only took my picture. The farther we went, the more the smell of damp dirt and moss filled my nose. The forest floor grew damper and felt squishy beneath my feet. Lieutenant Sun had quieted her crying, but her eyes were still rimmed in red. My Protectors were all grim-faced and serious.

The forest began to clear, and I saw a platform ahead with a simple, innocent-looking wooden box, which looked frighteningly like a casket. The platform sat over a dark and foreboding swamp. To the left was four rows of chairs, each filled with the High Council and their advisors, the tribunal, and the family of Miss Equinos.

Her mother looked up as I entered the field and yelled, "You deserve this. You evil Nip! You killed my baby." She collapsed on her husband's shoulder, sobbing. He stared right at me, and I could see in his eyes that he would enjoy watching his revenge. I looked away and hoped their daughter was alive and would be found soon.

To my right stood Starmon and Arameus. I met Arameus's gaze and held onto the only pair of friendly eyes in the crowd. Starmon walked forward and spoke. "Ora Stone, you have been tried and convicted by the tribunal for the crime of Nipping and breaching the Concealment Code. Under Conjuragic law, you have been condemned to death by The Kassen. Do you have anything to say before the sentence is carried out?"

I thought for a moment and shook my head. I said everything I wanted to say to Arameus right after the verdict.

"Very well," Starmon said.

The Protectors led me out farther onto the platform. Quivering from head to toe, every fiber of my being was screaming at me to run, fight, do something! My life couldn't simply end in a few moments. It was unreal. My heart buzzed too fast trying to cling to life. I thought of times in my life I had wasted. I was going to die because I did magic, all because I lost my mother's necklace. *Why didn't she tell me?*

We reached the end of the platform, the magical net was released, and I looked into the swamp waters and thought for a second of diving in. But I was surrounded by a couple dozen witches and wizards, all who knew how to use their magic. The thought of snakes and alligators caused me to hesitate, and my moment was lost. I eased into the simple dark wooden box floating on the water. It vibrated as I stepped inside, and Commander Stewart said, "Lie down."

I almost fell as I tried to obey, but my limbs were in panic mode and not listening to me anymore. With their help, I laid down, face up, in my makeshift casket, and I heard Arameus's choked sob. I knew it would cost him, but it meant so much to me. The Protectors backed away from me. Lieutenant Sun had a single tear running down her cheek, and Commander Stewart's eyes were moist.

I raised my right hand and waved goodbye to Arameus, hoping he could see. He let out a moan of anguish. I clutched the glass bottle in my left hand, hugging it close like a lifeline. Lieutenant Sun and Commander Stewart pulled the lid to the box over my feet, and it snapped into place. I closed my eyes, trying not to cry. I must be brave a while longer. I knew The Kassen was soundproof. Arameus told me I could yell and scream as soon as it sealed. No one would witness my fear. I'd been brave long enough. As soon as it was closed, I could fall apart, giving way to my fear and embrace it. The lid slid past my feet, above my legs, and rose past my waist. As it crossed my chest, the claustrophobia kicked in. A calming breeze flowed past my face and into the box. Lieutenant Sun and Commander Stewart paused looking confused for a few moments.

"Goodbye," I whispered. I didn't try to stop my tears now. They whispered at the same time, "Goodbye."

The lid slid into place and sealed shut with a click, then a hiss. I opened the glass vial Arameus slipped to me at the courtroom and put it to my lips. I drank the cold liquid, and it filled my belly with ice, spreading all over my body, numbing me to any pain that may come. I was bound inside The Kassen. Even my power had been petrified into stillness.

Encased in complete darkness.

My body shook as the box fell into the water, sinking into the swamp. All bravery gone, I succumbed to the panic, opened my mouth, and screamed.

Chapter Twenty-Four

My wailing continued. Over and over, my body wracked with screams. My power slept, not moving, undetectable. Despite the vial of numbing medicine, I screamed. I twisted and turned in the small space. I wanted out. I didn't want to die. I didn't do anything wrong.

Help!

I screamed over and over as my voice broke. I cried out for my mommy, for Charlie, for my John, Arameus, anyone. Over and over I cried as the swamp water leaked into the box.

Someone called my name. I listened hard. I heard it again. "Ora, use your magic. Break out of this box. If you don't do it now, you're going to die."

I pounded against the top of the box. I'd gone mad. Someone was talking to me. "Ora! Please listen. Open yourself up. Use what is inside you. Use what you were born with. Become who you are meant to be," the voice said.

"Help!" I screamed, my voice breaking from the ferocity of my yell.

"Ora, please!" the voice pleaded. The murky swamp water filled half the box. I was going to drown. I screamed and screamed, my voice gone, my arms and knees bloody from pounding the roof and sides trying to break out. I looked within myself, but I was too panicked to find the magic there. "I can't do it!" I screamed to my hallucination.

"You must."

"I can't," I called, shaking my head from side to side, the murky water lapping at my ears.

This was it. The water continued to rise. I tilted my head back. "Please," I whispered.

As the last bit of space was about to be overcome with the water, I drew in my last breath of life deep into my lungs. It was icy cold and tasted like a cool fall evening. Fully submerged in the dark water, my eyes closed and my chest burned for air. I grabbed my chest. I'd held my breath underwater before, but this was different, like something foreign was leaving my chest through my veins and spreading throughout my entire body. *This must be what it is like to die*, I thought.

My limbs moved, but I wasn't controlling them. I had become a puppet. A voice spoke inside my head, whispering in an unknown language.

Somewhere from deep within me, something pulled, deeper and deeper until I recognized it.

My magic.

It awoke, not a small part like before, but erupting like a volcano. The box ripped apart around me, and I floated deep in the swamp water. My limps moved, and the water parted from around my head, leaving a bubble of air. I gasped in several gulps of air, my body rejoicing. I cried out in relief. The voice in my head said, "Not yet."

The bubble disappeared as my body swam of its own accord, using my arms and magic to push me along. I wondered if perhaps I had died.

"No," the voice answered me, "you aren't dead, but we have to hurry."

I held my breath as I glided farther and farther into the water. My body stopped, and the bubble formed again. I took in several breaths and swam again. The farther we went, the less time I spent breathing.

The swamp bed separated into a hole. Using magic to dig through the dirt, pushing it ahead of me, I went into the hole. I was covered in the dirt, still being propelled forward but slowing. I couldn't see because the dirt was all round my face. I couldn't breathe again, this time suffocating from the earth. I urged the voice, *Faster! Faster!*

I held my breath, but I couldn't go on much longer. I escaped The Kassen but was going to die in the dirt. *No, we're almost there. Wait a little longer.*

My body turned and dug upward. My lungs couldn't hang on any longer. I inhaled the dirt. The awful murky earth filled my mouth, sending painful shards into my lungs. Pain spread from my chest as the steady beat of my heart stammered. It hummed inside my chest, beating before slowing. "No!" the voice screamed in my head. But I was so tired, better to stop.

My heart beat slower with each beat. My chest burned, filled with dirt, covered in darkness. Beneath my closed eyes, the darkness lightened. Was that the light at the end of the tunnel? My heart slowed and then paused, not beating again.

I left my body and floated above the ground. Beneath me, my mother and John stood with clenched jaws, staring into the distance, waiting. She wore Naiad robes, and John had on Sphere. My love for them poured outward, not hindered by doubt or any tiny human emotions. Something pulled at me from above. A feeling swept over me and told me I could go. Go on. Or I could stay. I floated for a while. Time felt gone, back there with my body.

My lifeless body erupted from the ground. Mom and John jumped back in surprise and then crouched to the ground, pulling my body out of the hole. My body looked unreal, like a doll. The dirt clung to my eyelashes and clothes. My lips were bloody, and my bald head was scratched. "No!" my mother wailed.

John pulled me into an embrace, sobbing over my body. He sat back. My body shook with the force of his sobs, snapping my head back and forth.

My mouth opened wide, and my limbs stiffened. It looked like I was having a seizure. The black tattoo on my arm, dulled from the dirt, began to twist and turn, receding into my skin. It vanished, but my body still shook. If I were still alive, I would be horrified as black tar mixed with dirt oozed out of my mouth, spilling over my cheek onto the ground beside me.

The thick liquid poured from my mouth, over and over, until it trickled to the last drop. The tar-like fluid formed beside me into the shape of a woman. The being spoke to my mom. "Perdita, you can still save her. She is over there." The woman in black pointed right at me, floating.

John looked up, confused. Seeing nothing, he leaned over my body. He pinched my nose, covered my mouth with his and breathed into me. My chest rose and fell twice. He felt my neck with his fingers and moved to placed one hand over the other, fingers intertwined and rhythmically pounded on my chest. He counted. Then he stopped, breathed into me twice more and felt my neck again. Repeating this pattern over and over calling my name in desperation, "Ora, please come back, baby! I love you. Come on! Come on! Please!"

My mom moved over to help, but there was no room. The woman in black reached out for my mom. She reached out and touched the hand covered in black oil. "Lailie, you're dying?" my mom whispered.

"Yes, my friend. I'm not meant to enter the body. It's not what I was made for." Lailie breathed, spewing the tar-like material.

"I'm sorry," Mom sobbed.

"Don't be, my friend. I am released. I've been here so long. I'm ready."

"I'll never forget you."

Lailie shook her head, her naked form beautiful. "Stop The Experimenter, Perdita. You have to."

"I'll try."

Lailie smiled before the woman's shape disintegrated, the only thing left a puddle of tar on the ground below Mom's feet. She bowed her head once as if in tribute and said, "Goodbye, my friend."

Mom turned from the blackness and crawled over to me. She watched John, the look in her eyes haunted and distant, the strain robbing her face of her beauty. Beside me appeared a radiant being, and I recognized Lailie, a vision in gold light. I had always known her name, but that was because I was caught in the in-between. She was wearing a long white gown, her black skin a sharp contrast.

"Ora," her voice rang like bells. "Will you stay or will you go?"

I felt the pull from beyond and also the pull from my body as soon as Lailie left me. It was my choice.

"I'm sorry you died for me," I said to her.

She smiled, at peace. "No, my child. I died long ago when my body was destroyed and my soul trapped in that form. I've been waiting for the day when I could leave, but I had to do it for a noble reason. That was the key to ending the spell. Don't be sorry. I want to thank you."

I felt the guilt leave me. And I knew I would go back. As soon as I thought it, I floated toward my body.

Lailie faded away, floating toward the sky. She turned and called out, "One more thing."

"Yes?"

"Tell Perdita I remember. Tell her my name is Tituba."

"The Tituba?" I asked, remembering her name from Arameus's story. She smiled again. "No, but I'm named after her. She was my ancestor."

She disappeared, and I slammed back into my body. Every part of me hurt like hell. My back arched as I sucked air into my lungs. John's arms were around me, holding me tight. John's voice was muffled as he cried into my ear, "Ora, You're back. You're back."

My mother cried and called my name. Their tears bathed me. Forcing myself to a sitting position, I wrapped my arms around both of them. We were on the top of a hill in the middle of grasslands, hidden from any watching eyes. As the sobs of relief quieted, we let go of one another. My mom stroked my face, and I said, "Mom."

She cried again, "Yes, my daughter. I'm your mommy."

In our close embrace, she whispered in my ear, "It's all my fault. I should've told you. I wanted to tell you a thousand times, but I wanted to protect you. I failed you, my baby. I'm so sorry."

"It's okay."

"I'll never forgive myself."

"Don't." I stroked her cheek, not believing she was really here and I was still alive.

My mom and I held each other for a long time, John rubbing my back. We separated and I threw myself onto John, and when he kissed me, I forgot. In that moment, everything was better as his lips pushed against mine. Despite the dirt and blood.

A cough from Mom brought us back to reality, and we pulled apart, smiled at each other, shy all of a sudden.

"Well," Mom reminded me, her lips pressed into a thin line. "We really have to get you into hiding."

In my relief, I'd forgotten I'd now be a fugitive, but at least Tituba had gotten rid of my black mark.

"John, turned around," Mom ordered. He gave her a quizzical look and did as he was told.

"Strip," she told me, and I opened my mouth at her. She sounded so much like Healer Tekden. She raised her eyebrows at me in a look I knew so

Across The Veil

well. Without further hesitation, I pulled the robes off my body and tossed them in the black puddle. I was damp and covered in muck and mud.

"Stand still." Mom waved her arms, looking rather silly, but the air around me vibrated. "Ready?" she asked.

Ready for what?

A floating puddle of water appeared above me and ran down my head, across my face, down my body, over my arms, and finished its descent down my legs and feet. It soaked into the ground. Inspecting my body, I discovered she had washed all the dirt and scum off with magic!

"Woah!" I exclaimed. My mom's a witch? But then again, I think I already knew. She laughed.

John moved as if to turn around, and Mom scolded him, "Stay put!"

"But I want to see magic," he complained. Mom let out a huff of annoyance and picked a bag I hadn't noticed before up off the ground.

"Put these on." She threw me a pair of Naiad robes like she was wearing. I slipped them on without question. She pulled out a blond wig and fastened it to my head. It hung to right above my shoulders and itched at once. "Don't scratch," she scolded.

She pulled out a small bottle. "Bend your head backward." I did as I was told. "Open your eyes wide. Good. Now look up."

I saw her hand over one eye. "Blink," she told me. I did then she had me repeat the same thing on the other eye.

She examined me until she was satisfied. "Perfect," she exclaimed.

John turned and let out a soft whistle. "I always thought you'd look hot as a blonde with blue eyes." A red flush stole across my cheeks. A shy smile played on my mouth. I noticed Mom's eyes were blue as well.

"One last thing." She lifted her hand again, and the wind blew against my feet. The ground rumbled, making me stagger.

She stopped and murmured, "Sorry."

She began again, and the air swirled around the ground, seeping into the pores, and lifting the dirt into the air, moved it over my Nip robes, and dropped it. She repeated this process over and over, raining dirt over the robes and tar. At the same time, the air pushed the ground, forcing the evidence underground, burying it. When she was done, she picked up the bag and looked at each of us. "Right. Ready to go?"

"Where are we going?" I asked.

"Back to our hotel. We make our escape tomorrow."

She turned without another word and took large hurried steps away.

I looked at John, who shrugged and smiled at me his face full of love. "I've learned to just roll with it."

I laughed. I wasn't out of danger yet, but I was closer. I smiled back at him, loving him with every fiber of my being. He reached out, grasped my hand, and we entered the grasslands following my mom.

He looked at me, his eyes sweet and warm, kissed my knuckles, and asked, "Will you marry me?"

My mouth spread wide, and I whispered, "Yes."

Chapter Twenty-Five

SABRINA MATERIALIZED IN FRONT OF THE GUIDANCE HALL. SHE didn't recall meaning to come here, but her brain was on autopilot. Her legs felt like rubber as if she were under the influence of the numbing potion. In fact, her whole body was numb, save for her heart. That felt as if someone were twisting it, and she could hardly breathe.

Flashes of Ora's face, pale with wide amber eyes darting from side to side, kept sneaking up on Sabrina. When Sabrina helped lower Ora into The Kassen, the girl trembled and her heart raced like a hummingbird. And there was nothing Sabrina could've done.

She was sure the tribunal would find her innocent. Sabrina went through the evidence herself. There was no way that girl was a Nip.

Sabrina didn't exactly know what she was, but she knew beyond a shadow of doubt she was not a Nip.

As soon as Sabrina entered the MDA, images of the Quad sealing The Kassen then releasing it into the water flashed before her eyes. It disappeared with bubbles erupting from the surface of the water. Sabrina ran to a nearby trashcan and vomited. Her retching so violent the blood vessels in her face broke causing the skin to burn. Someone appeared at her side pulling her braid out of the way. She slapped them away, straightened, and wiped her mouth with the back of her hand. It was Simeon. He looked crestfallen at her rebuke. She couldn't face him and sprinted to her office, flying past the onlookers.

Sabrina slumped in her chair, weak-kneed and sweating. She was staring at the wall when Leigh and the rest of the Quad appeared. Leigh asked her, "Do you need to see a Healer?"

Sabrina shook her head, but her stomach rolled again.

Leigh watched her for a long while before saying, "When everyone is ready, we'll need to fill out our reports, and this case will be closed."

Allyn asked, "Since she was guilty, do you think Bizard will be back?"

Leigh's face betrayed no emotion when she said, "He also was found guilty of his use of unnecessary force. My guess is he will be reinstated to the MDA, but either not on a Quad or on a lesser unit."

Sabrina couldn't wrap her head around it. She was supposed to fill out some paperwork and that would be it. The injustice done today would just be another file. The girl, another missing person. She said as much out loud.

Leigh leaned over a table, her hands clutching the ends. "It isn't our job to judge. Our duty is to Conjuragic and to the MDA. We did everything in our power to deliver unbiased evidence, and the tribunal found the accused guilty. Our job was then to carry out the punishment. You should be satisfied."

"I should be satisfied? Our oath is to protect the innocent, and today we helped kill an innocent girl. Where is the *protecting* in that?"

Leigh glared at Sabrina. "You forget yourself. Take the rest of the day off. You'll fill out your forms tomorrow. Now get out of my sight."

Jumping out of her chair, Sabrina stalked out of the office. *That two-faced liar. Telling me I should be satisfied when I know she feels the same way!* Sabrina couldn't go home. She needed to do some damage and made her way to the training yard.

Walter, the Master of Arms, waited at the head of the yard. When he caught sight of her, his face lit up in a broad smile that matched the rest of him. "Ahh Lieutenant, what brings you here today? Wanting to get some practice in?"

"Oh yeah."

He barked a laugh. "Okay what can I do ya for? Light and easy, medium, or knock 'em dead?"

She smiled, her eyes gleaming with the challenge. "Bring it on."

"Haha! I needed some action today. Good luck, dearie." He punched some buttons on the screen before him. She hurried inside, a door closing behind her.

The training room was pitch black. Her power bubbled to the surface, as natural as breathing. Lights flashed on, blinding her, but she expected it. Throwing her body in a sideways tuck and roll, she barely missed a tree trying to grab her from behind. It ripped its roots from the ground with a creak and blundered after her; the thick smell of dirt filled the room. Her breathing was steady as she balanced on the tips of her toes ready to move.

Sabrina, as always, could sense where the molecules of water were and called them to her. The tree gave a shutter as water seeped through its inner cells and trickled down the bark. In seconds, the tree changed from full and living to dried out and white. It crumbled to the ground at her feet in large chunks of dried wood.

Once it was dead, a gust of wind blew straight at her face. She pulled the water from the air to make a shield, but tiny droplets kept breaking away from her shield until she was forced to abandon it. Instead, she sprinted away from the onslaught of air and hid behind the remains of the tree. Once there, she pulled the water into a tight band, so close it formed a makeshift mirror. Its surface was clear and flawless. Gazing into the reflection, she spotted the source of the Tempest magic, an enchantment at the top of the room. Her power extended from her as soon as the plan formed in her head. Water seeped into the enchantment from around its corners and pulled together, like a noose, and the enchantment shattered. The wind died away.

Sabrina stood, panting with sweat on her brow. She thought the simulation was done until she felt a sharp slice down her back and warm blood flowing from the wound. She spun around, pushing a shield of water forward, but was greeted by a swordsman made entirely of water. Extending from its hands were ice swords. The water man swung as she dodged the down-swiping sword. She formed her own swords and parried. She ducked and swung, slicing through water only to emerge on the other side, its form intact. She went to block, and the second sword cut her arm. She screamed and backed away. How could she fight Naiad with Naiad? But then she knew. She dropped her sword and pulled the Naiad magic out of the swordsman. Its water was now hers. She let go, and the swordsman collapsed as if it had melted.

The doors opened and Walter emerged, clapping. "Well done, dearie. The best show I've seen in a while. I'd ask if you want to keep going, but its quitting time."

Sabrina nodded and leaned down, placing her hands on her thighs as she caught her breath.

Walter appeared by her side. "Here, let me help you." His used his magic on her cuts pulling her skin together as only a Sphere could. It was a handy part of their magic and was no small wonder so many Healers were Sphere.

"Thank you," she told him when he finished.

She made her way back from the training yard and grabbed her things. Leigh and the rest of her Quad were absent. Sabrina said a silent thank you for not having to face Leigh. Sabrina felt bad she'd quarreled with her. She had been out of line talking that way in front of the others. Duty was duty, after all, and Leigh had to maintain order. But that was what made her a great Commander. On the way out, she caught sight of Simeon walking out of the door. She jogged to catch up with him. When he noticed her, he flushed. Her earlier embarrassment returned to her, and she grew shy.

Simeon broke the silence by clearing his throat. "Ahem. I, um, heard you went home earlier because you were sick. Are you feeling better?"

She looked away, not quite able to meet his eyes as they descended the steps of the Guidance Hall. "Yeah, it was nothing. I'm sorry I was rude to you earlier. Thanks for trying to help."

They'd reached their usual spot where they went their own way. He shrugged and said, "No worries." He shuffled his toe on the sidewalk, and Sabrina knew he was stalling, just like she was. Their silence grew awkward, and he said, "Well, I guess I'd better be going. Goodnight Lieutenant."

He turned to leave and she called, "Simeon would you want to... maybe...go to The Spark with me? Get a drink or dinner or whatever?"

She had no idea what came over her. His gaze was surprised but pleased. "Sure."

"Really? Um, do you want to materialize?"

"Oh, I'm not so good at it. I have some Journey Dust."

"Okay. That's fine."

"Very good, Lieutenant."

"You can call me Sabrina."

Across The Veil

"Sabrina."

Her skin prickled at the sound of her name on his lips. They walked farther down the street to a travel booth. He stepped inside, closed the door, and placed some of the Dust into the payment slot. She paid attention to the code he punched in before the Dust floated around the air and he disappeared. She stepped in after him, put in some of her own Dust. The Dust was so old she hoped it still worked. She hadn't traveled by Journey Dust since before joining the MDA. She pushed in the same code and waited. The Dust puffed around her, and the sensation of the floor dropping away from her feet and falling followed. She landed seconds later, across town. Simeon opened the door, offering her his hand. She took it. "I haven't done that in forever. Don't miss that feeling of falling."

"I'm sorry."

She waved as if shooing his apology away.

The Spark was down the street. There was already a line forming. When she took her place in line, the bouncer, a broad-shouldered half-giant called out in a voice so deep that it felt as if it made her bones vibrate, "Protectors don't wait." He waved her to the front of the line.

Sabrina grabbed Simeon by his purple sleeve and said, "He's with me." It felt so good to say that.

The bouncer nodded, and they passed the line going right inside. Simeon elbowed her in the side and winked. "Impressive."

Rolling her eyes, she shouted to be heard over the music. "I'm glad they didn't bow and give the exaltation. I usually never go out in this." She gestured to her leathers, and she noticed Simeon took a little longer inspecting her skin-tight outfit than was needed, but she didn't mind. Instead, she let her eyes gaze around the club. The Spark had become the most popular dance club in Conjuragic, and Sabrina could see why. Even though it was barely six o'clock, the place was packed. There was a huge bar serving the best drinks in town, no matter your House or species. Or so the sign above the bar claimed. She spotted at least four bartenders, and they were barely keeping up. In addition to representatives from every House, there was also a Styx drinking out of a tankard as large a wheelbarrow and pixies sipping from thimbles. There were no fewer than three dance floors on three different levels. Tables and booths were scattered about. Some were so huge they could only be meant for giants and others so small Sabrina could have held them in her hand.

Off to the side, there was an all-girl Naiad band called The Beaoches playing a loud techno-beat song that made Sabrina want to dance.

"Let's get a drink!" she shouted above the music. Simeon nodded and followed her to the bar. One positive of being here dressed in her leathers was everyone got out of her way, giving her ample space, and it also meant she didn't have to wait in line.

"Can I get a hot cherry bomb?" she ordered. The bartender, a fierce-looking Sphere, raised his eyebrows but said nothing as he fixed her drink.

"I've never seen a Naiad have an Ember drink before," Simeon observed while ordering a Twisted Sister.

"During Protector training, I made friends with an Ember who introduced me to it. Besides, sometimes we put too much emphasis on how our Houses are separate. We should embrace each other more. It's what Conjuragic was made for." She flushed when she realized she had been lecturing, but it was a pet peeve of hers. She shrugged. "Sorry."

He waved while shaking his head. "No, I totally agree." He gestured to the bartender. "Excuse me. Can I change my order? I'll have whatever is this lovely lady's favorite Naiad drink is."

Sabrina flushed while the bartender glared, annoyed with their banter. "A Mermaid's Tail."

They waited in silence for their drinks. When they arrived, Simeon raised his glass and said, "To embracing our differences."

"And our similarities." They drank deeply and ordered another round.

"This is good." Simeon looked into his cup.

They sat at the bar drinking and exchanging small talk until the drink relaxed her tongue. "You wanna dance?"

Simeon's eyes grew wide, and his cheeks were red, whether from the alcohol or embarrassment, she wasn't sure. He gulped, making the lump in front of his throat bob up and down. He only nodded his agreement.

She allowed him to lead her to the dance floor, but he didn't touch her. He turned and rocked with the music. His moves surprised her. She allowed herself to get lost in the music and him. But the song ended, and when the next one started playing, it was a slow song. They stared at each other, and her heart did a little flutter when he reached out, grabbed her waist, and pulled her close. As they swayed with the music, she breathed in the smell of him, which reminded her of her father's soap, books, and something she couldn't quite place, but it felt like home. She didn't like to think on that.

When that song ended, another started, and they went right on dancing. They took breaks to get more drinks and talk. She found out his favorite books, plays, and music. His parents owned a small café in Paris, and his sister had just started Healer's school. She told him about her dad, the head of security at The Haven, and her sister who was a stay-at-home mom taking care of her twin daughters, Kayla and Emilee.

As they talked, she kept reminding herself they could only be friends. He was Tempest, and she was Naiad. They could only be friends. Anything else was illegal.

Simeon stared into her eyes as if trying to read something in them. It seemed as if he was building up courage for something. Her gaze drifted to his lips, and she felt a longing to feel them on hers.

"What happened today?"

His question surprised her, but her answer surprised her more. "For the first time, I was ashamed to be a Protector."

He didn't look at her with shock or shame, and for that, she liked him even more. It encouraged her to go on. She told him the entire tale and finished with tears welling in her eyes. "She was innocent, and I helped kill her."

His hand reached hers underneath the table and gave it a squeeze but didn't let go.

"If you had the chance to do it over, would you do something different?"

"I would've thought about rescuing her, but it doesn't matter. She's dead."

"Then remember her, and if you get the chance to save someone else, do it. For her."

Sabrina nodded and vowed to herself she would.

He grinned then and said, "Take it in stride 'cause it could be worse. You could be a gnome."

She laughed so hard her side hurt.

They talked long into the night, and Sabrina didn't even notice the crowd thinning.

It wasn't until the bouncer yelled, "Closing time in fifteen minutes," that she was aware of anything but Simeon.

Sabrina walked with him to the travel booth. He turned before going inside to bid her goodnight, but before he could speak, she leaned in and kissed him.

Chapter Twenty-Six

THE HOTEL ROOM WAS BEAUTIFUL BUT SIMPLE. PICTURES OF MAGICAL beings hung on the wall. One in particular caught my eye, a fairy sitting on a unicorn's back. The unicorn's head was turned as if they were in a conversation.

I breathed a small sigh of relief once we'd reached left The Meadow. They'd picked a place on the outskirts and put on their disguises. Before leaving The Meadow, Mom and John changed into the dark blue robes. John told me these were the robes humans wear out and about on their tour.

We used something called Journey Dust in a machine that looked like a telephone booth. We all squeezed in, John pushed the button for their hotel, and the floor fell out from under me. A blur of images flew past, and soon we stopped in a completely different spot, in the middle of Conjuragic city. Fighting the urge to run, I wrung my hands together, feeling way too vulnerable out in the open.

We moved right past the reception desk at the Feenwell Hotel and took the lift to their floor. Inside the room, I tried sitting, but I couldn't sit still long. I stood and paced, ignoring the looks John and Mom were giving me. My anger rose, and like always, my magic searched for a source to strike out at.

"I'm going to take a bath." I stormed out of the main room, slamming the door behind me. "Calm down," I whispered to the magic. It settled with a huff.

While waiting for the bath to fill, I yanked off the itching blond wig and stripped out of the Naiad robes. I stared at my reflection for the longest time. The bald head, sunken eyes, and each rib that stuck out. I'd seen myself in the infirmary and in Arameus's office, but this was different. I was in their custody; it was beyond my control, so I kept the horror of it locked away. Now I could fully reflect.

I stepped into the bath and sank into the scalding water. More tears flowed down my face. They should be tears of relief. Or fear, but no, I was pissed. Not at my magic or the Quad or even the tribunal. I was pissed at my mom. I said I'd forgiven her, but if she'd told me before, we wouldn't be here.

She should've told me. I should be telling John about The Meadow and how to use the Journey Dust. I knew I was being immature, but I couldn't help it. I had to try to relax. I closed my eyes and concentrated on my breathing, trying to meditate, but it wasn't doing any good. Soft music drifted toward me from right outside the door, and its melodies soothed me.

My mom was playing music on purpose. She knew me so well, and her comfort, even from behind the door, touched me. But I couldn't take her soothing. I was too angry, too hurt, had been through too much. I was just too…too… and I sank into the water.

I wanted to escape from inside my own head. I stuck my mouth and nose out of the water. It was dark and quiet and warm, and despite everything, I felt safe hiding here. I drifted off to sleep.

I awoke with a splash and a splutter. I'd sunk into the bath recalling being inside The Kassen. *Great Ora, drown yourself, why don't ya?* The last rays of sun were drifting through the windows. The water had lost all its warmth. My teeth chattered. I hopped out of the water, wrapping myself in a towel. I dried off, avoiding looking at my reflection.

A bag sat on the ground that hadn't been there before. Mom must've come in to check on me. I opened it and found my favorite warm pajamas—flannel, old, soft, comfortable, and smelling of home. I picked up the soft fabric, lifted it to my nose, and inhaled. My mom loved me, and she'd been protecting me. She never wanted this to happen to me. My anger receded with my bathwater that was circling the drain. I pulled on my underwear and pajamas, feeling more like myself than I had in a long time.

I left the bathroom, and John and Mom stood as if they had been waiting for me. I gave them a half smile, and their shoulders relaxed.

"I'm starving," I murmured, rubbing my growling stomach.

They looked at one another as if this was the last thing they expected me to say and burst out laughing. I couldn't help but join them.

Across The Veil

"Room service!"

My mom ushered me back into the bathroom to hide, but I peeked around the corner. She pressed a button, and a man's face appeared on a screen. She ordered our food, and I returned to the main room. Seconds later, there came a knock at the door. I ran back to the bathroom. Voices carried through the door, and my heart pounded. Cursing myself for not thinking of an escape route, I tried to recall every detail of the room. Just in case I had to make a break for it. But there was only the main door. Not the best position to be in. Drawing from my memory, I yelped when someone knocked at the door.

"It's okay. It's the food," Mom called.

She opened the door so I'd come out. The smells of warm bread and melted cheese wafted around me. She maneuvered past the two full-sized beds to the sitting area to the far left. I scarfed down salad while my mother plated the pizza. John picked up a remote. "Check this out." He pressed a button, and the far wall disappeared replaced by a giant stage with people acting out a play, except the background looked like a movie.

We watched in silence. This felt so odd, sitting around a hotel room, eating pizza and salad, and watching a magical play.

I devoured all my salad, half of my mom's, and five slices of pizza. It was so delicious: sweet sauce, nutty cheese, and spicy pepperoni. I felt some of my unease melt away as I sat with my family, laughing at the show, and eating comfort food.

After my mom cleaned up, I rose and crawled into the bed. I pulled the covers up over my chin and looked up at my mom. "I'm ready."

She nodded and sat down beside me. John looked confused and asked, "Ready for what?"

My mother smiled. She knew me so well. "She's ready for me to tell her about me, her father, and herself."

"Oh," John replied as he took a seat at the table. I liked him giving us our space, but also staying close enough to listen. He knew a lot more than I did, but he deserved to hear it all.

"Where to begin, my darling girl?" My mother looked far away considering her words. "I'm sure you have worked out by now that we're witches, but what you don't know is that we are different from the witches and wizards here."

There it was. Finally, she said it. I was not a witch born of a human.

"How so?" John blurted out.

Mom shook her head. "Shhh."

He turned sheepish and shrugged. "Sorry."

She smiled. "He always interrupts." And we giggled together.

Our laughter died away, and Mom let out a sigh. "My mother, your real grandmother, she was a witch, like the ones here. She was Naiad. I don't know why, but she was put in prison. She was kidnapped from there, and someone faked her death."

I imagined this unknown woman, in the horrifying prison, and I knew firsthand how easily this could have come to pass.

My mother's voice had grown soft. "She was taken to the homeland of Ember, the Pyre. Underneath the great volcano is another prison, a hidden one. The prisoners there are controlled by a wizard. I never knew his name. We were to call him Master. Others called him The Experimenter."

A shudder ran across her body, and I shivered with her. "He was very cruel. I know very little about the prison or his agendas, but I did know he'd heard a prophecy in his youth. I only knew a little of what it said, but something I overheard was, 'From the hands of two geminates, an all-powerful rock will be created.'"

"What's a geminate?" John blurted out.

"Shhh! Let her explain, okay, babe?"

"Sorry."

Mom gave me a sideways glance, thanking me. "So, his mission was to create this all-powerful rock to use to take over Conjuragic, or so we assumed. First, he needed to create geminates. A geminate is a witch or wizard who can control two cores of magic. The Houses are made up of witches and wizards who can control one core of magic: earth, air, water, or fire. It is forbidden here for two people from different houses to… mate."

"Why?" I asked, and then I smiled at myself. I was interrupting just like John. "Sorry, go on."

Across The Veil

Mom smiled, and I was stunned by how young and beautiful she was. Then something clicked. She used the water to clean me and then lifted the dirt to bury my robes and the remains of my black crystal. She must have Tempest and Naiad powers.

"It's forbidden for two reasons. The first is most of the babies are either miscarried or die shortly after birth, so it is very heartbreaking. The second is when the geminates do survive, they are very powerful, unpredictable, and hard to control. So even if a geminate baby does survive…it's euthanized."

The pizza threatened to rise in my throat. "These people kill babies! It isn't their fault. What…what's wrong with these people?"

"I agree, but from what I have learned, the geminates who did survive were very dangerous. I don't think they liked killing the infants either. That's why they made them illegal. But that was what my mom was for. She had several miscarriages before I was born—or so they tell me. I'm a geminate. There were many prisoners, and after several years, there were a few dozen geminates. We were hidden from the world, taught rudimentary magic by our parents, raised by our mothers. And when we reached a certain age, our parents were taken and… I can only imagine… killed."

Tears welled in her eyes. "My mom was a good woman. You would've loved her."

I hugged her close. John remained quiet, but he stared out the window, sorrow etched on his face. We locked eyes, and he moved to sit beside me and took my hand.

Mom continued. "So after our parents were taken, and it was just the geminates left, we were forced to work in groups, wielding our magic on various rocks and jewels trying to create this all-powerful stone. One day I worked with a handsome man, Philo Stone, your father. We fell in love, and in our own way, with our fellow geminates, we were married. We hid our romance, but one day I found out I was pregnant. I knew Master would take you if you survived. He would use you or kill you, and I would never see you again. I couldn't let that happen. After hours of planning, all of us, except a few who we didn't trust, tried to escape. The volcano erupted, and everyone but your father and I died in the lava.

Somehow we made it to a Transport gate. We tricked the gatekeeper, and we went through the Veil."

"So you made it?" I asked, smiling.

She stopped and took several deep breaths. "No one told us about the Veil…you have to hold yourself together. Literally. Your father, he…he didn't make it. When I made it to the human world…only parts of him came with me."

The happiness faded from her eyes. I could only imagine her life in the Pyre, the terror, finding love, and the courage it took to escape. Any remaining anger or resentment vanished. She'd spent her whole life tormented, born as a prisoner, escaping with her husband only to see him in pieces. Then she was in the human world, a world she knew nothing about, alone with no money, no place to go, and a child on the way. She spent our entire lives hiding from Conjuragic, protecting me with our necklaces. And I lost it, after I promised her I wouldn't ever take it off. And now she was back in Conjuragic, and if we were captured, we'd be killed, or if her Master finds us first, there was no telling what would happen.

"I'm sorry I didn't keep my promise, Mom." I collapsed into sobs.

She wrapped her arm around me, as did John. "It's okay, honey. I should've told you and taught you to control your powers. I wanted to protect your innocence a while longer."

We held each other and cried until our tears were gone. A knock sounded at the door. We weren't expecting anyone. I leapt out of bed and hid in the bathroom. I heard them straightening the room. Then the sound of the door opening and a man's voice. The door closed, and the voice grew louder. Arameus!

Without thinking, I jerked open the door and flew out of the room leaping into his arms. His eyes grew wide with shock.

"Arameus!" I yelled.

He pulled me back and looked at me, head to toe and back again. "Ora… you're alive!"

I grinned and nodded my head.

"You're alive!" he yelled as he picked me up and spun me around. "But how? What happened?"

"It's a long story, but basically, I was rescued." He put me down and stared at me as if I were a ghost.

"What're you doing here?" I asked.

"You asked me to find your mother and friend, remember?"

"That's right. So much has happened since then. Are you hungry? We have pizza."

He laughed, his eye twinkling. "No, I'm fine."

"Arameus, this is my mother, Perdita Stone." They shook hands.

"And John McCurry." They shook hands with more aggression. John appeared to be sulking.

"This is Arameus Townsend. He was my Defender during the trial. He's like a lawyer."

"Nice to meet you." My mom's eyes were rimmed in red, and I guessed mine were, too.

I nodded my head toward my mom. "She's a witch."

Arameus's face held no expression. "I guessed as much. Why didn't you come forth? You could have helped our case."

"I had my reasons."

Arameus's eyes narrowed, but he only said, "Fair enough." He turned to me and asked, "Are you okay?"

I nodded. "I will be as soon as we can get out of here."

"What's your plan?" he asked. Amazed, he was still willing to help me.

"Well, we could use a hand," my mom said.

"Anything for Ora. I failed her once. I don't intend to again."

John scowled.

"We came here on a tour. It would be better if we could return the same way. But if you could escort Ora, help her keep together?" Mom asked him, her eyes cautious.

"Of course, when do we leave?"

"The plan is to meet Todd, our tour guide, for breakfast, then leave right after. You could take her in the morning while we are at breakfast. We could meet up in a hotel by the gift shop. After we're back, we'll be off, and you can return home."

"Okay, what time?"

"Say 8:30?"

"I'll be there." He shook my mom's hand again. He turned to me, picked me up in a big bear hug. He kissed my cheek. "I'm so glad you're alive. I'll get you home tomorrow, where you belong. Don't ever use your magic again."

"Thank you, Arameus, I won't." I hugged him back.

He released me, wished farewell to my mom, nodded at John, and left. Mom announced it was time for bed. John had been quiet the whole time. I walked over to give him a hug, and he moved away. "What's wrong?" I asked him.

"Your friend?" he pouted.

I sighed. "John, I... It was just announced I was guilty, and they were going to take me to The Kassen to kill me. I... I couldn't bear to say boyfriend. It hurt too much. And now, it was too complicated. I'm sorry if I hurt you. You know I love you." I gave him my most pathetic look. He only pouted more. "John, don't be jealous. Arameus is kind. He worked hard to free me. I trust him, and we can use his help. And don't forget, I'm going home to marry you."

He pulled me into a fierce embrace. "I love you." He kissed the top of my head.

"Come on you two, off to bed," Mom scolded. I laid in the bed beside my mom, John in the other. I pulled the covers up around myself, all the way up to my chin. I sank low into the warm bed as the lights clicked off. John reached his hand from the other bed searching for mine. I obliged. I smiled as our fingers intertwined and fell into a deep dreamless sleep.

In only moments, another knock sounded on the door, urgent. I scrambled out of bed, running to the bathroom to hide yet again. This was growing old. A few moments later, my mom opened the door. "Come out."

I took cautious steps out of the bathroom. Arameus stood in the entranceway looking grim. "What's happened?" I asked.

"The Kassen has been found, no sign of your body. Your picture is all over the broadcast," Arameus announced. My blood ran cold.

"What now?" Mom asked.

"We leave now," Arameus said.

Across The Veil

"What about these?" John asked, pointing to the blue mark on his arm.

"I brought these." He pulled out two red bottles out of his robes. "Drink these, and they'll come out." Arameus handed a bottle to each of them.

Mom and John looked at each other, opened the bottles, and drank the liquid. I was reminded of how my mark was removed, and I would have preferred drinking something than watching it pour out of my mouth along with Tituba. They grabbed their arms and scratched. "It itches," John complained.

"It'll come out soon," Arameus explained.

Drinking the potions set everyone into action. We rushed around, throwing on our disguises, packing up our room. Arameus wiped the room down for fingerprints. Within a few moments, we were ready to go. I glanced at the clock. 7:30. We left the room, rode down the lift. When we reached the ground floor, I glanced in the direction of the sitting area. There was another large television-like projection, but this time, an anchorman sat at a desk with my picture filling up the top right hand part of the screen.

We left the hotel and hurried down the street. We turned down a nearby alleyway. "How're we getting through the gate?" I asked.

Arameus stopped short and turned to look at each of us. "You have to show them some magic. You got out of The Kassen, how hard can it be?"

"John is human," I explained and Arameus swore.

"Can't Perdita and I go back and return with the tour?"

"No, you drank the potion to remove your jewel. They'll be suspicious. Unless you can prove you have magic, they won't let you leave," Arameus explained.

We stood for a few moments thinking. John interrupted our thoughts and said, "I'll stay here. I'll hide, and when it's safe, you can come back for me."

"No, I won't leave you." I threw my arms around him.

I stepped back and heard it. "There she is! The Nip!" I looked down the alley, and a wizard pointed toward us, shouting at someone to the left.

We'd been spotted. There was no choice now but to run. The plan, so carefully laid out, was gone. We were running for our lives in a city full of witches and wizards, all trained since birth on how to wield their magic against our little group of my Defender, a human, and two witches relying only on instinct.

I glanced toward John. His face was full of panic, and I remembered all our moments, the good and the bad. I remembered how safe I always felt in his arms, how loved. And now we were here in this city where I was hated and hunted, none of it my fault. A stream of heat soared past my face, and we ducked. A jet of flame slammed into the building behind us.

"This way!" Mom yelled, pointing through a small opening in the newly created crack in the wall. We squeezed through, barely making it before the next fireball hit.

The blue jewel in my mom's arm popped out and rolled away. Arameus's potion had finally taken effect. I yelled, trying to tell her the jewel was gone. My words were drowned out by rumbling as the building shook, and a rock fell, hitting me on the side of the head. The room swayed as a warm puddle flowed with fierceness down my cheek. My Defender reached over, grabbed my hand, and hauled me to my feet.

"We have to keep moving!" He turned and ran. We followed his lead. He was raised in this city and knew it better than any of us. "We have to make it to a Transport gate. It's the only way out!" he yelled over the crashes of spells hitting the buildings.

My heart hammered as we dashed out of the building and into the next street. I ran and ran. My chest burned, and a cramp had formed in my side. I ran out of sheer panic blindly following Arameus. More shouting. We'd been spotted again. We kept going. Building after building flew by in a blur. We weaved in and out of the alleys, hearing the attacks coming at us from behind. A block of ice missed John by inches, and Mom was knocked down by a gust of wind. I reached out, pulled her up, and kept running. Sprays of fire flew past us. Turning a corner, another flame missed me by inches. A second before the fireball would've hit, a wave of water nearly knocked me down but squashed out the flames.

"Arameus!" I cried. "Do something!" He turned and glanced my way, occurring to him to use his magic, too. He threw gusts of wind while leading us through the living city. From beside me, someone screamed, "Stop!" Lieutenant Sun stood at the corner of a building her arms raised with water floating in front of her palms.

I shouted at her, "You know I'm innocent." Her eyes wavered for a fraction before she lowered her hands.

"Help me!" I pleaded.

She met Arameus's gaze. They stared in each other's eyes until they reached a moment of understanding. She waved indicating we should run toward her. We ducked into the building she emerged from and were off again.

"I can't believe I'm doing this," Lieutenant Sun muttered to herself.

Arameus was in the lead, followed by John, Mom, me, and Lieutenant Sun pulling up the rear. Arameus and Lieutenant Sun threw spells, protecting us. We were about to break through the streets directly across from a gate to cross the Veil. A gate to safety, to home. We sprinted toward the gate, except a gatekeeper pulled a lever to set up the barriers.

"Nooooooo!" Arameus screamed and threw a spell I didn't even see at the gatekeeper. A young Naiad's body was thrown backward and knocked unconscious. I couldn't believe it. We'd managed to lose all our pursuers in the chase. There was no one now. We were moments from being free. Then I saw it, running parallel beside us.

The black tailless cat from my cell.

The cat transformed. Its body twisted and grew. My steps slowed to watch this change. The fur stripped away, revealing a woman with pale skin, brown eyes, and long jet-black hair. The cat wasn't a cat at all. She smiled, the look fierce and superior. She raised her hands, and a chunk of concrete as large as a man erupted from the ground in front of her. With a flick of her wrist, the boulder hurled toward us, fast. It was headed straight for Mom. The boulder moved as if in slow motion. The air was stuck in my chest, and I knew it was the end. My mom was going to be crushed.

John shouted, sounding far away. "No!" He shoved Mom out of the way. She fell to the side. John stood in her place. For one heartbeat, time stopped.

The boulder roared back into motion. It slammed into John. His cry mingled with a loud crack. Both John and the boulder flew backward hitting the brick wall. The boulder slid down by John's feet. He fell limp over top of it. His eyes wide, glassy, sightless.

A thousand moments flashed before my eyes. The boy throwing rocks at his sister, our hands touching in his truck, the shy eye contact that followed, watching his lips and thinking what it would be like to kiss them, our soft first kiss on his bruised lips, lying on a woolen blanket looking at the clouds while wrapped in each other's arms, hearing him whisper I love you then squeezing my hand, and seeing him here in this place to rescue me and asking me to marry him.

And then to see him there, lifeless…the words wouldn't come to me. I couldn't think it, couldn't let the words form in my head. The pain would be too great. Someone grabbed my shoulder and pulled me up. I didn't remember falling to my knees.

"Ora, we have to go," Lieutenant Sun said. "He's dead. We have to go."

The words hit my heart with the same ferocity as the boulder hit John. *He's dead*. I heard it over and over and over. And then I heard the sound that drove away what little sanity I had left. *Laughter.*

The cat woman stood as at least a dozen Protectors ran toward us. There was nowhere left to run. We'd been caught. And the cat woman was laughing, laughing because she killed John.

My magic mingled with rage. Rage like I'd never felt. My entire being quivered as it sprang upward. An unimaginable power seared with need through me, awakening as it never had before. What had been a momentous amount of magic before was but a tiny spark compared to the magic that now exploded from within me.

My muscles filled and bones grew stronger, my hair grew back, lengthening, twisting its way past my ears and shoulders, snaking its way down my back. My vision burned white. I screamed, unable to hold it in. My hands balled into fists at my side. The ground shook beneath me.

The Protectors across from me all threw up their hands and sent jets of fire, water, earth, and wind toward me. I flicked a gaze toward them. Indifferent. My only thought was *no!* Their spells halted in front of me. Never reaching me. I tilted my head the tiniest fraction. The elements yielded under my command.

Across The Veil

My vision changed. Every molecule around me stood out. My magic rolled out of me, bending them to my will, balling the different spells into one enormous pulsating mass of energy.

The energy bounced off my magic, feeding it, merging with it. We had purpose. With a flick of my hand, the inferno flew at my enemies. Those Protectors had no chance. The energy passed through them. They stood motionless. Frozen in time. Until a gust of wind blew and their bodies crumbled in dust. Blown away in tiny swarms.

The cat woman had morphed back into the cat. Her small sleek form ran into the shadows. Relying on instinct, I threw different elements hurtling toward the alley where the cat disappeared. My magic and I wanted nothing more than to kill anything that had hurt John. Anything that might hurt my family. I hated this place and wanted it destroyed. I wanted it torn to pieces, brick by brick, and when this world was gone, never to be entered again, only then would I be satisfied. My magic reached deeper and further outward, pulling more and more energy around me.

This time controlled by my will to destroy the city, I set it loose, and it flew away from me, moving through buildings. Searching, searching for the source, the weak spot, and through the mass I saw what I was searching for, as if I had another set of eyes.

The heart of the city was just ahead, and I sent my spell into it, and with the force of an atomic bomb, the two energies collided. But mine was stronger and the heart pulsated once, twice, and then failed. The light that flowed throughout every building in the city flickered and died. The ground shook and crumbled around the heart of the city and spread outward.

The earthquake was massive. Buildings collapsed. Screams filled the streets. I turned my back on this despicable city and threw up my hand. The Veil ripped into existence, right ahead of me.

"You can't open the Veil here!" Lieutenant Sun shouted. "It will rip the world apart."

I couldn't care less about this world and smiled, satisfied. "Let's go."

Looks of fear swept over their faces. They eyed each other before turning. They grabbed one another's hands and stepped through the Veil. I followed.

This time I became one with the Veil. I sensed every fiber of it and the souls in it who were traveling. I knew their thoughts and feelings. I sensed the presence of those who were crossing over to the human world to find me. My power flickered and left me, traveling through the Veil, stopping the hearts of those who meant me harm.

Mom left the Veil, then Arameus, followed by Lieutenant Sun. Only a few made it through to hunt us, and then I was out.

I turned before the Veil could close, plunged my hands into it. My magic reached into it, expanding the infinity of the Veil, and slowed its flow. Slower and slower until it stopped. The Veil was closed.

I removed my hand, and the dancing rainbow of the Veil disappeared.

No matter what they did on either side, no one could get through. The gate between the human world and the magical world was closed. And I knew exactly how many were trapped in between.

My companions all wore an expression of shock and grief, and Lieutenant Sun stared at me. "What've you done?"

The rage inside me calmed. The magic controlling me relaxed and receded, not to where it was before, but under the surface, where I could bring it back whenever I wanted. My white vision faded to normal, and I collapsed with utter exhaustion.

The last word I heard myself say was, "John," before I was engulfed in blackness.

Chapter Twenty-Seven

Blackness surrounded and caressed me. Time lost all meaning as did any sense of self. I only knew I didn't want to surface. I hid as deep as I could. Occasionally drifting upward, voices spoke from what seemed far away.

"What are we going to do now?"

"I don't know. We have to wait for her."

Waiting for me, but I couldn't face them. I sank back into the depths of blackness where memory ceased to exist.

The darkness lightened, and I surfaced again. A hand smoothed my hair. I rose further, curious, but the pain in my heart returned, and I dove back down again.

The sound of panic stirred the emptiness. Screaming, a loud boom, the ground rumbling almost made me resurface, but soon it was quiet again, and I floated.

"We have to move."

"Where are they?"

"I've killed them, but more will be coming. We have to go." *Killed who?*

"But she isn't strong enough."

"Then we stay, and they can kill her where she lies."

"Where will we go?"

"If we're going after her friend, we'd better go now. Who knows what everyone stuck on this side knows. They might have studied her case. If so, they'll use her to draw us out." *Use who?*

Conversations swirled around me, but they were only voices. I heard their words. Some piqued my interest but held no meaning, no emotion behind them. Any sense of urgency had vanished with him.

Strong arms picked me up, but even that was too much. I screamed and crashed back into the darkness, hating myself for my cowardliness.

The darkness faded, and somehow, I knew I wouldn't delve into its depths again, though I wanted to.

Something was different. Something had changed.

I recalled being moved twice. But what was calling to me from beyond the darkness? Sounds of sobbing and the reason for the anguish was the same as my own. The same reason I hid in the darkness.

I rose and feeling returned to my body. At first my limbs were heavy, unable to make the smallest movement. It felt like forever before my ability to move returned, along with the heartache. The rate of my breathing increased from the panic, but no one noticed. The darkness encasing me reached outward, sensing people near, but not in the same room. The darkness tested its new freedom, tasting those around me, looking for danger. As it recognized the others, so did I. Then I realized what the darkness was. My magic, full and strong, no longer hindered by a crystal in my arm or blocked by an amulet. It had cocooned me.

I opened my eyes. I didn't know where I was. The room smelled of mold and Pledge, a sickening combination. A quilt covered my legs, and to my left was the door and windows by the end of the bed and to the right. The walls were wooden like an old cottage. On either side were two nightstands and a dresser up against one wall. All the furniture had a heavy film of dust. I sat, clutching my head as the room spun. Outside of the window on the right was a lake barely visible through the trees.

I stood on shaky legs. I had no idea how long I'd been unconscious, but my bladder was full, my mouth dry, and I was starving. Beside my bed was a small but clean bathroom. I entered and shut the door behind me. After I'd used the bathroom, I dared to look in the mirror. My hair had regrown and was longer than before.

I looked different, my eyes darker and haunted. Dark circles rimmed my eyes, and my cheeks were gaunt from weight loss. I stripped out of a simple cotton nightgown, and I wondered who dressed me, hoping it was my mother.

I got into the shower and washed away any remains of Conjuragic. I stepped out, wrapping myself in a towel. I ran the brush through my hair, enjoying this simple comfort, and left the bathroom.

Across The Veil

When I reentered the bedroom, my mother sat on the made-up bed. On her lap were clean undergarments, jeans, and a t-shirt. She handed me the clothes I didn't recognize without saying a word. I dressed in the bathroom before rejoining her in the bedroom. She still sat on the side of the bed. I sat beside her, and she took my offered hand.

"Are you ready?" Mom asked.

I shook my head no, feeling my eyes sting. We stood together and stepped through the door into an open concept living room, dining area, and the kitchen. The room was large and bright. The walls here were wooden as well. An odd little country cottage in the woods.

Lieutenant Sun was in the kitchen cooking. Charlie sat on the larger couch crying, facing away from me, and Arameus had his arm around her. When I walked in, Arameus and Lieutenant Sun looked up at me as if expecting something. I went to the couch, Arameus stood, and I took his seat beside Charlie.

"Charlie?"

Her sobs halted, and her head whipped around to look at me. Her face was healed! I was so relieved. We locked eyes, and she threw herself in my arms, and we both bawled into each other's arms. We managed a short conversation in between our sobs as only lifelong best friends could.

"I really loved him," I murmured.

"I know."

"I'm sorry I didn't tell you about us."

"I'm sorry they took you."

"I'm sorry you were hurt. I'm so happy you're okay."

"Me too. I love you."

"Love you, too."

Our sobs quieted, and we leaned back, resting our heads on each other. Mom watched us with silent tears running down her face.

"What's happened?" I asked. I remembered little from the darkness, but I didn't really want to know.

"After we returned, and you did whatever you did to the Veil, we hid out in a vacant house. We exited somewhere in Ohio. We were there about a day and a half when we were attacked," my mother explained.

Lieutenant Sun brought a plateful of grilled cheese sandwiches, a bag of chips, apples, and several plates. Arameus went to the kitchen and came with her carrying several bottles of water. They sat the food in front of us, and my mother plated the food.

"When we were attacked, Sabrina here was outstanding. There were two of them, and they didn't even get close," Arameus told me pointing with his thumb to Lieutenant Sun. He looked odd in a pair of old jeans and an AC/DC t-shirt. I glanced at Lieutenant Sun, who was eating, indifferent to the conversation. She was still beautiful with her blond hair hanging around her shoulders. Military style pants and boots with a simple gray t-shirt became her.

"After the attack, we had to leave. We arrived near Charlie's house in Raleigh, got a hotel room, and I stayed with you while Sabrina and your mother went to get Charlie," Arameus continued, as my mother handed me a plate of food.

"They almost didn't make it," Charlie whispered.

I looked to Mom for confirmation, and she nodded. "It's true. She was being watched by an assassin. As soon as we went in their house, the assassin broke through a window. Sabrina got burnt on her arm, but she overpowered him."

"What did you tell your grandparents?" I asked Charlie.

My mom answered for her. "After the attack, I talked to them. I told them all about us. About what happened with you. After the Protectors visited them, they'd erased any memory of Charlie's attack. All they were left with was your disappearance. I had to tell them about ..." My mother couldn't finish her sentence. "I told Evelyn and Jacob everything. I told them how their son died saving me. Told them how brave and kind he was. How I couldn't have saved you without him." Mom's voice broke as she discussed... *him*.

I still couldn't think his name. Tears welled in Charlie's eyes again, and I knew it was the sounds of her sobs over her brother that brought me out of the darkness. Her pain was my pain. I didn't have to face it alone anymore.

I forced my tears away so I could hear the rest of the story.

"It took a long time to convince them, but Charlie wanted to come with us. They finally agreed, and they're going into hiding," Mom explained.

Across The Veil

Arameus answered my wide-eyed expression. "I knew everything about your case, and the place they're going no one knows about. I learned everything I could about you, your family, and your friends. Any place you might be, and where they're going, I didn't know. They'll be safe."

"Okay," I whispered. "Do they know how sorry I am?" My voice threatened to break, but I held it in.

"Yes," Charlie answered. "We all do. I wish I had known about you and him... but I understand why you didn't tell me."

"How're you healed? Bizard said he wasn't going to have them heal you."

Sabrina answered, "When my Quad came to question her further for you trial, we discovered she hadn't been healed. Leigh was outraged and had a Healer come to her."

I pushed away the hurt for a few moments longer. I looked to my mom. "Where are we now?"

"We're in a summer cottage in North Carolina. We have no connections here, so we should be safe," she answered, looking around as if she still wasn't quite sure.

"You know we can't stay here." Lieutenant Sun spoke.

"I know," I said.

"What did you do to my home?" she finally asked, her voice full of anger.

I didn't answer, but we stared at each other for a long time. *I don't know.* She looked away and her voice softened. "I care about someone, too, like you did about him. I can understand why you were so angry. Why you did whatever it is that you did. I would've done the same."

"Thank you," I said, grateful she still understood. She had saved our lives three times already and proved to be a powerful ally.

"I want to know he is okay, my someone," she muttered, "and my family."

"I understand," I told her, and I did. I regretted what I'd done to Conjuragic. They were many innocent people there, kind people, who had families and friends.

"I'm sorry." Our eyes met and reached a silent understanding.

"Thank you," Sabrina said, and took a bite out of an apple. She chewed and swallowed. The silence continued for a while longer. "What're we going to do now?"

"I need to think. If that's okay?" I leaned down, picked up two plates of food, handed one to Charlie, and devoured my own. It tasted like cardboard, but I had to eat.

After I finished, I was allowed a small walk, Lieutenant Sun following a short distance behind. The summer heat was beginning to fade, but it was still hot. The walk around the lake with its peaceful waters reflecting the afternoon white clouds attempted to soothe me as did the birds singing and the quiet of the woods. I picked up small rocks and skipped them across the water. But this brought back memories of lake trips this past summer with John.

I sank to the ground and wailed, screaming my heartache over the loss of him. I loved him so much, and he was gone. I would never see him again, never hear his laughter, feel his arms around me, or his soft lips touching mine. We were going to get married, and the life I imagined in my brief period of freedom crashed down around me. I saw myself as a mother, perhaps with a little one running around, my belly swollen with the second. Growing old with this amazing man who loved me so much. He'd given up his life for me and my mother. Our whole future was gone in a second.

I cried and cried, lying down in the soft mud near the shore. I didn't care I was getting covered in sludge. I cried alone in my own misery. This was what I had been hiding from in the darkness. This pain, this loss, but I had to face it. I had to let it consume my body because it was what I needed. Other emotions emerged, anger at myself. I'd left him behind. I was capable of all this magic, and I didn't even think to get his body. I left him there. I knew he wouldn't have left my body if it had been the other way around.

Lieutenant Sun touched my shoulder and said, "The part of him you loved was already gone. You didn't leave him. He came with you. Can't you feel him?"

She knew exactly what I was thinking. I considered her words, and I felt all our love in the center of my chest. I thought about when I suffocated in the dirt, how the part of me that was me wasn't in my body, and I knew she was right. His body wasn't him, and I felt somewhat better. But I should've brought him home for his parents, for Charlie.

"Thank you, Lieutenant Sun." I wiped my running nose with the back of my hand.

She smiled her gentle smile. "Please, call me Sabrina."

As my sobs quieted, Sabrina stepped away to give me my privacy once more. I sat with my knees at my chest, my arms wrapped around them. The sky turned pink and purple with the fading sun. I thought back over my arrest, my time in the Nook, the trial, Lailie, John. I thought about my real grandmother, my mother and father, and their fellow prisoners, all those lives torn and twisted, all by one man.

A plan was forming, and I knew what I had to do. I didn't know how long it would take, but I knew I wouldn't spend my life hiding like my mother had. What I wanted was freedom and revenge for all those lives lost.

I returned to the cottage a while later. My little entourage quieted as Sabrina and I reentered the house. They all looked at me, waiting.

"I know what I'm going to do," I announced as everyone held their breath.

"What?" Mom asked.

"I'm going to make him pay."

About the Author

LEANN M. RETTELL was born and raised in West Virginia but now lives in North Carolina with her husband, three children, two dogs, and two cats. She is a full time family physician by day, full time sports mom by night, and writer somewhere in between. She is the author of the Conjuragic Series.

Made in the USA
Middletown, DE
15 May 2017